RETURN OF THE

RUSSIAN CZAR

NICHOLAS, CZAR OF RUSSIA, HEAD OF THE LARGEST ARMY IN THE WORLD, AND AUTHOR OF THE PROPOSAL FOR A CONFERENCE TO CONSIDER A GENERAL DISARMAMENT.
From his latest photograph by Downey, London.

Matt Drozd

mattdrozdbooks.com

Matt Drozd

TABLE OF CONTENTS

PRELUDE

"Czar Nicholas II was the last Romanov emperor, ruling from 1894 until his forced abdication in March of 1917. The duration of his rule was plagued by periods of political and social unrest. When he succeeded his father—Czar Alexander III—Nicholas II had little experience in government. He was widely seen as a politically weak, indecisive leader. His poor handling of the Russo-Japanese War of 1904-1905, subsequent 1905 uprising of Russian Workers (Bloody Sunday)—and Russia's involvement in World War I hastened the fall of the Russian Empire.

Czar Nicholas II married Princess Alix of Hesse, a duchy in the German Empire in 1894, shortly after his coronation. Alix, who would later take the name Alexandra Feodorovna, was a granddaughter of Queen Victoria of the United Kingdom. Nicholas and Alexandra had four daughters—Olga, Tatiana, Maria, and Anastasia—and one son, Alexei. Alexandra—with a brusque demeanor and distaste for Russian culture—was disliked by most of the Russian people. Her German ancestry and her devotion to Russian mystic Grigori Rasputin contributed to her unpopularity. She believed the self-proclaimed holy man could cure her son Alexei's chronic illness.

Alexei, the only son, and heir to the throne, suffered from severe hemophilia, and was often confined to bed. Hemophilia is an inherited disease in which the blood does not clot normally, causing excessive bleeding after any injury. (Many relatives of Queen Victoria inherited the disease, which was sometimes referred to as "the royal disease.")

Rasputin's powerful influence on the ruling family infuriated nobles, church leaders and peasants alike. Many saw him as a religious charlatan. Russian nobles, eager to end the cleric's influence, had Rasputin murdered on December 30, 1916.

Czar Nicholas II left Saint Petersburg in 1915 to take command of the failing Russian Army front in World War I. But by 1917, most Russians had lost all faith in the leadership ability of the czar. Government corruption was rampant and the Russian economy was severely battered by World War I. Moderates joined with radical Bolshevik revolutionaries in calling for an overthrow of the czar. During the Russian Revolution in November 1917, radical socialist Bolsheviks, led by Vladimir Lenin, seized power in Russia from a provisional government, establishing the world's first communist state." (1) All was now lost and sets the stage for the overthrow of the Romanovs, led by the Lenin and the Bolsheviks. Revolution is underway throughout Russia. Nicholas faithfully kept a diary. The following is an abbreviated version of what Nicholas wrote in his Diary about his last days as Czar. (2)

March 12, Monday: Disorders Started several days ago in Petrograd; unfortunately, even the troops have begun to take part in them. It is a sickening feeling to be so far away and to receive fragmentary bad news.

March 13, Tuesday I had a long talk with [General] N. I Ivanov, whom I am dispatching to Petrograd with troops to restore order. During the night we turned back from Malaia Vishera, as Liuban and Tono seemed to be occupied by the rebels.. Gatchina and Luga, too, reported to be in possession [of the rebels]. Shame and disgrace. How hard it must be for poor Alix [Empress] to go through all these events alone. Lord help us.

March 15, Thursday: In the morning Ruzski came and read his exceptionally long direct-wire talk. According to this, the situation in Petrograd is such that the Ministry of the Duma would now be powerless to do anything, for it must contend with the Social-Democratic Party, represented by the workers' committee. My abdication is required. I have agreed. All around me there is treachery, cowardice, and deceit.

March 16, Friday: Read a great deal about Julius Caesar. Alexeev came with the latest news. It transpires that Misha [Grand Duke Michael] has abdicated. God knows who put it into his head to sign such stuff.

March 17, Saturday: At 12 I drove to the platform, to meet dear Mother, who has arrived from Kiev. I took her to my own place and lunched with her and our own family. Today, at last, I received two telegrams from dear Alix.

March 19, Monday: I signed the farewell order to the armies. I went into the guardhouse to say good-bye to all ranks of the Staff and bureau. At my own house I bade farewell to the officers and Cossacks, of my guard, cavalry, and infantry. It nearly broke my heart. It is hard, painful, and sad.

March 22, Thursday: On the street, around the palace, inside the park, wherever you turn there are sentries. Went upstairs and saw dear Alix and the precious children. She looked cheerful and well. The children were lying in a darkened room, but were in good spirits except Maria, who recently came down with the measles.

March 23, Friday: In spite of the present circumstances, the thought that we are all together cheers and consoles. Later I looked through, arranged, and burned papers. Sat with the children till 2:30.

March 24, Saturday: I received Benckendorff. Learned through him that we must remain here for some time. This is a pleasant thought. Continued burning letters and papers.

April 5, Thursday: Sorted my belongings and books, and sorted the things I want to take with me in case I go to England.

April 9, Monday Kerenski arrived and requested that we confine our meetings to mealtimes, and that we sit apart from the children. This, he claimed, was necessary in order to placate the Soviet of Workers' and Soldiers' Deputies. I had to submit to avoid the possibility of violence.

April 20 Friday: The appearance of the soldiers, and their slovenly bearing have made a disgusting impression on all of us.

April 21, Saturday: Celebrated the 23d anniversary of our engagement quietly. Worked at the landing stage, on account of the mob.

May 14, Monday: General Kornilov has given up his post, Guchkov has resigned. Both give the same reason: the irresponsible interference of the Soviet Workers' Deputies, and certain other organizations that are far more radical. What is Providence holding in store for poor Russia? God's will be done.

June 16, Saturday: Kerenski arrived. He asked me to send to the Investigation Commission any papers or letters that have any bearing on internal politics. At this time, the incident of Alexei's rifle occurred. He had been playing with it on the little island and the soldiers, who walked in the garden, saw it and requested the officer to be allowed to take it away.

June 22, Friday: Exactly three months since I came from Mogilev and here, we are confined like prisoners. Just before dinner came the good news of the launching of an offensive on the southwest front. Our troops broke through the enemy's positions and captured about 170 officers and 10,000 men. The Lord be praised!

July 18, Wednesday: In Petrograd there are disorders these days, accompanied by shooting. Many soldiers and sailors arrived there to oppose the Provisional Government. Absolute chaos. Where are those people who could put a stop to strife and bloodshed? The seed of all this evil is in Petrograd and not everywhere in Russia.

July 19 Thursday: Fortunately, most troops at Petrograd remained loyal to their duty and order is again restored in the streets.

July 21, Saturday: The guards from the Fourth and First Rifles acted properly in the discharge of their duties, and did not shadow us during our walk. When I returned learned that Kerenski had arrived. In our conversation he referred to the probability of our going south.

July 26, Thursday: Following our offensive at Galich, many units, thoroughly infected by the contemptible defeatist propaganda, not only refused to advance, but in some sectors even left their position though they were not pressed by the enemy. Taking advantage of this favorable opportunity, the Germans, and Austrians, with small forces, broke our lines in southern Galicia, which may compel the entire southwest front to retreat in an easterly direction. This is dishonorable and heartbreaking. There has been a proclamation from the Provisional Government that the death penalty is in force in the theater of military operations for persons found guilty of treason.

November 2, Friday: Now all our people who wish to take a walk are forced to pass through the city escorted by the soldiers.

November 30, Friday: Heartbreaking to learn from the papers descriptions of what happened two weeks ago at Petrograd and Moscow. It is much worse and more dishonorable than before.

December 1, Saturday: Three delegates of our Fifth Army signed preliminary conditions of an armistice. Such a nightmare I never expected. How could these Bolshevik scoundrels stoop so low as to carry into effect their cherished dream of proposing peace without asking the opinion of the people, and at a time when the enemy is occupying large tracts of our country?"

Our story details as to what may have prompted Nicholas to write such a sobering diary. It begins with Nicholas returning from the ravages of war. Although our story is fictional in nature, much of its content is supported by factual research.

CHAPTER 1

THE CZAR'S FAMILY

The air in St. Petersburg smacks of uncontrollable turmoil. Those who were not demonstrating in the streets were fighting one another for morsels of food. A discouraged and beaten Czar Nicholas returns home after failing to fend off an advancing German Army. His return is hastened upon receiving word of the discontent of his people who were calling for him to abdicate.

Photo 1-Alexander Palace

Nicholas disembarks from his limousine to enter Alexander palace. His face is drawn and his demeaner smacked with defeat. The Alexander Palace, located in St Petersburg, is considered the pearl among the Czar's palaces and one of the main masterpieces in the world. "The art-critic I.E.Grabar wrote that "there are palaces bigger and more regal, but there is no palace having architecture more beautiful than the Alexander Palace" (3). It was a summer dacha for the Imperial Family in the nineteenth century, but it became a real home for the last Russian

Emperor Nicholas II and his wife Alexandra Fiodorovna during the last thirteen years of their reign. From this palace, the family of Nicholas II was sent from living a lavish lifestyle into enduring an agonizing exile in Tobolsk. Although the palace is magnificent in stature, it was difficult to ward off any advances by demonstrators and attackers.

It was a blistering cold day in Russia. Czar Nicholas, not knowing that he would soon become the last Czar of Russia, was returning to Alexander palace and to his loving family from the front lines during WWI. "His ancestor, Catherine the great, built Alexander palace in 1792. She built it on a plateau about thirty miles south of Saint Petersburg. It is an elongated two-story building with double wings on each side. Because his beloved Alexandra loved the thought of living here when they married, they decided to make it their permanent home in 1905." (4) Nicholas was returning home because he learned that his subjects were calling for his overthrow. To his surprise, his palace was over-run by his people. Surrounding the palace are large mobs of demonstrators demanding that he abdicate the throne."

Nicholas arrived at Alexander palace to find only a handful of guards and large mobs of demonstrators cursing the Romanov name. Many windows have been shattered throughout the palace. The few guards who were left struggled to make way for him to enter the palace. The demonstrators loudly shout their demands, "Down with Nicholas-down with the Romanov family." Nicholas needed to cover himself up for his protection as he struggled to get through the demonstrators, many of whom are pushed away by the guards as they reach out to beat on him. Several of the demonstrators succeeded in reaching through the guards to grab a piece of his clothing. Nicholas now realizes more than ever the seriousness of the situation, for it was the first time any commoner could get that close to a Czar. This is the first time in his life that he felt more like a commoner than part of the privileged class.

Nicholas lamented about what had befallen him, but he was forewarned that his people were becoming discontented for the past several years. "Against the advice of his consorts, he had been fighting a war his people were not behind. To add insult to injury, he caused the unnecessary massacre of 100 unarmed protesters during a peaceful assembly in 1905. Furthermore, he was responsible for his own coronation being a huge disaster. Because he did not go to a field to console the families of their loved ones who died in a stampede while celebrating his coronation, the people nicknamed him "Nicholas the Bloody." (5)

Nicholas's losing two bloody wars that he started with the Japanese and Germany was the crowning thorn that further eroded whatever semblance of control he still had over his subjects. With his taking the men away from their farms to fight unnecessary wars, the food system collapsed, and the transportation system fell apart. These disasters caused his people to riot and call for his abdication. He even lost support from his close confidants because he could not maintain a civil relationship with the parliament branch of the Government, dubbed the Duma. He outright refused to give them any power and even thought of disbanding them.

As he entered the palace, he frantically summoned the captain of the few remaining guards who are left to defend it. The guard captain hastily snapped to attention when Nicholas asked why the air smacked of chaos and disharmony?

Looking concerned, his captain addressed him with respect but not with the same respectful demeaner before the riots began. The guard captain has a lost look on his face and what he had to report was very disturbing." "My Imperial

Highness, the leaders of the mob say the Russian people have had enough of hunger and despair. They are demanding that you abdicate. I fear for the safety of you and your family."

Nicholas was totally bewildered and disbelief from the explanation of the guard. He could only think of his family's safety and questioned the guard as to the whereabout of his family. "Where is my family and are they safe?" The guard captain told him that they were barricaded in their apartment behind locked doors. He reassures Nicholas of their safety." "We have stationed guards outside the doors."

With the mayhem going on, Nicholas started to count the guards on duty and asked the captain of the guards for a head count. "Do you have enough men to ward off the mob if they decide to storm the palace? "Only for a short time," he responded. Many of your palace guards have defected to join the demonstrators because they will not take up arms against their fellow countrymen, some of which may be members of their own family."

Upon hearing this from one of the elite captains of his palace guards, he hastily entered the palace and went straight to his family's apartment. The apartment is huge with large murals of past ancestors and adorned with lavish furniture in gold brocade fabric. The thick ornate carpets were especially woven for the palace. A large glass chandelier hangs from the middle of the main sitting room.

As soon as Nicholas entered the apartment, he was greeted by a frightened Alexandra. Her beautiful blue eyes were red from crying, and she trembled with fear as she tried to explain her distress. Nicholas had to calm her, before he could understand what she was saying.

Alexandra wrapped her arms around Nicholas sobbing, making it difficult for him to understand what she was saying. She finally gained enough composure, making it easier for

Nicholas to understand her. "I cannot believe what is happening Nicki. Most of our servants have left us and there are only a few loyal guards left. The head of parliament, Kerensky, was here to inform me that the people are revolting and calling for our downfall. What are we to do?"

"If we cannot quelch this uprising Alexandra, then all is lost, and we will be at the mercy of a Provincial government organized by Parliament under the leadership of Kerensky. As bad as it is, we have a better chance with Parliament than with Lenin and the Bolsheviks." Nicholas kneels in front of Alexandra with tears in his eyes. Alexandra cradles his head to her stomach and starts to cry uncontrollably. It has been ages since Nicholas lost control of his emotions. The last time was when his father died and the reality of ascending the throne overtook him.

Alexandra tries to comfort Nicholas. She motions towards the living room of their apartment. "We are all here for you Nicki. Our children have been very worried about you and afraid you may have been killed in the war."

Alexandra and Nicholas entered the living room of the family apartment hand in hand. Their four daughters and one son were hugging one another and crying with fright.

Photo 2-Czar Nicholas, Tsarina Alexandra, and their children

The large colored tapestry that adorned the windows has been tied together to protect the family from any gunfire or rocks that are being thrown by the mob outside. This casts an even gloomier atmosphere over the situation. As the mob grows larger, the children continue to embrace one another and cry. Large paintings of czars that have gone before adorning the room.

As Nicholas stares at them, he keeps thinking where he went wrong. He stares at the large portrait of his father who gave him no direction on how to be a czar, only to ingrain in him the autocratic philosophy that contributed to his downfall. Repeatedly, he keeps thinking that he has disgraced the Romanov name and broken a long line that goes back centuries to Peter and Catherine the Great.

Looking at his surroundings, Nicholas peeks through the drapes at the demonstrators outside. Looking at the tattered clothing worn by the demonstrators and the desperation of their faces, he now came to realize what he had done to them. They were starving while his family lived in the lap of luxury. He comes to the realization why his people have grown to hate his family.

Power to the palace has been cut off and the rooms have become cold, dark, and the atmosphere smacks of despair and fear. Rocks are being thrown at the windows. The guards are leaving their posts in droves, making the palace more vulnerable to the mobs.

Nicholas turns his thoughts back to protecting his family and regaining his composure, finding it most difficult explaining to the children what has happened and trying to make them feel safe. Whatever may befall him, he realizes that he must focus on the safety of his children. As he turns to face them, he wraps his arms around them as they all hug one another.

All the children start talking at once. "Father, we are so happy that you have returned safely but chaos has gripped our country. We were herded into our quarters by the guards, and we do not understand what is happening. Most of the guards have abandoned us and the only protection between us and the mob outside is the captain of the guards, a handful of palace guards, and being barricaded in our apartment. What will happen if the guards are overcome by the demonstrators?"

The children are unaware that their father will be ousted as the czar of a country that spanned one sixth of the world and a dynasty that was once the richest of all monarchies. His abdication would end the three-hundred-year reign of the Romanovs and send them all off to their deaths.

The oldest of the Romanov children, Olga, speaks on behalf of her siblings. "We fear for our lives father. Many of the guards have abandoned their posts and those that remain have confined us to our apartment, saying that it is for our safety. What has happened to our beloved Russia and what does all this mean?

Nicholas places his hands on Olga's shoulders. Even though he knows that all may be lost, he cannot tell his family the truth. "Do not fear my children. This insurrection will be suppressed, and all will return to normal as it was before."

Nicholas, however, fears the worst and keeps what he thinks will be the outcome to himself. He was so proud of his beautiful daughters; Grand Duchesses Olga, Maria, Tatiana, and Anastasis. After nearly giving up on an heir, Alexandra gave him an heir to the throne which they named Alexei. Alas, Alexei was born with hemophilia which would cause him to bleed to death from a slight cut. They kept his disease a secret for fear the people would not accept him as the Successor to the Romanov throne."

"Alexandra was Queen Victoria's granddaughter and daughter of Louis IV, grand duke of Hesse-Darmstadt. She married Nicholas in 1894 and was the most dominant. She proved to be unpopular at court and turned to mysticism for solace. Through her near-fanatical acceptance of Orthodoxy and her belief in autocratic rule, she felt it her duty to help reassert the absolute power of Nicholas, which had been limited by reforms in 1905. "(6)

Alexandra became increasingly under the influence of Grigori Rasputin, a mystic monk whom she believed had saved Alexei's life by controlling his hemophiliac disorder. Rasputin solidified his relationship with Alexandra by making her believe that he alleviated Alexei's hemophilia through some mystical medicine and prayer. Later, the royal couple discovered that his mystical medicine was used in Russian villages to treat internal bleeding in horses." Rasputin rose through Russian society at the expense of Alexandra. His religious connections, coupled with his appealing charisma, gained the attention of some Russian Orthodox hierarchy and senior members of the Imperial family. This gave him access to Alexandra and her children.

Alexandra and Nicholas had sought out unconventional spiritual advisors, but Rasputin better met their needs by anticipating their inner thoughts and telling them what they wanted to hear. As a result, they wrongfully allowed him to provide political advice and to the dismay of the Russian elite, the imperial family even allowed him to make recommendations for political appointments."

"Allowing Rasputin to infiltrate the royal family caused suspicion among the Russian people. Along with Nicholas, they resented his power and grew to resent him. They finally discovered his deceitful tactics. Rasputin had cold calculating eyes and was strong. Instead of being a prayerful priest, he was a womanizer, a sexual pervert, and a drunk. Having known of his reputation and nickname "The Mad Monk," Nicholas and Alexandra should have known better than to put their trust in him.

"The husband of Nicholas's niece, Prince Yussup, finally rid the imperial family of Rasputin by arranging for his assassination. He invited Rasputin to his palace to meet his wife and then served him cakes and wine laced with potassium cyanide. Yussup was amazed that the poison had no effect. Yussup then grabbed the revolver of the Grand Duke and shot Rasputin numerous times. All these multiple gunshots still did not kill the mad monk. Because of Rasputin's toughness, they could not even end his life. In a final attempt, the assassins followed him after he staggered outside the basement and drowned him in the Tura River." (7)

"All the efforts to rid the Romanovs of this nuisance proved too late. Killing Rasputin did not improve the distaste the people held for the monarchy. Upon the rise of the Bolsheviks, Rasputin was used as an example of the corruption at the heart of the Imperial court. Instead of seeing his death in a positive light, killing him was seen as an attempt by the royalty to hold onto power. To the Bolsheviks and the poor, Rasputin represented the broader problems with czarism. This crazy monk contributed to the insurrection throughout Russia and the overthrow of the Romanov family. The President of the Provisional government went on to say that without Rasputin, there would have been no Lenin." (8)

Nicholas reflects on what went wrong to bring about his downfall. He now realized that his following the autocratic leadership example set by his father contributed to his eventual downfall when he took the throne at 27. He inherited a restless Russia from his father Alexander, who instilled in him the philosophy to rule Russia with an iron fist.

CHAPTER 2

THE CZAR ABDICATES

Realizing that his abdication was imminent, Nicholas felt compelled to talk with his brother Michael to devise a plan that would hopefully save the Romanov dynasty. Michael and his family occupied another wing of the Palace. As he was second in line to succeed Nicholas and Nicholas's son was very sickly, it was thought best that Michael and his family stayed nearby.

Only after Michael was assured it was Nicholas at the door did he remove the barricade blocking the door. Upon entering Michael's apartment, Nicholas found his brother and his family huddled together.

As Nicholas stood in front of Michael, he could see the fear and disbelief in his eyes. "Michael, I left our soldiers in the field only to return to this mess. What little remaining guards we have informed me that this lynch-like mob has surrounded the palace and many of our guards have joined them. I always thought that our people were pleased with us."

After all these years during the reign of his brother Nicholas, Michael never revealed that he resented his brother's autocratic style of ruling Russia. With his brother's imminent overthrow, he felt free to express his feelings.

"I have tried to tell you many times Niki that your autocratic approach to ruling Russia was making the people to hate us. I cannot blame you totally because your style of ruling was due to that which was passed on by our father and the reinforcement of it by your wife. Your alignment with that mad monk Rasputin only exasperated the problem. Your corrupt and oppressive policies antagonized our people day by day, giving them no choice but to revolt. Entering those no-win wars against the advice of our generals caused us to lose over one million of our young soldiers and even far more casualties among our people. As a result of your ignoring the home front and cries of our people, many of them starved."

As Michael spoke, you could sense his anger with his brother as well as his hopelessness and helplessness. He continually pounded his fist on the table while berating Nicholas and he ranted on and on about what he had done wrong. At the same time, Michael assumed no responsibility for not confiding this to his brother before. As Michael ranted on, Nicholas stood there, awe struck in disbelief that Michael felt this way. Just then, their uncle Nikolae walked into the room. Grand Duke Nikolae was not only their uncle, but he was also Nicholas's commanding general in World War I and the Grandson of Emperor Nicolas I. Because he struggled leading Russia's war effort against Germany, Nicholas dismissed him as Commander and took over commanding the military.

Nicholas turned to his uncle. "My uncle, what are we to do? With most of our army deployed on the front lines, we cannot quelch this uprising. The Bolsheviks are well organized and intent on overthrowing me."

The Grand Duke stared at Niki in disgust, shaking his head side to side. "I warned you about going into wars you could not win but you would not listen. You were more concerned with expanding your empire than taking care of the needs of our people. As a result, you have lost favor with the people Niki. They hold you personally responsible for all the misfortune that has plagued Russia over these past years. Because you isolated yourself from your subjects, they have no allegiance or love for the crown. You allowed that mad monk and your wife counsel you on matters they knew nothing of and ignored your trusted advisors, including me. The only possibility of saving the Romanov legacy is for you to abdicate the throne and name your son Alexei as your successor. If not, you and your family will suffer the consequences."

Nicholas and his brother just stood there in shock and bewilderment. After several minutes of complete silence, Nicholas spoke his mind. "Abdicate, if that is what will save the crown, I will do it, but I think I may have a better way."

Drawing upon his study of history and his lineage, he recalls to his uncle and brother how Catherine the Great came to power. "Our ancestor, "Catherine the Great, ascended the throne by plotting to overthrow her husband, Peter III, who was reputed to be a worst ruler than me. Peter was a hated Czar. Besides the people, he angered crucial allies including the Russian Orthodox church and the Country's military. Catherine then went onto lead our country into full participation in the political and cultural life." (9) Our father, brother Michael, reversed all that she institutionalized by imposing his autocratic style of leadership. Instead of my abdicating, we can stage a coup by having one of our family members overthrowing me, pacifying the anger and hate of the people."

His Uncle holds his hand to his chin in ponderance of what Nicholas proposes. "It is an interesting strategy, but it is too late for such a bold plan. Besides, Catherine had the support of her sizable army. With our troops hunkered down on the front lines, we have none and not enough time to muster any. No Niki, our only chance is for you to abdicate in favor of your son Alexi."

Nicholas raises his hand in opposition and waves off his uncle's suggestion. "Alexei is too young and fragile. If such a burden is placed upon him at such a young age with his medical condition, it will surely lead to his early death." Nicholas then turns to his brother Michael. "You are third in line to the throne after my son Michael. You must accept the crown!"

Michael stands there in shock with his jaw dropped as if unable to utter a syllable. "You want me to take the crown with that rabble outside waiting to send whoever sits on that throne to their death!? I never wanted to be Emperor of Russia. All these years, I was content to simply be a prince of Russia, providing my family with the comforts afforded the title. Being czar is never what I wanted for me and my family."

Michael turns away from his uncle and Niki. With a hand on his chin, he stares out the window at the demonstrators who are growing bigger and louder by the hour. He methodically realizes that his accepting the crown could put him and his family in harm's way. On the other hand, he rationalizes that wearing the crown may preserve the lifestyle and prestige his family has become accustomed to. Regaining his composure, he then turns towards Nicki and his uncle. "I will accept it on the condition that our parliament ratifies my accension to the throne and that you and your family leaves Russia until the fervor of the people subsides Niki."

Although reluctant to abdicate the throne, Nicholas feels relieved that it was settled. "Uncle, you are our witness to what we agree upon here today. Let it be written; let it be done Michael. I promise you that my family and I will be gone as soon as the crown is placed upon your head."

Nicholas then returned to his family to inform them of his decision to abdicate the throne. Alexandra and their children were in shock and could not even utter a word. Nicholas instructed his family to prepare for their departure from the palace and Saint Petersburg. His father and mother raised

Nicholas to be stoic in his mannerisms, which gave him the ability to show no emotions and keep his face expressionless. This was the first time; however, his face became distorted as his lips quivered, and a tear ran down his cheek. He looked like a downtrodden child who had been scolded by his parents.

After Nicholas announced his abdication publicly, chaos erupted. Nicholas wanted to send a message to his troops to submit themselves to the Provincial Government. He believed that apart from beating Germany, his troops were of prime importance to him. His message, however, was blocked by the Bolsheviks and never reached the troops. Reason for the Bolsheviks doing so was attributed to a rumor where Nicholas was thinking about enlisting troops to fight the revolution and create an alliance with the Germans. Chaos continued to erupt in Petrograd. The empress was accused by the Media of treason and having an affair with the mad monk Rasputin. Soldiers killed their officers, crime was rampant throughout the cities, and mobs looted and raped. Some of the ministers of the czar even asked to be imprisoned and placed under heavy guard for fear of being killed by the Bolsheviks.

Nicholas lamented over how his empire was being torn apart and how his family was treated. For the protection of him and his family, they were detained by the provisional government at their former residence in the town of Tsarskoye Selo, located south of Saint Petersburg. Nicholas's first thought for their survival was to ask his cousin King George of England to give them sanctuary in England. Afterall he his cousin and Alexandra is the granddaughter of Queen Victoria and daughter of Louis IV of Hesse Darmstadt."

Nicholas and King George of England were first cousins and extremely close. They even looked like twins, with the same blue eyes and beards. Nicholas would learn from Kerensky that King George would deny he and his family sanctuary because England was nervous housing the Romanovs due to possible uprising against the English monarchy. As a result, King George urged the British government to rescind any offers to protect Nicholas and his family, leaving him open to criticism that he sacrificed his family for politics." (10)

Photo 3-King George and Czar Nicholas

While deciding how to govern Russia, "the Russian Parliament (the Duma) took over the rule of Russia under the leadership of Alexander Kerensky. The Provincial leadership was comprised of the Duma and was far less vengeful and socialistic than the Bolsheviks. The Duma was an elected semi-representative body in Russia created by Nicholas in 1905. He created it when the government was desperate to divide the opposition during an uprising. Like his father, Nicholas limited their power because he did not want any restrictions or reductions on his own powers. By doing so was another example of him not empowering the people which contributed to his downfall. (11)

Kerensky enters the palace to talk with Nicholas about the fate of him and his family, no longer addressing Nicholas as Czar. "Your cousin, King George, and the French have denied giving you sanctuary Nicholas and there is too much turmoil here in St Petersburg to guarantee you and your family protection. We have arranged for you to be taken to Siberia for your safety. You will then be taken to the Border."

Initially, the Parliament planned to send the Romanovs to a small town in southern Russia where there was a comfortable Governor's house, and they would not be subject to mob violence. The change in plans to send them to Siberia was highly questioned. Especially as all the relatives of the imperial family who were sent to the Crimea south of Russia were eventually saved from any harm. In rebuttal, Kerensky defended his plan to send the Romanovs through the Siberian border was attributed to averting their assassination. Kerensky further defended the change to extremists interrupting him during a speech in the Parliament house, demanding the execution of the Czar. (12)

There was already a botched attempt to kidnap the czar and imprison him in the fortress of St. Peter and Paul. A Revolutionist from the far left, disguised as a Colonel, presented an order to hand the Czar over to him. It had an official seal and signed by a member of Parliament. Fortunately, the Commander in charge saw through his scheme and refused his request. Concerned for the safety of the royal family and the growing challenge of Bolshevism, the Parliament decided to suppress the increasing disorder in Russia. Such steps only lead to more rioting and increased the chances for overthrowing the government and executing the Czar and his family.

"It was speculated that the choice of Siberia by Kerensky was that he wanted to punish the Czar by having him experience the same cold winters as those banished to Siberia by the czars. Little did Kerensky know that he was signing the death warrant of the Romanov family by sending them through Siberia where the Bolsheviks would intercept them. The journey of the Romanovs to Siberia began a few months before the start of frigid winters. Siberia is a huge territory which occupies about 60 percent of Russia, four million square miles. Nichola's family would be facing subzero temperatures.

Thinking about what he and his family would be facing, Nicholas spent a sleepless night anticipating the long journey and cold winters. Alexei celebrated his thirteenth birthday the night before they departed. Besides the military escort, over forty court attendants volunteered to accompany the family. As a result, it took two trains to transport them and soldiers.

"Bolshevik revolutionaries led by Lenin took control of the provincial government. Catastrophic events followed their takeover. The parliament voted against Nicholas's brother ascending the throne. Eventually the Bolsheviks executed him. When word reached Nicholas of his brother's execution, the Romanovs thought their fate may also be cast in stone. On route to Siberia, they were intercepted by the Bolsheviks. Their escorts tried to ward them off but were outnumbered. "The Bolsheviks threatened the escorts with death if they did not give up the Czar and his family. Only the Royal family's physician, chambermaid, cook, valet, and a trusted sailor was allowed to accompany them. The Romanovs found themselves at the mercy of Lenin and the revolution leaders." (13)

CHAPTER 3

THE EXECUTION

Nicholas and Alexandra were in denial and refused to give up hope that their family would be saved. They were shuffled from house to house. Their new life was dramatically different from their regal life in St. Petersburg. Their guards repeatedly raped their daughters and threatened Alexandra with the same.

Their destination was Yekaterinburg which is the fourth largest city in Russia and far from their culturally rich home in St. Petersburg. Ironically, the city which was founded by Nicholas's ancestors will now mark the place where the last Russian Czar and his family will breathe their last breath. The family was to be kept in a house known as the Ipatiev House, a home that the Bolsheviks called "the house of special purpose." situated in the center of what was then a stark and barren city, a victim of the Bolshevik revolution. Once living in a regal palace, the family was now camped out in a dilapidated home that was once the former home of a famous merchant. With no maintenance, it now evolved into a ghastly dwelling with little heat and outside temperatures freezing or below. The house had no bed linens, lots of dust, infested with insects, and little furniture or silverware.

Photo 4-Ipatiev House-House of Special Purpose

"But as the events in Russia unfolded, this place became the scene of a darker happening and a mystery that remains unsolved to this very day. During their stay, the guards hassled them by drawing lewd images on the walls of the bathroom and covering them with obscene poems about Alexandra. During their entire stay in this despicable house, their daughters were sexually assaulted.

"Upon their arrival, they were greeted by a savory looking henchman in his forties, Yakov Yurovsky. His eyes were sullen, and he sported a beard and mustache. He would be the one to eventually coordinate and lead the killing of the imperial family. Yurovsky welcomed and greeted them with a stoic look as if there was nothing to worry about.

Lenin, Yurovsky, and the revolutionaries all saw the czars as a cancer that made it impossible for the working class to rise. Instead of owning up to ordering the murders of the family, however, Lenin devised a plan to divest himself from the killings by placing the blame on Yurovsky.

In anticipation of the arrival of Nicholas and his family, their rooms were made ready for a long stay. Unfortunately, the house did not have much creature comforts such as fresh bed linens, blankets, or towels.

The rooms were stark, cold, and drafty to say the least. The house temperature was in the forty-degree range while the outside temperatures hovered in the high teens to low 20's. Guards were posted in the hallways and surrounded the perimeter of the building. One guard accompanied each family member when they went to the bathroom. There was one incredibly young twenty-year-old guard, Jon Drukov, who always accompanied Anastasia. He protected Anastasia from being accosted by the other guards. Jon was kind and took a liking to her. She in turn liked him. He was not one of the Bolsheviks because he was hired as a mercenary and held no allegiance to the Bolsheviks and their cause. He grew more sympathetic to the Romanovs and did not think highly of the way they were being treated.

The Romanovs were housed on the upper floor while their guards were on the lower. permitted daily exercise in a walled garden and They were isolated from the outside by their windows being painted and the building being surrounded by a high wooden fence.

The trusted sailor voluntarily came along with the family even though he realized he may be putting his life at risk. His concerns proved right when the Bolsheviks had him shot for trying to stop one of them from stealing a gold chain from Alexei. Nicholas pleaded with Yurvosky to not kill him, but his words were ignored." (14)

Nicholas returned to his room to see Alexandra hopelessly sprawled on the bed sobbing. Her eyes were swollen and blood shot with tears. He took her in his arms and tried to comfort her while trying to devise a plan for the survival of the Romanov family.

It was difficult for Nicholas to not have any authority. "We must play along with them if we are to survive Alexandra. If they intend to kill us all, we must try to perpetuate the Romanov line by saving one or more of our children. One possibility would be Anastasia. The young guard Jon treated her well and appears to like her very much and Anastasia seems to feel the same way towards him. I must try to talk with him."

Alexandra tries to regain her composure. "I do not think we have much hope, but it is worth the try. Hopefully, you are right about the young guard, and he is willing to help us."

Nicholas looks towards the room where Alexei is housed. "I am going to Alexei's room to see how he is doing and to tell him good night."

Upon entering the room, Alexei speaks to his father in a disappointing and condescending tone. "Why did you not name me as your successor? I should have had my time as czar and the outcome may have been different. We may still be in the comforts of our palace and not in this despicable place and only God knows what our fate at the hands of these hoodlums will be."

All Nicholas could do was stare at Alexei and had little words of comfort. In his mind, he kept thinking that he should have named Alexei as his successor. On the other hand, he also thought that such a strain may have hastened his death.

Nicholas kissed Alexei on the forehead and bade him good night, returning to his own room. The room was dirty and stark compared to what they once enjoyed. It smelled and the linen was musty and torn. Upon entering, he could hear Alexandra crying again and felt much worse about placing his family in harm's way. The Romanov family has now endured seventy-eight days in this dilapidated home with no end in sight. What will befall them soon will be written in the annals of history.

"At midnight, Yurovsky entered the room of Romanov's doctor. The doctor was in the process of writing a letter to his family Yurovsky instructed the doctor to awaken the royal family and servants, so that they could ready themselves to be transported to another location. He gave the reason that the white army who opposed the Bolsheviks and the socialists were preparing to battle with one another in the streets. The doctor followed his instructions and awakened the Romanovs to alert them of the move and to start packing. Hearing this, the Romanovs were pleased that they were moving to another location. Their stay at the house of special purpose was more than they could bear.

After giving marching orders to the doctor, Yurovsky then goes to his office to talk with another one of his henchmen. "I am waiting word from the Kremlin. They are discussing what to do with the family, either execute just Nicholas and Alexandra or the entire family."

"They have information that a division of the white army that is loyal to Nicholas, is on its way here to free him and his family. Lenin wants the executions to take place as soon as possible so there is no chance for the white army to reinstate the czar and defeating our revolution."

Even though the counter revolutionary White army was larger than the Red army, the Red army won out in the end. This was attributed to the White army encountering major problems in organizing their campaigns and the Bolshevik Red army had more drive and energy because of their cause to overthrow the government." (15)

It seemed like hours but within a short time the phone rings and the caller sealed the fate of the Romanov family. Receiving the order to execute the entire family, Yurovsky loads his revolver and organizes a firing squad.

In the meantime, Nicholas goes into each of his family's rooms to arouse them. "Wake up Alexandra my love. Thank god that they are going to move us to another location."

After packing their bags, the Romanovs along with their doctor and three servants were first led down the courtyard and then through an entrance to a basement room at the rear of the building. Because Alexei could not stand on his own, chairs were brought in for Alexei and Alexandra. The others stood behind and to their sides. The room was stark and cold with no windows for ventilation. All were drowsy from being awaken in the middle of the night.

After patiently waiting for their escort, the family could hear footsteps of what they perceived to be several men approaching the room. Suddenly, the double doors swung open and Yurovsky appeared along with a group of men bearing weapons and knives. Nicholas looked with a puzzled expression on his face thinking why many armed men came to escort them.

Yurovsky stared directly at the family and reads an official written statement from the Kremlin. "Because of crimes against the state Nicholas Romanov, you and your family are sentenced to death. Yurovsky also noted that relatives of the Romanovs attempted to rescue the imperial family and failed, thus they were justified in executing them immediately without trial.

Hearing this, Nicholas rose to confront their executioners. "With his hands on Alexis and Alexandra, he pleads with Yurovsky…. No…no…please do not punish my family for any violations you feel that I may have caused. They are innocent of any wrongdoing. I beg you to not do this to my beautiful family."

"The rest of his family joined in pleading for their lives, but their pleas went unanswered. Their captors then turn on them ignoring the pleas and cries of the family, attacking them first with bullets, then with the butts of their guns, bayonets, and even their own heels and fists. Yurovsky personally shot Nicki and his heir Alexei.

The jewels that Alexandra and her daughters sewed into their dresses at first blocked many of the bullets. First to drop was Anastasia, followed by the rest of the family. The remainder of the family cascaded over one another, each of them falling on top of the shell-shocked Anastasia. With Anastasia falling first and in a state of shock, the henchmen could not clearly see her to ascertain whether she was alive or dead. Each of the royal family reached out to grasp one another's hands while they lay wounded and barely alive on the floor, their life's blood slowly draining from them. Seeing they were still alive, Yurovsky personally finished the royal couple while the remainder of the family was knifed and crushed with the henchmen's boots and butts of their weapons. The killers kept shooting into the Romanovs. It was more of a slaughter than an execution. The last words of Nicholas to his beloved wife were "I love you" and I am sorry that I failed to protect our family. The killers were convinced that they were all dead. At least they thought they were all dead." (16)

What may have looked like an impromptu execution was in fact a carefully thought-out planned act of murder. For days, the Bolsheviks had been preparing for the murders. They stocked up benzene and sulfuric acid to destroy the bodies of the royal family beyond recognition.

Yurovsky orders his guards to bring up the truck to take the bodies to the mine shaft where they will dispose of them.

Guard Jon Drukov did not take part in shooting the Romanovs but was ordered to help transport the bodies to the mine where there was a team of Bolsheviks who would desecrate the bodies beyond recognition and then drop the remains down the mine shaft. Jon was the only guard riding in the back of the truck with the bodies and one driver was in the cab, who did not have clear vision to the back of the truck. As the truck slowly made its way to the burial site, Jon heard a groan beneath the pile of bodies. As he gently peeled away each of the Romanov bodies, he heard another groan again. He was totally surprised that the groans came from Anastasia. She was still alive, but her one arm had several wounds. She survived the massacre because she fainted before receiving a fatal gunshot and was hidden under the bodies of her family. Because her eyes were glazed over from going into deep shock, the Bolsheviks took her for dead. Mistaking her for dead, the henchman did not bother to fire follow-up shots into her. She only incurred bullet wounds on her one arm and shoulder but was in shock after being wounded and witnessing the slaughter of her family.

Another reason for Anastasia's survival was attributed to her mother's instruction to sew family jewels into their garments. Besides jewels, Anastasia sewed the official crown seal of the czars that was used when signing official documents. It was made of solid gold and strong enough to ward off the bullets and knives.

Jon quickly pulled her from the remainder of the stacked bodies of her family and slid her to the rear of the truck. As he cradled her in his arms, Anastasia laid there whimpering about her family and moaning from her wounds. Lovingly holding Anastasia in his arms, Jon whispered in her ear. "Be still and quiet Anastasia or the driver will hear you and alert the Bolsheviks that you are still alive. I will protect you and help you escape the wrath of these killers. When we stop at the next crossroads, I am going to lift you out of the truck and hide you in the woods until it is safe to move you again. I must continue with the truck for now or they will be suspicious and may launch a search for you and me throughout the city."

Jon gave Anastasia a comforting hug and kiss before jumping back into the truck. After the Bolsheviks completed the gruesome task of mutilating and burying the bodies, Jon made his way back to where he hid Anastasia only to find that she had tried to escape by herself. She was trembling with fear and her arm was in severe pain. Realizing that she needed some medical care, his only hope was to enlist the help of those who still held allegiance to the Romanovs. There were many in Russia that remained loyal to the Romanov family, and he was housed with one such family. He took Anastacia by the hand and slowly walked back to the city.

"Do not fear Anastasia, I will not let them hurt you again. We need to find a safe place to hide. Hopefully, the killers are too dumb to count the bodies and discover that there is one missing. The only way we can survive is to enlist the help of those sympathetic to preserving the Romanov dynasty."

With tears running down her cheeks, Anastasia looked into Jon's eyes. "How do I know I can trust you Jon. You were one of the guards that kept me and my family prisoner in that terrible house. I appreciate your saving me from what would have been a terrible death, but how can I be sure that you will not return me to the Bolsheviks for ransom?

I would rather die here than bear more of the suffering that befell me and my family."

Jon hugs Anastacia and looks into her eyes. "Right now, we do not have much choice. We can try to save ourselves by walking out of these woods to seek help from those who still supports your family or stay here where the Bolshevik will find and kill us. Which do you prefer?"

Too weak and afraid to be by herself, Anastasia painfully grabs Jon's hand as they slowly walk along a dirt path towards the city. As she walked, the gruesome visions of her family being slaughtered continually haunted her. She could not stop whimpering.

Jon thought their only hope was to seek help from the lady that housed him, who was a former maid servant of Alexandra, Madeleine Zanotti. The Bolsheviks spared Madeleine because they needed someone to maintain the house of special purpose.

CHAPTER 4

COMING TO AMERICA

After an arduous walk to the city, Jon is careful not to walk the main streets. Instead, he walks in the back alleys. He knocks on Madeleine Zanotti's door while keeping a watchful eye for any Bolsheviks. She opens the door and is surprised to see Jon standing there with a young girl. "Jon who is this young girl."

"Mrs. Zanotti, we desperately need your help. This young lady has been wounded by the Bolsheviks and we need a place to hide while I find a way for us to escape Russia.

Madeleine holds Anastasia's face in her hands, Recognizing her immediately she gasps.

"My god, Jon, you have one of the daughters of the Czar. It is Anastasia! I used to hold her in my arms when she was a little girl when I tended to Alexandra. Do you realize that you are endangering us by bringing her here? How did you free her from the Bolsheviks?"

Madeleine was unaware that the Romanovs had been murdered. Like many others who knew the Romanovs were in captivity, she thought they were not going to be harmed. Jon then described the dreadful murders of the Romanovs at the hands of the Bolsheviks.

After learning of the Romanov's terrible ending and recalling Alexandra's kindness towards her when she was her maid, Madeleine was inclined to help Anastasia. She had fond memories of how Alexandra took an interest in the lives of all her Household help, right down to the last little servant. The Czarina often helped them in times of trouble in ways no one knew. Even though Alexandra was the czar's wife, she treated her maids with respect regardless of their class in life. She would visit a sick maid as readily as one of her ladies-in-waiting. Even when Alexandra was in captivity, she contrived to have a present made and got the commander of the prison guard to send it to Madeleine for her 25 years of service to her and her family. Remembering all this, Madeleine was determined to return Alexandra's kindness by doing all she could to help the last surviving child of Alexandra.

"Bring her in quickly Jon. I have no mercenaries staying here because the Bolsheviks said that they no longer needed them. It all makes sense from what you have told me about the murders. You and Anastasia can be safe here while we devise a plan to get you both to safety."

Anastasia's wounds needed immediate cleansing and bandaged. None of the bullets were lodged in her arm as they cleanly pierced through her arm. Luckily, no bullets had hit any major arteries. Jon watched as Madeleine cleaned and bandaged Anastasia's wounds. From watching and learning from the doctors who treated Crown prince Alexei's bleeding, Madeleine had the knowledge to clean and bandage the wounds.

It took some time for word to spread of the Romanov's fate. News that Nicholas and his family had been assassinated completely overshadowed the political victories Lenin and his fellow revolutionaries had achieved. Ironically, murdering Nicholas, Alexandra, and their children disgusted many Russians how they were mercilessly slaughtered. Also, ten percent of the Russian population remained loyal to the czar because they benefited as being part of the privileged class, many of them formed an underground network to help and protect one another. Even today, there is a contingent of Russian society that wants to restore the monarchy, including an oligarch who funds a school designed to prepare Russians for a future monarchy. Despite Nicholas's short comings, some Russians even yearned for the day he or one of his successors would return to power.

Several days had gone by since the massacre of the Romanov family. Jon and Anastasia have been holed up in the basement of Madeleine's home while she contrives a way to get them to a safe place.

Speaking to Jon and Anastasia, Madaleine has an idea how to get them to safety. "I can place you in touch with those that can help you escape the clutches of the Bolsheviks Jon, but you must promise not to tell anyone that I helped you if you are captured. Get a good night's sleep and we will discuss it in the morning. Before you go to bed, we need to clean and bandage Anastasia's wounds better. They are healing but we cannot take a chance on their getting infected."

Jon nods his head in agreement. "Agreed in both cases Mrs. Zanotti. We are so grateful for your help. Forgive us for placing this burden on your shoulders. We simply have no one else to turn to for help."

Anastasia chimes in. "Thank you from the bottom of our hearts. I cannot believe that any human being could be so cruel as to kill my family in cold blood. My brother and sisters were never aware of what transpired during our father's rule. Even the cruelty that he may have inflicted on others does not justify what these heathens did to my brothers and sisters. I pray that a descendant of ours may someday return to lead Russia down the right path and atone for any sins or hurt caused by my ancestors."

Madeleine and Jon nodded in agreement. "We too will pray for this to happen."

That night, Jon and especially Anastasia slept little. The pain radiated from her wounds, and she had nightmares about the slaughter of her family. There was too much hurt right now to calm her fears.

When Jon and Anastasia woke up the next morning, they could not find Madeleine anywhere. They started to have fears that Madeleine may have betrayed them for ransom money. After several hours of anxious waiting, Madeleine appeared accompanied by two men, who identified themselves as former members of the Duma, Pavel

Milyukov and Alex Guchkov. They were once members of the noble class and had to go underground to save themselves. It was there, along with others, where they formed a movement to protect those being hunted by the Bolsheviks.

Pavel starts the dialogue. "Do not be afraid Jon and Anastasia, Madeleine told us everything. We are here to help. Some of the blame for not protecting your family from their fate must be placed on the president of our Duma, Kerensky. The members of the Duma agreed to provide your family with safe passage out through the southern border of Russia, but it was Kerensky who decided to send your family thru Siberia, the far eastern part of Russia. It seemed that he wanted to punish your father for his misgivings that caused the overthrow of our government. Also, one of the escorts we assigned to take your family to safety betrayed our trust by alerting the Bolsheviks of the route taken. That is how the Bolsheviks intercepted your family and diverted you to this place where they could cover up your execution."

Alex Guchkov then entered the conversation. "First, we will need to obtain credentials with new passports. We have arranged for you to travel by vehicle to the city of Novosibirsk in southern Russia where there is little if any infiltration of the Bolsheviks. From there, you will board a train to the western border of Russia where you can gain entrance to Poland. In Poland, our people will assist you to garner support from either the British or American embassy. Our people are preparing the necessary documents which will identify you as brother and sister with assumed names."

A sedan pulled up to take Anastasia and Jon to Novosibirsk. The driver turned out to be Alex Guchkov. "Hurry Jon and Anastasia. We must get on the road as soon as possible before any of the Bolsheviks in the town recognize either one of you. In anticipation of the white Army descending on the city, the Bolsheviks are bringing up more troops in preparation for a battle between the two armies. We do not want to get caught in the middle of it. If the white army could only have made it in time, they could have saved your family Anastasia. We cannot take the chance that the White Army will prevail."

Anastasia and Jon thanked Madeleine and the two patriots for their help. They only had one change of clothing provided to them by Madeleine. The underground gave them Russian, British, and American money. Anastasia reached for her dress and pulled the jewels and royal seal she had sewn in it. Jon looked surprised but was pleased that they could sell the jewels to help pay for their passage to either England or America.

As Jon held Anastasia in his one arm, he went over some pitfalls they must avoid. "I am relieved that the underground people sent us through the southern route to avoid St. Petersburg and Moscow Anastasia. With your father's hobby of taking so many photos of your family and releasing them to the media, you could easily be recognized. I think their plan for us to skirt the southern region of Russia and head for Poland is a good one. There, we can seek help from the American or British Embassy. Hopefully one of the two will grant us asylum and arrange for safe passage to either America or Great Britain."

Anastasia places her hand on Jon's hand. "I trust that you are right Jon. You have been good to me, and I do not want to endanger your life. If they discover that I am still alive, they will not only kill me, but they will torture and kill you too. I think it best for us to part ways and that will give you a better chance to save yourself."

Jon grimaces at the thought of leaving Anastasia by herself. "In no way am I going to leave your side Anastasia. Whatever befalls you will also be my fate. We will either make it together or die together."

When Jon and Anastasis finally reached the Border between Russia and Poland, they are surprised to see that the Bolsheviks have replaced the border guards with their own people. The railroad station they needed to reach was within walking distance but was surrounded by the Bolsheviks.

The three of them sat in the car staring at the border guards they had to broach to reach Poland. Finally, Alex spoke up with a plan. "It is too dangerous to depend on the passports that we gave you in the hope that they will fool them. Our only possibility is to overtake a soldier of the Bolsheviks and dress you as one of them Jon. Those that are off duty seem to be hanging around that bar and restaurant. Follow me."

Alex led them into the bar and directed them to find a booth in an obscure location. He then spotted a young officer having a drink at the bar. Alex went up to him and started a conversation. "I admire you guys who serve in uniform. Can I buy you whatever you are drinking Comrade?"

The soldier nodded his head with approval. Alex then got into a conversation about the revolution. Most Russians in those days were heavy drinkers and were borderline alcoholics. After several large drinks of Russian Vodka, the young officer slumped over the bar and passed out from drinking too much. Some of the other soldiers came over to take care of him but Alex waved them off. "This man is my son. I will make certain that he gets back to the barracks. My other son will help me."

Alex motioned Jon to give him a hand. They drooped an arm of the officer over each of their shoulders and carried him out the back door. The back was a dark alley. Alex and Jon carried the officer in a narrow hallway between the bars and stripped him of his clothes. Jon then put them on. Alex told Jon to keep his own clothes because he will have to get rid of the uniform once over the border.

Jon and Anastasia bid Alex farewell and thanked him for all his troubles. They then start for the border crossing. Alex watches from a distance to see if they make it all right. Jon tells Anastasia to follow his lead and let him do all the talking. "Hopefully, they will not ask for your papers because you are being accompanied by one of their own. If they ask for your passport, delay giving it to them by pretending you are searching your pockets for it."

The line was quite long because many upper-class Russians wanted to escape the wrath of the Bolsheviks. Many were being turned back for questioning and being searched for any valuables they may be taking from Russia. If the Border guards found them hiding anything or they were on the list of those wanted for questioning, they were taken into custody.

After waiting their turn for four hours, Jon and Anastasia finally reached the guard post. Because they thought Jon was one of their officers, they did not question him or ask for his papers. They then turned to Anastasia, asking for her papers. Immediately Jon spoke up. "She is my sister. I am taking her to visit our family in Poland."

The one guard still insisted on seeing her papers. This was of great concern to Jon because the border guards were closely scrutinizing papers and stopping anyone that had questionable ones. Jon did not know how good the underground was at forging documents.

Suddenly, the commander of the guards approached Jon and Anastasia. Jon looked in the eyes of the commander of the Border guards and rebuked him for asking to see her passport. "If I were on Border duty and your sister was traveling with you in uniform, I would not even consider asking for her papers." After intently looking from head to toe at Jon and Anastasia, the commander ordered the border guards to let them pass. Within twenty steps, they were out of the Bolsheviks reach and on to a new life.

Finally making it to Poland they thought that their journey would go smoother. Little did they know that the embassies were closed for a holiday and at the train station, they encountered a large contingency of Russian refugees in the same predicament as them. Everyone was trying to board a train and needed to find a place to stay until they could board one. In those days, people who were fleeing Russia were classified as Emigres rather than refugees.

"Emigration implies permanent departure from one country and settlement in another and suggests a choice by the émigré not to return to the native country. Émigrés are thus differentiated from refugees, who are seen as people forced from their homeland in abnormal circumstances, usually under threat of violence, who will return once normal life resumes. In the case of those who left the Russian Empire in the aftermath of the First World War, the line between émigré and refugee was blurred. Most Russian subjects who ended up living outside the borders of the empire had been captured as soldiers or had fled and sought refuge from military defeat, hunger, deprivation, or political persecution. It was frequently unclear to international relief organizations and authorities as to who they should classify as a refugee awaiting repatriation or an émigré who would not return. Those who remained abroad often resettled several times in different countries and considered themselves temporary exiles, expecting to go back as soon as the Bolshevik regime collapsed. "(17)

Whether Jon and Anastasia would be classified as émigré or refugee was of critical importance. Their being classified as Émigré can give them more priority to access embassy services.

The next train Jon and Anastasia could book a passage on would be three days out. They searched frantically for lodging, but everything was booked. Another couple that was in the same situation said that someone suggested the red cross. When hooking up with the red cross, they were referred to a Russian Orthodox church.

The Pastor greeted them upon their arrival and gasped when he looked into the face of Anastasia. From photographs taken by Anastasia's father and viewed by people around the world, he immediately recognized her. "My god, you are one of the grand Duchess of the Romanov family. We received word about the abdication of your father and the murder of your family and thought you were all dead."

Anastasia explained how she escaped the wrath of the Bolsheviks. The pastor stopped her in the middle of her explanation. "Knowing of your families' strong religious beliefs and how our church revered your family, you need not explain further or fear that we will reveal your identity. You can stay here for a few nights out of the cold while you wait for the embassies to open, and you can board a train.

This was the first time Anastasia did not have to bear freezing rooms and fear of being raped or killed since her family's incarceration.

The next morning the pastor placed Anastasia and Jon in touch with a Foreign Officer at the American Embassy who gave them the necessary passports to leave for England and hopefully from there to America. From England, they boarded a boat for the United States.

Like all immigrants, the first thing they saw coming into New York harbor was the Statue of Liberty. Soon afterward, their boat docked at Ellis Island *(Photo 5)* to be processed into the United States.

Photo 5-Ellis Island-Immigration in Processing

"Ellis island, a federally owned island in New York Harbor, situated within the U.S. states of New York and New Jersey. It was the busiest immigrant inspection and processing station in the United States. From 1892 to 1954, nearly 12 million immigrant arriving at the Port of New York and New Jersey were processed there under federal law. The south side of the island housed a hospital where immigrants that were suspected of having illnesses could be treated." (18)

After Jon and Anastasia were processed through Ellis Island, they settled at first in New York city. Shortly thereafter, they married. Anastasis kept her first name but took Jon's last name.

Jon and Anastasia lived in New York during what was known as the gilded age of New York. Living in New York City in the early 1900's was exceedingly difficult. The city's population was 3.4 million. It was not a peaceful city and there were only pockets of serenity. It was a loud, fast-paced, expensive, and crowded city. In a short period of time, New York was becoming a city of skyscrapers, subways, and the development of central park. They were building massive bridges to connect the once isolated boroughs. More than a million poor immigrants that were crammed into tenements were in view of luxurious fifth avenue mansions built by half of the millionaires in the country. Jobs for the immigrants were menial and low paying, denying them insufficient funds to keep body and soul together. It did not take Jon and Anastasia long to realize they had to seek a better life elsewhere. Jon decided to contact an aunt who migrated to the steel valley of Pittsburgh. After discussing their plight, the aunt urged them to come to Pittsburgh. There they could live with her until they secured a job and had enough money to get their own place.

The address in Pittsburgh given by Jon's aunt turned out to be in Steel Valley. Upon arriving, Jon and Anastasia were greeted by the bellowing smoke from the Steel Mills. Homestead was fast becoming the steel capital of the world. As jobs were more plentiful than in New York, Jon found work in the steel mills. Anastasia and her sisters were taught sewing by her mother which gave her the skills to be a proficient seamstress and the opportunity to open a small seamstress shop. Word spread quickly about her skills and many of the wives of affluent mill bosses brought their alterations to her. She never revealed her identity to them.

Jon and Anastasia's love for one another grew stronger. Shortly after buying a home, Anastasia gave birth to a son and a daughter thereafter. Their son got married and had children. The oldest of those great grandchildren bore a son which they named Alexei. They chose Alexei because of a story Anastasia told them about the heir to the Russian throne who was never given the chance to ascend the throne. Anastasia asked her children to name one of their sons Alexei. One of her grandchildren decided to do so. Anastasia continued to guard her heritage for fear that it would put her family in harm's way. She never revealed to either her son or grandson that they were heirs to the Russian crown. Not long after Alexei was born, his father was accidently killed in the steel mill where he worked. Unbeknownst to Alexi and his family, this technically made Alexei the heir to the Romanov throne.

CHAPTER 5

GROWING UP

Alexei, who is now six years old, is entering his first year of grade school. He is the youngest kid in the class and because of his size and age, he is very meek. The other kids in the class looked down upon him and two boys bullied him constantly. The bullies called Alexei a wimp. Every day he went home crying to his mother about how badly he was treated. 'I am so tired of being picked on mother. Every day I go to school, the same two kids bully me every day. They even make fun of my name "Alexei. Why did you name me Alexei mom?

His mother gently pats him on his head. "Actually, it was a wish of your great grandmother Anastasia. 'For some reason, she was intent on having a descendant named Alexei. Now Nicholas, think of a way you can get even with the bullies without having to fight them. A good way may be to embarrass them in front of the class."

That night while lying in bed, Nicholas produces what he thinks is a good way to get even with the Bullies. Before going to school in the morning, he eats a lot of food that normally gives him gas. When he is in class, he goes near the bullies and expels some gas, leaving a very smelly odor and then quickly walks back to his desk.

Classmate Janey is the first to smell the odor. "ooow, who expelled gas? It is coming from Jack and Billy." All the kids join in by pointing a finger at Jack and Billy who now have very red faces. By doing what Alexei did took them down in the eyes of his classmates but it did not stop them from bullying him. Likewise, it did not elevate

Alexei in the eyes of his classmates. To them, he was still a meek little guy that was insignificant.

Another day, Alexei is talking to his mom about a little girl that he likes by the name of Kathy. "Mom, I really like this girl in my class, but I do not know how to talk to her. I sent her a shamoogram but she never thanked me. She will be singing in the school play tomorrow."

His mother smiles. "My goodness Alexei, you are sending her a shamoogram is quite a commitment. Ladies like to be complimented on their beauty and they like boys that make them laugh. Every girl also likes flowers, especially after performing on stage. I will buy a rose when I am out shopping today for you to give to her."

"But mom, would that not make me look that much more like a pansy to other boys in the class?" "Maybe so Alexei but what do you care about what the other boys think if you win the lady over in the end. Have you not heard the saying, a rose does not answer its enemies with words, but with beauty."

Alexi especially liked this little girl that sang the song "Me and my shadow" while holding a teddy bear. She had shiny black hair with big olive eyes. Her voice was sweet and soft. She was by far the most liked little girl by all the boys in his class. Standing in the center of the stage with lights on her made her picture perfect. You could not hear a pin drop among the little boys. They were fixed on her. After she completed her song, all the boys surrounded her trying to get her attention and favor, including Alexei. Because of Alexei's height, he tried jumping up and down on the outside of the circle of boys to get her attention. "Kathy-Kathy-Kathy, I would like to give you a flower for your great performance." Once again, however, Alexei was overshadowed by the bigger and more athletic boys.

Alexei's one nemesis, Jack, grabbed the rose from Alexei's hands and gave it to Kathy while Jack's friend Billy held Alexei back. Tears start dripping from the eyes of Alexei and flowing over his cheeks. Kathy gives Jack a hug, thanking him for the rose while Alexei's heart sinks. He turns away despondent while Jack and Billy laugh and make fun of him. Another setback in the days of Alexei.

At the start of another day, Alexi finds himself in another position to get closer to Kathy. The teacher asks for volunteers to clean the blackboards, and Kathy is one of the first to put her hand up. Alexei is the first boy to raise his hand and is readily picked by the teacher. Finally, Alexei sees a great chance to get close to Kathy. To his dismay, however, Jack blurts out a point to the teacher.

"Teacher, Alexei, and Kathy are not tall enough to reach the top of the black board. I can clean the top while Kathy cleans the bottom."

You have a point, Jack. Sorry Alexei but I will have to select a taller boy." Alexei drops his head and desperately asks the teacher to reconsider. "I can stand on a stool to reach the upper part of the black board." Once again, Alexei loses out to Jack. Alexei sadly watches as Kathy is engrossed in cleaning the blackboards with Jack while Billy smirks at him.

Time marches on and Alexei finds himself in high school still struggling with his shyness. His high school is old, built in the early 1900's, and situated on a hill above the steel mills.

Some of the students used to make fun of the school by saying that the building was so in need of repair that you had to walk close to the walls for fear that the floor may cave in. The building had no air conditioning, and the windows of the classroom were stuck and hard to open. The classrooms were badly in need of repair and the desks and lab equipment were antiquated. The cafeteria was small and always had a food odor that filled the halls during lunch time. There was a small playground and both it and the school were closely surrounded by low-income homes. Close by was one of the old libraries funded by the steel baron Andrew Carnegie. The students were always playing tricks on their teachers and fondly nicknamed them. The biology teacher was nicknamed "Bugsy."

Alexei was a late bloomer in physical size. Even though he has grown taller and stronger, he is still looked upon as a wall flower and backward. He was not polished like the other kids in the class. Some of the kids in his school, like Jack and Kathy, came from influential and wealthier families unlike his own. He came from the Steel Valley of Homestead where thanks to his neighborhood friends like Joey, he learned how to defend himself and settle his differences in the streets. Eventually he became known as a fierce street fighter. His type of fighting was more like a kick boxer where you used every part of your body including anything or anybody you could grab. Most of his friends were like him, rough around the edges and hardened street fighters. Other kids in his school, like Jack and Billy, settled their arguments in a more gentlemanly boxing style.

The class bullies remained Jack and Billy. They not only picked on Alexei, but they relentlessly picked on other kids in school. Besides the two of them, they had a group of athletes who always joined in the bullying.

Alexei was one of those kids who never participated in any activities. He would look at cute girls from a distance but never dated any of them and he rarely went to any high school dances. Whenever he did, he stood on the side of the dance floor by himself. He still had a crush on Kathy but never told her. To his dismay, she was quite friendly with all the guys in her class but never acknowledged that he existed.

Finally, one day, he thought he would use the same approach he saw in a romantic movie where one of the young actors in the movie did what he considered a cool thing. On the last day of school of his junior year, he gathered the courage to walk up to Kathy who was surrounded by her friends and kissed her on the lips. He then took her hand and said "I have been wanting to do that for a long time. "

Kathy's response was quite surprising. "What took you so long? I always thought you had a girlfriend or did not find me attractive. That is why I ignored you all this time."

Alexei was so startled by her reaction that he was clueless as to what to say or do next. He just stood there without being able to say anything. His gut reaction was to kiss her again. Instead, he thought his next best move was to walk away. "Oh, I hear our teacher calling me." Alexei quickly walks away from Kathy while Kathy just stood there with her mouth wide open. From a distance, Jack saw what Alexei did and became jealous of Alexei.

At the start of his senior year, Alexei caught Kathy looking his way in class and wondered if she felt anything towards him. As Alexei sat in class staring at Kathy, the teacher saw he was distant and decided to wake him up. To do so, the teacher enforced a school code that students could not put their hoodies over their head while in class.

"Alexei, you are not paying attention! Remove your hoodie from your head now and I want to check the pocket in your hoodie. You can hide a lot in that pocket, and I better not find anything in there that is not permitted by our school. You know all too well that our school has rules against wearing hoodies because of what students may be hiding in them."

Alexei pulls the hood back from over his head. "I understand the rule teacher, but it is not fair. My pants have pockets. Should I take my pants off too?" The entire class laughs, and the teacher cannot think fast enough of a comeback. She is silently snickering. "Do whatever you want with your hoodie Alexei but keep your pants on!"

The teacher was young and beautiful, and Alexei was secretly infatuated with her. After being brazen enough to rebut her about his hoodie and pants, Alexei saw his chance to express how he felt about her. He raises his hand and stands up in front of the whole class, respectively asking her permission to say something.

The teacher looks puzzled at him. "You have my permission to speak Alexei." At first Alexei shyly drops his head looking at the floor with his hands folded behind him. He then looks directly at her. "I think you are one of the most beautiful ladies I ever saw, and I wish I was older so I could ask you out on a date."

The teacher and the class were stunned. She blushed at his comment but by giving him permission to speak and what he said was complimentary, there was no way she could discipline him. "Thank you for the compliment, Alexei, you can sit down now." She suddenly thought of a come-back this time. "By the way Alexei, here is a quarter, call me when you have turned twenty-one."

The entire class just sat there also in total amazement knowing that Alexei, being such a shy and backward guy, could have the guts to say such a thing. Alexei simply took the quarter and clinched it in his fist and said, "I will do that but by the time I am old enough to call, I will need more than just a Quarter."

After class, Jack with some of his friends cornered Alexei in the hallway. "You think you can kiss my girlfriend and get away with it. I will meet you in the Alley after school tomorrow and we will see how tough you really are you wimp!"

The students settled their differences by fighting it out in the alley. Alexei's mother told him to only resort to fighting if it meant defending himself and Jack knew nothing of Alexei's Street fighting skills. Alexei knew that if he did not show up, Jack would hunt him down and mock him in front of the whole school. Thinking about what his mother taught him not to fight unless his back was against the wall, Alexei felt that this was such a time. To the surprise of Jack, Alexei accepted his challenge but tried to reason with Jack.

"I will meet you after school Jack, but do you think our fighting will resolve anything. Perhaps you may want to rethink about fighting me." Jack just continued to stare angrily at Alexei. "Rethink about fighting you! No Way! Are you trying to weasel your way out? You are a coward! You are going to feel a lot of pain and humiliation. After I finish with you, I will expect an apology for me and my girlfriend Kathy."

Alexei knew Jack's reputation whereby he would show up with Billy and a bunch of his friends to intimidate his opponent and if it appeared that he was not winning, his friends would step in and beat up his opponent. Knowing this, Alexei approached his good friend Joey who was also rough around the edges and tough as nails. "Joey, I need you to be my second in a fight after school tomorrow and bring some of our friends. The guy that I am fighting is the class bully and has a reputation for his friends ganging up against his opponent. They have been known to jump in the fight if their friend is losing."

"No problem, Alexei, I will be there with a bunch of our friends. Who are you fighting and who started the fight?" "His name is Jack, and a bunch of his friends may pile on Joey. He started the argument and wants to beat me up to impress his girlfriend who I like. "

"I know that guy Alexei. I once had a run in with him over something that was completely his fault. He is a big bully. I cannot think of anything I will enjoy more than beating up Jack and his friends if they try to pile on. We will see you there tomorrow."

The next day in school, Jack and Billy reminded Alexei of their fight after school. Alexei told them he would be there but wondered if he knew that he was not the wimpy kid Jack thought he once was. "I will be there Jack but realize that I am not the same meek kid I once was in grade school." Hearing this, Jack laughed at Alexei. "I cannot wait to get you in the alley and make you pay for humiliating me in front of Kathy. After I get through with beating you up, I will expect you to apologize to me and to her in front of all our classmates."

The day went very slowly for Alexei. Jack and Billy spread the word about the fight so most of the students were expected to show up. Even though Alexei was confident that he could defend himself, he was not looking forward to fighting Jack. He knew, however, that he had no choice. Alexei kept thinking that hopefully his mother would not be mad at him for defending myself. That day, Kathy confronted Alexei in the hallway and urged him to just apologize so he would not get hurt. Her reason for doing so was the feelings she had towards Alexei, and she was very sincere to protect him from being hurt.

"I have no choice but to show up Kathy. If I do not show up, he will continue to humiliate me in front of the entire school. I asked him to rethink fighting me, but he just laughed and called me a coward in front of a lot of our classmates. Now word has spread and a lot of them are going to show up to see if I back out."

The bell to end the last period finally rang and Alexei started walking slowly out the doors and down the alley by himself. By now, most of the school heard about the fight and to Alexei's surprise, there was a huge body of students lined up along the alley way when Alexei turned the corner. When he arrived at the center of the Alley where Jack and his friends were waiting, Joey and their neighborhood friends were nowhere in sight. Jack's girlfriend Kathy stood close by with a concerned look on her face. She was pleading with him to apologize and walk away.

Jack confronted Alexei. "Are you ready to fight coward? You are about to pay for trying to cut in on me and Kathy. Remember what I said. I expect you to apologize to me and her after I give you a good beating."

Just then, Kathy chimed in to try to help Alexei. "Stop this nonsense, Jack. Alexei did nothing wrong and needed no apology. You are not fighting him for me. It is about your ego. Alexei has always been polite to me and has never tried to separate us." "Stay out of this Kathy. It is time for Alexei to take his medicine. Since first grade, he has always been a wimp and had his eye on you."

Alexei stood in front of Jack, sizing the number of Jack's friends surrounding him. He knew that even if he got the better of Jack, Billy and his friends would jump in, and he would suffer a lot of hurt. He was in a no-win situation. As Alexei was looking to the one side to size up the situation, Jack showed his true colors as a dirty fighter by sucker punching Alexei to the side of his head. Alexei went down with his head pounding off the pavement. When Alexei got back on my feet, Jack was in a boxer's stance and started to plummet him with punches. Knowing his friends were not there to back him up, Alexei feared that Jack's friends would jump in if he became the aggressor. All he could do was fend off the punches of Jack and cover up from getting hit. Jack knowing that he had the backup of Billy and his friends, he kept beating on Alexei without any let-up.

Suddenly, Joey and a bunch of Alexei friends showed up. The friends were of the typical ethnic middle European stock with staunch builds that came from lifting weights. They were much bigger and stronger than Jack's friends. Jack knew that Alexei lived in a hard section of the town but never knew he had such street fighter type friends or that Alexei could fight. You could see the fear in the eyes of Jack's friends as they backed away from Joey and his friends. Jack had a puzzled look on his face when he looked around and saw that his bullying friends had backed down. All he could see now was Alexei coming in closer and raising his fists and a show of anger on his face. Knowing that Joey and his friends would keep anyone from piling on, Alexei prepared to unleash a volley of punches.

The backing of Joey and their friends was all Alexei needed to take control of the situation and apply his street fighting skills. Jack's eyes started to widen as Alexei spoke to him. "Now we will see who the coward is and who will be making the apologies Jack. It's time to pay the Piper. I will now give you a demonstration on how we fight in the streets of the Steel Valley."

Jack was waiting for Alexei to swing a punch, but it was not coming. Instead, Alexei jammed his right knee into Jack's stomach. As Jack buckled over, Alexei gave him an upper cut punch to the jaw and a hard elbow to the side of Jack's head. Jack quickly went down moaning in pain. Normally, Jack's training in street fighting would have him jump on top and continue beating him until he begged for mercy. Alexei could see Jack had enough as he covered up his face with his hands and rolled to the side in a ball-type tuck. Jack put up his hand. "No more, I have had enough Alexei."

All the students that were watching could not believe that Alexei was such a good fighter. As a lot of them were also bullied by Jack and his friends over the years, they were cheering Alexei on. Alexei's side glance at Kathy revealed that she approved of Jack being given a lesson in humility.

Alexei held Jack to the ground with his left hand and readied his fist to hit him with his other. "Now Jack, about that apology. I agree with you that it is time for an apology, but it will be given by you instead of me. First, you need to apologize to Kathy for doubting her loyalty."

Jack slowly got up off the ground and was very embarrassed about the outcome. "I apologize Kathy. To avoid a thrashing from Alexei, Jack then also apologized for calling him a coward. To show he was a better person than Jack, Alexei then brushed off Jack's clothing and handed him his jacket. "Thank you Jack and I would assume that you and your friends are finished bullying students in our school."

At that revelation by Alexei, all the students cheered and surrounded him with pats on his back. Joey gave Alexei a wink of approval and Alexei returned it. Kathy approached Alexei to give him a kiss and a hug despite Jack's objections.

Alexei's remaining days in high school were not that eventful except for him being the equipment manager for the football team. Alexei never tried out for the high school football team because he was cut by the Junior High football coach, and his mother was concerned that he would get seriously injured if he played football. The high school had a good team but suffered some losses due to it not having a good kicker. One day during practice, the coach caught Alexei punting the football over sixty yards and kicking field goals with ease. He approached Alexei and asked him why he never came out for the team. Alexei just stood there and shrugged his shoulders. The coach then urged him to suit up for practice the next day. He never realized that Alexei could also catch a football and tackle far better than any other player.

After talking his mother into playing, he showed up for practice. Because he only played sand-lot football in his neighborhood, none of the team ever saw or knew he could play. He just sat on the bench watching the team practice. The coach was using Billy, the bully, as a running back. Recalling the times that Billy also bullied him, Alexei thought it was his chance to get even with Billy. Alexei quickly went up to the coach and asked him if he could work in the practice as a linebacker. The coach nodded his head in approval.

Alexei ran out on the field and got set in the linebacker position, just waiting for the quarterback to lateral the ball to Billy. He could not wait to tackle Billy. Billy just looked at Alexei as if he were going to easily run right over him. Finally, his chance came. The quarterback handed the ball off to Billy who came straight through the center of the line. Alexei moved to meet him straight on. He tackled Billy so hard that the impact was so loud that everyone watching gasped in horror. Alexei quickly stood up while Billy just rolled over in pain moaning. Alexei reached down to help Billy up. "Now we are even Billy." The coach came over and placed his hands on Alexei's shoulders. "Where did you learn to tackle like that Alexei? Where were you two years ago?" Alexei humbly answered the coach. "From playing pick-up football on empty lots in my neighborhood coach." The coach beamed with delight that he found a hidden talent. "That was awesome! I never saw anyone tackle as good as that. You are now our starting linebacker and kicker for the section championship game on Friday night Alexei."

When the championship game came around, the stands were packed with students and avid football fans. Alexei played phenomenally well in the linebacker position. Midway through the second quarter, his chance came to punt. When the ball was centered to him, the ball was centered too high for him to reach it. It barely touched his fingertips. He had to run back to pick it up before an onslaught of tacklers reached him. Everyone in the stands and on the bench gasped at his fumbling the ball which rolled past him. You could hear some of the players on the bench and people in the stands verbally booing him and the center. He quickly picked the ball up and to the amazement of the fans, he punted it over sixty-five yards.

His next opportunity to shine came when his team was a field goal behind with the other team having possession of the ball on the 40-yard line with less than one minute left in the game. The coach called Alexei over and looked him in the eye with both hands on his shoulders. "There is only one chance to win this championship game Alexei and that is for you to do the same thing you did to Billy in practice, make their runner fumble the ball by your tackling him as hard as you can."

Alexei could feel the pressure. The ball was snapped and the runner for the opposing team tried an end around. The runner could see Alexei coming at him from the corner of his eye. Alexei hit him with all his might. The ball came loose, and Alexei recovered the fumble. The fans went berserk with cheers. The coach took time out and again put his hands on Alexei's shoulders. "Alexei, do you think you can kick a 40-yard field goal?" "I do not know Coach. I think I can kick the distance but am not sure about my accuracy." The coach looked intently at Alexei. "The championship is riding on you Alexei.

Alexei turned to the ball holder and expressed his fears. "I cannot believe that he put me in this predicament. All eyes are on me, and I almost peed myself with fear of not making the field goal." Alexei stood on the field looking at the goal posts which seemed a mile away. The center snapped the ball on three to the holder and Alexei kicked it. To his dismay, the ball was blocked and rolled right back to him. He grabbed the ball one-handed and started running around the end. The opposing team was focused on rushing the line to block his kick, so he had a clear path to the goal posts. After avoiding three tacklers and out running a fourth, Alexei made it into the end zone for the winning touchdown. The fans again went wild, chanting Alexei's name. The team and coach picked Alexis up on their shoulders.

When the senior prom came, Alexei asked Kathy to go with him. She turned him down and opted to go with Jack at the urging of her parents. Kathy's parents felt that because of Jack's family wealth, Jack was much better suited for her. Jack was also destined to attend one of the ivy leagues schools and afterwards go into his family's business.

Graduation came quickly. Jack arranged to have Kathy sit next to him. Each student received a round of applause as they received their diploma. Alexei received the most for winning the football championship and standing up to the class bullies. After returning to his seat, Alexei thought it would be big of him to congratulate Kathy and Jack on graduating with high honors, but both ignored him.

CHAPTER 6

DUTY CALLS

Upon graduation, Alexi flunked out after attending a year of college. As a result, he enlisted in the Air Force and learned leadership from his drill instructor who spoke with an English accent. After processing through the Welcome Center at Fort Knox basic training, the drill instructor introduced himself to their platoon as "Sergeant Badman. His steel cold eyes looking at them from under his smokey bear hat, sending chills up and down their spines.

Photo 6-Drill Instructors with basic training recruits

Fearful comments came from many of the recruits including the word "Mummy," meaning they wished they were home with their mother. They were especially concerned in those days because many drill instructors were post-Vietnam soldiers who had serious psychological scars and were drug users or alcoholics. Some of them would think nothing of hitting the young recruits in the head with the butt of a rifle if they stepped out of line. They were a mixed bunch of recruits, some drafted, others reserve, and career soldiers. Some among them were Attorneys, drafted into the army for a two-year stint. When Alexei asked the college graduates why they did not go for a commission, their answer was "No way, I am getting out after I serve my two years."

After Alexei's first stint serving as an enlisted in the army, he returned to college and earned an undergraduate and master's degree. It was shortly thereafter that his childhood sweetheart, Kathy, had married his nemesis, Jack. Realizing his hopes of ever being hooked up with Kathy was lost, he met a young lady who he married and had two sons.

It was soon thereafter that the outbreak of the Persian Gulf War occurred. Being patriotic, he volunteered to come back into the military after what was probably the longest break in service of the military, over 20 years. He earned a commission as a first Lieutenant in the Air Force even though he was over the age of commissioning.

He was assigned to the Pentagon, rising through the ranks to Lt Colonel, and served at the highest level of the military command. Not long afterwards, terrorists used commercial aircrafts to level the world trade centers and flew into the inner rings of the Pentagon. Alexei volunteered to return to active duty, serving for the Chairman of the Joint Chiefs of Staff, the Secretary of Defense, and the State Department. While there, he learned military strategy and foreign policy. He became a member of the military team that provided key input to the Chairman of the Joint Chiefs of staff, the Secretary of Defense, and the President of the United States. From there, he went on to be one of 50 officers to serve at the State Department and volunteered to be deployed into the middle east and South Korea to protect American embassies and troops.

As a result of where he served, he became experienced in military tactics and strategy and learned the inner workings of the Department of Defense and the State Department. During his stint at the Pentagon, he deployed twice into harm's way. As a result of his willingness to volunteer for whatever was asked of him, he had no personal or social life for six years. He put his country before himself by placing his life on hold and barely saw his two sons during his tour of duty. Luckily for him, his mother took care of his sons while he deployed to the far corners of the world. He was referred to be the Secretary of the Army but was not selected because the President had a friend he wanted.

It was a huge let down for Alexei when he returned to civilian life. Upon his return, he lost his wife giving birth to their second son which devastated him and left him indifferent to life. To boot, he was at the top of the military command structure and then returned to the Steel Valley where he first started and led a mundane life. Unknowingly, he was a victim of severe Persian Gulf Syndrome which is commonly known as combat stress. Coupled with this infliction and the loss of his wife, he became socially and mentally distraught. It drove him to live a reclusive life, including isolating himself from many of his friends and family. He and his two sons took up residency with his mother. It was ironic that he found himself living in the same house and neighborhood that he grew up in as a boy.

With all his college degrees, he could not obtain a high paying job because of his mental state and the steel valley economy was in a recession. To support his two sons and pay for their college education, Joey helped Alexei get a job in the steel mills working long, tedious hours tending the hot furnaces. His life became very mundane with no social life, disassociating him further from life and distancing him from his family and friends. He just could not get his life jump started again. Alexei started to realize that his life was reverted to how he was when he first started elementary school and that was when everyone thought him backward and boring. No one was even aware that he was a war hero. He kept thinking that Kathy may have made the right decision to opt for Jack instead of himself.

The only stimulation of Alexei's mind was keeping abreast of current events and reading history books. What caught his interest the most was the invasion of Ukraine by Russia. He kept thinking this is the same situation that he once read in the history books about the last Czar of Russia fighting two wars he could not win. He knew that his great grandmother was born in Russia during those trying times and recalled some of the stories she passed down through the family in carefully thought-out written notes about the downfall of the Romanov empire and the murders of Czar Nichols's family.

The details in her notes about the Romanov family were uncanny. Alexei wondered how her notes could be so concise and realistic, written as though she was a member of the family. Her description of the palace, the family, and how the Romanovs ruled seemed very real. She brought the Romanov family back to life by writing every detail about their personalities. She seemed to know everything about them, and her description of Czar Nicholas and Alexandra's relationship was uncanny. Even more intriguing was how she described the murders of the family beyond what was written in the history books. She also seemed to support that one of the daughters survived the slaughter. Some of the Anastasia notes bore tear drops as she wrote about their tragic ending. On the last page of her notes what may have been a mark made by some sort of seal, which is used for official documents."

Alexei's life and that of his family was further thrown into turmoil when he lost his job due to the mills closing. His only source of income was money from his father's pension and some insurance money given to his mother by the Steel Company. He was forced to work odd jobs to supplement his family's income.

CHAPTER 7

RUSSIA IN TURMOIL

Russia was exiting its long cold winter months. Red square, situated in the middle of Moscow, was covered with snow.

Photo 7-Snowy night in Moscow's Red Square

normally colorful against the Moscow sky, even historic St. Basil cast a dark image with voluminous clouds seeming to frame its silhouette closely against the Kremlin. The people of Russia were not only coming out of a long and cold winter, but they were also becoming cold towards their President, Vladimir.

"Russian President Vladimir Dimitri's approval rating fell in April to a historic low as the coronavirus crisis engulfs the country, along with the rest of the world. Dimitri's approval rating fell to 59% in April, down from 63% in the previous month, according to a poll conducted by the independent Levada Center in Russia." (19) Much of this was due to his handling of the coronavirus virus more so than the Ukraine invasion. It is the biggest problem he has faced since taking power.

A billionaire once challenged Vladimir to a fight with winner taking all regarding Ukraine, meaning Vladimir would have to pull his troops out of Ukraine if he lost. It would have been an interesting match with high stakes. Vladimir is a man turning 70, balding, approximately 5 foot 5 inches tall and weighs around 160 pounds. Holding a black belt in judo, he is an experienced fighter and keeps in shape by exercising on a regular basis. In sharp contrast the billionaire challenger is in his early 50's, 6 foot 2 inches tall and accomplished in Jiu-Jitsu, Kyokushin karate, taekwondo, and judo. Even though Dimitri would probably never accept the challenge, Las Vegas started placing odds on the match, making him the underdog.

As to Vladimir's education and background, he studied law at Leningrad State University, later serving 15 years as a foreign intelligence officer for the KGB (Committee for State Security, including six years in Dresden, East Germany.) In 1990, he retired from active KGB service with the rank of lieutenant colonel and returned to Russia to become prorector of Leningrad State University with responsibility for the institution's external relations. Soon afterward, Vladimir became an adviser to the first democratically elected mayor of St. Petersburg. He quickly won the mayor's confidence and became known for his ability to get things done. As a result, he was promoted to deputy mayor.

In 1996 Dimitri moved to Moscow, where he joined the presidential staff as deputy to the Kremlin's chief administrator. From there, he moved up in administrative positions. In July 1998, the President of Russia made him director of the Federal Security Service, the KGB's domestic successor, and shortly thereafter he became secretary of the influential Security Council. Searching for an heir to assume his mantle, Russia's then President appointed Vladimir to be prime minister in 1999.

Although he was virtually unknown, Vladimir's public-approval ratings soared when he launched a well-organized military operation against secessionist rebels in Chechnya. Wearied by years of their Presidents erratic behavior, the people of Russian appreciated Vladimir's coolness and decisiveness under pressure, thus ensuring his success in the December parliamentary elections.

On December 31, 1999, the prior Russian President unexpectedly announced his resignation and named Vladimir Dimitri acting president. Promising to rebuild a weakened Russia, the austere and reserved Dimitri easily won the March 2000 elections with about 53 percent of the vote. As president, he sought to end corruption and create a strong and regulated market economy. (20)

"Vladimir strongly objected to U.S. Pres. George W. Bush's decision in 2001 to abandon the 1972 Anti-Ballistic Missile Treaty. In response to the September 11 attacks on the United States in 2001, he pledged Russia's assistance and cooperation in the U.S. led campaign against terrorists and their allies, offering the use of Russia's airspace for humanitarian deliveries and help in search-and-rescue operations. Nevertheless, Vladimir joined German Chancellor Gerhard Schröder and French Pres. Jacques Chirac in 2002 to oppose U.S. and British plans to use force to oust Saddam Hussein's government in Iraq.

Overseeing an economy that enjoyed growth after a prolonged recession in the 1990s, Vladimir was easily reelected in March 2004. In parliamentary elections in December 2007, Vladimir's party, United Russia, won an overwhelming majority of seats. Though the fairness of the elections was questioned by international observers and by the Communist Party of the Russian Federation, the results nonetheless reaffirmed Dimitri's uncontested power. With a constitutional provision forcing him to step down as President in 2008, he personally chose his own successor. Although facing strong opposition, he ran for a third term as President and won. In January 2020 Vladimir announced his intention to modify the Russian constitution in a way that would scrap term limits for presidents, paving the way for him to remain in office indefinitely.

In late 2021 Dimitri ordered a massive buildup of Russian forces along the Ukrainian border; additional units were dispatched to Belarus, ostensibly to engage in joint exercises with the Belarusian military. Western governments raised concerns about what appeared to be an imminent Russian invasion, but Vladimir denied that he had any such plans. By February 2022 as many as 190,000 Russian troops were poised to strike into Ukraine from forward bases in Russia, Russian-occupied Crimea, Belarus, and the Russian-backed separatist enclave in Moldova. In addition to Russia's buildup of troops, amphibious type units were deployed to the Black Sea under the guise of previously scheduled naval exercises. On February 21, Vladimir recognized the independence of the self-proclaimed people's republics of Donetsk and Luhansk, effectively voiding the 2015 Minsk peace agreement. In the early morning hours of February 24 Vladimir announced the beginning of a "special military operation," and explosions could be heard in cities across Ukraine. The President of Ukrainian declared that his country would defend itself, and Western leaders condemned the unprovoked attack, promising swift and severe sanctions against Russia." (21)

This brings us to how the invasion of Ukraine evolves into turmoil for Vladimir and the global community starting to question his intentions and soundness of mind.

Vladimir is sitting in his office waiting for his chief of staff, Jon Sanyo. The office of Russia's president is not like the oval office of the president of the United States. It is wood paneled with a large conference table and only two seats, one at each end of the table. The entrance to his office is adorned with two large iron doors guarded by two of his special security people. It does not have the creature comforts such as a fireplace and couches. Along with his office,

Russia's presidential residency is located inside the walls of the Kremlin.

Reportedly, Vladimir has two identical offices. One located in the Kremlin at the center of Moscow and the other at his summer palace. "The Kremlin is a fortified complex of buildings which was founded by the Rurikids dynasty. The Rurikids ruled parts of Russia spanning twenty-one generations or seven hundred years, making them one of Europe's oldest royal families. Inside the walls of the Kremlin are five palaces and four cathedrals, including the Grand Kremlin Palace that was once the Moscow residence of the Czar. Surrounding the walls of the Kremlin are the Moskva River, Saint Basil's Cathedral, Red Square, and the Alexander Garden.

The word Kremlin translates to meaning a fortress inside a city. It was a former home of what was the old Soviet Union. Now it has transitioned to become the seat of government of the Russian Federation. "(22)

Jon Sanyo, Vladimir Dimitri's chief of staff, enters the President's office. The President of Russia empowered his chief of staff to manage the federal bodies of the state and department heads, coordinates the activities of Presidential advisors, proposes federal laws, and acts on behalf of the President in his absence. Dimitri is a man in his sixty's and has a stout build. He is highly intelligent, highly respected among the Kremlin hierarchy. His career path was through the Ministry of Foreign Affairs (MID). The MID is a Russian federal executive body responsible for drafting and implementing government policy and legal regulation in the field of foreign relations of the Russian Federation. It would be comparable to the U.S. state department which is also accountable to the President of the United States. Sanyo is supposed to hold allegiance to Russia, but he serves at the pleasure of the President which is Dimitri. The Kremlin is a fortified complex of buildings which was founded by the Rurikids dynasty. The Rurikids ruled parts of Russia spanning twenty-one generations or seven hundred years, making them one of Europe's oldest royal families.

Inside the walls of the Kremlin are five palaces and four cathedrals, including   the Grand Kremlin Palace that was once the Moscow residence of the Czar. Surrounding the walls of the Kremlin are the Moskva River, Saint Basil's Cathedral, Red Square, and the Alexander Garden.

Prior to be appointed as Vladimir's chief of staff, Sanyo worked in Russia's Tokyo Embassy and in the Second Asian Department of the Foreign embassy. He worked his way up to Chief of the Government staff after holding various positions. He was trusted by Dimitri and was the closest confidant to him. If the President chooses to select another chief of staff, Sanyo will simply have to resign.

Sanyo points to a news article that appeared in a local newspaper. "For the fourth day in a row, our country has experienced more than 10,000 new cases of the coronavirus from the previous day. Because the people are not pleased with the way you are managing the Coronavirus, Vladimir, your approval rating has dropped to 59% compared to your 63% approval rating the previous month. This is the lowest since you came to power.

Throwing the paper on the floor, Vladimir points his finger at Sanyo. "You are supposed to be controlling what is printed in our newspapers. If that is so, how could such an article be written and get past our sensors? I cannot understand how the people can criticize me for how I handled the Coronavirus. I supported the Cabinet's proposal to introduce a nonworking period. In some regions where there was a threat of the virus spreading, I even directed that the non-working period could be extended if needed."

Sanyo advise was so respected by Vladimir that he was the only government official that could get away criticizing him. Sanyo leans over Vladimir's desk and places both his hands on the desk directly in front of Vladimir. "You know that I have done everything to suppress the media as you have asked but this is the day of high tech. Most of our young people have cell phones which give them a window to the outside world. We cannot control the internet. You have done a lot to combat the virus, but the people see that the daily coronavirus mortality rates are surging and topped 1,000 for the first time over the weekend amid sluggish vaccination rates. The people are also disgruntled about a litany of issues such as our shrinking economy due to the war in Ukraine. The Czech Republic expelled eighteen of our Russian diplomats because they suspect you might be behind an explosion in their country. Our people are also not happy with you because they think that you are behind torturing your opposition, tampering with national elections, suppressing freedom of speech and religion, not supporting human rights, and not protecting the environment. The list goes on and on. Even our party is becoming impatient with us. Need I say more Ivan?"

Enough Jon! I am trying my best to regain the confidence of our people and our party. We have been cut off by the west to surplus vaccines. As far as the war in Ukraine goes, it is too late for us to turn back now. To bolster the economy, we need to gain more support from countries like China, Iran, Belarus, and Syria. You would think the staged photo of my saving some geese by flying an ultra-lite aircraft would show the people that I am a leader that wants to protect the environment. Surely there must be something else we can do to calm the fears of our people.

Sanyo shows an expression of frustration. "I cannot think of anything except finding someone else we can blame for this mess. Over the weekend, I started reading some Russian history and how prior leaders managed similar situations. The problem is that we cannot rely on what past leaders put in place because they espoused communist rule. Our people have become too sophisticated to accept such an autocratic government again. Our youth even mock Lenin when they visit his tomb. One young person even wrote a humorous letter to the editor of one of our papers which I must admit was very hilarious. It was a letter mocking the body of Lenin that he wrote to a girl that he knew in the states.

"One most recent Russian history lesson we should have learned from is the huge mistake for trying to occupy "Afghanistan under Brezhnev's leadership. We suffered 15,000 military casualties and the loss of two million Afghan people. The other catastrophic mistake by former Russian leaders goes much further back in history, to the last Tsar of Russia, Czar Nicholas. Against the advice of his consul, he entered two wars that he could not win, WWI against the Germans and the other against the Japanese. He became so enthralled in the wars that he forgot about the needs of his starving people. The result was 1.5 million Russian casualties, his forced abdication of the throne and eventual execution. The odd thing is that many of our people now liked the mystique of having a Czar and some have even formed an organization to reinstate a Czar." (23)

Sanyo keeps philosophizing. "How will you justify to families all the body bags that will be coming back from Ukraine? Do you really think that all those body bags will bolster your image, Vladimir?"

Pondering what Sanyo had said and with his finger pointed at him, Vladimir's eyes widened, and he stood up from his desk. "Jon, what you have just said is interesting and brilliant. What if we used someone else as a scapegoat for sending our troops into war? A puppet, someone that I could manipulate, pull the strings, and still be in control."

Sanyo shows an expression of question. "What are you suggesting Vladimir? Are you pointing that finger at me to be the scape goat? Do you want my blood also? I will do anything for you but that I will not do!"

Vladimir snickers at Sanyo. "No…no…Jon. You do not occupy any seat of power. What we need is someone who holds leadership rank in Russia, someone like a King or Queen or in our case, Jon, a Czar. Look at the way Britain is set up. The Queen has limited powers, and the Prime Minister runs the day-to-day functions of the country. The Queen is just a figure head in the government. However, it is a huge money maker for the British government. It brings billions into the economy every year."

Sanyo looks bewildered at what Vladimir is proposing and questions his reasoning. "Putting it mildly Vladimir, have you lost your mind. As you know the last Russian leader that held power was Czar Nicholas II. They thought all his heirs were killed by the Bolsheviks in the early 1900's but were never sure there were any survivors. Rumor always was that the youngest daughter, Anastasia, may have survived. How do we find an heir and how do we sell this to our parliament, the Duma? Even if they agreed to such a wild idea, they would have to amend our constitution to reinstate the Czar.

"A descendent of Anastasia's family may work if she survived but we must exhaust all possibilities to discover whether the story is true that Czar Nicholas's youngest daughter survived the wrath of the Bolsheviks. If the story is true, one of her descendants will be the true heir to the throne."

Dimitri walks around the room with his hand on his chin and thinks aloud hoping to gain consensus from Sanyo. "Changing the constitution would be easy enough, our party of United Russia has most votes in the Duma, we should have no problem. We will sell them on the idea that we can expand the Russian empire and pump billions of tourism dollars into the Russian economy by all the pomp and ceremony of having a Czar, just like the Brits do with the royal family. As head of State, the King or Queen of England no longer has a political or executive role. Whoever the monarch is, they play a less formal role. The sovereign simply acts as a focus for national identity, unity of pride, gives a sense of stability continuity, and supports the ideal of voluntary service. Of course, I will not permit whoever we select as Czar to overshadow me or have political power."

Vladimir continues to state his case for reinstating the Czar. "I do not know if you are aware that the Russian Orthodox Church was supportive of the Czars. Coupled with our huge financial support for the church, its Patriarch will surely go for it. Do you realize that over 85% of our people belong to this church? If we can convince the church's Patriarch, we will win the people over by giving our Czar proposal a good chance. The Duma will also like this because they will win more support from the church."

Sanyo shakes his head and tightens his lips. "I am not sure if this is a good idea but if you insist, we need to put it in place as soon as possible before your ratings plummet further. When doing so, please do not point the finger at me if this plot goes south." With that, Vladimir and Sanyo start intense lobbying to collect the votes needed to amend the constitution. Vladimir summons the speaker of the Duma, Veslav Vlodinesky, to his office. "Veslav, we want to amend our constitution to reinstate a Czar as a figure head of state and we need you to get the Duma to ratify it."

Vladimir presents his case and how it will not only shield himself from any criticism over Ukraine and the virus but will also protect their party and the Duma from any fallout should they not be successful in Ukraine. He also stresses the economic boost to tourism by using the tremendous tourism dollars England generates by having a Queen. It may even bring back into the fold some of the satellite countries that were spun off under our former Soviet leader.

Veslav looks at Vladimir like he has lost his mind but after given the benefits of such a bold plan, he doubtfully shakes his head in agreement. "I will go along with your proposal and push it through the Duma but there is one thing you must promise me in return Vladimir Dimitri. In fact, I want your solemn word. By the way, do you have any idea where any descendants of the Czar may be. We cannot crown just anyone. It will have to be a direct descendant of the Romanov family if there even is one, and you will have to convince the people that this is good for Russia and the church. The person you present must have a legitimate claim to the throne. The only positive note is that because there are not any people left that overthrew the Romanovs, there should be little if any resistance."

Vladimir smiles at Veslav. "Leave finding a direct descendant up to me and Dmitri. I will leave convincing the Duma up to you and the leadership of our party. Now, what promise do you want from me Veslav?"

"That you will not reunite any former Soviet providences by force, and you will eventually pull out of Ukraine. We cannot afford to go against the will of the people, the majority of which did not want to invade Ukraine and see so many of our young soldiers returned to us in body bags. Our people do not want to see the blood of their children shed again like in Afghanistan."

Dimitri hesitates because he knows deep down, he cannot keep that promise but then he never keeps his word. Dimitri always lied with tongue in cheek for he knew in his mind that he was not ready to pull out of Ukraine. He intended to stay under the guise of a peace keeping mission.

"Veslav, you and the Duma have my word that I will pull out of Ukraine as soon as they promise not to join NATO. We wanted to stop Ukraine from joining NATO. We do not want foreign forces based inside their borders, do we?"

"The United States and NATO are not aggressors Ivan, so why do we even have to try to occupy Ukraine?"

With that, Dimitri went silent on discussing Ukraine any further and started some small talk about family and friends. After bidding Veslav goodbye, he summoned Sanyo again. "I want you to use all the resources available to us for locating a descendant of Czar Nicholas. Get our Federal Security Service Involved."

Sanyo thinks about what he knows of the mystery surrounding the murders of the Romanov family. "My interest has always been history Ivan. From what I have read, and we just discussed, the youngest daughter, Anastasia, may have survived. The best place to start our search is in Yekaterinburg where the family was kept captive. If the rumors hold true, we may find descendants of Anastasia or at least descendants of the Czar's servants. They may still reside near the house of special purpose where the Romanovs were last imprisoned."

Sanyo and a team from the Federal Security Service were off to Yekaterinburg. Before leaving, however, Sanyo had all the documentation and photos pulled from the national archives on the Romanov family as well as the servants. Upon arriving in Yekaterinburg, they interviewed families of ancestors that lived near the home where the Romanovs were imprisoned. After days of interviews, they came across a great grandchild of Madeleine Zanotti, Alex Zanotti.

He closely resembled the photo of Madeleine Zanotti from the archives and the documentation validated his relationship. "Yes, I recall my grandmother telling me a story that was told to her by her mother, my great grandmother Medeleine Zanotti. She told her about a young man who came to her in the middle of the night with a young girl that my great grandmother she identified as the youngest daughter of the Romanov family. The young man said that he saved the girl after she was shot, and they needed to escape Russia. My great grandmother put them in touch with some Czar loyalists who helped them escape."

Sanyo face glowed with this discovery and anxiously asked Alex for further information. "Did your great grandmother reveal the young man's name?" "I believe my great grandmother may have written his name in her diary. Let me get it."

Alex goes upstairs to fetch his great grandmother's diary and hands it to Sanyo. Sanyo quickly goes through the pages until he comes to a part that describes exactly what Ivan just told him, including the name Jon Drukov. There was a detailed description of what happened on that dark night long ago when the Romanovs were murdered. Sanyo hastily calls the ministry of transportation to have their people search all the train logs between Yekaterinburg and the Poland border. He also calls the British department of transportation to ask them to search for the name of Jon Drukov in their passenger manifestos for ships departing in the early 1900's for the United States following the revolution. The Brits had all their manifestos dating back to the beginning of the 19th century online. They came back with information on several men by the last name of Drukov. The manifestos showed the four by the name of Drukov boarded ships destined for New York City.

The media reports that Russia is seeking the heir to Czar Nicholas's throne. The Russian people become infatuated with the idea. The Kremlin is bombarded with people claiming to be heirs. Television stations air interviews with people claiming to be descendants of the Czar. The stories go viral throughout the world.

Vladimir is becoming impatient. Finally, the call comes into him from Sanyo that they have information on where Anastasia may have settled. "You must quickly move Sanyo, the war in Ukraine is heating up and the people want this virus curbed. They are now caught up in the idea of reinstating a Czar. "Take a team to New York and find where these two ended up. Track them down as soon as possible Jon."

CHAPTER 8

SEARCH FOR THE HEIR

Sanyo calls for a helicopter and orders the Moscow Air base to ready an Antonov An-225 Mriya, nicknamed the Candor and load it with three SUV's. The Candor is the world's second heaviest cargo airplane. Ironically, it was designed by a Ukrainian and then became

Photo 8-The Candor-World's 2nd heaviest cargo plane

part of the Soviet fleet. Later the same aircraft was destroyed in the Battle of Antonov Airport by the Ukraine military during the 2022 Russian invasion of Ukraine. The enormous aircraft was parked at an airfield near Kyiv when it was attacked by "Russian occupants," Ukrainian authorities said, adding they would rebuild the plane. (24)

Sanyo then turns to his team of investigators. "We are off to New York City. Make certain that you document all the information on these people and arrange clear passage with the air space in the United States, so they do not think we are on a clandestine mission."

Normally, the passengers on board would be cleared through standard customs but because the aircraft is military, the U.S. Customs boards and searches the aircraft before any passengers and vehicles are offloaded. After Customs cleared Sanyo and his team, they were off to the New York customs office. They were told that there was no need for them to come to their office. "Ellis Island has an online searchable database, created by the Statue of Liberty/Ellis Island Foundation, of 22.5 million arrivals to New York between 1892 - 1924. Registration is required but free, and you can view scanned images of actual passenger manifests. You can also purchase copies through the site." (25) Sanyo and his team spend two days in a New York hotel room researching documents from Ellis Island. Finally, they find four men that meet the profile. Two are in New York, one migrated to Pittsburgh, and another to Chicago.

The easiest would be to interview the two living in New York city close to their hotel. The arrival of this Russian caravan at the doorsteps of the suspected people was a site to behold, causing great curiosity and commotion among their neighbors. It was mind boggling to see these black SUV's with security people driving into neighborhoods where the common folk lived. It was fast becoming a tale of looking for who would fit Cinderella's shoe. Only in this case it was a crown.

Two of the descendants in New York had a different story, and both tried to produce evidence that linked them to the throne. The men tried to lay claim by offering false documents and family photos that had no resemblance to the Romanovs. One had a photo of their ancestor in a Moscow crowd watching the Czar and his family in a parade, another had a photo of Czar Nicholas that could be purchased anywhere, another had Russian military medals that their ancestors earned while serving in the Czar's army. After comparing their DNA to the DNA samples that they collected from the bodies of the Romanovs, they concluded that there was no family connection whatsoever.

The next one they chose to visit was a descendant of the one that migrated to Chicago. He did not pretend to be an heir to the throne. He was a descendant of a servant to the Czar's family that escaped to the United States after the Bolsheviks occupied the palace. After a lengthy conversation with Sanyo, the Chicago man did give him a lead. He spoke about stories his great grandmother told him that she heard from another servant friend named Madeleine. According to the story, a young man saved a young girl from being killed by the Bolsheviks. The servant Madeleine corresponded with this couple while she was still alive. After spending a brief time in New York, Madeleine said they wrote her a letter with a return address in Pittsburgh. His great grandmother thought the young girl's name was Anastasia. When Sanyo heard this, his eyes widened. "We are off to Pittsburgh. No use wasting any more time here. I phoned Vladimir and briefed him. He wants us to push on."

Upon arriving in Pittsburgh, they chose to land at a local county airport to avoid commotion and it was close to the steel valley where Jon Drukov and his wife settled. A commotion could hardly be avoided, however, for the sight of a large military aircraft with Russian insignias cruising at a low altitude in a landing pattern was a remarkable sight. It was truly a strange sight to see this huge transport with Russian emblems on the wings and tail sections. Concerned that they were being invaded by the Russians, the people in the vicinity of the airport called the police. After checking with the airport, the police discovered that they were of no threat and had clearance to land. The local news media quickly noticed their arrival and used their news helicopters to track the landing of the transport.

As soon as Sanyo's plane landed, a plethora of news stations approached the aircraft for an interview. Sanyo intended to avoid interviews at all costs so he pre-arranged to have U.S. Customs come aboard for their clearances. After being cleared, the belly of the plane opened and out sped Sanyo and his security team in the three black SUVs with the Russian seal on the doors. The news reporters, however, did not miss a step by following behind. In view of the war in Ukraine and the rumor that Russia was looking to reinstate a Czar, this may turn out to be the story of the century. The sight of these black SUV's followed by all the news vehicles was truly a sight to behold

The steel valley where Jon and Anastasia settled grew out of the industrial revolution and once was the steel capital of the world. Andrew Carnegie, himself an immigrant from Scotland, helped grow the steel valley. Like himself, the labor also immigrated from all corners of the world. "Most of the workers, however, came from the European continent. The promise of work to feed their families drew them to the steel valley. The valley is comprised of Munhall, Homestead, Braddock, and West Homestead boroughs. The Monongahela River flows along the boundaries of the towns and joins the Allegheny River to form the Ohio River. In the early years when the steel mills were booming, men had to change their shirts twice a day because of the dark bellowing smoke. "(26)

The Russian caravan, closely followed by the news media, wound through the main street of Munhall, and came to an elementary school known as the park school. It was here where all the ancestors of Anastasia and Jon attended their first six years of school. Within one block, Sanyo and his men came to the home where Jon and Anastasia lived. The same home now housed their descendants. It was a typical home for the steel valley with a detached garage and front porch.

As soon as Sanyo and his team exited their SUVs to walk up the steps, the news reporters surrounded them, and the neighbors started to come out of their homes to see what all the commotion was about. The news reporters pushed microphones and cameras in their faces, asking many questions. "Why has a Russian transport aircraft landed at our county airport instead of our larger international airport? Perhaps you are here about Russia's search to find the heir to the Romanov throne?" Sanyo was always quick and creative when addressing such questions.

"Oh, we are here just to tour the steel valley to learn more about how they revitalized a steel town. The Prince of England did the same many years ago. Days before his visit, a group of British and American architects studied the towns in the Steel Valleys and subsequently delivered a report suggesting several ideas, including the creation of a garden festival on the ground where steel was once produced. We are more interested in job creation.   We stopped by this home because we understand there is a former foreman in the mills that lives here, and we want to gain his insight as someone who worked in the mills." One could readily see the news media was not buying Sanyo's reason for the visit.

Sanyo's security was quick to push the cameras and people of the neighborhood away and set up a secure perimeter around the home. Sanyo ascended the stairs to knock on the door. The reporters and neighbors stood on the street and sidewalk in wonderment.

Upon hearing all the commotion outside, the great grandson of Anastasia, Alexei Drukov, came to the front door just when Sanyo was about to knock on it. "Can I help you? What is all this commotion about?" At first, Sanyo said nothing. He just stood there staring at Alexei wanting to better visualize the similarities between Alexei and his distant grandfather, Czar Nicholas.

Sanyo stood awe struck because he was thinking back centuries during the ceremonial and revered time of the Czars and realizing here is a man who may have the same blood and genes flowing through his veins as the great former rulers of Russia, Peter, and Katherine the Great. Alexei, a middle-aged man, was of slight build and physically fit. Sanyo continued studying the face of Alexei to see how much he resembled the Romanovs. Alexei was as handsome in stature as Nicholas, had a full head of hair, in his late fifties, six foot one, and had a chiseled physique due to his military background that engrained in him a rigid morning of exercise.

It was uncanny to Sanyo that his posture and facial features came close to mirroring that of Czar Nicholas except that Nicholas was younger than Alexei when he met his death. All Alexei needed was a beard and mustache and one would readily see what Nicholas would have looked like at an older age. It was strange seeing the two-standing toe to toe saying not a word at first. Alexei was 6-1 in height and Sanyo was only 5-9, making Sanyo look up to Alexei. From studying photos of the Romanov family, Sanyo could easily see from photos the similarities in the features of Alexei to Czar Nicholas and Alexandra. While standing in front of Alexei, Sanyo reached in his pocket and pulled out photos of Nicholas and Alexandra. He held them up next to Alexei's face to compare the three. Alexei stood patiently while waiting for Sanyo to give him an answer to what brought him to his home and his weird behavior. "I do not know who you are sir, but I would appreciate an explanation. Why are you and all these people at our front door? Also, I would like to know what these photos are all about?"

Sanyo is still awestruck by the fact that he may be looking at a direct descendent to the Romanov family and possibly the next Czar of Russia. "I am Jon Sanyo, Chief of Staff to the President of Russia. And your name is sir?" Alexei is still puzzled about why they are here. "I am Alexei Drukov, and this is my mother's home. Who have you come to see and why is all this security surrounding our home?" Sanyo takes one more step forward closer to the door. "May I come in so we may talk in private?"

Alexei motions for Sanyo to enter his mother's small home. "We are in search of the direct descendants of the last Czar of Russia, Nicholas II. Are you the great grandson of Anastasia Drukov?"

Alexei, still with a puzzled look, identified himself. "I am, she was my great grandmother but what do you mean that you are looking for a direct descendant of Czar Nicholas?" Like everyone in the world, I have read where Russia is in search of an heir to the Romanov throne but why come to our home?"

Sanyo places his hand on Alexei's shoulder and poses another question. "Are you the oldest living descendent of your great grandmother Anastasia Drukov who migrated to the United States in the early 1900's?" "I am. My father would have been but was accidently killed in the mills."

Sanyo offers Alexei his condolences but smiles with delight that he may have found the heir to the Russian throne. "This may come as a surprise to you Alexei, but the next Czar of Russia might be you if we can verify that you are the great grandson of Czar Nicholas's youngest daughter. If so, you will be the next in line to ascend the Romanov throne. We believe your great grandmother Anastasia was the only Romanov who survived the wrath of the Bolsheviks."

Photo 9-Gathering of Neighbors

While Alexei and Dimitri are talking, the crowd outside is growing. Neighbors had come out of their home and people who saw the caravan of reporters followed the caravan to Alexei's house. Alexei's first love, Kathy, and her now husband Jack, also joined the crowd. Alexei just stands there in disbelief for several minutes with his lower jaw dropped. He has a perplexed expression on his face. Hearing all the commotion, Alexei's mother joins Alexei and Sanyo at the door. Finally, Alexei gains his composure to speak.

"Most believe that the survival of the Czar was only a myth made into a fairytale. My mother has told me the many stories that my great grandmother spoke of during her days when Russia was ruled by a Czar. Perhaps you can enlighten this gentleman with the stories Great Grandmother told you mother."

"My mother said that somehow her mother Anastasia was familiar with the Romanov family. The way she talked about them was like she knew them personally. She talked about the slaughter of the Romanov family in detail as though she was in the same room where they were killed. Anastasia also spoke about how the Romanov family lived as royals. At the time, my mother thought it was very strange how she knew so much about their personal lives, like she was talking about her family. " Alexei now questions Sanyo. "Knowing how Czar Nicholas died, why would anyone want to assume the mantle of the Romanov family? I would think that anyone who puts on the crown could encounter the same fate as Czar Nicholas and his family? I do not think anyone would want that fate.

"Those were different times Alexei. This is a new Russia where people are not starving and thinking revolution. Many are no longer living that remember those sorrowful days. There has been much publicity in Russia about the crowning of a Czar. The Russian people are infatuated with the day to day lives of the royal family in Britain and the publicity of the coming of a new Czar has them excited. The Russian Orthodox church has canonized Nicholas and would welcome the return of a Czar." Sanyo tries using reverse psychology to get him to accept the challenge.

"Of course, I can understand if you are not up to the task and feel that you cannot manage such responsibility. We have also done some preliminary investigation into you, Alexei, and you have been somewhat of an introvert most of your life. I cannot imagine that a true descendant of the Czars would turn his back on his people. Czar Nicholas may have been a terrible leader, but he had the courage to accept the responsibilities of the crown."

Hearing what Sanyo said, Alexei's mother excuses herself to find the small chest that was handed down to her by her grandmother Anastasia. She hurriedly brings it to Alexei and Sanyo. "Alexei, this belonged to your great grandmother and in it is all she left behind in this world. She made my mother promise that it would only be opened if our heritage were ever in question. I think that this is that time. Alexei took the box in hand and opened it in front of Sanyo. It was an object wrapped in cloth, a document, and an envelope containing a handwritten note.

With a questioning look, Alexei slowly read his great grandmother's note aloud. "My loving family, it is now time for you all to know who we are and who our ancestors were. I am the Grand Duchess of the house of Romanov, the youngest daughter of Nicholas and Alexandra, and one of you is the heir to whatever may be left of the Romanov dynasty. I will not bore you with what is already written in history books but if the day ever comes when one of you is asked to re-claim the throne, it is your responsibility to do so. Especially as the Romanov lineage and the good name of our family must be restored. The Bolsheviks may have turned their backs on us, but our family never turned their backs on the people of Russia. It is in your blood to answer the call to service. I asked one of your sons to be named after my brother Alexei who would have been next in line to ascend the throne. Hopefully, this letter along with what I have left in this chest will validate that you are the true successor to the Russian throne. With all my love, Anastasia Romanov."

With that, Alexei reached into the envelope and pulled out a birth certificate certifying Anastasia's birth to Czar Nicholas and Alexandra. He then pulled out the cloth covered artifact. Both Alexei and Sanyo gasped at the site of what turned out to be the royal signature seal of the Czars. All the pieces now fill into place including why he was named Alexei. They could not believe their eyes.

Seeing that, Sanyo excused himself to phone Dimitri. "I am 100% certain that we have found Nicholas's descendant Vladimir. His mother produced a small chest with a letter, document, and the Czar's seal. This proves Anastasi Romanov was his great grandmother and he is next in line to the throne." "I believe you Jon, but I think it best to confirm his identity. Use the DNA samples that were taken from the bodies of the Romanovs and the DNA sample that was donated by Prince Philip of Great Britain who was related to the Romanovs."

After Alexei's mother convinced him that he needed to take his place in history, Sanyo got Alexei to agree to a blood sample and sent it out for DNA testing. It only took two days to confirm that Alexei was indeed a descendant of the Romanovs. Vladimir then instructed Sanyo to bring Alexei to Russia. "All is confirmed Alexei that you are the heir to the Romanov throne. We are ordered back to Russia and need your answer."

As they talked, the news media reported that Vladimir launched a massive attack on Ukraine. Military and civilian lives were already lost, and it was now a full- scale war in Ukraine. What was happening in Ukraine resonated in the mind of Alexei. Alexei was savvy on current events and like many Russians, he was dead set against the invasion and hoped he could change the course of history. His great grandmother's words resonated in his mind about assuming his responsibilities if called upon. He knew that he could not shirk the wishes of his great grandmother. At the same time, he wanted to avoid for him and his two sons what happened to the last Czar of Russia. Alexei turns to Sanyo and speaks to him in Russian.

"I will accept your offer under these conditions and that is that I choose and bring my own security, and they need to be always armed no matter who is in my presence and are compensated the same as any of your Russian security and the United States secret service. I would also want to request a small contingent of Secret Service from the White House to intermingle with and train my security people. I want to choose where I reside and have my security positioned as recommended by the White House Secret Service. Next, my security people will not be expelled from Russia if contentions flair up between the U.S. and Russia. Lastly, I will require that Russian allow me to have dual citizenship, meaning my sons and I will become citizens of Russia while maintaining our U.S. citizenships." For his security, Alexei had in mind his tough longtime friends under the leadership of his closest friend, Joey.

"I am impressed that you speak fluent Russian Alexei. That will be of great help in being accepted by the Russian people. The power is vested in me to consent to all your wishes and arrange all you ask. Before we leave for Russia, we will have a small orientation for your security. Let me tell you how it works for those that protect our leaders. The special service responsible for the security of the Russian president is called the Federal Protective Service The requirements for this position do not include real war experience. Combat experience is not applicable in their work. During war, you attack whereas a bodyguard only needs to anticipate threats to protect. *(Russia Beyond)* Hopefully yours will do the same."

"Yes, I speak Russian. Because my great grandmother spoke little English, her children and then her children's children learned to speak Russian from their parents. I learned from my mother who spoke Russian as well as English in our home. My mother and I even taught Russian to my two sons. Because they were not raised when my grandmother was alive, they are not as fluent in Russian as I am, but they speak conversational Russian and can read it."

Sanyo nods his head. "The command of the Russian language by your sons is outstanding, especially as one of your two sons will secede you to the throne. As I mentioned, I am vested with the power to grant all your demands Alexei. As far as Russia is concerned, we agree. Now that we accept your conditions, select your people, and tell them to prepare for the trip. We leave in two days from your county airport. In the meantime, we will leave security to protect you until you get your security in place."

Sanyo and his people go to a local hotel while Alexei starts to prepare for his departure. His first order of business is to explain to his sons what has transpired. Before he can pick up the phone, Alexei receives a call from the White House. The CIA has already briefed the President on what has occurred, and he is offering whatever assistance Alexei may need. Having served under the Secretary of State and the Chairman of the Joint Chiefs of Staff during 9-11, Alexis knows that everything has changed for him now. He must walk a fine line between the United States and Russia. He and his two sons must now also owe allegiance to Russia. To maintain ties with the United States, however, he asks the White House that he and his sons be granted dual citizenship. The White House complied.

He explains to his two sons how dual citizenship works. "Dual citizenship is a legal status in which a person is concurrently regarded as a national or citizen of more than one country under the laws of those countries. We will retain our citizenship here in the United States while also becoming citizens of Russia. Luckily for us, U.S. law does not require a person to choose one citizenship over another and if it did, the White House informed me that they will grant a waiver. I am leaving for Russia in a couple of days and will send for you and your grandmother once I get settled and it is safe for you to come." Both boys nod their heads in agreement and wait for their father's departure.

Alexei explained to Sanyo that he will need a handful of secret service to train his security that will be accompanying him to Russia. The White House assured Alexei that they will send a team of their best security. Because of what is going on with Ukraine, however, the White House warned there may be some resistance by Russia to allow U.S. secret service into their country.

Alexei phones Joey. "Hopefully, you have been watching the news, Joey. I never knew until today about my heritage. I feel like I am living in a fairy tale. It is like a dream where I cannot wake up. Because of what happened to the last Czar of Russia, I am very skeptical and untrusting of Russia's President and his henchman. Hopefully my fairy tale dream will not turn into a nightmare Joey." "They are allowing me to organize my own security, and I would like you and some of our other trusted friends to be part of it. You will be paid generously including your expenses. We will also need to leave some security behind to protect my mother and sons until they join us in Russia."

"Joey is speechless. Like Alexei, he and their other friends lost their jobs when the mills closed, and they went through their life savings and what little pension money that was given to them. Joey never married so he can leave freely. "I am ready Alexi!"

Alexei urges him to come over to his home as soon as possible. "Pick about ten friends that we can trust and along with them, get your affairs in order and pack your bags. All of you will receive training from a handful of Secret Services men who will be accompanying us. The Russians will also provide some training on security procedures and orientation to Russian life." "Say no more Alexei, we will be there for you and will do everything we can to protect you. "

The next day, the white house sent ten of their most experienced secret service people and Joey shows up with ten trusted friends. The secret service brought ample weapons and security equipment including a couple trained canine dogs. They also brought the necessary documentation to allow them entry into Russia.

As Alexei prepares to leave for the airport, the entire town gathers outside his home. Included among the crowd is the former love of his life in high school Kathy and her husband Jack. Jack and Kathy are in the same financial boat that Alexei was in when the family business went bankrupt with the closing of the mills. The financial stress has aged Kathy beyond her years. As Alexei prepared to enter the limos, he walked through the crowd to greet Kathy and Jack.

He gazes upon them with a serious yet forgiving look. The expressions of surprise on Kathy and Jack's face were payback to Alexei for all the humiliation and disappointment that he suffered at their hands. Kathy takes Alexei aside and whispers into his ear kiddingly. "Hopefully the kiss you gave me in high school turned you from the frog into a Czar Alexei." Alexei smiled at her and gave her a friendly kiss on the cheek. He then shook Jack's hand. Being a compassionate and caring person, Alexei is already thinking of ways he can help them. Jack Kiddingly told Alexei that "I can tell my kids and grandkids a great story line. A Czar once knocked me on my butt." Alexei and Jack had a good laugh before walking to his waiting limo. Before getting inside, everyone cheered and applauded him.

Alexei caravan was cleared to move quickly back to the airport. The local and state police blocked all the roads. People were standing alongside the road waving at Alexei as his Limo drove by them. Upon arriving at the airport, there were people that came from neighboring towns to see them off and catch a glimpse of the Russia aircraft, which resembled a spaceship from another world. Alexei and his security team could not believe their eyes as to its size.

The mouth of the aircraft dropped (Photo 9) and out walks Sanyo

Photo 10-Antonov An-225 Mriya receiving passengers and Cargo

to welcome them aboard. Many of his neighborhood showed up along with Kathy, Jack, and his other one-time nemesis Billy. As Alexei and his team board the aircraft, he gives one more wave to his neighbors and blows a kiss and a smile to Kathy. Suddenly realizing she still cares for him; she does the same in return. The start-up sound of the engines was deafening and the sight of this large aircraft preparing for takeoff was overpowering. When the aircraft turned to taxi for takeoff, the exhaust from the engines almost blew everyone over. The Candors powerful engines require only a short runway to take off and they were out of sight in minutes.

Their aircraft made good time. It did not take long to enter Russian air space and obtain the necessary clearances to land. Alexei and his team were mesmerized by what they could see outside the windows of the aircraft. The ground was covered in snow. It looked like a snow scene in the movie Dr. Zhivago.

Upon landing, Russian news teams and a throng of Russian people were waiting. Alexei's became the topic of interest among the Russian people and the world. Shop owners were excited about what it would do to bolster their economy. With Russia being shut off from the world because of the Ukraine war, the people were hoping that the return of a Czar would remake the world's image of Russia.

Sanyo's orders were to bring Alexei to Dimitri's office at the Kremlin immediately upon landing. As they walked across the runway to the waiting sedans, camera flashes from the news people were blinding. People were leaning over the fences hoping to shake Alexei's hand.

Sanyo motioned for Alexei to hurry, but Alexei turned to walk towards the people. Sanyo's team rushed to head him back to the limos, but Joey and his people blocked them. Alexei walked up to the people and reached over the fence to shake their hands. The well-wishers went wild with excitement. The news cameras caught all the action and were televising it. The people kept chanting Alexi's name. It went more viral when Alexei yelled back to them in their native language of Russian, ya russkiy…. I am a Russian. The news media featured the story in every newspaper and on all television stations throughout the world.

CHAPTER 9

HERO MEETS VILLAIN

Upon their arrival in Kremlin square, it was snowing even though Spring was around the corner. "The term Kremlin means fortress in medieval Russa and was usually located at a strategic point along a river separated from the surrounding parts of the city by a wooden fence. Later the wooden fence was replaced by a stone or brick wall with ramparts, a moat, towers, and battlements. In the case of Russia's seat of power, it was surrounded by a tall concrete bricked wall located in the center of Moscow. The main entrance is located through the Kutafya tower, where most visitors queue to enter. The second entrance, which is much less used, is located by walking through the Alexandrovsky gardens. This second entrance is the quickest entrance to the Armory chamber and the Diamond Fund. The Kremlin is open to the public where they can tour the Armory Chamber, Tsar Cannon, Tsar Bell, artillery pieces, and a large exposition of Russian wooden sculpture and carvings.

Moscow's Kremlin (photo 10) was built between the 14th and 17th centuries and was once the residence of the Great Prince and was also a religious center. It hosted the most important historical and political events in Russia. It was once the residence of what they called in the days of early Russia, the great prince. Now it is the primary residence of its President. The Kremlin has over fifteen buildings and is surrounded by 1.5 miles of concrete walls 21 feet thick. It is protected by twenty defensive towers and protected by an elite military regiment known as the Presidential Regiment. Nearby is Lenin's tomb.

Inside the Kremlin are the Arsenal which houses antique military trophies and weapons worth billions of dollars, an event theater with 800 rooms, Ivan the great bell tower, cathedral square, the Grand Kremlin Palace which houses the throne room of Czars from the past and the personal residents of the Russian presidents." (27)

It is well after visiting hours but in preparation for the arrival of Alexei, the guards have been waiting to open the huge iron doors for him. The heavy bronze doors are reflected in the moonlight to make them look intimidating but quickly open as soon as Alexei and his accompaniment arrive. Sanyo orders were to bring Alexei immediately to Vladimir's office upon his arrival. "The Presidential Executive Office of Russia is situated in Moscow where it occupies several buildings in Kitay-gorod and inside the Kremlin. Part of the offices of the Presidential Executive Office are located in an Art Nouveau building at Moscow's Staraya Square. It is next to the former seat of the Central Committee of the Communist Party when Russia was known as the Soviet Union.

On the 25th of March 2004, Dimitri undertook a major reorganization of his office by decree. He eliminated five of his seven deputy chiefs so he could better control the news media, he merged the Press Office and the Information Office. He put in place a document called Revision Number Six, which he couched as a reform document. Revision six rejected the possibility of direct prohibition on opposition activities and independent mass media activities. Saying that Russian society was not ready for mass media, they proposed that Domestic Policy Directorate of the Presidential Administration will use the combination of public and secret activities. Secret activities were to be carried out with the direct use of special services which was Dimitri's Federal Security Service. This document is what gave Vladimir the oversight on the news media and his ability to hide the atrocities of the Ukrainian war." (28)

"According to the 1991 amendment to the 1978 constitution, the President of Russia was the head of the executive branch and headed the Council of Ministers of Russia. According to the current 1993 constitution, the president is not a part of the government of Russia, which exercises executive power. However, the president appoints the prime minister. In most other countries, the Prime Minister is elected. The Russian government issues its acts in the way of decisions and orders. These decisions and orders must not contradict the constitution, federal constitutional laws, federal laws, and Presidential decrees, all of which must be signed by the Prime Minister. Such a structure gives Vladimir more control over the government and executive orders." (29)

To enter Vladimir's office, a visitor must go through a series of check points and eventually end up in a waiting room prior to entering through two huge bronze doors guarded by two of Vladimir's elite military. Upon entering the waiting room, Alexei spots a beautiful young woman sitting off to the side. He acknowledges her presence by a friendly salutation, and she does the same. Alexei then introduces himself as Alexei Drukov and she in turn introduces herself only by her first name only, Lina. They briefly start a conversation before Vladimir's staff interrupts them by signaling for Alexei to enter Vladimir's office. Alexei bids Lina good evening and gets up to enter the President's office. As he enters, he looks back to Lina and their eyes lock on one another with a sense that there was a mutual attraction. Even though Lina was up on current affairs, she did not tie Alexei into being the heir apparent to the Romanov throne.

As the guards open the doors, Vladimir is seated at his conference table surrounded by generals who were briefing him on the Ukraine war. Alexei thought it unusual that Vladimir allowed people to sit that close to him. From all the news reports he read, Vladimir always greeted visitors at the end of a long table, with him sitting at one end and the visitor at the other. One could see Vladimir's dissatisfaction with his generals as to how the war was progressing. Strewn on the table were maps and military documents.

When Alexei entered his office, Vladimir and the generals stood up to greet him. "Welcome to Russia Alexei, home of your ancestors. Forgive me for not spending much time with you right now. I am sure you have read about our conflict with Ukraine." Vladimir introduces the generals to Alexei. He then briefs Alexei on the progress they have made in the war, most of it exaggerated to Vladimir's favor.

Vladimir hid the true casualty rate from the people, and many did not know whether their child may be among them. "The number of Ukrainian and Russian troops killed or wounded since the war in Ukraine began in February 2022 is nearing 500,000, the New York Times reported on Friday, citing unnamed U.S. officials. Russia's military casualties are approaching 300,000, including as many as 120,000 deaths and 170,000 to 180,000 injuries, the newspaper reported. Ukrainian deaths were close to 70,000, with 100,000 to 120,000 wounded, it added." (30).

Vladimir was especially happy to see Alexei because he could now set him up for being the scape goat on anything that went wrong in the war on Ukraine or for any of his directives that went wrong. Giving him a misleading brief was the first step in doing so. To start, Vladimir offers justification for Russia to attack Ukraine. "Ukraine, while not a formal NATO member, has been a loyal partner to NATO and sent troops on NATO missions—and they desperately want to join the Alliance. We want Russia to have a veto of any further NATO expansion and want military troops removed from former members of the Cold War Warsaw Pact. This would include countries like Poland, Romania, Bulgaria, Hungary, and others.

Vladimir then presents Alexei with his game plan to bring Ukraine to submission. My generals are tactically innovative and have a variety of options in front of them. The commanders you see here before you are experienced through a wide variety of combat scenarios, most recently in the ongoing civil war in Syria and of course during their engagement in Ukraine itself. The combat in Ukraine continues both overtly in Crimea and covertly in the Donbass region towards the southeast of the country.

At first, we considered a blitzkrieg. Traditional blitzkriegs included the mix of weaponry and offensive warfare designed to strike a swift, focused blow to an enemy using mobile, maneuverable forces, armored tanks, and air support.

"In our invasion of Ukraine, we are going beyond the traditional blitzkrieg. We intend to ramp it up to what we used against the invasion of Georgia. "Our blitzkrieg will require not only the 100,000 troops currently on the border, but an additional 75,000 who would "fall in" on prepositioned equipment that the U.S. showed the world in intelligence photos.

This approach would include heavy air strikes against Ukrainian command and control, artillery bombardment, strikes from naval vessels in the Black Sea, and surface-to-surface missiles. All of this would be accompanied by offensive military cyberattacks against Ukrainian defensive weapons systems, communication capabilities, and against parts of the nation's electric and utility grids.

Helicopters would move shock troops quickly forward behind Ukrainian front lines. They would confuse and destabilize Ukrainian coordination and higher command authorities. Heavy infantry units would then cross the weakened border and thrust deep into southeast Ukraine as far as the Dnieper River. This would end up consolidating Donetsk, Luhansk, and Mariupol. Eventually we envision this approach will help us create a land bridge connecting Russia with Crimea. We will be able to occupy a significant portion of the Black Sea waterfront which gives us access to another freshwater port.

At that point, we intend to pause, assess the situation, and decide whether to push forward to Kiev to effect regime change before pulling our troops back. We would go on to annex the southeast of the country, support a puppet regime in Kiev, and wait for the response of the west. This is the riskiest but also the highest payoff for us and is a 20% probability of leading to a quick victory and limiting the loss of our soldiers and artillery." (31)

While Alexei is listening to Vladimir expound on the Ukraine invasion, his thoughts were focused on a Moscow's 2008 invasion into Georgia which resulted in the conquest of two small provinces. of that small, western aligned democracy. similar invasion by Moscow in 2008, which resulted in the conquest of two provinces of that small, western democracy. It was a straightforward offensive attack against the tiny nation of under four million—Russian tanks, troops, bombs, fighter jet, infantry, and artillery strikes provided the heavy punch.

"In 2011 Vladimir invaded Crimea and used what has come to be known as "hybrid warfare," conducted by mix of non-uniformed soldiers and high-end special forces. They were sophisticated enough to launch a cyber-attack against command centers that included electric grids and social media. The Ukrainian crisis altered the security paradigm in Europe by forcing NATO to revise its stance towards Russia, as it employed a wide array of military and non-military tools and tactics called "hybrid warfare." To counter Russian hybrid warfare in future, the NATO Alliance implemented functional and structural changes known the Readiness Action Plan (RAP) and endorsed the New Strategy on Hybrid Warfare. This paper will study Russian hybrid warfare activities, and the preparedness of an Alliance shaped by the RAP and the New Strategy on Hybrid Warfare. It discusses whether this new NATO will be able to deter Russia from resorting to hybrid warfare against a NATO ally. While the Alliance has enhanced its military capabilities, the Allies' ability to achieve consensus on a response is the factor most likely to deter and dissuade Russia from engaging in hybrid warfare." (32)

Alexei looks over the Ukraine maps and documents strewn all over the conference table and feels compelled to include his observation. He was not one to hold back his opinion when serving on the joint Chiefs of Staff. "You know Mr. President that I served at the highest level of the military command structure at the Pentagon. If you do not mind, I would like to provide some insight as to what happened to American when it chose to take up arms against another country."

Vladimir nods his head to give Alexei the go ahead but the frustration on his face said otherwise.

Alexei quickly took advantage of the opportunity. "We used to have a saying after we briefed the Secretary of Defense and the Chairman of the Joint Chiefs and the saying was always "Lessons Learned," meaning what have we learned from previous war strategies? I always wondered about that because we never learned from the prior wars such as Vietnam or from your military actions for that matter. We made the same mistakes when it came to Afghanistan. Yes, we should have gone in and make the terrorists pay for killing innocent American's, but we or Russia should never have occupied the country. We suffered similar losses when your forces assaulted Afghanistan, and the country reverted to the Taliban. We study history but for some reason, we never learn from it."

"After wasting much money and sacrificed many young lives, we had to settle for an embarrassing exit from the country. To add insult to injury, we lost billions in equipment and had to leave innocent Afghans behind that helped our troops. The more prudent and honorable way we should have left was to create a green zone around Kabul and kept the Taliban at bay until we evacuated our equipment and those Afghans that supported our cause. Did Russia experience similar losses?"

"I see the many similarities between you and czar Nicholas when he tried to do battle with the Germans and Japanese. Common knowledge should have prevailed. He did not have the planning or the weaponry to support the mission and nor does Russia. As a result, he paid the price by having to abdicate his throne due to his failures in war while at the same time ignoring the needs of his people at home. Your invasion of Ukraine will cost many lives on both sides and the result may be the same as before you invaded. Are you willing to bet the lives of our young people and those innocent people of Ukraine? I think that I can sum up what I am saying from the quote by a former president of the United States, Truman. "If we do not eradicate war, war will eradicate us from the face of this earth."

Vladimir squirmed while he listened to Alexei. "Thank you for your insight, Alexei but I think that our end state will not be the same as what happened to you and us in Afghanistan. We will prevail in the end." Alexei looked at Vladimir with a questionable look on his face. "Well then, I guess you are willing to bet your presidency, our beloved young of Russia, and the lives of many innocent people living in Ukraine and Russia?"

Alexei could sense that Vladimir did not want to hear the disastrous way his assault on Ukraine could end up. Instead, he wanted to hear from Alexei and his generals that his plan was on target. The generals could not say anything for fear of losing their commissions, but you could sense from the generals that they agreed with Alexei rather than Vladimir. Alexei knew that Vladimir wanted to end their conversation.

Vladimir was taken back by Alexei's comments. With eyebrows raised, he gave Alexei an unpleasant stare, gritting his teeth, hesitating before saying something he may regret. He does not even respond to his comments. Instead, he points towards the door. "I would imagine you and your security are tired from your long journey Alexei. My staff will show you and your people to your quarters. They have planned for you to stay within the walls of the Kremlin, in the Terem Palace until you decide where you wish to make your permanent residence. You may be interested to know that the Terem Palace was once the main residence of the Russian Czars in the 17th century. When it housed the Czars, the third story was occupied by the czarina and her children, and the fourth one contained the private apartments of the czar. There is ample room for both you and your security people. Now you will have to excuse us, Alexei. We have some important matters to address. I hope you have a pleasant night, and we can talk more in the next day or two about your ascension to the throne."

Alexei gave a disconcerting look, turned, and walked out. Outside Vladimir's office Joey and his security stood watch for Alexei's return. As Alexei walked out into the waiting room, he looked around for the young lady he had just met but could not find her. He gave a disappointing sigh because he wanted to ask for her contact information. Joey could sense a feeling of frustration in Alexei. Not knowing that Lina dates Vladimir on occasion, Alexei looks at Joey. "Story of my life Joey, I never seem to be able to hold onto a beautiful woman." Joey gives Alexei a pat on the back. "You win some and you lose some Alexei. Hopefully, there will be a win coming your way soon."

Alexei thanks Joey and says he has greater concerns. Alexei explained his frustration with Vladimir to Joey as they walked down the corridors of the Kremlin to where they were going to be housed, the grand palace.

After leaving the waiting room, Alexei and Joey were shown to their quarters. In the meantime, Lina came back into the waiting room and looked around to see if Alexei was anywhere in site. Just then, Vladimir came out of his office to offer Lina his arm. Lina was waiting for Vladimir; they had dated for quite some time after she won her Olympic gold medals. With the help of Vladimir, Lina became the current head of the National Media Group, a pro-Kremlin empire of television, radio, and print organizations. She was also a former member of Parliament and because of her relationship with Vladimir, NATO also targeted economic sanctions. Despite all that Vladimir helped to bestow upon her, she was looking for a way to distance herself from him. She felt her relationship with Vladimir had relegated her to nothing more than an escort. The only reason she continued to see him was because of what he had done for her and her family. Tonight, they were going to another boring state dinner where she would have to give the air of enjoying herself and belittling herself to be the "candy" on Vladimir's arm.

Walking into the grand palace of the Kremlin, Alexei and Joey were awed by the architecture as they walked through some of the corridors of the palace. It was laden throughout in gold and red finishes. Alexei could not help imagining what it was like when occupied by his ancestors. The quarters of the Czar had numerous bedrooms, large enough to house Alexei and his security. When not occupied by dignitaries, it was on tour but always kept in the same décor as when Czar Nicholas and his family occupied it.

Photo 11-Grand Palace of Kremlin

The suite of rooms was redone with oak parquet floors, wool rugs, and silk draperies, and even spittoons that were used by the imperial family and courtiers. When Alexei curled up in the antique bed, he began feeling like he was sleeping in a museum. After such a long and tiresome trip, he felt he could sleep anywhere. In the middle of the night, he was awakened by voices. He raised his head off the pillow and did not see anyone. Even though he did not believe in spirits, he started to have thoughts that they did exist. He recalled the tale that some people who slept in the Lincoln bedroom at the white house experienced a spiritual revelation. He just rolled over and ignored whatever he heard.

The next morning there was an early rise for Alexei and his people. With the Czar's living quarters preserved as they were in the 17th century, it had no televisions or electronic modems where one could connect to the outside world. Visitors could only use their cell phone if they could reach connectivity via the orbiting satellites. The housekeepers directed Alexei and his people to a dining hall in the lower part of the palace. It was there they found televisions and web access.

Alexei and his team were introduced to a typical Russian breakfast along with some variations on common American breakfast foods such as Russian pancakes and millet porridge. The Russians often start the morning off with coffee or tea, eggs, sausage, and buttered bread. Available were many sweet dishes of morning pastries and other sugary treats called by different names than the typical American breakfast.

Joey and the other security opted more for the American dishes whereas Alexei chose the traditional Russian dishes so as not to insult anyone. He felt compelled to adhere to Russian traditions. One of the most interesting breakfast experiences was how they prepared the tea. Making Russian tea is a bigger process than brewing American Tea. To brew authentic Russian tea, it takes about three hours, and you drink it with cinnamon sticks, cloves, and juice from pineapples, lemons, and oranges. Alexei found it tasty and commented to the waiters that once you had such great tea, you would not want coffee.

The waiters turned on the TV because they thought Alexei would like to catch up on Russian news. Without commenting openly, Alexei and Joey found it to be more propaganda than objective news reporting. Alexei and Joey could readily see that Vladimir's kept the Russian people and its parliament in the dark on the Ukraine war by controlling the news media. The media was bent on telling a story that Russian troops were there on a peace mission and portrayed the Ukrainian hierarchy as despots, suppressing freedoms of Ukrainian people.

At that moment, in walked Sanyo. "Hopefully, you do not think that I abandoned you last night, but I have not seen my family for quite some time. Do you have any questions of me?" "I would like to walk around Moscow Sanyo, and I would like to visit the city where Czar Nicholas and his family were murdered.

"A couple of unusual requests but no problem, we will make it happen Alexei. I will make all the arrangements. For now, feel free to walk around Moscow. Would you like me to arrange a tour, including one of Lenin's tomb."

Alexei was appalled when Sanyo suggested a tour of Lenin's tomb, the man who ordered the execution of his relatives. "There is no way that I would even think of giving Lenin any respect by visiting his tomb. I agree with a former Russian President who said they should bury Lenin. I would add, it should be in an unmarked grave.

CHAPTER 10

ALEXEI TOURS RUSSIA

Alexei thanked Sanyo for his offer to accompany him but said he would rather go incognito with only his friend Joey. After finishing their breakfast, Joey and Alexei set off walking the streets of Moscow and spoke to people they met as they walked, hoping not to be recognized. After walking a few miles around the city, Alexei and Joey start realizing that Moscow is a huge and heavily populated city. Despite this, they were not going to let size stand in their way to exchange some pleasantries with its citizens. The residents of Moscow are nicknamed Muscovites. The only problem was that Alexei and Joey did not realize how large Moscow is, and not only the capital of Russia but it is its largest city. It is a vibrant city, adorned with palaces straight out of a fairytale. Even the metro system is full of rare and breath-taking art.

Awaiting Alexei and Joey as they wander are streets that lead to marvelous sites from ancient cathedrals to royal estates including the summer havens of the Czars and their family. Wherever they look they see a modern city but realize they are walking in the same footprints of old Russia, where the Bolshevik Revolution took place. Moscow is glowing with a rich culture, exceptional theaters, and exciting nightlife.

"Moscow stands on the Moskva River in Central Russia, with a population estimated at 12.4 million residents within the city limits, over 17 million residents in the urban area, and over 20 million residents in the regional metropolitan area. The city covers an area of 970 sq mi, while the urban area covers 275 sq mi, and the metropolitan area covers over 10,000 sq mi. Moscow is among the world's largest cities; being the most populous city in Europe, the largest urban and metropolitan area in Europe, and the largest city by land area on the European continent.

The Kitay-gorod (Photo 11) is a historic quarter of Moscow and a major tourist attraction. Within the Kitay-gorod is red square where ceremonial parades are held. In the center is Lenin's tomb, which is also a major tourist attraction because people come not out of reverence for Lenin but instead out of curiosity. The body of Lenin is one of the oldest preserved bodies on display in the world. A previous President was going to bury the body but changed their mind because it proved to be a huge draw from tourists visiting Moscow. At the south end of red square is the Cathedral of St. Basil built in the 1500's." (33)

Photo 12-Lenin's Tomb

Talking with Muscovites, Alexei and Joey learned that inner "Moscow functions like a typical central business district, where most of the government offices, hotels, shops, theatres, museums, and art galleries are located. Scattered within the garden ring of Moscow are luxury apartments for Russia's elite. More convenient and nicely furnished studios, as well as one-bedroom apartments, will set you back for at least $507 per month in the suburbs, and as much as $1,859 in the city. Moscow has grocery shops on every corner: big ones, small ones, local ones, organic and vegetarian." (34) Finding food items that Alexei and Joey are accustomed to won't be a problem. "Prices on imported goods might be a problem, however, because on average they are two to three times higher than Russian products. On the other hand, there are many domestically grown vegetables, fruits, fish, and meats of excellent quality, and prices are affordable. Prices for specific items vary depending upon the store. Commuting in and around Moscow takes a significant share of your time and money. The cheapest option is to buy a monthly pass for all forms of public transportation (buses, trams, and metro), which will cost $33. It is always good to grab a cup of coffee on the way to the office. In Moscow this might cost you $2-5 on average depending on what you like. It was cheaper to have a cappuccino in McDonalds or at local cafes than at Starbucks or other international coffee chains but due to the Ukrainian War, McDonalds closed all its stores. The cinema is one of the most popular and affordable forms of entertainment in Moscow, and the average cost of a ticket in the evening is $5-6. Bar hopping is another. A concert by a famous international music group costs $50-67, a ticket to the Bolshoi Theater is $84-118; and to the circus is $33-67." (35)

Alexei gets his first opportunity to strike up a more in-depth conversation with a Muscovite by pretending to share some interest in a shop window. He asks him if he was born in Moscow and what are his thoughts about invading Ukraine? Fortunately for Alexei, he speaks fluent Russian. "About 30 percent of Russians speak English to one degree or another: 20 percent can read and translate using a dictionary, 7 percent are familiar with English, and 3 percent are fluent." (36)

The Muscovite speaks very openly with Alexei and Joey. "I was born and raised outside the city of Moscow. For a regular citizen it is hard to understand what is true and what is false, who is right and who is wrong," he said. "Most people I know are "harsh critics of Vladimir's actions" and sympathize with Ukraine where some of us have friends and families. What I know for sure is that no one wants war."

I served in the Russian army and was one of many deployed to fight the war in Afghanistan. I know what it is like to sit next to a close friend and see a bullet piercing his heart. Many of us knew that we could not win such a war. "It turned into a bloody war that resulted in the death of one million civilians, 90,000 Mujahideen fighters, and 18,000 Afghan troops. On our side, we lost about 15,000 men. As more Soviet soldiers were being killed or wounded in a war that dragged on forever, our then president started to refer to the Afghanistan war as a "bleeding wound." (37)   After ten years of fighting with no end in sight, our leaders decided to pull out of Afghanistan. The Afghan war was like your wars in Vietnam and Afghanistan. Nothing good ever came out of them. Yet, our current president has ignored what history has taught us and that is you never go into a war unless there is a direct threat to Russia. I am dead set against shedding the life blood of our youth for a war that has no real meaning."

Alexei thanks him for his insight and continues their stroll through Moscow. They come to a lady who appears to be in her thirties walking with her young daughter. "What do you think of Russia wanting to reinstate the Czar?"

The lady laughs at first and then ponders an answer to the question. "It certainly is the talk of Russia. Like many Russians, there are few if any that remember what it was like to live when the Czars ruled Russia. There are many, however, who remember what it was like to live when we were a communist country. I for one am too young to know the difference between either of the two except for what my parents told me. Having a royal family seems to work quite well for England, bringing in a lot of tourism dollars and the enchantment of having the pomp and ceremony of what it may entail.

Alexei thanks her for her thoughts and starts to walk away. As he starts to walk, she calls out to him. "Hey, have we met before? You look familiar to me." Alexei turns around and speaks the truth but does not reveal his identity. "No ma'am, we have never personally met before, but it was great meeting you and your daughter."

Their next stop was a Moscow shop. The shop owner happened to be on site and personally greeted Alexei and Joey. Alexei asked him how small shop owners are surviving the embargo placed on them.

"Not that well, especially the small business owners. Many of the small Russian shops have closed, most of the branded stores have left. Small shops are having great difficulty getting products to sell. "Ordinary Russians faced the prospect of higher prices and crimped foreign travel as Western sanctions over the invasion of Ukraine sent the ruble plummeting, leading uneasy depositors to line up at banks and ATMs on Monday in a country that has seen more than one currency disaster in the post-Soviet era. The value of our ruble has plummeted, and the savings of most people have eroded. Tourism has dropped dramatically because most countries have banned travel to Russia. We are economically dependent on other countries and apart from the financial hardship caused by the pandemic, we are still feeling the consequences of the sanctions from 2014. These latest sanctions will just make it even worse for everyone. Large stores like TSUM have survived because it is the signature fashion department store of Russia and an historic site that has been in existence for more than 110 years. TSUM features collections of more than 700 leading global brands of clothing, shoes, bags and accessories, fine jewelry, and timepieces, as well as perfumes and cosmetics." (38)

Alexei looks at him with a sympathetic look. "Do you think reinstating a Czar will be of any help to attract more tourism?" Do I think we should bring back the Czar? Do you realize that the British having a monarchy brings in billions of tourism dollars. The shop, restaurant, and hotel owners cannot wait until the Czar is put back on the throne.

This time, Alexei and Joey turn to walk through Red Square. The sun is setting over the city. As they walk through the square, it is snowing. They kept hearing but could not see some sort of bird flying overhead in the falling snow making a hawkish sound. The next thing they heard is the huge doors to the Kremlin open and shut. Out from the Kremlin fortified compound come goose-stepping soldiers. The cleats on their boots resonated throughout red square with each step they took. The goose step is a special marching step that is performed during formal military parades and other ceremonies. While marching in parade formation, troops swing their legs in unison off the ground while keeping each leg rigidly straight. The step originated in the Prussian military drill in the mid-18th century and was introduced by German military advisors in the 19th century.

Alexei saw these two events to be another opportunity to make conversation with another muscovite. He approached a man who was in his eighties, tall and well dressed. He was not the typical eighty-year-old and was very approachable. "Good evening, Sir. What are the birds that fly overhead making a crowing type noise? We cannot see them through the heavy snow."

The man was eager to address Alexei's answers but first proudly showed him two medals that he displayed on his chest that were awarded to him while serving in World War II. Normally the older generation of Russia speak only Russian and a little broken English. In the case of this man, he spoke eloquent Russian and English. Like many Russians his age, they liked to show people their battle ribbons. Alexei and Joey complimented him on his medals and thanked him for his service to his country, especially as the Russians fought on the side of the Americans during World War II.

He explained to Alexei and Joey what they heard overhead. "The sound of the bird is a falcon who still flies in Moscow and has the strength to fly in blinding snow. They are indigenous to Russia." (39) Alexei asks the man if the falcon is the national bird of Russia. "There is no such a thing as a "national bird" in Russia. The national emblem of Russia, however, has a two-headed eagle." Alexei asks him what he thought of the war in Ukraine?

The older man placed his hand on his chin. Those of us who are World War II veterans fought for a more valiant cause than what is happening in Ukraine. We fought so hard during WWII because our country was in danger of being taking over by Germany. Strange as it may be, WWII was the second time our country had to fight off the onslaught of Germany. The first time was when Czar Nicholas was in power. The interesting thing is that Czar Nicholas of Russia and Kaiser Wilhelm of Germany were both grandsons of Britain's Queen Victoria. Both Victoria and Nicholas felt that their relative, Kaiser Wilhelm, was hot-headed, conceited, and wrong in his approach. In the early hours of July 29, 1914, Czar Nicholas II of Russia and his first cousin, Kaiser Wilhelm II of Germany, begin a frantic exchange of telegrams regarding the newly erupted war in the Balkan region—and the possibility of its escalation into a general European war. Eventually Nicholas and Wilhelm became embroiled over something that could have been resolved by the two simply sitting down at a bargaining table. Instead, it escalated into the first World War. Nicholas's plea for peace went unheard. The Kaiser declared war on Russia and eventually Russia lost, contributing to Nicholas's abdication of the throne. (40) It seems that many of our youth are forced to die for causes that are not in the best interest of our country. I believe that the war in Ukraine is one such cause."

The older man went on to say, "It seems that egos and ideology take precedence over common sense." Pointing across the square, he gives Alexei and Joey some background on the soldiers who are goose stepping to guard the tomb of the unknown soldier. "At one time, that same ceremonial guard was assigned to guard Lenin's tomb, but it was abruptly removed by the order of the former president who wanted to crackdown against the legacy of communism and saw Lenin's tomb as a symbol of communism. That same President took the bold step to end communism and implement a democratic system in Russia. As a result of his efforts, the people had great hopes that our autocratic type of government had come to an end. Now the new President is taking it entirely upon himself to commit Russia into senseless wars. Russia may sadly have been thrust back into the past when it had an autocratic form of government. As a result, Russia is now ostracized by most of the world countries and is shedding the life blood of its youth needlessly."

Alexis and Joey were amazed that this older gentleman spoke so openly and with such elegance. They both shook the hands of the man, thanking him for being so frank. The older gentleman was more aware of his element than they thought when he kept ahold of Nicholas hands and looking intently into his eyes said, "You are welcome my Czar. Hopefully, you will be the one that has the courage to instill some common sense into our leaders."

Alexis stood there in amazement. "You knew who I was all along?" The older man smiled and said, "I may look old, but I keep up on current events. Besides being a WWII veteran, I hold a doctorate degree in history and teach at Moscow State University. May God and the people of Russia be with you Alexei." Before leaving the man, Alexei asks him for his contact information and the man hands him a business card. Without divulging the reason for asking the older gentleman for his name and address, Alexei intends to send him an invitation to his coronation.

Alexei and Joey started back to their quarters. Alexei looks at Joey shaking his head. "From what we are hearing, Vladimir has lied to the Russian people about the invasion, and he has used the news media to keep them in the dark Joey. We need to be careful what we say when around Vladimir, especially as he has us outgunned and we are not in our normal element. From what I read; Vladimir had the constitution amended to reinstate the Czar. We need to get ahold of that amendment to see what powers if any have been granted to me. I have a feeling that my powers will be limited, like the queen of England."

The very next day, Alexei and his security boarded a Russian aircraft which took them to the location where Czar Nicholas and his family were murdered. They traveled the very same route as the Bolsheviks had traveled when they mutilated and burned the bodies of the Romanov family. Alexei and his security just stood there in silence trying to visualize what horrors the family, especially the children, went through at the hands of the Bolsheviks. Joey looked at Alexei and made a comparison of how they defended kids that were being bullied in the steel valley. "I know it is not the same, but I almost wished we were here back in the early 1900's to defend this family." Alexei, Joey, and each of their security friends expressed how they wished they could have been there to take the Bolsheviks to task for their murderous actions. On their way back to Moscow, they were all silent while haunted by thoughts of what it must have been like for the family to be subjected to such inhuman treatment.

The next day Sanyo pays a visit to Alexei to inform him that the Russian Orthodox church wishes to invoke the old tradition of overseeing the coronation. Sanyo further said that the church and Vladimir would like to perform the ceremony as soon as possible. Vladimir's underlying motives to use Alexei as a scape scope was his reason for moving up the coronation.

Alexei agreed to the coronation being held in two weeks. With that, he planned to bring his mother and two sons to Russia for the ceremony. In the meantime, he asked to visit St. Petersburg and the summer palace of the Czars. Sanyo granted his request by making the arrangements to have him flown to St. Petersburg.

"St. Petersburg, city and port, extreme northwestern Russia. A major historical and cultural centre and an important port, St. Petersburg lies about 400 miles (640 km) northwest of Moscow and only about 7 south of the Arctic Circle. It is the second largest city of Russia and one of the world's major cities. St. Petersburg has played a vital role in Russian history since its founding in 1703. For two centuries (1712–1918) it was the capital of the Russian Empire. The city is remembered as the scene of the February (March, New Style) and October

113

(November, New Style) Revolutions of 1917 and for its fierce defense while besieged during World War II. Architecturally, it ranks as one of the most splendid and congenial cities of Europe. Its historic district was designated a UNESCO World Heritage site in 1990. The city is also home to the 87-story Lakhta Centre, the tallest building in Russia and Europe and one of the tallest buildings in the world. Area city, 550 square miles (1,400 square km). Pop. (2010) 4,879,566; (2012 est.) 4,953,219. The National Library is one of three national public libraries in Russia. It is ranked among the world's major libraries and has the second biggest library collection in the Russian Federation, a treasury of national heritage, and is the All-Russian Information, Research and Cultural center." (41)

The permanent residence of the Supreme Court of the Russian Federation is also in the city of St. Petersburg. (Photo 12)

Photo 13-Aerial view of Russia Supreme Court in St Petersburg

There are 115 members of the Supreme Court. Supreme Court judges are nominated by the President of Russia and appointed by the Federation Council. Another constitutional clause giving Vladimir never ending power. (42)

Alexis surmises how the Supreme Court of Russia is structured. "If the affairs of the Supreme Court of Russia are conducted by the Russian President, which means Vladimir could control Russia's rule of law and thus put him in the driver's seat when it comes to deciding major disputes in Russia." Alexis has an uneasy feeling about this.

Another place Alexei always wanted to visit even before he learned of his heritage was the winter palace of the Czars. the official residence of the Russian emperor from 1732 to 1917. "Winter Palace (Photo 13), former royal residence of the Russian tsars in St. Petersburg, on the Neva River.

Photo 14-Czar Winter Palace in St. Petersburg

Several different palaces were constructed in the 18th century. It was restored following a fire in 1837, though the destroyed interior was redesigned. The palace is now part of the Hermitage art museum. The storming of the palace in 1917, as depicted in Soviet art and in Sergei Eisenstein's 1928 film October, became an iconic symbol of the Russian Revolution." (43)

The emperors constructed their palaces on a monumental scale that aimed to reflect the might and power of Imperial Russia. From the palace, the tsars ruled over almost 1/6 of the Earth's landmass and 125 million subjects by the end of the 19th century. In 1905 the Bloody Sunday massacre occurred when demonstrators marched toward the Winter Palace. By this time, the Imperial Family had chosen to live in the more secure and secluded Alexander Palace and only returned to the Winter Palace for formal and state occasions.

With a grin on his face, Alexei turns to Joey and his security and tries to visualize aloud what it must have been like for his ancestors to live in such an intimidating structure as the winter palace. "I can almost see myself trying to find my way to the kitchen to get a cup of coffee and of course, the cinnamon raison bagel I eat every morning. It would take most of the day just to find my way out of the palace." Joey laughs and notes that Alexei would have been even more lost because there were no coffee shops that he could frequent.

Alexei and his security toured the city for two days and greeted many of the people they came across. This time they were not able to be incognito. The News media quickly noticed his visit and sent their crews to cover Alexei's tour of the city. At every spot they visited, throngs of people would warmly encircle him. Even though he exposed himself to assault, Alexei emersed himself in the people, standing shoulder to shoulder with them. He especially acknowledged and kidded with the children, picking up some of the babies and cradling them in his arms. The news aired video across Russia of him reaching out to the people, shaking their hands, and greeting them in their native tongue. The people went wild with excitement, and one could sense the love building for Alexei. It was not long before they began chanting, "our Wonderful Czar Alexei."

Among the many sites they visited, they toured the state hermitage museum, grand Peterhof palace, Catherine palace and park, and Alexander Park. The State Hermitage Museum was founded by Catherine the Great and has the largest gallery space in the world.

Peterhof' palace has approximately thirty rooms and looks truly imposing when seen from the Lower or Upper Gardens. Peter the Great built the Catherine palace and park for his wife Catherine. The garden boasts terraces, stone staircases, arbores, and ponds. Alexander Park is one of the first public parks established in St. Petersburg. On its breathtaking grounds are housed an interactive children's theater, music hall, planetarium, and festival theater.

As Alexei stood on an historic bridge in Alexander Park leaning over the railing, he spoke to Joey and his security of some horrific outcomes that could besiege the people of Russia. "I cannot help thinking what could become of magnificent cities like this if Vladimir carries out his threat to use nuclear weapons. All these treasures throughout many European and North American countries would go away in minutes and the only thing that would be left are ashes and deadly radiation. More importantly, millions of innocent people would needlessly die."

Alexei and his team gazed out towards St. Petersburg, trying to visualize what would be left if Vladimir launched a nuclear war. After touring a few more revered sites of St. Petersburg and conversing with more of the people, Alexei boarded his plane for their return trip to Moscow.

In the meantime, Vladimir has seen the news where Alexei is winning over the people. He calls Sanyo into his office. "Sanyo, this guy Alexei is fast becoming a celebrity! He is like a rock star!

Sanyo shrugs his shoulders. "This guy seems to genuinely like and care about people Vladimir. Even my wife and kids have come to like him!." Vladimir gives Sanyo a disgusted "whatever" look.

CHAPTER 11

CORONATION PLANS

Like the British monarchy being crowned in a service conducted by the Church of England, the Czars of Russian have been crowned in a service conducted by the Russian Orthodox Church. Vladimir summons Sanyo to discuss the coronation. "Brief me on how the coronation will be conducted Dmitri. Who has the lead on it, us, or the church?"

Sanyo sits in front of Vladimir with his planner in hand. "The church took it out of our hands and has everything planned. They informed me that history will substantiate that the coronation of the Czar rests with the Russian Orthodox church. They said that the only thing we must do is show up at the cathedral. If you have anything special to inject, I will try my best, but it is better that we do not interfere with the church protocol. It could anger the clergy and reduce their support for our invading Ukraine." Vladimir looking out the window. "You are right Sanyo. It is better for us to go along to get along. Allowing his coronation in ceremonial style by the Russia Orthodox church will legitimize him as the next Czar."

Coronations of Russian Czars involved a highly developed religious ceremony in which the Czar was crowned with regalia during a five hour ceremony. The Arch Bishop anoints the Czar with chrism, a mixture of oil and balsam and blesses his reign. While months or even years could pass between the initial accession of the sovereign and the performance of this ritual, church policy held that the monarch must be anointed and crowned according to the Orthodox rite to have a successful tenure. As the church in the past rested on the position that the church and the state were one in the same during the days of Imperial Russia, the coronation of the czar vested him with political legitimacy. It was equally perceived as conferring a genuine spiritual benefit that mystically wedded sovereign to subjects, bestowing divine authority upon the new ruler.

Even when the imperial capital was located at St. Petersburg, Russian coronations were always held in Moscow at the Cathedral of the Dormition in the Kremlin. The last coronation service in Russia was held on 26 May 1896 for Nicholas II and his wife Alexandra Feodorovna. The church intended to use the Russian Imperial regalia that survived the Russian Revolution and the Communist period which are currently on exhibit in a museum at the Kremlin Armory.

"Starting with the reign of Ivan IV, the ruler of Russia was known as "Czar or Tsar" rather than "Grand Prince"; When Ivan was 16, he was solemnly crowned Ivan IV in the Moscow Assumption Cathedral. Subsequently, he expanded the title of ruler and became the Grand Sovereign, Tsar and Grand Prince of all Russia. He believed this was how to elevate himself to the level of an emperor." (44) Peter's decision reflected the difficulties other European monarchs had in deciding whether to recognize the Russian ruler as an emperor or a mere king and reflected the czar's insistence on being seen as the former. However, the term "Czar or Tsar" remained the popular title for the Russian ruler instead of Emperor.

"During Nicholas II coronation and Tsars before him, the Tsar was met at the Red Porch, where he took his place beneath a large canopy held by thirty-two Russian generals, with other officers providing additional support. Accompanied by his consort (under a separate canopy) and the imperial regalia, he proceeded slowly toward the Cathedral of the Dormition, where his crowning and anointing would take place. After the service, the Emperor and Empress proceeded under canopies back to the Red Porch of the Kremlin, where they rested and prepared for a great ceremonial meal at the Kremlin's Hall of Facets. During their procession back to their Kremlin palace, later rulers (starting with Nicholas I) stopped on the Red Staircase and bowed three times to the assembled people in the courtyard, symbolizing what one historian has called "an unspoken bond of devotion" between ruler and subjects." (45)

The church wanted to also use the original jewel studded crown of the Czar which is kept under guard in the Kremlin. "Beyond its historical significance, the Imperial Crown of Russia is a testament to the artistic prowess of the craftsmen who meticulously designed and assembled it. In 1920, the crown's estimated value was $52 million." (46)

Normally, the crown was placed on the Czar's head by the Archbishop of the Russian Orthodox Church. Catherine the great broke tradition by taking the crown and placing it on her head. When Alexei learned of the coronation plans of the church, he decided to also break with some of the tradition. As far as the royal robes, he only wanted the traditional military tuxedo with no sword, again symbolizing that Russia should only resort to force in defense of their country and not be the aggressor.

Instead of being crowned with the jewel studded Czar's crown, he opted for a simple gold crown that had no jewels, like the one pictured in movies of King Arthur. He also insisted that a young Russian boy and girl place it on his head. He wanted his two sons to stand by his side. Rather than a canopy held by the general he wanted school children of every age, including some college students, to walk from the red porch of the palace into the church alongside him. Alexei thought this would symbolize his commitment to the betterment of children and the importance of education unlike the last Czars who were focused on war, not the people of Russia. Instead of the standard four-hour ceremony, Alexei stipulated that the ceremony could last no more than two hours and that only contemporary songs popular with the people of Russia were to be used.

When Vladimir heard that Alexei wanted to emphasize Russia was not a waring nation, he became infuriated. In sharp contrast, he wanted to depict Russia as a strong nation that is heavily fortified.

Alexei wanted to invite all of Russia, but he knew that was impossible. Instead, he asked that screens be set up in whatever cities and towns wanted them where the Russian people could watch. Lastly, he wanted to address all of Russia from the pulpit after he was coronated. The church and Vladimir had no choice but to agree to all his requests.

The coronation was fast approaching, only one week away. Alexei greeted his mother and two sons upon their arrival. The newspapers wanted a photograph of him with his family. Alexei agreed to accommodate them but wanted them to appear more like a typical Russian family.

After the photo, Alexei sat with his mother and two sons in his quarters talking about how fast this has come about, and it does not seem real. Alexei looks out the window at the cathedral where he is about to be crowned the next Czar of Russia. He turns around to talk to his family. "Can you believe that Anastasia kept our heritage a secret all these years. It is amazing to find out that our family tree dates back 300 years to the days of Peter and Catherine the Great. Even more amazing is that their blood and the blood of other monarchies runs through our veins." Alexei was referring to "Royal intermarriage" which was the practice of members of one royal family marrying into another royal family, who often had common ancestors and common blood lines of descendants. It became widely practiced as a way of ensuring all members of a royal family were descended from royalty as opposed to commoners.

"Except for my service at the Pentagon, I have led a very mundane life. I would never have thought in a million years that I would be the one that bridges the gap that will return the Romanovs to the throne of Russia. This all seems like a dream to me. I am having great difficulty adjusting to my new identity. I am struggling to determine how to best use this title bestowed upon me. I do not want to let it go to my head and lose sight of who I always wanted to be and how I need to conduct my life. I want to use my life to better the lives of others and be a good role model for others to follow. I keep thinking about what happened to Czar Nicholas and his family. I do not want to ever do anything that would put any of you in danger."

Alexei looking at his mother. "It scares me thinking of the fate of Nicholas and his family. This all seems like a dream, and I am not sure if it may end up being a nightmare. I do not want that for you or my sons. Alexei's mother looks at him shaking her head. "I knew no more than you did until we opened the locked box left by your great grandmother. I kept my word to my mother and your great grandmother Anastasia by not opening the box until we deemed it necessary to do so. As to your endangering us Alexi, your upbringing and outlook on life will never let that happen. You have too much compassion and love instilled in you."

Looking at his family, Alexei digresses further. "Even though this is a new Russia, there still lurks treacherous leaders like Vladimir. This is a man whose aggressive policies combined with his KGB background have made him a decisive player on the world stage as well as a dangerous man. On the other side of the spectrum, he is struggling to turn around a flagging economy and declining population. "Many in the U.S. government saw him, during his stint as Deputy Mayor of St. Petersburg, as someone who was tough on crime and potentially helpful to U.S. interests. He worked hard to rid organized crime in St. Petersburg. His honeymoon with the West started to fade as his rule became authoritarian and his foreign policy more confrontational." (47)

"Now, Vladimir has changed his spots where he is attacking another peace-loving country under the false pretenses of peace keeping and I sense that he wants to reinstate me as the Czar as part of some devious plan that he has concocted. I am trying to understand why this has all come about and where it is heading. Sometimes I think it would be better to give up this fairy tale and return to America to protect all of you. On the other hand, we cannot turn our backs on the people of Russia if Vladimir continues to take them down this tumultuous road. We need to keep the dialogue open with America by maintaining our U.S. Citizenship while respecting the people here by becoming citizens of Russia."

Alexei two sons nod their head in agreement and the older of the two speaks his mind. "We are with you Dad and willing to accept whatever fate that may befall us. Hopefully, we can do something to stop the bloodshed now occurring in the Russian Ukrainian war. I cannot help thinking about what the outcome may have been if our Romanov ancestors never left Russia, and we were born in Russia. We would have been drawn into the war and may have become one of the many casualties. Yes, we need to stay and try to stop these winds of war."

Alexei ponders what his one son just said. "First and foremost, no two countries should settle differences by force. I absolutely condemn Vladimir Dimitri waging war on Ukraine. At the same time, I cannot help but ponder the history of corruption in Ukraine by their leaders. Rather than just relying on the news media, I researched the facts reading publications from such organizations as "Carnegie of Europe."

"Carnegie of Europe states that corruption is an inadequate word to describe the condition of Ukraine. Since the country achieved independence in 1991, the problem is not that a well-functioning state has been corrupted by certain illegal practices; rather, those corrupt practices have constituted the rules by which the state has been run. Ukraine's political system is best described as prisoners of the state. Business and politics have been fused, the rule of law has been weak, and all transactions, from managing a business to serving in an elected office, have incurred illegal taxes or rents. Formal political and bureaucratic offices are held on a basis of dependence on powerful experts, who exact rents and pay incomes to members of their networks, thereby robbing the state of revenue at every stage.

Whatever the case, we must try to stop the fighting at all costs and hopefully the political chaos in Ukraine and Russia will be resolved by new leaders." (48)

"An article by Hillsdale college entitled "Complications of the Ukraine War" says it all. "If you had to give a one-word answer to what this Ukraine War is about, you would say Crimea. The peninsula of Crimea juts out into the middle of the Black Sea where the great powers of Europe fought the bloodiest war of the century between Napoleon and World War I. Its location makes it a defensive superweapon. The country that controls it dominates the Black Sea and can project its military force into Europe, the Middle East, and the steppes of Eurasia. Since the 1700s, that country has been Russia. Crimea has been the home of Russia's warm water fleet for 250 years. It is the key to Russia's southern defenses. This is why Vladimir wants it back under the Russian flag.

Crimea found itself within the borders of Ukraine because the year after Stalin died, his successor Nikita Khrushchev signed it over to Ukraine. Historians now hotly debate why he did that. But while Crimea was administratively Ukrainian, it was culturally Russian. It showed on several occasions that it was as eager to break with Ukrainian rule as Ukraine was to break with Russian rule. "Some 95.5% of voters in Crimea have supported joining Russia, officials say, after half the votes have been counted in a disputed referendum." (49) Alexei emphasizes that "NATO needs to become more pro-active in settling this conflict peacefully instead of pumping more war materials into it."

CHAPTER 12

CZAR PROTOCOL

The next morning, one week before the coronation, a representative of the Russian Orthodox church met with Alexei and his two sons to brief them on how the coronation will proceed. "Good morning, everyone. I am here to provide you with the procedure of the coronation ceremony according to how past Czars were crowned. To start, you will make a processional entrance on horseback into the city the day before the coronation, accompanied by multiple cavalry squadrons while thousands of church bells ring. You will stop at the most revered icon in Moscow to say a prayer, the chapel of the Icon of the Blessed Virgin of Iveron."

"Following your entry into the city, you and your family will attend a reception to be held for diplomats the evening before the coronation. During the evening, heralds dressed in medieval clothing read out special proclamations to the people. We are receptive to your not wanting to wear any imperial regalia as was done in past czars, but the state banner will be consecrated and brought to the throne hall in the Kremlin for the procession to the cathedral. One custom you do not have the power to invoke is to do what past czars did Alexei and that was to pardon captive prisoners and proclaim a three-day holiday for the people." (Trove Newspapers-The Coronation of the Czar. Vast Preparations, Prisoners to be amnestied, flogging to be abolished, London May 18, 1896-50)

"You may be surprised to learn that Russia does have girl scouts and boy scouts. As you requested, you will be met on the morning of the coronation at the Kremlin Palace's red porch by a group of scouts and college students. You will then proceed slowly toward the Cathedral of the Dormition, where you will be anointed, and your crowning will take place. The regalia items in the parade will be the chain of the Order of St Andrew, the banner of state, the state seal, the Orb, the Scepter, your crown, all which are arranged in the strictest of order. The First Called Order of St. Andrew will be conferred on you. It is the highest order conferred by both the Russian Imperial Family (as an Order of Knighthood) and by the Russian Federation (as a state order). (51)"

"When you reach the cathedral door, you will be met by the Orthodox prelates and as you requested the Metropolitan Bishop of Moscow, instead of the Patriarch of the Russian Orthodox Church. The bishop will hold out the cross for you to kiss, while another will sprinkle you and the cross with holy water. Upon entering the cathedral, the priests will bless you and all the items used in the ceremony. You will then ascend to the raised platform of the cathedral dais where a throne has been set for you to sit on, the same throne used by Tsar Michael I, the first Czar of the Romanov dynasty in 1613. The coronation ceremony will then begin." (52)

Alexei shakes his head in confusion and exhaustion just hearing what he must do in the ceremony. "Isn't there an abbreviated version of a coronation ceremony? One more thing that I want to happen is setting up screens in town squares throughout Russia where the people can watch the coronation. We can distribute medallions commemorating the coronation at no cost to the people. When doing so, we must avoid the stampede that happened on the day of Nicholas's coronation. Also, I want to alert guests that the only gifts that will be accepted are contributions to the local children's hospital and Russian families that have lost loved ones in the Ukrainian war and can no longer support themselves. As far as the reception and the ball following my coronation, I wish the organizers to be frugal on the money spent. I would rather some of the monies saved go to charities throughout Russia."

Unlike czars that went before him, Alexei wanted to modify the old ritual so he could demonstrate that he was a servant to his people. To do this, he reaffirmed his request that the crown be placed on his head by a young Russian boy and girl.

The church representative thought his suggestions were great and agreed to make his wishes happen. "We will arrange such a telecast and at your request, we have already reduced the coronation to a two-hour ceremony verses the five hours that former Czars underwent. We can do a walk for a couple of days before the coronation. When we do the walk through, we can brief you on the rest of the ceremony." With that, the representative bids Nicholas and his family goodbye.

Alexei wants to learn about the coronation ball following the coronation. He asks that they send the planners in to brief him. Within an hour, the head planner comes before Alexei. The planner begins to tell Alexei the details. "Like the Czars that have gone before you, "your banquet will be in the Granovitaya Palata, the council Chamber of Muscovite rulers."   (53). The walls are adorned with historical frescoes, and a special table elevated above everyone else will be set for you, your mother, and your sons. No one else will dine with you at your table and a toast will be made in your honor. Only a few foreign sovereigns will attend the ball. As to other sovereigns who will not be attending, they have designated their princes as their representatives. After you dine, you will select a lady to be your dance partner for the first dance and all others will stand on the sidelines until you motion for them to join you on the dance floor."

Alexei ponders what the planner just said, and he shakes his finger in the air to make a point. "I have no problem with what you have just said overall but for two exceptions. There will be no special table for me and my family. I do not want to look like a privileged class so we will dine at a table with others. I want food and drink booths set up in red square and all other squares throughout Russia where people will watch the coronation. I want carnival rides or something special in place for the children. The evening should end with displays of fireworks. You can solicit contributions from corporations and any wealthy Russian families so there will be no cost to the people of Russia."

The Planner looks at Alexei in a delightful way. "You know, I have always wanted to plan a national event for Russia. I think we can make it happen, and I can think of some corporations and wealthy families that will cover the costs. I will get right on it."

Equally important was how Alexei and his sons were to support themselves. To answer this question, the Duma or Russian Parliament sent Russia's minister of Finance and Federal Treasurer of Russia to brief Alexei on his income and any wealth of the Romanov family that he may claim. "I am here to answer any questions you may have about how your discretionary money will be funded and any remnants of your ancestor's wealth Alexei. After much research of records when the "House of Romanov fell in 1917, your ancestors had an estimated value of anywhere from $45 billion to $300 billion in jewels, money, and palaces. Much of this wealth was grabbed by the greed of the Bolsheviks, making dozens of them rich." (54)

"The crown jewels play an important part in the coronation story because the czar crowns himself in the coronation, and that is the moment when he takes full power. The Romanov dynasty ended in 1917, amid the chaos of a world war, a revolution, and a civil war. Regina says the fate of the crown jewels raised a furious debate among the Bolshevik leadership, which was badly in need of money. Some of the revolutionaries saw the jewels as symbols of centuries of exploitation — gems that ought to be sold to benefit the workers. Historian Igor Zimin says much of the collection was preserved by curators at the Kremlin in Moscow, who were able to convince the leaders that the gems had enormous historical significance Zimin, the head of the history department at the St. Petersburg State Medical University, says there are records of auctions of some of the lesser pieces from the collection dating from around 1927. There are even memoranda about Soviet agents being caught while traveling with diamonds in their luggage. The jewels of the Russian Diamond Fund are on display in the Kremlin in Moscow — or most of them, anyway." (55)

Photo 15-Crown Jewels

"Prior to the outbreak of the Great Patriotic War in 1941, the Alexander Palace housed more than 52.5 thousand *items, of which more than 44.8 thousand* items were lost during the war from 1941 to 1945. From the 7.7 thousand items which survived, a significant part of the items is currently in the collection of numerous museums throughout Russia. Among these were 5,615 items that were moved from the Alexander Palace to the Pavlovsk State Museum Reserve. On the other side of the coin, Russia has spent $30 million to renovate just one of the palaces, the Alexander palace." (56)

"Now as to your yearly allowance that you can spend at your discretion Alexei. According to Imperial-era Russian law, every member of the Romanov family was assigned an annual 'basic income.' Starting in 1884, when Nicholas became tsesarevich, heir apparent to the Russian throne, the sixteen-year-old future ruler was assigned a stipend of 100,000 rubles, in your dollars it would equal $1,664.59 American. When he became Czar, the amount doubled. We know that in 1896 his personal funds totaled 2 million rubles and 355,000 francs or American $38,643 dollars in 1884. Today, that would be effectively worth $1,167,850 in American dollars. The Duma decided to pay all the expenses of running the monarchy and give you the discretionary annual allowance of $1,167,850 dollars per year to spend as you wish." (57)

Alexei nods his head with approval. "That is an extremely generous amount of money." As far as the palaces and jewels, I am pleased that they reverted to the people of Russia. Hopefully, they are being put to good use to benefit our people." "They are Alexei. Tourists flock to see inside the palaces, and they have become one of our biggest tourist attractions, generating a good amount of revenue."

It is the day before the coronation has arrived. In keeping with tradition, Alexei proceeds to the palace stables outside the city where a strong white thoroughbred and an entourage of military escorts awaits him. Normally the Czar would ride directly from the stables into the city. Instead, Alexei breaks with tradition by informing his military escort that before riding directly into Moscow, they will first spend the day riding through some of the outlying towns and villages to greet the Russian people. At the suggestion of the commander of the military escort, they select two of Russia's most picturesque villages.

"Sviyazhsk is the first, located in a lagoon of the Volga River. This natural enclave contributes a lot to its beauty, but this is not its only attraction. It is often referred to as an island since the 1955 construction of the Kuybyshev Reservoir downstream at Tolyatti, but it is in fact connected to the mainland by a causeway. You can visit a monastery that, after its restoration and restitution as a religious building, is now in use and inhabited by monks. Only the historical center of the town survived and is located on an imposing high cliff." (58)

"The epicenter of the Rostov Kremlin is the second. It is a kingdom ruled by the impressive bell tower of the Assumption Cathedral, whose bells weigh thirty-two tons each. A bishop named Iona Sysóyevich decided to create a dream city. He built his own palace and built streets and buildings that today look like decoration. This is one of the best examples of wonderful Russian villages beyond Moscow and St. Petersburg." (59)

The townspeople were unaware that Alexei chose to visit their villages, so it was a site to behold to see ten riders on horseback galloping into their city followed by an entourage of television cameras and reporters.

Alexei and his guard's road to the center of each town and dismounted from their horses to greet the people. He was immediately encircled with people and emersed with news coverage. The people were amazed that they could shake hands and some even patted him on his back. Alexei greeted them in Russian and walked part way through each town, stopping to greet people in shops and restaurants. They immediately embraced Alexei and applauded his visit. Images of his visits were televised throughout Russia and even those in other towns and cities felt a distant presence as if he were in their town.

On their way back to Moscow, they came across a car that broke down on the side of the road with a good-looking lady inside. Alexei dismounted offering a hand to the driver and upon looking closer, he discovered it was Lina. "Weren't you the guy, I saw in Vladimir's waiting room?" Alexei looks closer. "Yes, and you were the lady?" They both laughed and reintroduced themselves. Lina looks inquisitively at all the riders on horseback surrounding Alexei. "What is this all about Alexei?" Alexei responds while trying to jump and start Lina's vehicle. "Oh, my friends and I are just out for a ride today. I very much enjoyed our conversation in the waiting room and am new to Moscow." Before Alexei could get another word out, the other riders were urging him to move along. They told Alexei that he was on a tight schedule. He climbed back on his horse and before he rode off, he asked her where she lived. She yelled her address to Alexei as he rode off towards Moscow. When he tried looking it up later, he could not find it because he must have the spelling of the street wrong. Another missed opportunity in the day of Alexei. Whether he got it right or not, he still did not realize that Lina dated Vladimir and did not know the potential problem that may cause.

Once again, Vladimir caught the news feeds and called Sanyo into his office. "What have we created Jon? This guy has become more popular than any royal, movie star, politician, or any celebrity for that matter! In the short period of time, he has been in Russia, he has even become more popular than even me! The funny thing is that he seems genuine. Hopefully, his popularity wains." Sanyo just stared at the television and did not say anything.

Continuing the tradition of coronations, Alexei and his military escort road into Moscow and were again greeted by throngs of well-wishers while heralds dressed in medieval clothing read out special proclamations to the people. Balloons were sent into the air. The people encircled Alexei with cheers of "Long live our Czar Alexei."

Alexei worked the crowd shaking hands and hugging little children. His security showed great concern but knew there was no way to hold him back. People started lining the streets like they were watching a parade and Alexei kept walking from street to street until he finally came to the gates of the Kremlin.

Before entering the Kremlin, he positioned himself in front of the tomb of the unknown soldier where two Russian soldiers stood guarding the tomb. Hundreds of people gathered around. The guards allowed Alexei to walk to the front of the platform to

Photo 16-Russia's Tomb of the Unknown Soldier

address the people. "I am sure that like America's unknown soldiers, there are thousands of young Russians that are among the

132

unknown soldiers throughout our land that paid the ultimate price with their lives to protect Russia. There are many parents who never saw their child again after they answered the call to bear arms. We must not fight wars that are not in defense of our homeland or in defense of a valiant cause. The youth of our nation must be allowed to live a full life without the threat of unwarranted conflicts. Our military should not be sent into harm's way without knowing the truth of what they are fighting for and that it is a righteous and just cause. To quote Dwight Eisenhower, "Every gun that is made, every warship that is launched, every rocket that is fired, signifies in the final sense a theft from those who hunger, those that are not clothed. The world in arms is not spending money alone. It is spending the sweat of its laborers, the geniuses of its scientists, and the hopes of its children." (60)

The people cheered Alexei and kept chanting his name, "Czar Alexei, Czar Alexei, Czar Alexei"! The television carried his speech and all who watched across Russia were pleased that Alexei took such a bold stand when he could feel the wrath of Vladimir who was heralding the Ukraine war as a peace keeping mission.

Alexei applauds the people and thanks them for allowing him to speak his piece. He then turns and along with his escort, he disappears behind the Kremlin walls to return to his quarters to prepare for the evening of festivities that were planned prior to his coronation. Before doing so, however, he climbs to the top of the wall facing red square and gives everyone one more wave.

Alexei returns to his quarters to prepare himself for the next event in his coronation festivities and that is to greet dignitaries at a reception to be held in the great ballroom of the palace. He is pondering what to wear when a Butler enters the room. "You look confused Czar Alexei." The butler does not look the part of someone who is trained in the art of serving nobility. He is not dressed like one and is a man in his forties, a bit pudgy, and looks much like the everyday Russian on the street.

"I have been assigned to be your personal Butler. My name is Nikolai." Alexei eyes up the Butler and expresses his reluctance to have a personal Butler. "Other than when I was a little boy, I never had anyone dress me Nikolai." Nikolai is fluent in both English and Russian and speaks to Alexei in English. "I can understand you're not wanting to have someone help you dress but I have served the hierarchy of Russian leaders for years and think I can be of great service not only as your Butler but as a confidant." Alexei pauses and then sets some stipulations. "Okay Nikolai, I will agree to utilizing your service, but we must bring our interaction down to more like a friendship basis. I will tell you what. If you agree to call me Alexei instead of Czar Alexei, I will call you Nikolai instead of Butler Nikolai."

Nikolai laughs and agrees to the arrangement. Both men shake on it. "Now Alexei, let me make some suggestions on what to wear tonight. We have stocked your wardrobe with more formal clothing that should be worn at formal receptions. This is what you will be wearing for the coronation which is a duplicate of Czar Nicholas's military uniform. For tonight, however, I would suggest this less formal uniform. It is both comfortable and not so regal. You may meet a special lady tonight." Now it is Alexei's turn to laugh. "Because my two sons have always come before my social life, I have not dated since I lost my wife years ago." Nikolai smiles. "Perhaps now is the time to start. There are many beautiful ladies in Russia that would find you attractive not only as a Czar but as a former soldier." With that, Alexei made Nikolai relax in a chair while he dressed himself. "Well Nikolai, what do you think of my duds." Nikolai nods his head with approval. "You look the part and all you have to do now is act the part."

Alexei has a puzzling look. "You know what really funny Nikolai is?" Nikolai gives Alexei a questioning look. "What is funny Alexei? "Soon, I am supposed to take on the role of a Czar, but no one has told me how I am supposed to act the part when I officially become the Czar." Nikolai squeezes his lips together, conveying a look of dissatisfaction with the powers to be. "I guess I should tell you that I initially became a Butler to support myself while pursuing my doctorate in history and government. I had much time researching background information in many libraries, including your library of Congress.

I chose as my thesis the protocol of the czars and how they evolved through history to abdication by your great ancestor Nicholas. One of the premises of my thesis is how Nicholas could have averted abdication of his throne. I would assume that is why they chose me to be your Butler. I can give you some insight into the formalities of being a Czar, but I cannot convey to you the basics of how to make your subjects love you as a person. From what I have seen on television, you seem to have a good grasp on being loved by the people. You are better loved than any Czar that has come before you in the Romanov chain. Whatever the case, I can provide you with some insight on the formalities of how past Czars have acted, their duties, and the protocol of royalty."

"In the eyes of most Russian people during the very first Czars, the Russian Czar could not commit any sin or wrongdoing, because he was God's emissary on Earth. Now, over one hundred years have passed since the last Russian monarch abdicated the throne. But the collective Russian memory of a ruler as someone whose power draws its source not from the law or the will of the people - but from God himself - lives on. Except for Nicholas, the Russian people were used to blaming anyone but the Czar for their woes. Instead, they blamed the Russian aristocracy and the ministers. Every civilization throughout human history has had its own take on the relationship between God and rulers." (61)

"In Ancient Egypt, the pharaoh was considered the earthly embodiment of the god Horus. In Ancient China - which did not have a monotheistic religion, the emperor was proclaimed as the 'son of heaven,' his authority being perceived with humility as if it were destiny. In the Roman Empire, the emperor would perform sacrifices on behalf of his people, asking gods for mercy, fortune, a good harvest and so on. In this respect, the ruler took on the role of his people's foremost priest. In Russia, the clergy of the Russian Orthodox church began to look to the Czar as the defenders of their faith and looked upon them as supreme heads of Orthodox Christianity. That is why the Russian Orthodox church has canonized and martyrized Nicholas and his family. Furthermore, the secular ruler carries the role of God's emissary. The role of the Czar is both imbued with absolute power and has absolute responsibility to God. So, what do we have as a result? The Czar must obey God's laws, but the earthly ones he can simply write himself. Pretty neat for the Czar but not so much for his subjects, is it not Alexei!" (62)

Nikolai continues his indoctrination. "Part of the Czar's responsibility to God meant steering the country out of crisis whenever its faith was in peril - such as presiding over religious matters and organizing meetings, as well as acting as a judge in any quarrels between the church hierarchy. With absolute power, however, absolute responsibility also came, and the ruler knew well that his life was to be devoted to this duty. The Russian coronation ceremony was the visual proclamation of this pledge. Coronation is a Western word, but in Russian, the process is called "chrismation or anointment to tsardom." In essence, the Czar is wed to the tsardom. Anointing the Czar in the coronation ceremony was a symbol of his being wed to tsardom and to his people. As all weddings are made in heaven, so is the Czar wed to his tsardom and his people. He cannot abscond from this holiest of unions. That is why, following Nicholas II's abdication, many Russians simply refused to believe that the Czar could have abdicated at all – such a move was deemed unfathomable." (61)

"As a result of having absolute power Alexei, Czars governed by decree and functioned as the head of state and lead policy maker in the kingdom of Russia. They issued declarations or proclamations, and his ministers, governors and bureaucrats implemented them. Russia had several high-level political bodies or councils, but they had no power like the Czars. Their function was limited to only providing advice. Because Czars did not have to follow their advice, this is what got Nicholas into trouble. His advisors were right, and Nicholas was dead wrong, for not following the advice of others to not fight two unwinnable wars." (63)

"Now let us talk about your specific power and duties as outlined in the amendment that Vladimir and Parliament wrote into the Constitution Alexei. I have read the amendment that reinstates you as Czar and it does not provide you with much power. Your duties and responsibilities are much like the Queen of England. They include opening each new session of Parliament only in ceremonial fashion, granting Royal Assent to legislation, and approving and making Proclamations. Your office as Czar is known as a constitutional monarchy. This means that you are head of State in title only, the ability to make and pass legislation resides with our Parliament and our President. Even though you will not have a political or executive role, you will play an important part in the life of the nation. You will function as a focus for national identity, unity, and pride, giving the people a sense of stability and continuity. You are to recognize people for success and excellence and support the ideal of voluntary service. In all these roles, you are to be supported by members of your immediate family. In your case, your two sons will mirror your roles. From what I have researched, I would assume that you have come to the reality that you will be a figurehead with little or no power. On the other side of the coin and I do mean coin, the Russian hierarchy expects that reinstating you as Czar will bring in much tourism dollars and divert attention from President Vladimir's acquiring territories of countries such as Ukraine. When telling you all this, please do not tell anyone what I said about President Vladimir. If you do, I will emphatically deny it. I cherish my freedom and do not want to end up in some Siberian prison like all the others that opposed Vladimir." (64)

Alexei looks at Nikolai in amazement and is trying to comprehend all that he has said. Nikolai is not finished and continues his instructions. "Now let us talk about some protocol and etiquette for tonight. There will be several sovereigns in attendance during tonight's festivities and you will be expected to follow protocol when greeting and talking with them. Please note that you are not one of them until you are officially ordained."

"You cannot touch any of them or you cannot be the first one to reach out to shake their hand. They must initiate a handshake first. Likewise, you must not talk first. Allow them to initiate the conversation. This includes while you are standing or sitting at the dinner table. You will not see thirteen people sitting at a table because there are a few royals in attendance that are very superstitious, and they are concerned that dinner guests might be reluctant to be among the unlucky. Believe it or not, there are dining manners when sitting at a table. You must avoid going to the bathroom once you are seated. If you find it a dire need to do so, simply excuse yourself and do not say you are going to the bathroom. When leaving, also remember to cross your knife and fork. Hold your knife in the right hand and the fork in the left. This tradition dates to when men would carry their swords and daggers in their right hand. Simply placing your napkins on your lap is only part of proper etiquette. You need to fold your napkin in half and use its concealed part to wipe away any food stains. If seated to the right of a royal, one is considered the guest of honor and will be the first to chat with them. However, if placed on the left, one must wait before engaging in dialogue. Because you are not yet ordained as the Czar, they will seat your sons to the left. You may be interested to discover that couples will be split up when entering the dining room to invite more conversation at the table. When finished eating, your utensils are to be put at an angle, specifically placing the handles of the silverware at the bottom right side of the dish." (65)

Alexei gives a sigh of frustration and exhaustion after hearing all this. "I will tell you what Nikolai. Let us dress you up as the Czar and send you to the reception tonight." Nikolai laughs but says he would rather go in a plain tuxedo. A friendship is forming between the two.

"It is time for you to be promoted Nikolai. You will no longer be known as my Butler. I am promoting you to be head of protocol and my personal first secretary." Nikolai looks sideways at Alexei with a grin. "I now realize more than ever Nikolai that I need someone to guide me through the royal stuff while not losing sight of being a Czar of the people. In essence, I want to represent the people of Russia with dignity and respect but at the same time, I never want to let my being a Czar go to my head." Nikolai nods his head in agreement.

Alexei finishes donning his Tuxedo and asks Nikolai to give him a once over to make sure everything is in place. "It is uncanny that you resemble an older version of Nicholas. You will wow the guests.

Alexei looks down at the floor and appears to be embarrassed to ask the next question. "Nikolai, there is one more area that you can help me with and that is ballroom dancing. You see, I was a wall flower at school dances and never learned how to dance, especially ballroom dancing. It is my understanding that I must start the dance tomorrow evening at the coronation ball." "No problem, Alexei. Take my hands. I will lead first and then you will lead afterwards." Alexei and Nikolai spent the next hour practicing and Alexei caught on quickly. As the two men were finishing, the doors suddenly opened, and Alexei's two sons enter the room dressed in tuxedos. They were surprised to see their father dancing with another man. Alexei and Nikolai drop their hands quickly and explained.

"Ah, my two handsome sons. It is not the way it looks. I want you to meet my new consort and secretary, Nikolai. He has not only taught me royalty protocol, but he has also given me some quick dancing lessons." Nikolai greets them both with a hardy handshake and comments on how great they look. "It is approaching the time for the three of you to make your grand entrance to the ballroom. Before you go, however, let me convey the same information to your two sons Alexei." Alexei and his two sons descend the staircase into the grand ballroom of the palace where the guests are enjoying refreshments and an orchestra. Along with his mother, Alexei and his two sons, form a reception line to greet everyone.

As the line moves along, a familiar lady catches the eye of Alexei. Her beauty radiates above all the other ladies in attendance. He could not wait to speak to her again. Directly behind her is Vladimir. Vladimir introduces her to Alexei as his significant other. Lina rebukes Vladimir by saying she is his significant other. Alexei and Lina look intently at each other. Alexei was ecstatic that he met her again.

Lina was infatuated with Alexei even though this was only their second encounter. All those waiting in line also gazed at her beauty and sensed the electricity between Alexei and Lina. They stood staring at one another until Vladimir finally broke their silence. "Lina was once an Olympian and gold medalist Alexei." Still caught up in her beauty, Alexei finally thought of something to say, "I am quite impressed Lina. What was your Olympic event?" "I was a gymnast Alexei." Alexei, who had always followed the Olympics, was extremely impressed. "I watched all the Olympic gymnast events on television and cannot believe that I am finally meeting one that is a gold medalist. What do you do now?" "I am a media manager."

With that, Alexei broke the protocol and kissed Lina's hand. Vladimir was taken back by this but said nothing. Lina smiled and returned his kiss with a curtsey. Lina and Vladimir moved on to give other guests who were patiently waiting in line to meet Alexei.

After all the guests exchanged greetings, they sat down to dinner. Alexei was seated at the same table as Vladimir, Lina, and numerous sovereigns. The conversation focused on their countries, giving Alexei little opportunity to talk. When it came to him, one of the royals at the table asked Alexei where he was born and raised. "I was born and raised in a small town in Pennsylvania. I worked in the steel mills and was part of a military team that went after the terrorists."

One of the royals made a rude remark. "So, you grew up living a miniscule life as a common laborer to now find yourself the Czar of

Russia. How quaint." Immediately Lina spoke up to rebuke the royal. "Many Russians have worked menial jobs to provide themselves with the opportunity to live a better life. In all due respect, I would venture to say that royals have never had to work a laborer's job to support themselves." Vladimir tried to hush Lina, but she did not stop with just one comment. "Please let me speak my mind Vladimir. Unlike us, people of royalty are born with a silver spoon in their mouths." Alexei smiled. Seeing that Lina was willing to speak her mind in his defense, he decided to back her. "I always wondered what God would ask me if I was killed in action and went before him. I was certain that the question was not going to be how much money I made or what my status was in life. Instead, I thought the question would be what difference did you make or how did you contribute to the betterment of this world"? Lina smiled at Alexei for supporting her. The royal then apologized. Vladimir just looked down and Lina gave him a disappointed look. Everyone bid one another good night

CHAPTER 13

THE CORONATION

The morning of the coronation came fast. Czars in the past wore flowing red robes with gold sewn throughout the fabric. Instead of the traditional robes and military uniforms worn by past czars, Alexei chose to dress himself in his formal dress uniform that he wore when serving in the United States Air Force. Because there were no insignias that would denote the uniform of an American officer, he felt that it would not offend the Russian people. His reason for not wearing the uniform of past czars was that he wanted to portray the image that he is truly a contemporary royal that did not hold an autocratic philosophy. His uniform also did not require him to bear a sword, portraying the image of a warring czar. Instead, he wanted to convey the image of a peace-loving czar.

It was a beautiful sunny day and a short walk to the Red Porch of the Palace. Upon arriving, he was greeted by the group of children and teenagers as he requested. He was also greeted by the priests who were going to conduct the coronation ceremony. The priests greeted Alexei with his first name instead of greeting him with the title of Czar. Only upon being anointed and crowned will he be addressed with the title Czar.

Alexei took the time to personally greet each one that was to accompany him on his walk to the cathedral. As he and his escort stood on the porch, he could hear the people gathering outside to watch the coronation on many huge television screens' setups around the square. Breaking with tradition again, he walked with his escorts towards the gates of the Kremlin instead of walking to the cathedral as planned. He directed the guards to open the gates, and he walked out among the hordes of people waiting for the ceremony to begin. The people, being respectful of him, his sons, and his escorts; opened a large pathway for them to walk from one end of the square to the other while waving, shaking hands, and welcoming the people in their native tongue. The crowd kept cheering on his name. When he made it back to the gates, he turned and waved.

From there, he walked to the Cathedral of Dormition (Photo 16) where he was greeted by the bishop. From 1547 to 1896 the coronation of Russian monarchs took place here. In addition, the cathedral is the burial place for most of the Moscow Metropolitans and Patriarchs of the Russian Orthodox Church; it also serves as a part of Moscow Kremlin Museums. The cathedral was packed with dignitaries and news media.

Photo 17-Cathedral of Dormition where Czars are crowned

As requested by Alexei; half the cathedral was filled with everyday citizens of Russia who were selected randomly from a poll. Although the United States and Great Britain did not send a delegation, they knew Alexei opposed the war outwardly. Instead, their ambassadors attend.

Alexei was concerned that there were still long lines of people waiting to get into red square, but the time was at hand to start the coronation. Always thinking of others rather than himself, he asked some of his security guards to see if they could assist those trying to enter the square.

The Metropolitan bishop, bishop of Moscow, started the ceremony. The ceremony began with contemporary songs chosen by Alexei, "On Wings of Eagles" as Alexei walked down the aisle. Upon reaching the altar, the Metropolitan invited him to recite the Nicen-Constantinopolitan Creed which is the defining statement of belief in Christianity and is part of the profession of faith. After that, Alexei was given a book containing a prayer for him to read prior to the bishop pronouncing a blessing upon him. Further hymns were sung, and three scripture lessons were read, two of which were read by his sons, and the third by his mother.

At this point in the ceremony is where prior Czars were robed in Purple, but Alexei declined being robed in any royal clothing. Bowing his head, the chief celebrant read two prayers over him. These two prayers originated in those found in the Byzantine coronation ritual.

Following this the Czars of past directed the bishop to hand them the diamond studded Crown, some who chose to place it on their head themselves. As requested by Alexei, the crown used in his ceremony was a duplicate of the one used by King Arthur in a movie entitled "Camelot." It was forged out of gold with no jewels laden in it. Past Czars would have placed it upon his own head as the prelate invoked the name of the Holy Trinity. This was in keeping with the custom inherited by the Byzantine Emperors. The placing of the crown symbolized the direct continuation of the Christian Roman Empire's power came directly from God." (66) Alexei motioned to the bishop to hand the crown to the two small children as planned, children, who took it in their hands.

As rehearsed by the children and Alexei, the children pointed it at the people and then raised it towards the top of the cathedral, symbolizing his allegiance to god and the people of Russia, before placing it on his head. When doing so, the two children recited a statement given to them by Alexei. "The people of Russia trust that you will always protect our mother Russia and place the wellbeing of its people above all else. You pledge to a commitment of service before self-Alexei." Alexei first placed his hands on his heart and then on the shoulder of each child. "My two sons and I promise with all our hearts that we will never forsake the people of Russia."

The Metropolitan then recited a prayer over Alexei that was recited over all the czars that had gone before him. 'Most God-fearing, absolute, and mighty Lord, Czar of all the Russia's, this visible and tangible adornment of thy head is an eloquent symbol that thou, as the head of the whole Russian people, art invisibly crowned by the King of kings, Christ, with a most ample blessing, seeing that he bestows upon thee the responsibility for his people." (67) Here again, Alexei requested that the words "responsibility for his people be substituted for "the entire authority over his people." Alexei felt that this signified his responsibility to be an advocate for the people instead of being an autocratic ruler like his predecessors.

Next Alexei received his scepter and orb, given to him by the Metropolitan, who invoked the Christian Trinity and then recited these words: "God-crowned, God-given, God-adorned, most pious Autocrat and great Sovereign, Emperor of all the Russia's. Receive the scepter and the orb, which are the visible signs of your commitment to service given thee from the most high over thy people, that thou mayest rule them and order for them the welfare they desire." (68) Alexei directed that the words "commitment to service" be substituted for "autocratic power" in the ceremony because he never wanted to be known as an autocratic leader.

The next part of the service was supposed to come after Alexei received the crown, scepter, and orb. "Czars of the past would seat themselves upon the throne, holding the Scepter in his right hand and the orb in left hand. He would then take the crown off and briefly place it upon the head of his wife before returning it to his own" (69). In the case of Alexei, however, he had no wife. Instead of taking a seat on the throne, he stood at the same level as the guests. He lifted the crown off his head and pointed it towards his two sons and then towards the people. He then repeated what the children had done by raising it above his head in both hands and looked up towards the dome signifying his obedience to God and the people. "I accept this crown in the name of the people and ask God to bless me and my people. This crown belongs to the people." He hands the crown back to the two small children who in turn hand it back to the Metropolitan. Normally the symbol of placing it on a wife's head is to signify her sharing his dignity and responsibility for the nation's welfare. Instead, Alexei decrees before the guests that the symbol of giving the crown back to the children is to remind the President and other leaders everywhere that they share in his responsibility for the nation's welfare. Hearing this, Vladimir squirmed and stared at Alexei with contempt.

After receiving Holy Communion, previous Czars returned to their thrones whereas Alexei chose to take a seat at the same level as his guests next to the choir. Prayers were read after Alexei and his two sons received Holy Communion. Following this, past Czars receive homage from his family and notable guests. Instead, Alexei walked into the guests seating area to hug his mother and then returned to the altar to do the same to his two sons. The dismissal was read, as the Archdeacon intoned a special blessing for the Czar and his family, with the choir singing "Many Years" three times. This concluded the portion of the coronation conducted inside the cathedral, but other ceremonies were yet to come.

Alexei and his two sons slowly walked down the aisle acknowledging his guests standing in the pews. He locked eyes with Lina, and she nodded her head and smiled with approval of the coronation ceremony. At the conclusion of the coronation, past Czars and their entourage proceeded to the Archangel and Annunciation cathedrals within the Kremlin walls where further rites were conducted. Following this, the newly crowned monarchs proceeded under canopies back to the Red Porch of the Kremlin, where they rested and prepared for a great ceremonial meal at the Kremlin's Hall of Facets. During their procession back to their Kremlin palace, later rulers stopped on the Red Staircase and bowed three times to the assembled people in the courtyard, symbolizing what one historian has called "an unspoken bond of devotion" between ruler and subjects.

Alexei liked the tradition of bowing to the people, so he decided to invoke the tradition of stopping by the two cathedrals. Instead of returning to the Kremlin to rest, however, he turned and looked at the Kremlin Gates again. Sensing what he was about to do, Joey and his security looked at one another with great concern. "Oh no, Alexei might go into the square." Alexei started to give a signal to the guards to open the gates. He went straight for the Kremlin Gates and right into the square to walk among the people. Joey and the security knew that Alexei was very spontaneous and was determined to greet the people. Immediately, they had backup security surround Alexei and his sons as they stepped into the square and started walking among the large throngs of people.

The attention of the people quickly switched from the large screens to Alexei coming out of the Kremlin gates. They were shocked to see Alexei and his sons appear. The crowd becomes ecstatic but respectfully do not rush him. Instead, they form a path to allow Alexei to walk between them safely with his security at his side. Alexei uses both hands to wave at the people, stopping every so often to go to the people when he sees little children. Kneeling on one knee and giving the smaller ones a hug, Alexei asks their names.

He then goes to the large screen where there are microphones. He picks one up and speaks to the people as he walks among them with his sons by his side. The news media follows and televises his movements.

"I share your concerns that I was born and raised in a country other than Russia. The Czars that came before me put themselves and their ambitions before the best interests of the Russian people. Please rest assured that I will live and die amongst you and lay down my life for you and for the good of Russia. You have my devotion and brotherly love. I come before you when our young people are shedding blood in a foreign land, and I know many of you are questioning why. When questioning whose war it is, please know it is not mine. I will never condone our dominance over another peaceful nation or transcend their borders without cause. Should any foreign power invade the borders of our great country, however, make no mistake that I will take up arms and fight along your side. When doing so, we must be merciful and never inflict pain on the innocent, only on our aggressors."

Wherever and whenever without resolve, I will live and die amongst you all and for our homeland. I am with one mind like you and have the heart and soul of a different Czar than the Czars of my ancestors. I will always put you and service before myself. If any of my two sons succeeds me, you can rest assured they will be committed to doing the same. Lastly, to re-coin the words of a famous U.S. President, YA rodilsya russkim, ya russkiy, ya prozhivu russkuyu zhizn, I UMRU RUSSKIM. "I was born a Russian, I am a Russian, and I will die a Russian."

After his speech, trucks loaded with candy, food, and gifts for the children appear in the square. The men in the trucks step down from the truck and started handing out the candy, food, and books. The trucks not only appeared in red square but every square throughout Russia where there were television screens and Russian people watching them. Remembering the casualties caused by Nicholas when he was crowned, he wanted to avoid the same catastrophe. Alexei secretly requested the surprises in the squares at the same time he met with the head planner to discuss the royal ball. Alexei and his two sons joined the truckers in passing out the candy, food, and books. People were amazed that this man who was just crowned a Czar and his two sons, one of which would one day pick up his mantle, were getting down to the level of the people. The cameras quickly noticed it and the scene was televised into all the other town squares and Russian homes. After spending a couple of hours mingling with the people, Alexei, along with his sons and security boarded some of the trucks to return to the Kremlin to greet visitors and dignitaries that came from afar. They prepared for the evening's reception and banquet. The paparazzi were quick to interview Alexei two sons. "What are your thoughts on your father becoming a Czar of one of the most powerful countries of the world? Will you follow in his footsteps?"

The older of the sons answered without hesitation. "I see no difference in our father. He is the same person now as he was when we lived in the Steel Valley. My brother and I were raised to show the same compassion and respect towards others, and we will not be any different. If my brother or I follow him, we also will be honored to serve the people of Russia the same way as my father." A reporter asked Alexei which of the palaces he would take as his residence. Will it be the luxurious quarters of the primary residence of Nicholas or one of the other Romanov palaces?

"I will use the smallest summer palace instead of the larger palaces, the one where I can live close to the people of Russia. I am also currently looking for a home where I can seek sanctuary when I want to be alone by myself or with a special person that may someday come into my life. I want to better understand the people and learn of their needs.

A reporter questions Alexei about whether his sons will take up permanent residence in Russia? Alexei nods his head yes. "My two sons will be living between here and the United States until they get their affairs in order. Within six months, they will become permanent residents of Russia. Once they join me, they will take an active role in helping the people of Russia."

"I will not make the same mistakes as Nicholas. The Russian people deserve a Czar that is their advocate and has a hand on the pulse of their everyday needs and concerns. I believe that to be a good leader, you must also be a good follower. I will surround myself with those who do not tell me what I want to hear but will tell me what I need to know. Unlike most royals, I know what it is like to work as a laborer and struggle to put food on the table for your family. I think that I can avoid many of the pitfalls of Russian Czars that have gone before me."

Just then, Alexei realized that what he is saying in opposition to waging wars was a direct criticism of Vladimir and his top Generals. Whatever the case, the words of Alexei were immediately televised throughout Russia and the news media followed up by featuring him on the news reporting everything he was doing and saying. The response of the people was overwhelming in support of Alexei and his two sons. After Vladimir watched the news feeds that evening, he angrily spoke to Sanyo. "Did you hear what he said. This was not what we expected. He is not the docile person we thought he would be when we plucked him from the United States."

Sanyo shrugs his shoulders, being incredibly careful to choose his words wisely, so he does not offend Vladimir. "Hopefully, he will tone down his rhetoric Vladimir. I am afraid that because he has become a very likable storybook type figure in the eyes of the people, there is not much we can do to curve the appetite the people have for him. The people will not tolerate any harm coming to him and if there is confrontation between you and him, they will side with him. All we can do now is hope that he does not tarnish your image."

While Vladimir thought his speech was a threat to his governance of Russia, Sanyo also felt a bit endeared to Alexei. Lina and others also found Alexei's words most refreshing and humble. Lina never met anyone like this and wanted to get to know more about Alexei.

After the coronation ceremony, Alexei gave in to the planners by being open to hosting a banquet and ball. The planners arranged for a royal meal to be served in the Kremlin's Palace of Facets with Russian subjects and foreign representatives. Traditional Russian food will be served in various parts of the palace, including black sturgeon caviar harvested from the surrounding seas of Russia. The following morning, a reception for ambassadors will take place where Alexei will accept greetings from dignitaries in the Andreevsky throne room.

Thinking it might be of interest to Alexei, Nikolai handed Alexei an historical excerpt from the diary of Nicholas that he came across when doing research at the University. In his diary, Nicholas II described what happened during those days: *"We woke up with wonderful weather. Unfortunately, I did not have time to take a walk because of the reports of Lobanov and Goremykin. Went to dinner at 11 o'clock. Breakfast with Mom and D. Fredy. We walked with them. We are deeply sorry to leave Alexandria; exactly that minute when the weather became summer, and the green began to grow rapidly. At 3 1/2 we left for Moscow and settled in the Kremlin in our former rooms. I had to take the whole army of retinues of the princes who had come. At 7 o'clock we went with the whole family to the all-night vigil to "I will save for the golden lattice". Dined at 8 1/2 Mom and left early to her. Confessed in the bedroom. May the merciful Lord God help us, may he support us tomorrow and bless on peace-working life!!! 14 May. Tuesday.*

Great, solemn, but heavy in a moral sense, for Alix, mom and me, day. From 8 am they were on their feet; and our procession began only on 1/2 10. The weather was fortunately wondrous; the Red Porch represented a radiant look. All this happened in the Assumption Cathedral, although it seems like a real dream, but do not forget all my life!!! Returned to his half past one. At 3 o'clock the same procession went again in the Faceted Chamber to the meal. At 4 o'clock everything ended quite well; a soul full of gratitude to God, I completely rested afterwards. Dined with Mom, which fortunately stood the whole test. At 9 o'clock went to the upper balcony, where did Alix ignite the electric illumination on Ivan the Great and then the towers and walls of the Kremlin were lit up consistently, as well as the opposite embankment and Zamoskvorechye. We went to bed early." (Nicholas II diary) Alexei looked at Nikolai perplexed. "Hopefully his diary will give me some insight into what Nicholas was thinking!"

"Nicholas began keeping a diary in 1882, at the age of 14. The last entry in his diary is dated July 13, 1918, just four days before he and his family were executed. He named more than a thousand people who lived both within the Russian empire and abroad. His diaries are a personal and official document reflecting the daily events in his life. They rarely reflect any emotion or any kind of political judgement or evaluation. Only during the last months of his life when he was a prisoner, did he record his pain for the fate of his beloved family and Russia." (70) It was Yeltsin that honored the family of Nicholas by giving them a burial fit for a Czar."

Alexei placed the papers on his coffee table and thanked Nikolai for showing it to him. He left for the palace's Hermitage Theater as was the tradition of the Czars. The venue was being performed by the world-renowned Bolshoi ballet. During the performance, Alexei kept glancing at Lina who was in attendance with Vladimir, and she returned the glances. He tried not to be so obvious, but Lina's beauty made it difficult.

CHAPTER 14

THE ROYAL BALL

From there, Alexei and his sons were directed to form a reception line in the grand ballroom. People were properly announced by a herald who thumped his staff when each guest entered the ballroom. Vladimir's limo and security escort pulled up to the entrance. As they ascended the steps to the great staircase that led down into the ballroom, Lina was reluctant to be seen as the girlfriend of Vladimir, so she used the excuse that she needed to freshen up. It forced Vladimir to enter by himself. Along with leaders of other nations, he was given the fanfare befitting a head of state.

The herald, thumping his staff, announced numerous dignitaries which included royalties across the world. The list included mostly royals from other countries, a member of the British royal family, the Danish, Morocco, and many other countries. Because of the Ukraine war, elected officials from other corners of the world refused to attend but some did send their ambassadors who were stationed in Moscow.

After Lina saw that Vladimir was seated, she was the last to enter the ballroom. She walked through the double doors at the top of the staircase while the herald announced her. All eyes, including Alexei, became fixated on her beauty. Lina was very athletic, and her figure was very conditioned from hiking and biking the Russian countryside. Her erect posture and graceful entrance gave her a look of royalty. She had brown eyes with long auburn hair and was one of the most decorated gymnasts in history. Vladimir had been dating her on and off since he and his wife divorced several years ago but he was not committed to only her. He openly dated other ladies. She truly was the prettiest lady among all who attended the coronation ball. The herald thumped his staff again three times, announcing the entrance of Lina. She was dressed like a princess. Her gown was a flowing Jet black, and her tiny waist was accentuated by a gold belt. Her high-heeled shoes were gold in color. The dress flowed as she walked down the steps. All eyes, including Alexei's, were on Lina. When she reached the ballroom floor, Lina was at one end of the ballroom and Alexei was at the other end.

Alexei older son noticed how his father was fixated on Lina and saw the scorn Vladimir had for his father. "Dad, you are too obvious. She is a beautiful lady but do not forget who brought her." Alexei was so drawn in by her beauty that he did not even hear his son. Just then, the herald announced that the Czar would choose a lady for his first dance. Alexei asked Vladimir for his permission to select Lina. Vladimir reluctantly nodded his approval.

Without hesitation, Alexei walked straight towards Lina and bowed to her at the bottom of the staircase. "May I, may I, may I." Alexei was so mesmerized by her beauty that he could not get the rest of the words out. He seemed to revert to his boyhood shyness where he was unable to ask a lady for a dance. Lina was so taken back by his shyness that she at first stared into his eyes. Finally, she smiled and finished the sentence for him. "Have this dance." Alexei finally became unfrozen by her thoughtfulness. Smiling, he nodded his head and said "Yes, yes…. that is what I am asking." The orchestra started playing a contemporary song.

Photo 18-Beautiful lady dancing at a Ball

Alexei gently placed his one hand around Lina's tiny waist and when their hands touched, it was a magical moment for them both. He and Lina danced alone on the floor as all eyes watched them, with many of the ladies wishing their husbands would dance with them. Vladimir stood there with a dagger-like stare. As Alexei moved Lina around the dance floor, Lina commented that all eyes are fixated on him. "No Lina, all eyes are on you. How could anyone resist such a lovely lady that radiates such beauty." Trying to sound causal he added, "how long have you been with Vladimir?"

"We have been on and off as a couple since he met me at an athletic event and no, we are not engaged or in a committed relationship. I am completely turned off by him after I caught him cheating with another lady and he does it openly." Alexei starts thinking that he may have a chance with Lina. As Alexei smoothly moves Lina around the dance floor, Lina starts to question him. "How does it feel to come from a small town in America and suddenly become the Czar of one of the most powerful countries in the world?" "I still feel that I am living a fairy tale Lina. After returning from being on active military duty and losing my wife, I became a recluse. I became disassociated with life. I have loved no one since. I find myself now wanting to be open to a new relationship. Can I see you at least as a friend Lina." Lina nods her head in agreement. "Of course, I see no harm in our being friends with one another."

Upon Joey seeing the electricity between Alexei and Lina, he saw the need to keep Vladimir occupied. To do so, he urged Sanyo to start introducing Vladimir to numerous dignitaries. Just before the dance ended, Alexei danced Lina towards the balcony doors and disappeared onto the balcony. Alexei held out his arm to Lina. "Would you please accompany me for a brief walk my lady?" Lina looked at him with her big brown eyes. "Of course, I cannot refuse a royal command of my Czar. Where are we going?" Alexei smiles "We are going to greet the people and join them in the celebration around the city Lina." Enchanted by the spontaneity of Alexei, Lina quickly agreed to join him. Joey and his security team followed closely behind but gave them the space they needed.

They walked out into the courtyard of the Kremlin. The guards were surprised to see Alexei and Lina out so early in the morning. They immediately came to attention, but Alexei put them at ease. Lina especially liked the fact that Alexei took the time to talk with the guards and asked them if they needed anything.

Having people congratulating Alexei on his walk made him want to help the Russian people that much more. Lina commented on his popularity. "The people love you Alexei. They cannot get enough of you and are really into the idea of resurrecting the Czar." Alexei laughs but takes a more serious approach. "You know Lina, I want to vindicate my family's good name, but I want to highlight the good of their long reign and not resurrect the bad. Too many innocent people died under the Romanov's reign. In sharp contrast, I want to save lives, like those that are at risk in Ukraine. According to our constitution, I do not have much political influence, but I can play a big part as a positive role model to our elected officials. Hopefully, this will change the bad image we have on the international stage of nations to one of a kinder and gentler nation. Pardon me for what I am about to say but I think Vladimir is taking us in the wrong direction." Lina comes back quickly with an observation. "I like what you are saying Alexei. You and Vladimir are on completely opposite sides of the spectrum, and I honestly think you are on the right side. The people will get behind you if you lead them down a path of prosperity and peace."

Lina was obviously smitten with Alexei. Having spent a brief time with Alexei, she suddenly started to realize what it was like to be with someone that placed others before themselves. Her relationship with Vladimir grew out of pomp and ceremony and being infatuated with his position. In sharp contrast, she seemed more drawn to the sensitivity and humbleness of Alexei than the coldness and indifference of Vladimir.

As they walked, Alexei thought it was an opportunity to ask Lina out. "I have not had much opportunity to savior Russian life outside the walls of the Kremlin. It would be great to see more of our great country with someone who knows it well. Will you accompany me this next week Lina"?

Hesitating for a moment, she wanted to accept his invitation but felt it was not proper to accept it now. "When I was a little girl, my parents and the Olympics gave me the opportunity to taste the outside world. Since I met Vladimir, most of my life has continued to be sheltered. I once loved to hike and bike in far corners of Russia but now have forgot what life is like outside the Kremlin walls and Vladimir's palace on the Black Sea. Could I give you an answer later Alexei?" "Of course, Lina, you can let me know anytime. We have all week for you to decide."

As it was declared a national holiday, the city was packed with people. To keep people from shoving their way to food like the stampede that occurred during the coronation of Nicholas, Alexei had his planners strategically space food trucks and rides throughout the city to make them easily accessible to the people. As soon as he stepped into the square with Lina, they were surrounded by well-wishers. Alexei reached out to greet everyone and thanked them for coming to his ball. Alexei introduced Lina to the well-wishers as if she were his date for the evening. Lina liked the down-to-earth approach of Alexei and did not deny that she was his date. She felt the whole evening was like a fairy tale, only this time she was with a newly crowned Czar instead of a prince like in the fairytale Cinderella.

Suddenly, fireworks erupted all around the square. Alexei and Lina stood there among the people watching them. The entire square lit up and reflected their silhouette in the warm night. Alexei could not keep himself from glancing at Lina and likewise, she returned the glances.

The moonlight was bright, and the night winds were warm. Alexei walked with his hands in the pockets of his hoodie and offered his arm to Lina. She graciously accepted his offer. "You probably wonder why I did not accept your kind offer at the ball to tour some of the outlying areas with you Alexei. Being with Vladimir, I did not think it proper to make a date with another man." Alexei liked what Lina just said, thinking this lady is an honorable person. "I can understand and very much respect you for not doing so Lina. Do you feel it appropriate to give me an answer now Lina?" Lina leans in towards Alexei and rests her head on his arm, smiling she says "of course, I would like to accompany you Alexei." Lina could only rest her head on his arm because she was a petite 5 foot 3 and Alexei was 6 foot 1. "Great, I will make all the arrangements Lina." "No Alexei, I will make all the arrangements including picking you up. When I do, please make it just you and I, no security." Alexei looks sideways at her and responds "Okee Doki." Lina laughs, "Where did you pick up that slang?" "It's what we call Pittsburgher." The two of them strolled around Red Square, chit chatting like they knew each other for years. They discovered that they shared a lot of the same interests, including hiking and biking.

They stopped in front of St Basil's (Photo19) cathedral which was brightly lit and shined against the moonlit sky and fireworks.

Photo 19-St. Basil's Cathedral in Red Square at night

Alexei and Lina stood in front of it staring at its beautiful colors and design. Lina told Alexei that the Blessed, church "constructed on Red Square in Moscow between 1554 and 1560 by Tsar Ivan IV (the Terrible), as a votive offering for his military victories over the khanates of Kazan and Astrakhan. The church was dedicated to the protection and intercession of the Virgin, but it came to be known as the Cathedral of Vasily Blazhenny (St. Basil the Beatified) after Basil, the Russian holy fool who was "idiotic for Christ's sake" and who was buried in the church vaults during the reign (1584–98) of Tsar Fyodor I.. St. Basil's Cathedral is Moscow's most famous artistic work of architecture. Also called "Pokrovsky Cathedral" or "The Cathedral of Intercession of the Virgin by the Moat", it is the most recognizable Russian building. This Cathedral means to Russians the same as the Eiffel Tower means to the French, being an honorable symbol of their past, present, and future. Strange thing is that it was designed by an Italian architect and not a Russian architect. Myth has it that Ivan had the architect blinded so he could not design another one like it." (71)

Next, they stopped in front of Lenin's tomb. Lina told Alexei that "two days after Lenin died in 1924, an architect was tasked with building a structure suitable for viewing of Lenin's body by mourners. A wooden tomb, in Red Square by the Moscow Kremlin Wall, was ready in two days, and later that day Lenin's coffin was placed in it. More than 100,000 people visited the tomb in the next six weeks. Later, the powers to be had this more elaborate one built, and Lenin's body was transferred to it." (72) "Lina noted that most young Russians do not revere that for which Lenin stood. He is the old Russia, and the youth look to the new. They only visit it out of curiosity to see a well-preserved stiff. Alexei chimes in. "I would not visit it or give him any respect after what he did to the beautiful family of my ancestors." Kiddingly he says, what I might do is send a postcard of it to an old friend of mine, Joan, who lives in New York. Joan is always looking for "Mr. right." On the card, I would write, Joan, we found the "right guy" for you, he is not very lively, but he is a big party man." Lina laughs, loving his sense of humor.

When the fireworks were over, Alexei took the hand of Lina. "I must return you to your date for the evening, Vladimir. It would be rude of me to not do so." Lina responded. "Vladimir does not make me feel like his date. As the saying goes, I lost that loving feeling for him quite some time ago." Alexei thinks again to himself that he may have a chance with Lina

When they reached the doors of the Ballroom, Lina reached up and pulling him down closer to her, she gave him a kiss on his cheek. As he turned to walk into the Ballroom, he felt ten feet tall. Upon his arrival, Joey was frantically waiting for him. "Where in the heck were you all this time brother? This is not the Steel Valley, and you are no longer a simple person. We were worried." "Sorry Joey but I just had a great walk with a wonderful lady. Time for me to get a bit more sleep before my day begins." Suddenly, Vladimir came and pulled Lina away and ordered his security to bring his car around. He left without bidding Alexei and his family good night. At the end of the night, Alexei and his sons thanked everyone and returned to their quarters.

Alexei slipped into the bed and was fast asleep in no time. At approximately 3:00 in the morning, there came a knock at the door. At first, Alexei thought it was a dream. He normally sleeps in the buff, so he hurriedly slipped on some lounging pants but not a top. Slowly opening the door, he was surprised to see Lina. Alexei looked at her and then the antique clock on the wall, "What time is it, Lina?" "Why I think it is time for us right now Alexei." Alexei looked at her with a questioning look. Lina stared at his chiseled muscular torso and was surprised to see some deep scars on him. She gently ran her hands on some of the scars, asking Alexei how he had gotten them. "I rarely talk about the scars but since you asked Lina, I was attacked by the Taliban in the middle east." Her face went solemn. Lina reached for his hand, telling him that she could not sleep and asked if he would like to take another walk with her. Alexei was never one to turn down an invite from a beautiful lady. "Of course, I would like to walk with you Lina. How on earth did you get past all the security?" "I have been in and out of the Kremlin so many times when Vladimir and I were an item, most of the guards know me." Alexei does not question Lina further, he just nods. He slips on some casual clothes, including a hoodie so no one would recognize him outside the Kremlin walls.

Alexei awoke later that morning in deep thought. He could not believe that Lina paid him a visit in the middle of the night. Once dressed for the day, his thoughts turned to the Ukrainian people and the young Russian soldiers who were losing their lives over a senseless war.

CHAPTER 15

ROMANCE BLOOMS

As promised, Lina came to pick Alexei up for their tour in a sleek sports car. The guards were quite surprised to see what they thought was the girlfriend of Vladimir coming to pick up Alexei. She looked completely different than how she looked at the coronation ball. She had long flowing hair to the middle of her back with high heeled boots and shorts. The security guards could not keep their eyes off her. Alexei, as he promised her, snuck out without alerting his security. Lina opened the door to her car. "Come Alexei, we are going to see some of your people where they enjoy themselves the most." "I am at your disposal Lina. It is amazing. Depending on how you wear your hair, you look quite different today. No matter how you wear your hair or how you dress, you are one of the most beautiful women I have ever met." Lina blushes with the compliment, thinking to herself that she never received a compliment from Vladimir. Alexei hesitates before getting into Lina's car. "Hopefully Vladimir does not mind your accompanying me."

Lina just looked at Alexei with a disgruntled expression. "As I said before Alexei, I am no longer committed to Vladimir. We now go out to formal receptions when he needs a date, but I have him drop me off at my home. Vladimir may seek my company on occasion, but he does not own me Alexei. I am now simply a companion to him and not his girlfriend. This is a beautiful sunny day, let's not waste it talking about what Vladimir may think."

Lina was a fast driver that took some chances. She tended to push her car to the limit. Alexei held on to the dashboard as they cornered many tight bends. Lina looked over and smiled at Alexei. "Evidently you do not drive fast cars on tight turns Alexei." "I never even owned a sports car Lina and where I come from, there were few roads with tight corners." First stop was a street carnival known as Maslenitsa. Lina explains to Alexei that "Maslenitsa is normally celebrated during the last week of Lent but also at other times during the year. This is a weeklong celebration and is also called Pancake week. The golden pancakes symbolize the sun, the end of winter, and the beginning of spring. Pancakes are made with ingredients that allowed Russians to eat them even if they were fasting during the Lenten season. In some regions, each day of Maslenitsa had its traditional activity. Monday may be the welcoming of "Lady Maslenitsa". The community builds the Maslenitsa effigy out of straw decorated with pieces of rags and fixed to a pole formerly known as Kostroma. It is paraded around, and the first pancakes may be made and offered to the poor. On Tuesday, young men might search for a fiancée to marry after Lent. On Wednesday sons-in-law may visit their mother-in-law who has prepared pancakes and invited other guests for a party. Thursday may be devoted to outdoor activities. People take off work and spend the day sledding, ice skating, having snowball fights and going on sleigh rides. On Friday, sons-in-law may invite their mothers-in-law for dinner. Saturday may be a gathering of a young wife with her sisters-in-law to work on a good relationship.

Many countries with a significant number of Russian immigrants consider Maslenitsa a suitable occasion to celebrate Russian culture, although the celebrations are usually reduced to one day and may not coincide with the date of the religious celebrations." (73)

Lina has an ulterior motive for bringing Alexei to this celebration. Maslenitsa symbolizes a time for working on good relationships, she hopes that Alexei takes the hint that she may wish to build a more solid and meaningful relationship with him. Lina had been here many times before, some of the street vendors greeted her with open arms and a hug. Suddenly, someone shouts Alexei, "Czar Alexei is among us!"

The people quickly surround him and Lina. One of them chides Lina. "Is this your new boyfriend Lina?"

Lina blushes. One can tell quite soon if there is a mutual attraction between two people and the interaction between them was becoming more than just a friendship. When asked if he were her boyfriend, Lina would only say he was a friend. Friend or not, Lina would occasionally reach out to hold Alexei's hand. Actions speak louder than words and their loving looks, and soft touch of one another's hands said it all. There definitely was a fondness growing between Alexei and Lina.

Lina goes over to a booth of one of the Vendors. "Let us buy a picnic basket here and find a nice place in the country to sit and have a pleasant lunch Alexei. In fact, I know the perfect place. After going there, I have two other surprises I want to share with you."

As Alexei and Lina walked back to the car, many people recognized Alexei from all the press and photos taken of him. Before they reached the car, a crowd surrounded him wanting to shake his hand. They all saw the televised comments of Alexei and thanked him for wanting to be their advocate and live among them. Some asked him for an autograph like he was a movie star. Alexei gave attention to their children first, picking them up and giving them a hug. Alexei kiddingly asked a few of the small ones if he could have their binky. The reluctant looks on the children's faces made the people laugh and feel that much closer to him.

Lina just stared in amazement as to how the people took to him so quickly and the obvious magnetism between him and the people. Suddenly, there were paparazzi who took many photos of Alexei surrounded by the people and their children. Lina thought that surely these photos would appear on the national news media throughout Russia. Little did she know that she was captured in the photo alongside Alexei and that Vladimir would also learn of their little escapade.

After exchanging hugs with the parents and their kids, Alexei and Lina drove to a special place that her parents often frequented. Lina and Alexei stand on a hilltop overlooking the countryside "That village over there is Tarus Alexei. That is the Oka River bordered by a small village. The town has never changed because its residents declined railroad construction. It has become the home of many famous writers and artists. (*Visit Russia*) It is where my mom and dad went when they first dated and later, they took me to picnic there when I was a little girl. I still come here often when I want to be alone but would now like to share it with you Alexei. It is so inspiring with the valley, the river, and mountains in the distance. You can sense the solitude yet hear the river and the wind blowing through the valley with eagles soaring above it."

One of the things you must do in Tarusa is to walk along the river, especially as it being a warm sunny day. Lina takes Alexei by the hand and walks him towards the river. For quite some time, they walked hand in hand and simply talked about their lives. They suddenly realized that they had a lot in common. After a long walk along the river, Alexei and Lina walked back to the car and got the picnic basket and a blanket that Lina conveniently loaded in her car. She spread the blanket on the ground overlooking the valley and set out two plates with wine. After enjoying some tasty food and a tall glass of wine, Alexei lay on his back and Lina laid next to him face down, looking into his eyes.

Lina rests her chin on her hands and starts to reminisce about her past. "I used to come here not only with my parents but with my first and only true love." "Do you still stay in contact with him Lina?" "I cannot talk with him in person. I can only talk with him in my prayers Alexei. You see, he was one of our young people killed in those senseless wars." I am sorry to hear that, Lina." Alexei sat up and comforted her with a hug but refrained from kissing her. Lina, however, had closed her eyes in anticipation and with the hope that he might kiss her. Lina regained her composure. "Time to go to our next fun place Alexei." "Okay, let's go but where are we going?" "You will see when we get there Alexei." Lina drives that much faster because she does not want to be late for her next surprise.

After about an hour's drive, she pulls up to the Bolshoi Theatre. Lina informs Alexei that they are going to see one of the finest performances of Swan Lake by one of the most accomplished ballet troupes. They perform in a very historic concert theater. "The Bolshoi was founded in 1776 and is one of the crown jewels of Russia. Before having this magnificent theater, it held its performances in a private home. It was renovated in 2009 at a cost of over one billion dollars. The Bolshoi Ballet is an internationally renowned classical ballet company and is recognized as one of the foremost ballet companies in the world." (74)

"I have read a lot about the Bolshoi Ballet Lina because my great grandmother, Anastasia, passed along stories of how she used to attend many of their performances with her parents who I finally discovered was Nicholas and Alexandra. Her story about the Bolshoi was another part of the puzzle that affirms her story about her being a Grand Duchess in the Romanov heritage." "Come Alexei, the performance is about to start and a friend of mine who works for the Ballet company gave me seats in one of the premier boxes."

People who were attending the performance were dressed in suits and gowns, some men in Tuxedos. Alexei and Lina had no time to change so, being dressed in casual clothes, they were a strange site to behold and stood out among everyone else. Once inside their box, however, they were not as visible. Swan lake is one of the premier performances of the Bolshoi. The music and dance is enchanting. Alexei glanced occasionally at Lina as she sat focused on the performance. She was so much into the performance that it brought a tear to her eye. Alexei wiped it away with a gentle touch of his hand. She turned to Alexei with a smile and quietly thanked him. She then placed her hand on his and he turned his hand upwards to hold hers in the palm of his. Their hands did not move from one another's all evening. When the performance was over, they quickly exited the box and darted for the front doors so no one would recognize them. Once they were outside, Alexei turned Lina towards himself and gave her a hug and thanked her.

Lina nestled her head on his chest. "We are not done yet Alexei. I have another surprise for you whenever you have a free evening. "I am very much looking forward to it Lina." Lina then drove Alexei back to his quarters. When they arrived, Alexei posed a question to Lina about what she thought about Vladimir invading Ukraine.

"One thing I have learned Alexei and that is not to discuss or make suggestions when it comes to how Vladimir runs our country. I personally do not know what his true intentions are when it comes to Ukraine. As you can see from the news here, most Russians have been kept in the dark. Those of us that are savvy with using the internet and cell phones know what truly is going on with the war. The atrocities that Vladimir has inflicted on the Ukrainian people are beyond my imagination. I saw a different side of him when we first met after my winning a gold medal at the Olympics. I fear he is on a course of self-destruction and does not care if he takes Russia and others with him. If it were up to me, I would not be waging war on others. I am more a lover than a fighter. Enough said, Let us instead reflect on what a great day we had together."

"Sorry about even bringing it up and putting you on the spot. I agree, let us not talk about it anymore and concentrate more on having a great time again when we get together next time. "By the way, the palace is drafty and too much like a museum for me. I am going to look for a large house in the city that I can renovate for a getaway home. I want to find something where I can sit in front of a fireplace with someone special. I do not want to end up like many other royals where they are constantly in the public eye and having to portray a certain posture to the public. Sometimes I simply enjoy going to a nearby coffee shop and hanging out with the locals. I want to find a home that is in a neighborhood close to where Russian families live and has fireplaces in a great room and the primary bedroom. Would you like to look for a house with me and help decorate it, Lina?"

Thinking that someone may someday share a home with him, Lina quickly responds. "I have always wanted to renovate a house Alexei. When do we start?" "I have some meetings in the morning Lina. Would some afternoon work for you?" "Of course, Alexei, call me when you would like to look at some houses."

Upon returning to his quarters, Alexei searched the palace for Joey and his security. He found them in the billiard room. Joey knew Alexei like a brother and could sense he was smitten by Lina. "What is going on with you, my brother. Did you have a great time with Lina? When you ducked out on us, we were worried that you may have encountered some trouble." "Everything went great Joey. I had a great time with her. She is not at all like I envisioned, and she is not into Vladimir anymore. Like most young people her age, she is very fun-loving. Enough about Lina, there must be something we can do to stop the carnage that is going on in Ukraine and the loss of our young soldiers. The sanctions imposed by the West and the United States are leading to the economic ruin of Russia.

CHAPTER 16

THE SOVIET UNION LEADER

We must do whatever we can do to stop it even if it means removing Vladimir from office."   Joey scratches his head and then comes up with a suggestion. "If it ever comes to where Vladimir needs to be removed from office, it would probably be best to expose his heinous acts and then let the people remove him from office." Alexei nods his head in agreement. "Agreed, but for now the people are clueless when it comes to the true reason Vladimir invaded Ukraine. He has shut down any truthful broadcasting about Ukraine.

We need to devise a way to oust him from power and I have a plan. To implement it, we will need support from inside Russia. We will have to organize a coalition of leaders to facilitate a coup to overthrow Vladimir.

First, we will have to contact owners of television, radio, and newsprint. Second, we need to find a list of those Oligarchs that are losing money because of the sanctions. They in turn may have connections with the crime bosses who also want to preserve their wealth. Over 10% of the Russian population engages in the illegal market. The reason Vladimir does not try to reign them in is because he has concerns that they could overthrow or assassinate him.

Next, we need to find a former political leader that is still highly respected among the people, one that can enlist the support of ranking military leaders in Vladimir's army that opposes the war. I have in mind a former president of the old Soviet Union before its breakup, Mical Gorbousky. He was the last leader of the Soviet Union and is a strong critic of Vladimir. Bobrovsky is in his 90's and still lives in Moscow. Another one we need to contact is Ivan Tombosky. I once read that Ivan was a Russian Opposition Coordination Council member. He is the leader of the Russia of the Future party and founder of the Anti-corruption foundation. He was recognized by Amnesty International as a prisoner of conscience and received an award for his work on human rights.

In the same article, I read about another opposition leader who was jailed by Vladimir, Michail Navalka. Vladimir had him and some of his top allies jailed as terrorists and extremists. Michail is up for a new trial, and we may be able to talk to him under the guise of our wanting to visit and help prisoners. Vladimir had him poisoned while he was speaking in Europe and then had him arrested on false charges after he returned to Russia. Thousands of his followers across Russia staged the biggest mass protests across Russia when he was arrested. Many of those that demonstrated on his behalf have now become staunch followers.

One of our biggest obstacles is the patriarch of the Russian Orthodox church world-wide. He was elected in 2009 by the ROC Local Council as Patriarch of Moscow and Primate of the Russian Orthodox Church. He only received 508 of the 700 votes cast. He has not condemned the war because he receives considerable funding from Vladimir, thus being controlled by him. We need to have him replaced by another key Russian Orthodox leader and that is the ecumenical patriarch of the Russian Orthodox church in Ukraine. Forty-one percent of Russians are members of the Russian Orthodox church and follow the teachings of Patriarch Frill. Replacing him with a leader that is against the war in Ukraine will help rally the Russian people to oppose the war.

Lastly, we need to enlist the support of former special ops soldiers. They will prove to be of great value in opposing Vladimir because they understand the mindset of the Russian military and how to infiltrate the security of Vladimir. We may want to look for soldiers that served in the special op's forces of the Ukrainian army. The Ukrainian military special ops were formed under the command of the Soviet military intelligence service. The Ukrainian special ops were modeled like the forces of the Russian special ops. With Vladimir being a former KGB agent, the Ukrainian special ops can readily understand the mindset of his security. *(Wikipedia)* Perhaps we can find some people sympathetic to our cause that can offer some suggestions."

"I think it best to start with the last President of the Soviet Union, Mical Gorbousky. He is highly revered by the Russian people and is one of the most significant figures of the second half of the 20th century. He is the recipient of a wide range of awards, including the Nobel Peace Prize. He played a major role in ending the Cold War and introduced new political and economic reforms in the Soviet Union. His reforms led to both the fall of Marxist–Leninist administrations in eastern and central Europe and the reunification of Germany. Some often criticized him for facilitating the dissolution of the Soviet Union—an event which weakened Russia's global influence and precipitated an economic collapse in Russia and associated states. Others applauded him for breaking up what could have become a dangerous adversary. I will make an appointment to introduce myself."

Gorbousky divides his time between a seaside home owned by the state and a flat that he owns in London. Alexei decided to travel to see Gorbousky in his seaside Villa where Gorbousky spends most his time. Despite his avid campaigning against Party privileges, Gorbousky had no hesitations having a three-story holiday home built for himself on the Black Sea coast. The dacha contained a private beach, rooftop solarium, marble floors, cinema, dance floor, tennis courts, and a self-watering peach grove.

Most notably, Gorbousky's dacha was the location of his three-day house arrest during the failed coup d'état by the KGB and hardline Communist Party members in 1991. At first, Alexei thought it not wise to ask Gorbousky for his support at this time. He had to acquaint himself with Bobrovsky first and gain a sense of how he felt about Vladimir and the war.

Upon Alexei's arrival, he was surprised that Gorbousky had little security. When Bobrovsky visited the United States as President of the Soviet Union, he was protected by his own security, the Secret Service, the U.S. Park Police, the Metropolitan Police, and the Maryland State Police. Like many U.S. Presidents who left office, he now has a small security of two around the clock for life and a small staff of servants. Alexei was surprised to see that gibbously was in decent shape and had a sharp mind for a man in his 90's.

Alexei was greeted by many cameras and television crews. It was big news for the Russian people to see the last leader of the Soviet Union and the next Czar of Russia together. Bobrovsky was as surprised as Alexei to see the overwhelming show of interest. In addition to the news, half the village turned out to get a glimpse of the new Russian Czar.

"Greetings Alexei and welcome to my home. I have read much about you and how you have earned the admiration of the Russian people. Although I am in my 90's, I never lived under the rule of any Russian Czar. Like you, my concept of life under the Romanovs is what I read in history books. I am certain that you have a lot of questions on how to be a Russian celebrity. Other than that, what brings you to this part of Russia and what role do you want to play in the lives of our people?"

"I traveled here to specifically meet the last great leader of the Soviet Union and the one who had the courage and vision to go back to the old values of Russia and resurrect its traditional boundaries."
"How diplomatic of you Alexei but you overstate my accomplishments. Many others, like President Vladimir, believe that I should have never broken up the Soviet Union. It is ironic that empire builders like Vladimir want to reunite the old Soviet Union at all costs, even if it means spilling the blood of innocent people and our soldiers."
"You seem opposed to Vladimir's invasion of Ukraine ."

"Very much so Alexei. Because I was born to a poor peasant family of both Russian and Ukrainian heritage, I have a fondness in my heart for the people of Ukraine. Also, I learned early in my Presidency that it was foolish to invade a country that posed no immediate threat to Russia. After I became the General Secretary of the Central Committee of the Communist Party of the Soviet Union, I planned for the withdrawal of the Soviet Union from the Afghan war. I tried to consolidate the People's party of Afghanistan's hold over power in their country to stabilize Afghanistan and to save face for withdrawing our troops. I directed that our military and intelligence organizations work with the Afghan government and the rebel factions to improve their relations with one another. I worked vigorously to improve the diplomatic relationship between the USSR and the U.S. when it became clear that a policy of consolidation did not work."

"Unlike Vladimir, I am not an empire builder. I understand that it was impossible for Russia to advance in the eyes of the world unless we embraced fundamental changes, including the breakup of the Soviet Union. Especially as the resources of Russia were being drained by trying to keep the Soviet empire intact. If it were up to me, I would have used sensible negotiations to reach an agreement peacefully between our country and Ukraine. I can only imagine how the families of those young dead soldiers and all the refugees fleeing Ukraine feel."

Alexei is pleased with what he is hearing and starts to feel that he can be more open with Gorbousky. "Do you stay in touch with any current or former military leaders Mical?"

"Yes, I do Alexei. I frequently get together with some of the current generals who served under me as young military officers, including one retired general that was one of the most decorated Generals that ever lived, General Leopold Ivoshovsky. He was my Chief of Staff of the military and became Chief of Staff as my successor. His views parallel mine in that he does not believe in invading a country that is no threat to Russia, and he is dead set against the war in Ukraine. Like America's General Colin Powell, he still commands the respect of the Russian people and current military leaders. It is rumored that many generals now serving would follow his lead no matter where it may be or against whoever."

"After his retirement, he became the chairman of a national officer's organization and published an appeal on their web site demanding that Vladimir reject any war in which Russia would be alone against the United forces of the West. He also called upon Vladimir's retirement. "

"Although Ivoshovsky is retired, he has been politically active as an extreme, anti-democratic nationalist leader. The ideology of his organization is a mixture of Soviet nostalgia, religious orthodoxy, and patriotic conservatism. His organization even called upon the ouster of Vladimir because they felt that he was corrupt and incompetent."

"Their support to any cause would be critical for two reasons. Their controversial web postings have withstood any opposition where others have been taken down within 24 hours by Russian censors. Moreover, their position has been reposted on other websites and has been viewed almost one million times. This suggests that Ivoshovsky's appeal is very strong and that he enjoys substantial political support despite any opposition from Vladimir."

"Second, Ivoshovsky and his society are supported by hardline Russian military figures and the Russian military intelligence agency. Traditionally, Vladimir has been comparatively soft on hardline nationalists, and he failed to quelch a longstanding annual nationalist march in Moscow's Pushkin Square. Therefore, Ivoshovsky appears to be the last man standing, and his harsh attack on Vladimir's Ukraine policy appears authentic and deserves great attention. The most reliable Russian media under the control of Vladimir has been cautious not to depose or censor Ivoshovsky. Bottom line is that Ivoshovsky is dead set against the war in Ukraine. Why do you ask all this Alexei?"

"I cannot go into much detail for now, but I share your and General Ivoshovsky's views on the war in Ukraine. Can I count on you and General Ivoshovsky to join me and others in deposing the Ukraine war? "Hearing this, Gorbousky was taken back and initially refrained from answering Alexei. "What do you want of me Alexei? Please speak directly to the point instead of beating around the bush. What you are alluding to brings back those tumultuous days when I broke up the Soviet Union. They were borderline revolutionary. I think I know where you are going with this and let us say if I am right, you can count me in."

Making certain that the two of them are only within earshot, Alexei decides to be open with Gorbousky. I want to build a plan to stop this insane invasion by Vladimir even if it means ousting him from power." Gorbousky's eyes widened. "As I said before, you can count me in. At my age, I cannot fear whatever may befall me for trying to save lives and the integrity of our country. Please be careful, however, who you share your inner secrets with." Knowing that he has put all on the table and feeling that Gorbousky does share his vision, Alexei briefs him on how he envisions the plan to unfold.

Alexei spent the remainder of the afternoon visiting Gorbousky. The former Soviet Leader took him on a tour of his villa and the village. Alexei had a good feeling that when the time came, Gorbousky could prove of great value in stopping Vladimir. Alexei would have enlisted more of Mical's support but for now he knew the timing was not right to lay out a complete plan. He first needed to recruit other respected leaders against the war. After spending another half hour, Alexei excuses himself. "I will contact you as soon as the other pieces of the puzzle are in place Mical." Mical bids Alexei farewell and Alexei starts his return journey to Moscow.

Recalling he had a date with Lina tomorrow, Alexei thought it would be an opportune time to visit some of the rich Oligarchs with Lina at his side. Not wanting to place Lina in harm's way, however, he was not about to reveal his plan to her, and he did not want word to get back to Vladimir that Lina was with him. Alexei's secretary was able to arrange a meeting with two of the top oligarchs in Russia, Russian billionaires Mikhail Ferdinand and Oleg Demetris, both of whom have risked their safety by breaking ranks with Vladimir, calling for an end to Russia's war in the Ukraine. Ferdinand, who was born in western Ukraine, wrote a letter that stated he wanted the bloodshed to end. Because they openly opposed the war in Ukraine, their yachts were not embargoed. Thus, they felt comfortable to meet Alexei on Ferdinand's yacht which was docked along Russia's coast in a secluded marina.

Alexei calls Lina to invite her for a trip to the coast for a cruise on an Oligarch's yacht. Lina accepts but asks Alexei to delay it for one day because she has planned a special evening for the two of them. Alexei asks Joey to schedule the meeting with the Oligarchs for the following day and leaves to pick up Lina at her home. As soon as Lina enters his Limo, Lina flashes two tickets in front of him. "What are these tickets for Lina?

Lina smiles at him. These are for a dinner performance of the greatest circus on earth. The Russian Circus of Moscow is the oldest entertainment institute in Russa. Russia has two circuses; the Circus Nikulin is the old circus that features animal acts and the Bolshoi Circus which features trapeze and acrobatics.

"Our circuses are not the typical circuses. They are very symbolic and have meaning. One of them has a flying trapeze troupe which depicts fallen Soviet World War II soldiers who fly up into the sky as cranes.

The show is set to classical music and focuses on the story of the soldiers. The performers work hard to reveal the very souls of the Soviet people. The circus building has five arenas (equestrian, water, illusionist, ice rink, and light-effect), eighteen meters below the floor, which can be readily staged following the performance of another.

Photo 20-Moscow State Circus

The current production is entitled Babushkin Sekret (Grandmother's secret) and is based on the Russian story of the twelve Chairs. The cast includes clowns, acrobats and jugglers, and also features a wide variety of acts that involve perch poles, static trapezes, aerial silk, Chinese poles, and high wire techniques.." (75)

Before the show, I am treating you to a delicious meal with a panoramic view of Moscow at one of our finest restaurants. You can almost reach the stars and night lights of Moscow.

To ensure a more intimate evening with Lina, Alexei took only Joey and another highly skilled bodyguard. When they arrived at the restaurant, Alexei arranged for Joey and his colleague to have dinner at a nearby table. Upon entering the restaurant, you see huge panoramic windows and life-like trees. The high point of the restaurant is when the windows open to give diners a breathtaking view of Moscow and the opportunity to feel the warmth of the evening air. It is the only restaurant in Moscow where the upper sections of the windows are fully open to view the city.

Joey and his partner are seated two tables away from Alexei and Lina. Coming from the small town of Homestead, Alexei and Joey are not used to such exquisite dining. Alexei wears shaded glasses to cover up his identity and requests a table in a far corner of the restaurant with a great view. Despite Alexei trying to conceal his identity, the owner of the restaurant recognizes him and sends him a complimentary bottle of his finest wines. He follows up by personally visiting their table and offers his personal service. Alexei and Lina thank him for his hospitality and dedication to providing great service to his clientele.

Alexei reaches for Lina's hand and exclaims. "Is not this wonderful. Other than Pittsburgh, I have never seen a city with such a view. I used to dine in a restaurant like this at the top of the US Steel building in Pittsburgh. You are spoiling me with all these outstanding arrangements Lina." Alexei held on to Lina's hand and Alexei gently raised Lina's hand to his lips and kissed it.

After enjoying some wine and dinner, Lina says that they need to leave for the circus to catch the opening act, which is spectacular. She asked for the check, but the waiter told her that the owner said it was on the house, including Joey's tab. Alexei wanted to pay the check but knew if he did, Lina would be hurt as she wanted to treat Alexei. Alexei asked the waiter for the owner and thanked him profusely for taking care of their checks. "The pleasure is all mine, Czar Alexei. It is an honor to have you join us for dinner. As the Czarina did my great grandparents a kind favor many years ago by providing them with food when their cupboards were bare. I am honored to return the favor."

Joey brought the car around for Lina and Alexei. They arrived at the circus minutes before the first show was to start. Lina was excited to see the reaction of Alexei while he watched the show. Russian Circus traditions include clowning, juggling, acrobatics, contortion, and animal acts (especially bear acts, such as bears who juggle with their feet). Stylistically, the Soviet circuses were different from their Western counterparts. Lina told Alexei that she especially wanted him to see the show because the Moscow spanned centuries and performed for his ancestor Czar Nicholas, Emperors Maximillian of Mexico, Dom Pedro of Brazil, the Emperor of Japan, and Indian Rajahs. The ringmaster recognized Alexei and welcomed him and his friends to the circus. All the audience stood and applauded him. Lina beamed with pride and complimented Alexei on being given a standing ovation.

After the two-hour show finished, Lina suggested that they stop at a local pub for some refreshments and a taste of the Russian night life. She explains that Moscow nightlife can be both fun and confusing. At night, restaurants often turn into clubs, and there is an infamous face control policy to enter some night clubs. Under this policy, the club will only admit the most beautiful, well dressed, and cash laden. "The one we are going to is one of the most famous in Moscow, the Moscow Space Bar. It is one of the top ten bars in the world. It has breathtaking views of Moscow and special cocktails that make you forget the rest of the world. Each club has its own venue. Some posh clubs offer all night dancing and others have great food menus and exotic dancers. For music lovers, the musical nights of Moscow make the nightlife of Russia attractive as well. Some nightclubs have entertainment with ballet performers and opera shows. I love to dance and hopefully you do too, so we are going to a posh club where we can dance to the wee hours of the morning."

Joey rolls his eyes fearing for the safety of Alexei and Lina. Where he and Alexei comes from in the Steel Valley, he is more familiar with bar fights and drunkards. Whatever the case, Joey knows that he and Alexei must abide by the wishes of Lina. They arrive at the club, which admits people under the face control policy. Joey and his counterpart lead the way and are first in line. The bouncer stops them because he does not find their appearance that attractive. Joey was much bigger and stronger than the Bouncer and Alexei knew that Joey had a reputation for not accepting a no from anyone. Seeing Joey folding a fist, Alexei quickly moves between Joey and the Bouncer. The Bouncer was about to argue with Alexei until he recognized that he was the new Czar. "What are you doing here in a night club that may place you at risk? Please do not get me wrong. We are one of the more plush and classy night clubs in all Moscow but sometimes our patrons become a bit pushy and overbearing." Seeing that Alexei very much wanted to dance, he explains his situation to the Bouncer. "Where I come from, all night spots have overbearing clientele. I may be the Czar, but Joey and I consider ourselves no different than anyone in your club. In fact, I helped fund my college education by being a bouncer in a college bar." The Bouncer looks at them fondly and steps aside, waving them to pass on in.

Although Alexei is only a social drinker, he ordered a round of wine for the four of them. He then asks the waiter to send a glass of wine to the Bouncer and thank him on his behalf and his friends. The Bouncer stepped inside the door and quietly toasts Alexei. Alexei toasts him back, gently reaching for Lina's hand to take her onto the dance floor. Joey and his partner watch their backs from a distance. Lina comments on Alexei dancing. "I cannot believe that you enjoy fast dancing and do not even seem to tire or break out in a sweat Alexei." Alexei gives Lina one of those cool gestures of pointing to his and her feet. "I was always too shy to ask a girl to dance back home but my mother taught me fast dancing. To recoin a phrase Nancy Sinatra once sang, these boots are made for dancing." Lina's laugh was infectious. She looked like a shy schoolgirl when she laughed, her eyes sparkled.

Alexei excused himself to use the bathroom. A man approached Lina while she waited for his return. He was rough and crude with tattoos on both arms. He was not Russian and had several men with him. He grabbed ahold of Lina and started pulling her towards the dance floor. Lina tried desperately and politely to get away from him, but he would not let her go. He was starting to make a scene. Joey, covering Alexei's back, could not see what was going on with Lina. Alexei returned to find the crude man bullying Lina into dancing with him. Not wanting to make more of a scene, Alexei addressed him in a gentlemanly way. "Sir, can you not see the lady does not want to dance? Besides, she is with me, and I would appreciate your leaving her alone." Joey and his partner now had a strong bead on the troublemaker. The man pushed at Alexei and kept grabbing at Lina. That is all Alexei needed. Alexei grabbed the man and threw him aside like a feather. As the man started towards Alexei and Lina again in a threatening way, the Club Bouncer stepped between them. The man backed off and walked out the door with his friends, not seeing that Alexei had Joey and another security person with him. Lina was shaken and suggested they leave.

Joey and his security always walked about ten yards behind Alexei when he was with Lina so they could have some privacy. When they were walking out into the parking lot to get their car, the tattooed foreigner and five of his friends were waiting for them. "You are going to pay for getting us thrown out of the club." Alexei told Lina to get into the car and lock it. Alexei had enough of this guy and warned him to back off. "You need to move on before the six of you get hurt my friend." The foreigner laughs. "It seems that we have you outnumbered six to one." Alexei nods towards Joey and his partner. "You may be right that you have us outnumbered but you definitely do not have us out gunned." As the foreigner and his friends look towards Joey, he sees them brandishing "Glock 17 handguns, one of the deadliest semiautomatic handguns. It was used by the Austrian army because its reliability will work in demanding conditions and has an automatic fifteen-round magazine." (76)

Angry that these men offended Lina, Alexie insists that they apologize to her." The foreigners mumbled an apology to Lina and then dispersed. Joey, Alexei, and their other bodyguard got into the car to drive Lina home. When they arrived, Lina was still badly shaken. "I am fearful that these men may have followed us home Alexei. Please stay with me tonight." "Okay Lina, let me talk with Joey. I am going to stay with Lina tonight and I need you to position a car across the street with two of our men around the clock Joey."

Alexei asked Lina as to which room he should sleep in? "With me of course Alexei. I will feel safe with you sleeping by my side." Alexei looks questionably at Lina. "Do you think that we are ready to spend the night together?" "Yes, I do Alexei." "Okay Lina, I guess I can sleep in my clothes." Lina gave him a got to be kidding look.

The night in bed together was very frustrating for Alexei. He very much wanted to be intimate with Lina, but he thought it proper to restrain himself. Alexei would push to one side of the bed and Lina would pursue him, snuggling up close. Occasionally they would wake up gazing into each other's eyes. Lina would fall back to sleep where Alexei lay there marveling about her beauty. Alexei woke up before Lina. Before going out the door, he invited Lina to join him tomorrow evening on the yacht of the Oligarchs. Lina blew him a kiss when he was going out the door. "I cannot wait until tomorrow, Alexei." Alexei told Lina to pack an overnight bag.

CHAPTER 17

ALEXEI MEETS OLIGARCHS

Sitting in the billiard room, Alexei tells Joey and his security people about what is happening with ships owned by the Oligarchs who have supported the war. Joey looks puzzled when Alexei mentions Oligarchs. "Oligarchs, what are Oligarchs Alexei?" "Oligarchy is a form of power structure in which power rests with a small number of people. These people may or may not be distinguished by one or several characteristics, such as nobility, fame, wealth, education, or corporate, religious, political, or military. Russian oligarchs are business oligarchs of the former Soviet republics who rapidly accumulated wealth in the 1990s via the Russian privatization that followed the dissolution of the Soviet Union. The failing Soviet state left the ownership of state assets contested, which allowed for informal deals with former USSR officials of Russia and Ukraine. Many of these businessmen imported or smuggled goods such as personal computers and jeans into the country and sold them on the illegal market at a hefty profit. During the 1990's, these same businessmen emerged as what are called Oligarchs. They started from having nothing and became well-connected and rich entrepreneurs. "(77)

Some of these Russian oligarchs have bought some of the largest and most extravagant "superyachts" on the planet." (Photo 20) Their spoils are gleaming symbols of how Russia's elite have profited under the government of Vladimir. The ships of the Oligarchs that have supported the war have shown up at ports around the world. They span the length of a football field or longer, come outfitted with helipads and swimming pools."

"As one of the Oligarch's yachts linked to Vladimir was preparing to flee a port, the French officials seized it. They also intercepted one of the cargo ships last weekend, and a Malaysian port refused to let another Oligarch dock at their port."

Photo 21-Russian Oligarchs seized Yacht

Alexei told Joey that "The yacht we will be visiting tonight has not been confiscated because its owner has spoken out against the war. They docked in the nearby Port of Moscow by bringing it up through the canal system. With the canal, Moscow is connected to Russia's Unified Deep Water System, a large system of canals and rivers in European Russia, which created access to five seas: the White Sea, Baltic Sea, Caspian Sea, Sea of Azov, and the Black Sea. As such, it is sometimes called the "port of the five seas". Apart from transportation, the canal also provides for about half of Moscow's water consumption, and the shores of its numerous reservoirs are used as recreation zones. (78)

Upon their arrival, Alexei sensed that Ferdinand and Oleg seemed taken back that Alexei brought Lina. Alexei relieved their concerns by asking Ferdinand to arrange a tour of the yacht for Lina.

Alexei did not want to tip his hand so soon should any attempts to stop the invasion to remove Vladimir from office. He speaks cautiously without incriminating himself. Ferdinand takes the initiative to speak first. "Greetings Alexei. It is great to have you aboard, but we were wondering what brings you to visit us when your people contacted us for a meeting?" "I wanted to touch base with some of the doers and shakers in Russia Ferdinand. I particularly wanted to gain your insight as to the sanctions and how they will affect the economy in Russia and if we have already seen some adverse effects."

Ferdinand shows frustration by gritting his teeth and lips. "How the sanctions are affecting Russia depends on whose tea leaves you are reading. Some say the short-term financial impact of the sanctions on Russia's economy has been substantial but appears to have dissipated since May. "Russia's currency is losing value, falling 40 percent against the U.S. dollar since December 2022. To stabilize the currency, the Russian central bank held an emergency meeting in August and raised interest rates from 7.5 percent to 11 percent."(79) "On the other side of the spectrum, the reason Russia has been able to weather the previous round of sanctions, and likely will weather this storm as well, is due to the interactive effect between economic sanctions and the value of Russian exports. Russia is the world's third largest producer of oil and liquid fuels at 10.5 million barrels per day which is roughly 11 percent of global supply. Russia is also the world's second largest natural gas producer, at 25 quadrillion British thermal units.

"Oil is a global commodity traded in USD, and natural gas contracts often have prices indexed to oil prices. What this all means is that as the value of the ruble relative to the USD falls, the price of Russia's major exports increases in the local currency markets.

"Unlike the United States and other western nations where oil and gas production are controlled by private companies, Russia's oil and gas production is managed by state-owned enterprises." (8) This means Vladimir holds the purse strings when it comes to the oil. This in turn effects other European countries like the scarcity of energy now being experienced in Germany."

Oleg chimes in on the conversation. "From a political point of view, they had little effect on the ongoing invasion of Ukraine. To add to what Ferdinand said, the sanctions combined with many U.S. and European companies discontinuing business in Russia, are going to eventually have a truly devastating effect on the Russian people. Soon, the people of Russia are going to face extreme shortages and high inflation. To boot, the American people will also face inflationary prices. Vladimir is supplementing needs by soliciting support from Countries like China and North Korea."

Alexei poses a question that could lead him into asking their support to remove Vladimir as President. "Is there anything you can do to get Vladimir to the table to formulate a peace with Ukraine and order a cease fire? "

Ferdinand is quick to respond. "We have tried but he is bent on going all the way. It seems he has a death wish and is willing to take us all with him. It may be because he could have a deliberating health issue and is not concerned about his demise, only his place in history. We have even explored about calling for new elections to remove him from office, but our parliament is afraid to oppose Vladimir. Before we reveal more about Vladimir and his invasion, we would like to know your views Alexei."

Sensing that Ferdinand and Oleg are at wits end like most businesspeople, Alexei decides to risk all by making the ultimate suggestion. "It appears that the only way to stop this insane invasion is to remove the one person who has caused this mess and that is Vladimir."

Ferdinand and Oleg were taken back and surprised at Alexei being so frank and outspoken. Because everyone close to Vladimir was guarded, they were not used to such openness. "We feel the same way. Every other approach we have taken has failed. We are not the only financiers that have discussed this with him, but our words have fallen on deaf ears. What do you propose? We are open to any suggestions that will end his insanity."

Alexei starts introducing his plan. "If we go ahead with a plan that I have in mind to remove Vladimir from office, we will need to do it within the constitution framework of Russia and must enlist the support of leaders like the two of you. One component I thought about is recruiting some former members of the Russian underground. From what I have researched, "there are 6,000 crime families with 200 of them having a global reach. A French criminologist, said that it is one of the best structured criminal organizations in Europe, with a quasi-military operation." (81) Vladimir and his administration have fears of them infiltrating the government. If this is true, we need the military component of those that are not hard-core criminals and one of their retired bosses who has gone legitimate and would support our cause because they share our concerns. Do you have any connections to someone like this, or do you know of anyone who can reach out to that someone?"

Ferdinand seemed reluctant to discuss any connection to the crime bosses of Russia or even offer any names. Suddenly Oleg chimes in with a name. "Simon Kodkavich………. Simon Kodkavich."

Ferdinand is taken back to Oleg offering Kodkavich's name. "Be careful what you say Oleg. You cannot go down that path where you may put you and your family in danger. Simon does not want anyone to resurrect his past by pointing a finger at him."

Oleg stands up in response. "This is bigger than me and what is best for my family and Russia. Simon Kodkavich was one of the biggest crime bosses in Russia and is likened to a Godfather in an American crime family. The interesting point is that like Ferdinand, Kodkavich is Ukrainian born and still has much family living in Ukraine. Kodkavich quickly built a well-organized criminal organization in the same venue as the American mafia families, but he and his family have now gone legit, owning a lot of businesses. Many in his organization can be trusted because they are his relatives and never involved in criminal dealings. He lives in Moscow and from what I am told, he still maintains contact with one of the largest Russian crime groups. He protects him and his family by retaining former special operation forces who have left the military. His special ops people have the same training as a Navy Seal. Some of them were former members of the Russian and Ukrainian special ops. He demands loyalty and trust so the men that he now employs have never been involved in organized crime. In fact, they are very patriotic because of their military backgrounds. Simon has no love for Vladimir because Vladimir tried to incarcerate him when he was cleaning up St. Petersburg as the vice mayor of that city."

Alexei perks up with what he just heard. "This is exactly what we need if we are to topple Vladimir from power, we will need an established organization in Russia that has a network of strong men and fire power. Can you list Simon's support, and can you trust him? Surely his family's wealth has also been sanctioned." Oleg nods his head yes.

Alexei walks across the deck thinking. "Another thought, we need is to enlist the network of the jailed opposition leader, Michail Navalka. I would imagine that Kodkavich being a former crime boss has an in with the prisons and can get word to Navalka about our plan. In fact, he may be able to help Navalka escape from prison. With Navalka free to work his network, he should be able to rally a great deal of support across Russia in opposition to Vladimir. Lastly, we will need the television and radio media to get the truth out about what is happening in Ukraine."

Ferdinand offers input on media support. "Garnering the support of the television and radio media is the easiest of this puzzle because several Oligarchs that are sympathetic to our cause own them. They will rally to our cause if they are certain our plan will not falter. Ferdinand takes his turn in the dialogue. "Yes, Oleg and I can do all this but when doing so, we need to keep our families in harm's way. Both Oleg and I will need to get our families safely out of Russia and the way to do this is aboard my yacht without it being confiscated while enroute to a safe port. "

"I will have my contacts at the Pentagon give your and Oleg's ships and family safe passage to whatever port you choose. In the meantime, Oleg, you contact Kodkavich and arrange a meeting."

"We are not staying tonight, Alexei. Why don't you and Lina stay on the yacht overnight and enjoy the yacht on us? The sunset and sunrise are spectacular. We have several spacious staterooms, a helicopter, swimming pool, wine room, and a speed boat at your disposal. In the meantime, we will arrange a meeting between you and Kodkavich." Alexei thanked them and showed him his overnight bag.

CHAPTER 18

A MOONLIGHT DANCE

Just then, Lina returned from her tour. Alexei told Lina of Ferdinand and Oleg's kind offer to allow them to spend the night aboard their yacht and enjoy a dinner and some wine on them. "Would you like to spend the night watching the Sun go down and Moonlight come up." Lina gave an enthusiastic nod of approval. "I think it would be wonderful to spend the evening on the water and have dinner and breakfast watching the Sunset tonight, and the Sunrise tomorrow, Alexei." Seeing Lina's beauty, you could see the envy in the faces of Ferdinand and Oleg as they departed to put their part of the plan into action. Alexei and Lina retired to their respected cabins to change for a casual night.

So as not to put Lina in a compromising situation, Alexei asked one of the crew to show Lina to the best state room and then direct him to another. After dawning some casual clothes, Alexei and Lina met for dinner on the upper deck overlooking the ocean and having a clear view of the sunset, with the sun glimmering on the water. The ship's chef prepared a gourmet dinner along with the appropriate wine and dessert. The steward turned on some classical dance music which played softly in the background and the steward, along with Alexei's security, gave them some privacy.

When they finished dinner, they took a walk along the docks overlooking the water and evening sky. Upon returning to their dock, Alexei took Lina by her hand, and she turned, facing him and the moon shining over his shoulder. The warm breezes made Lina's hair gently wave in the moonlight. The moon made her eyes sparkle and cast both their shadows on the dock, making it one of the most eventful and romantic evenings either one has ever spent. Both realized that much more than fate threw them together and that they were perfectly matched and meant to be with one another.

Watching Alexei and Lina from the yacht, Joey thought he would give Alexei a little help to woo his lady. He quickly pulled out his iPhone and brought up the song "How do I live without you" by Celine Dion and has the crew put it on their loudspeakers. Alexei looks up and gives Joey a thumbs up. Joey and the crew then gave them some privacy by going below to play cards.

Looking into Lina's eyes and taking both her hands into his, Alexei asks "Can I have this dance my lady?" This will be my first dance with a lovely lady looking at a moonlit sky overlooking the water." Lina laughs with her cute schoolgirl giggle and answers, "mine too. Why let me check my dance card to see if I can fit you in Alexei? Yes, I do have a space, and you may have this dance."

Alexei reverses his baseball cap so he can place his cheek next to hers. Both look like a couple of lovesick young romantics on their first date, like two kids at a high school dance. They danced slowly on the dock, lovingly embracing one another, cheek to cheek. Slowly, Lina's lips turned to kiss Alexei on the cheek and Alexei returned the kiss. Lina whispers into Alexei ear how much she enjoys being with him and Alexei sings romantically into hers. He quietly sings some lyrics to the Celine Dion song that is playing over the loudspeaker. "Lina snuggled closer to Alexei and whispered into his ear. I never had such a lovely romantic evening in my whole life."

Alexei softly sings the words of the song into Lina's ear as they dance. *"How do I get through one night without you? If I had to live without you, what kind of life would that be? I need you in my arms, need you to hold, you are my world, my heart, my soul, If you ever leave Baby, you would take away everything good in my life, How do I live without you? How do I breathe without you? How do I ever survive without you? Without you, there would be no sun in my sky, there would be no love in my life, Baby I don't know what I would do, I'd be lost if I lost you."*

Lina loved every minute of it. She could not believe how romantic Alexei is. She has never experienced anything like it with any other man, especially Vladimir. She feels like she is living a dream from a fairy tale romance.

When the music stopped, the two of them continued to hold hands and faced one another. Lina was first to speak. In all my life, I have never had a romantic evening like this. When my parents discovered that I had exceptional athletic ability, they decided to send me to special schools where my whole life was consumed in training to compete in the Olympics. Not long after winning a gold medal, Vladimir overwhelmed me with his power and wealth. He used me for show and controlled my very existence. All we did was attend state dinners and never had an evening alone except in the bedroom and that was not like two romantic lovers. I started feeling used, like a prisoner."

"I am so sad to hear this, Lina. I would say that my life was not much different. After school, I lived a mundane life. I did not date through college after coming back from the service. I never had time for romance until I met my wife, and she died giving birth to our second child. When my wife died, I did not date anyone. I was devastated by her death and my boys were so young, I wanted to be there for them." "We certainly have a lot in common Alexei. Besides Vladimir, I only had one other relationship in my life and he was killed in battle."

After their dance, they went to the rear of the boat to look at the moon and the stars (Photo 19). Even though it was a warm night, Lina used the excuse that she was chilled so Alexei would wrap his arms around her while they looked out over the water. The moon shined bright, and the warmth of the ocean air felt great. Alexei and Lina had magic between them but were very reluctant to express themselves. Looking at the stars, Lina voiced a nursery rhyme taught to children by their mothers. "Star Bright, star light, first star I have seen tonight, I wish I might, have the wish I wish tonight. Turning around to look into the eyes of Alexei, Lina finishes the rhyme, "and my wish is that we spend the night together."

Alexei puts his arms around Lina and pulls her to him. "There is nothing I would rather do than to make love to you Lina, but Vladimir still believes that he is in a committed relationship with you. It is not right for me to start an intimate relationship with you under the circumstances. You need to be up front with Vladimir and make certain that he understands you no longer care for him." "I have done exactly that Alexei. He just will not let go. He is very controlling. It is like he feels he owns me!" "Perhaps the best way to hit the message home with Vladimir is to give back any personal items he has given you, such as jewelry Lina." "Good idea Alexei. I can give back to him an expensive ring he gave me. I really have strong feelings for you and would hope that we can build a loving and lasting relationship." "I feel the same about you Lina."

As midnight approached, Alexei decided it was time to at least put his arms around Lina and give her a passionate kiss. Lina returned an inviting kiss. Both found it difficult to walk away from one another. Every time they tried to walk away from one another, one passionate kiss and loving hug led to another.

"We better stop here for now Lina." "Thank you for thinking of and respecting me Alexei. I think you are right, and I will finalize it with Vladimir and make certain he understands that it is over between us." Finally, they let go of one another and go to their cabins.

CHAPTER 19

THE CONFRONTATION

Early next morning, Alexei and Lina joined one another again on the top deck to have breakfast and watch the sun rise. Afterwards, Alexei took Lina home. Upon their arrival, a bunch of black SUVs surrounded by security guards was waiting for them. Out of the limousine came Vladimir who approached Lina and Alexei. "Where have you been Lina"?

"Out for the evening but it isn't any of your business where I was Vladimir." "Out for the evening-none of my business! I thought we had an exclusive relationship, Lina." "We never agreed to such a relationship and what about other ladies you have been seeing Vladimir? You told me several times that you wanted to see other ladies. I guess exclusive to you means only one way and that is your way!" Alexei chimed in to protect Lina from insults. "We were with some friends, and everything was proper. Nothing happened Vladimir." "Stay out of this Alexei or you will end up like Czar Nicholas and his family, only your demise will not be so quick."

As Vladimir said this, he shoved Alexei. His shoving action caused Vladimir's security forces to surround Alexei. This action in turn prompted Joey and his team to draw their weapons. Alexei and Lina quickly tried to calm the tense situation. Surprising, the head of Vladimir's security tried to avert trouble. "Sir, I think it best that we leave and return to the Kremlin." This angered Vladimir further and he dressed down his chief of security. "Mind your own business. You work for me and will follow my orders." You could see the loss of respect for Vladimir in the eyes of his security forces.

To avert the situation from escalating, Lina put herself between the two men asking Vladimir to discuss this in private. To respect the wishes of Lina, Alexei directed Joey and his men to stand down.

Lina pulls Vladimir by the arm. "We need to talk in private Vladimir." "Talk, talk about what? The only words I want to hear from you Lina is that you are committed to our relationship." Vladimir just glared with hate towards Alexei but did not want to be caught in the middle of a fight, especially as he knew that Alexei's guards were more resolute than his men. Also, Vladimir's security was not supportive of his actions. Vladimir said nothing more and left in a huff.

Lina turns to Alexei. "Thank you for sticking up for me Alexei. You and your men can leave now. I will be okay." The danger was over, so Alexei and his men respected the request of Lina and leave.

Early next morning, Alexei was scheduled to have a meeting with the head of the Russian Orthodox Church, Patriarch Chrill. Before leaving, he decided to call Lina to make certain that she was all right. Lina answered with light humor. "You missed me Alexei to call so early in the morning. Yes, I am all right. Now you can see that it is impossible to have a calm and sensible conversation with Vladimir." "Yes, I saw firsthand Lina. Would you have dinner with me when I return from my trip?" "Of course, Alexei"

Alexei and his security left for St. Petersburg cathedral, the cathedral that housed the tombs of Czar Nicholas and his family. Before leaving, Alexei directed some of his security to make certain that Lina was safe. Upon landing in St. Petersburg, throngs of well-wishers greeted him. Alexei had become a rising star among the Russian people. Chrill decides to meet Alexei at the Cathedral.

CHAPTER 20

ALEXEI MEETS THE CLERGY

"Greetings Alexei. I would imagine that you came to pay your respects to your ancestors. Because of their commitment to our faith, the Russian Orthodox Church holds Czar Nicholas and his family in high esteem. Come, let us take you to the crypt where you can see where your ancestors lie in state. The remains of your ancestors lie beneath the floor of the crypt." Alexei and his security stood in quiet reverence when they entered the cathedral. Alexei appreciated that the former Russian president gave his family a proper burial of honor.

Chrill takes Alexei by the hand. "Let's just you and I visit the tomb for it may be more solemn if you and I walk down to the crypt and just the two of us talk awhile." "This is good your eminence because I would like to talk to only you in confidence and be protected under the church's law of–penitent privilege." Chrill gives Alexei a confused look because he knew that according to church law, he is sworn to secrecy, "Are you saying you want me to hear your confession Alexei?" "Yes, something like that your Eminence."

Alexei and Chrill walk down a long staircase to a lower part of the cathedral where the remains of many patriarchs and the ancestors of Alexei lie in state. There were many sarcophaguses' including one that housed Nicholas and his family. Surrounding the sarcophaguses are many photos of Nicholas and his family, including photos of the skulls and bones of the family. The Russian Orthodox church lovingly preserved the remains because they canonized Nicholas II and his family. They did so because of the family's humbleness, patience, and meekness in face of being executed in such a barbarous way.

Chrill explains the history of the royals buried in the vault and two of those that were not. "We stand on the site where most of the graves of the Romanov rulers from Peter the Great onward are entombed Alexei, with Peter's grave at the front right. Originally, only the Czar and the immediate family could be buried in the cathedral, but Nicholas Ist decreed that grand dukes and their families could also be buried here.

"Peter and Paul Cathedral, which houses the tombs of all Imperial Russia's rulers, including Peter the Great, Catherine the Great, and the last Russian monarch Nicholas II. The Grand Ducal Mausoleum, next to the cathedral, was built in 1896 to hold the tombs of the lesser Romanovs, as well as the Beauharnais family (Dukes of Leuchtenberg), who had married into the Romanov family." (82)

Photo 22-Peter & Paul Cathedral-Tomb of Czars

The remains of only two Romanov Czars did not make it into the Peter-Paul Fortress, Peter II, and Ivan VI. Peter II reigned as Emperor of Russia from 1727 until his premature death at the age of 14. He is buried in the Moscow Cathedral Archangel. Ivan VI was an

197

infant emperor of Russia who was overthrown by his cousin Elizabeth Petrovna in 1741. He was only two months old when he was proclaimed emperor and his mother named regent, but the throne was seized in a coup after a year. Ivan and his parents were imprisoned far from the capital and spent the rest of their lives in captivity until he died in his early twenties. The remains of Nicholas II and his family were re-interred here in 1998. (83) So, you see Alexei, you are standing among a good bit of your blood line. Now my question is what brings you to St. Petersburg and why did you ask for a meeting with me?"

"I will get straight to the point Patriarch Chrill. Before I do, I want you to understand that I consider what I am about to say is protected by your allegiance as a priest to keep what we say entirely confidential. Alexei did so to prevent Chrill from reporting their conversation to Vladimir. The clergy–penitent privilege, is a rule of evidence that forbids judicial inquiry into certain communications (spoken or otherwise) between clergy and their congregation. Chrill agrees that their conversation will be protected by the priest-penitent privilege.

Alexei thanks Chrill for agreeing to adhere to the churches rule of clergy-penitent privilege and begins with a question. "What are your views on the war in Ukraine. Do you oppose or condone it?"

Chrill is taken back by Alexei question but answers it willingly but not to the liking of Alexei. "Rest assured Alexei I am not in favor of war, but Ukraine needs to be taught a lesson. Their evil ways include allowing many practices contrary to our religion. I am in total support of what our President is doing to stop Ukraine."

"President Vladimir has been supportive of me and our Church. I know of your stance on pulling out of Ukraine. Pointing to the remains of Nicholas and his family, Chrill makes a point. "Be careful of what you say and do Alexei. If you continue to involve yourself in the business of Ukraine, something like this could happen to you. I do not think that you would want to end up like your ancestors." Hearing this, Alexei knew exactly where Chrill stood on Ukraine. His only hope now was to neutralize Chrill's position until he could have him replaced as the head of the church. "Is that a threat your eminence? I would think that a leader of the church would not take such an unorthodox position!" "Let's consider it more a suggestion Alexei!"

He did not want the Patriarch to alert Vladimir. To stop the shedding of innocent blood, Alexei felt compelled to leave Chrill with something to consider and at least try to neutralize him. "Your eminence, let me read some excerpts from an article that appeared in an American newspaper. When I do so, I would like to remind you that this is part of my confession and according to the biblical oath you have taken, you cannot share what we talk about here today with anyone, including the President." With a surprised look on his face, Chrill slowly nods his head in agreement.

Alexei commences to read the newspaper article. *"Patriarch Chrill has provided spiritual cover for the invasion of Ukraine, reaping vast resources for his church in return. Now, in an extraordinary step, the E.U. is threatening him with sanctions.*

Today, Chrill stands apart not merely from the Pope, but from much of the world. The leader of about 100 million faithful's, Chrill, a man in his seventies, has staked the fortunes of his branch of Orthodox Christianity on a close and mutually beneficial alliance with Mr. Vladimir, offering him spiritual cover while his church — and possibly he himself — receives vast resources in return from the Kremlin, allowing him to extend his influence in the Orthodox world.

To his critics, the arrangement has made Chrill far more than another apparatchik, oligarch, or enabler of President Vladimir, but an essential part of the nationalist ideology at the heart of the Kremlin's expansionist designs.

Chrill's role is so important that European officials have included him on a list of individuals they plan to target in an upcoming and still in flux — round of sanctions against Russia, according to people who have seen the list." (84)

"Is this the legacy you want written as your epitaph your Eminence? I thought the church was nonpolitical and put the sanctity of life above all else. I will leave the article with you to ponder. Again, I would ask that on your oath as a priest, that you keep our conversation confidential and not share it with anyone." Chrill is shockingly bewildered at Alexei being so direct and critical of his position but reluctantly nods his head again and takes the article.

You could sense that Chrill was bought and paid for by Vladimir, but the newspaper article gives him much food for thought. Alexei could not stand spending another minute with Chrill. He turns to leave Chrill standing alone in the burial vault. As Alexei turns to leave the Patriarch in the tomb, Chrill calls out to Alexei. "You leave me a lot to ponder Alexei. I will ask God for guidance." Alexei slightly shakes his head yes in agreement. "I am certain that God will answer you truthfully your Eminence and that is that you must take a stance against the war in Ukraine. While asking for his guidance, you should also ask God for his forgiveness for not speaking out against the war. "

Upon emerging from the Crypt, Alexei motions for Joey and his security that he wanted to leave. On the way back to the airport, Alexei reports the stance of Patriarch Chrill to Joey. "At first, I did not believe what I read in the newspapers that the head of the Russian Orthodox Church supports Vladimir's invasion of Ukraine. I now believe it and I cannot fathom that a world-church leader would condone killing innocent people and soldiers. If Chrill does not change, then we must remove him as the leader of the church."

"Russia only has 1/3 of the church membership where the remainder of the world has 140 million people, with Ukraine having 24 million." (85) "We need to have the spiritual leaders of the church to vote for the spiritual leader of the Orthodox Ukraine church. I am certain that he will send a message to the Russian people and the world that the blood shed needs to stop in Ukraine. Especially as the Ukraine Patriarch dubbed Vladimir the anti-Christ."

CHAPTER 21

HOUSE HUNTING AND THE GENERAL

Upon returning to Moscow, Alexei remembered that he promised to take Lina house shopping. He called Lina to see if she was available tomorrow afternoon. Looking forward to seeing him again, she immediately said yes. Remembering her grandmother's adage about not keeping a lady waiting, Alexei picked her up at noon sharp. Alexei had three houses to look at with Lina. Each had similar layouts. A separate two-bedroom fully equipped guest house where Alexei's security could be housed. A basement with billiards and bar for entertainment. A theater room, small gym, dressing room, family room with wide screen TV. a great room with stone fireplace, master bedroom with fireplace, jacuzzi tub, huge walk-in dressing rooms large enough for two, wine cellar, laundry room, and large deck off each floor. As each of them were in serious need of upgrade and renovation, they were being sold at bargain prices.

After visiting each of the three, Lina liked them all. Alexei left the choice up to her. After selecting one of the three, Alexei asked her if she would help him pick out colors and materials for the upgrades. By doing so, he thought it would give him the opportunity to spend a lot of time with Lina. Lina's eyes widened with excitement as she gave Alexi a hug. "I have so many wonderful ideas that work with any of the houses Alexei. It will be great redoing any one of them together." As she said this to Alexei, Lina kept thinking about how she and Vladimir never shared an experience like the one put forth by Alexei. After making a down payment for the one Lina selected, Alexei dropped Lina off and returned to his quarters to prepare for his meeting with General Leopold Ivoshovsky at his home in Moscow.

Ivoshovsky lived on the outskirts of Moscow in a home surrounded by an iron fence. As a former chief of the General Staff of the military under Gorbousky and his successor, Ivoshovsky was the top-ranked military officer in the Russian armed forces. He is also the central "interpreter" of the military's needs for civilian leadership. "Like the Joint Chiefs of Staff of U.S. forces, the relationship of the general with the minister of defense and Russia's President is one of the pillars of Russian civil-military relations. The efficacy of contemporary Russian military leadership depends on the link between the minister and the chief. The former must balance out the military requests and civilian demands and limitations to achieve civilian objectives, while the latter must effectively couple military needs with the minister's orders" *(Center for International Strategic Studies)*. Upon taking over the Presidency, Vladimir forced Ivoshovsky into retirement because they did not share the same philosophy.

Ivoshovsky is waiting in his door when Alexei arrives. "Good morning, Czar Alexei, it is truly a pleasure to meet you. I have heard much about your exploits." Ivoshovsky invites Alexei into his study which is decorated wall to wall with his medals and photos of him with high-ranking Russians.

"I have also heard a lot of good things about you Leopold. "Your medals sure do exceed mine. I am quite impressed." Ivoshovsky looked at the medals and then Alexei. "Russian officials love to bestow medals upon their military and the military loves to receive them, even though they may not necessarily deserve them Alexei."

"How have you escaped the wrath of Vladimir by being so outspoken Leonard? Are you not concerned that you would suffer the same fate as others who have gone against him?"

Leonard sports a big grin on his face. "Vladimir may have forced me into retirement, but he does not mess with me because he knows that a good portion of the military supports me. I treated my troops well and with respect. In turn, many are more loyal to me than Vladimir. Vladimir wanted to invade Ukraine long ago when I was Chief of Staff, but I refused knowing that it would cause many deaths among our troops and many civilian casualties. You know that we military officers study military history in our war colleges. All one must do is read the carnage that resulted when Nicholas fought two needless wars. It is not a secret that I would like Vladimir to be gone from power. That is why he pushed me outside his inner circle."

This was all Alexei needed to hear. He now knew that he could be open with Ivoshovsky about his plans to oust Vladimir from office. "Can we trust one another and speak frankly Leonard? Like you, I am concerned about the fate of Russia, and I want to do something about it before it is too late. We are trying to form a coalition of leaders to depose Vladimir and drive him from power and we would like your support. Former President Gorbousky is enlisting the support of other Generals, and we would hope you would join us."

"I have been very instrumental to place some restraint on Vladimir using the pen and do not want to jeopardize my progress Alexei. If you can get a workable plan in place and key leaders support it, however, I will also accept whatever risk that may befall us. Remember the military saying, Lessons Learned" We do not want the same failed results when some of Hitlers inner circle tried to remove him. Let us make sure all the parts are together before we execute the plan."

Alexei and Ivoshovsky spent the next two hours getting to know one another. Feeling comfortable that he could trust Ivoshovsky, Alexei bade him farewell and assured him that he would soon be in touch. Each gives the other a firm handshake.

CHAPTER 22

THE FORMER CRIME BOSS

His next visit would be the former Russian crime boss, Simon Kodkavich. "Organized crime in Russia began in the Russian Empire, but it was not until the Soviet era that it emerged as leaders of prison groups in forced labor camps, and their honor code became more defined. With the end of World War II, the death of Joseph Stalin, and the fall of the Soviet Union, more gangs emerged in a flourishing black market, exploiting the unstable governments of the former Republics. In 2012, there were as many as 6,000 groups, with more than 200 of them having a global reach. Criminals of these various groups are either former prison members, corrupt officials and business leaders, people with ethnic ties, or people from the same region with shared criminal experiences and leaders. A former director of the FBI, said that the Russian mafia posed the greatest threat to U.S. national security in the mid-1990s." (86)

The meeting with the former crime boss was arranged by Oleg. Kodkavich lives in a sprawling mansion on the stretch of Khamovniki between Boulevard Ring and Garden Ring, known as the Golden Mile. It is downtown Moscow's most expensive housing area. In Rublyovka, government officials and wealthy businesspeople live in homes which cost up to $80 million. (87)

To get to Kodkavich's mansion, Alexei and his security had to pass through heavily guarded iron gates. The security stopped him at the gate and asked if anyone was packing weapons. Joey and his colleagues pulled out their weapons and Joe commented. "You mean like this?"

The guards informed them that they cannot enter unless they checked their weapons at the gate. Joey started to argue with the guards, but Alexei stopped him and asked the guards if at least Joey could accompany him to the main house while the rest of his security stays at the entrance with the guards. The one guard phoned the mansion and received approval for him to do so. Joey and Alexei were driven up a long and winding road to the mansion. Several guards were posted around the mansion with fully automatic weapons. Alexei asked the driver several questions, but he did not respond. He kept his eyes on the road, pulling up to the front door.

A butler greeted them at the door and directed them into a large ornate living room. After a short wait, an elderly man in his eighties entered the room. His stature was erect for a man of any age and his eyes were fixed on them. "What do I owe to the being a host to the new Czar of Russia? Oleg did give me an overview of the reason for your visit but said that you would go into the details when you arrived. Well gentlemen, the ball is in your court, and I am waiting for the details."

Alexei and Joey surveyed their surroundings and were quite impressed with what they saw. The walls were adorned with expensive paintings. On the surface, Kodkavich appears warm and open, but Alexei was told that underneath he is a calculative man who rarely reveals his true emotions to anyone except a trusted few. He is cunning and ruthless, and his greatest ability is his far-reaching vision. What interested Alexei the most in gaining his support is that he can plan an enemy's demise years in advance. On his dark side, Kodkavich justifies his former criminal actions by viewing established society as being more unfair than his world of crime.

Alexei goes into detail on the plan that he feels will end the carnage in Ukraine and why he feels Kodkavich, and his contacts can prove of great value. Kodkavich walks around the room with chin in hand. "Most of my life has been dedicated to padding my pockets using the crime syndicates. In the process, we have paid off politicians and key members of the political parties in power. I became sick of what I did at the expense of the Russian people and that is why I went strictly legit. As far as Vladimir is concerned, he was the most ruthless and untrusting of the politicians we had to deal with. I still must maintain a large and trained security force to protect me and my family from corrupt politicians and threats from a few of the Russian Mafia because of what I know. As for the Mafia people, they pose no threat to me because I kept my word when dealing with them and did not expose them.

As far as Ukraine is concerned, I was born and raised in Ukraine. Many of my family members still live in Ukraine and a good many of them are casualties of Vladimir's selfish ambitions. What you are proposing Alexei will not only give me the opportunity to atone for my sins, but I will be able to avenge those family members I have in Ukraine. I am all in Alexei."

Alexei and Joey stand up and embrace Kodkavich. "Thank you for your support, Simon. Alexei goes over one of the key roles he can play immediately and that is helping Mchail Navalka to escape from prison. Mchail is critical to rallying his followers to support the overthrow of Vladimir. Helping prisoners escape is one of my specialties Alexei. "I will have my people work on it immediately." "When the time comes Simon, we will also need you to use your special ops people to overpower the security defenses of Vladimir and taking out the generals who are loyal to him.

Alexei now needed to wait for word to come back from all who he met with to solidify his plan. His thoughts now turned back to Lina and her well-being. He phoned her again. Her voice was calm and welcoming. "I hope you are no longer stressed over what happened the other day, Lina." "Everything is fine Alexei. It is great to hear your voice."

Just then Joey interrupted Alexei. "The news just reported that Queen Elizabeth passed away Alexei. She was 96 years old. They are putting into effect the plans they have been exercising for a long time for her funeral. Invitations have gone out all over the world. Thus far no one from Russia has been invited to the service. Because you are a distance cousin to the Queen, you may receive an invitation. Especially as England did send a delegation to your coronation. "

Sure enough, Alexei received a phone call from Nikolai that Buckingham Palace sent him an invitation to attend the services for the Queen. Alexei looked at Joey with wonderment. "What do you think Joey, should we go or not." Yes Alexei, you need to go because it will give you an opportunity to network and enlist support from the United States and Great Britain to remove Vladimir." "Right on Joey. As a young kid, I watched the Queen as she matured into being one of the greatest monarchs to ever rule Great Britain. Little did I ever imagine in my wildest dreams that we were related and that I would be attending her funeral. She was such a great and gracious lady."

CHAPTER 23

BRITISH COUSINS

Alexei gets ready to leave for Britain but thinks it best to bring a delegation with him. He invites Gorbousky because he once had a distant friendship with the queen and future King Charles. Alexei thought about Vladimir but knew that would not go over big with leaders of nations that oppose his invasion of Ukraine. Instead, he used Britain's distaste for Vladimir as an excuse to invite Lina.

He phoned Vladimir and gave him the opportunity to appoint Lina as his representative. "Are you taking Lina as my representative or are you taking Lina because you want more time to be with her Alexei?" "Look Vladimir, it is up to you, but I cannot think of anyone else that would better represent the people of Russia. With her being an Olympic gold medalist that competed against and intermingled with British Athletes, she will be well received by the royal family and the British people. I will give you my word that everything will be proper." Vladimir reluctantly gave his consent. Alexei phones Lina to invite her to the services. Lina enthusiastically accepts the invitation and tell Alexei that she will be ready whenever he wants to leave.

Alexei picks Lina up and meets Gorbousky at the airport. They are pleasantly surprised to see that the Russian parliament arranged to have an aircraft waiting to transport them to Britain. Parliament realized that Alexei has become extremely popular and needs an aircraft that will safely transport him to the far corners of Russia and other countries. They thought it fitting to commission an airplane like the one used by the President of Russia. The Ilyushin Il-96 is a shortened, long-range, and advanced technology development of the Soviet Union's first widebody airliner.

The Il-96 features supercritical wings, is used as the main Russian presidential aircraft. The aircraft is designed specifically to protect Russian leadership at all costs through a worst-case scenario. It can transmit encrypted messages from any altitude to any point throughout the entire world. It is nicknamed 'the Flying Kremlin.' *(88)*

Upon Alexei and his delegation arriving at Heathrow Airport, a driver and car sent by Buckingham Palace meets them. Nikolai planned for Alexei and his delegation to stay at a hotel, but the Royal family insisted that he stay at Buckingham Palace. They missed a huge reception for dignitaries hosted the night before by the new King.

Upon arriving at Buckingham palace, they were greeted by a royal footman. "The footman is the head of the Household, supervising the team responsible for services at Buckingham Palace (Photo 22) and overseeing operational activities.

Photo 23-Buckingham Palace

He manages team schedules, travel planning and daily tasks, and ensures that exceptional service is provided, whether for a small lunch or a state banquet. As for organizing elements of the Queen or King's programs, the Lord Chamberlain Office takes the lead.

Buckingham Palace has served as the official London residence of the UK's sovereigns since 1837 and today is the administrative headquarters of the Monarch. Although in use for the many official events and receptions held by The King, the State Rooms at Buckingham Palace are open to visitors every summer. Buckingham Palace has 775 rooms. These include 19 State rooms, 52 Royal and guest bedrooms, 188 staff bedrooms, 92 offices and 78 bathrooms. In measurements, the building is 108 meters long across the front, 120 metres deep (including the central quadrangle) and 24 metres high. More than 50,000 people visit the Palace each year as guests to State Banquets, lunches, dinners, receptions, and Garden Parties. His Majesty also holds weekly audiences with the Prime Minister and receives newly appointed foreign Ambassadors at Buckingham Palace." Alexei was awe struck by the size and grandeur of the palace. (89) The Palace has fifty-two royal and guest bedrooms, all full of guests. Those invited to stay in the palace included the King of Norway, the Grand Duke of Luxembourg, the King of the Netherlands, the King of Belgium, the King of Spain, the King of Sweden, Queen of Denmark, and sheikhs from the Mideast. Many other dignitaries were also provided with rooms at the Palace if they chose to stay.

Because Alexei was related to the Queen, he was given a two-bedroom suite. Gorbousky was given his own room. The housekeepers assumed that Alexei and Lina were a couple, so they did not make up the other bedroom. Keeping true to his word to Vladimir, Alexei requested that the other bedroom be made ready for Lina. After a long flight and enjoying some refreshments in the sitting room of Alexei and Lina's suite, they all turned in for the night.

Just as Alexei was falling off to sleep, his bedroom door opened, and Lina climbed into bed with him. "This place is so big; it reminds me of a mausoleum. No wonder the former wife of Prince Andrew did not enjoy staying in Buckingham Palace. What is one to do if they want a midnight snack? I just cannot sleep by myself in such a large and poshly decorated bedroom by myself." Alexei laughed; he could not say no after looking into her sorrowful eyes. "Okay climb in but remember we are only snuggling up against one another." The bed was so huge that he thought he was assured of a good night's sleep. Every time he moved over to the other end of the bed, however, Lina snuggled right up against him. After a while she stopped. He suddenly realized that he was getting used to having her warmth next to him, so he moved over holding her back against his chest and wrapping his one arm around her. She gently placed her hand on his.

They woke up the next morning with a tap on the door. It was a maid. "Your breakfast will soon be served in the sitting room your excellency." Alexei phoned Gorbousky and invited him to join them. They then dressed and left for the services in West Minister Abbey. The streets were lined with thousands of people and large screens were set up in Hyde Park and other parts of the country.

Alexei, Lina, and Gorbousky were ushered to a prominent seat in the church close to the President and former Presidents of the United States. All sat quietly while they waited for the caisson carrying the Queen to arrive at the church. The service was magnificent and befitting a Queen that was the longest serving monarch in England. "Over eleven million people in the United States watched the funeral of Britain's Queen Elizabet. the first time TV cameras were allowed at the funeral of a British monarch. The BBC said most people in Britain tuned in to the event. Viewership across BBC networks and its Player streaming service peaked at 22.4 million people. About 32.5 million watched at least three minutes, making it the biggest audience since the closing ceremonies of the London Olympics in 2012." (90))

The service was concluded with a sermon from the Archbishop of Canterbury and hymns, followed by a two-minute silence within Westminster Abbey and across the nation. Afterwards, the national anthem was sung and all in attendance, except Alexei, started the return to their quarters to prepare for their departure the next day. Instead, Alexei had Joey corner the U.S. Presidents chief of staff and ask him for a brief meeting at the back of the church.

Upon greeting him, Alexei gives him a brief overview on how he wants to neutralize Vladimir to stop the war in Ukraine. Recalling his promise to Ferdinand and Oleg about providing safe passage for their families, Alexei requested for their safe passage. The Chief of Staff was pleased with what he heard from Alexei and assured him that NATO would do all it could to support his efforts, and the U.S. would arrange for the yacht's safe passage. The two men shook on it and returned to their respective quarters.

That night, there came a knock on the door of Alexei and Lina's suite. When Alexei opened the door, he was surprised to see the Queen's youngest son, Prince Edward. "Could you please accompany me for an hour or two Cousin Alexei?" Alexei was surprised to hear a prince of England address him as a cousin when he only knew Edward from what he saw on television or in the tabloids.

For years before discovering he was the heir to the Russian throne, he could only dream about what it was like to be a member of the royal family. Now, the son of a great queen was standing before him, addressing him as a cousin. "Of course, I will go along with you Cousin Edward." Edward smiled and replied. "It is funny to find a long-lost cousin, no pun intended." Alexei and the Prince walked out of the Palace to a waiting limo. The limo took them to Windsor Castle. Alexei was surprised to learn from the prince that there was a royal library housed at Windsor Castle and that was their destination.

"The current Royal Library was established by William IV (r.1830–37) in a series of three rooms adapted from the State Apartments at Windsor Castle. These three rooms are referred to as the Upper Library and consist of Room I, adapted from Queen Catherine of Braganza's state bedchamber; Room II, formerly the private bedroom of the Tudor monarchs; and Room III, Queen Elizabeth I's indoor walking-gallery." (91)

Alexei found it very intriguing that the prince would take the time to show him through the collection. "I once watched a documentary you did on your uncle, the duke of Windsor. Your presentation was outstanding and very impressive. You need to do more of it." The prince thanked him and said that this is one of the main reasons that he wanted to show some documents in the royal library to Alexei."

I feel compelled to set the record straight that my great uncle was very loyal to England. "For now, however, I need to show you something special in the collection that I discovered when researching my great uncles' papers, the Duke of Windsor. It is a sheet torn from the diary of my great uncle and buried in another manuscript. He wrote about how his father, King George V, told his cousin Nicholas that he was sorry and apologized for not giving him and his family sanctuary. The uncanny thing about George and Nicholas was that they looked much alike.

My great uncle wrote in his diary that Nicholas told him that he should never have abdicated his responsibility as ruler. I think my great uncle had second thoughts about revealing that Nicholas thought it irresponsible for a monarch to shirk his duties by abdicating. This is why he tore this page from his diary and hid it beneath another manuscript. I believe his documenting such an admission by Nicholas in his diary might someday come back to rekindle his regrets and tarnish his own reputation. "

He wrote in his diary that his father's decision to not give Nicholas sanctuary agonized him for the rest of his life and the murder of the Russian royal family, your ancestors, shook his father's innate feelings of decency. "George V had personally planned to rescue Nicholas with a British cruiser but then abandoned the rescue. His reason for doing so was attributed to the growing labor unrest, the rise of socialism in Britain, and Nicholas being dubbed as "bloody Nicholas" after he ordered the shooting of peaceful demonstrators in St. Petersburg. Faced with all the turmoil going on, George V felt that giving his cousin Nicholas sanctuary might compromise his position as King and subsequently bring down the British monarchy." (92)

"I guess my reason for sharing all this with you Alexei is to ease what I perceived to be a burden of guilt and sorrow by King George V. As an historian, it also gives me the opportunity to share and discuss it with a direct descendant of the Romanov dynasty. You see Alexei, I never told anyone about this admission of regretting to support Nicholas II by George V because I did not want it to rekindle all those hurtful and unanswerable questions as to why an ancestor of mine did not act to save the lives of those he once cherished. Furthermore, I felt compelled to explain to you on behalf of my family about George V not taking the necessary steps to save yours. Especially as his inaction helped to create a huge disconnect in the Romanov's claim to the Russian throne. All King George V had to do to protect the possibility of your family's right of succession to the Romanov crown was to give Nicholas and his family sanctuary. By taking the path of least resistance, however, he may have denied your family the possibility of someday retaking its rightful place on the Russian throne. Furthermore, it may not have plunged Russia into a communistic type of government. I cannot keep from thinking what it may have been like if the same situation would have happened to my family."

Alexei continues to ponder what he read in the Duke of Windsor's diary and what has been said by Prince Edward. "Thank you for revealing this to me cousin. I am inclined to agree with you that it would be best to leave this document as one of those voids in the annals of history. It would do no one any good to publish such a document. I tend to follow the philosophy of an old-time comedian. When he reached the ripe old age of one hundred, he was asked what he thought about his life when looking back on it. He simply said, "I never look in a rear-view mirror." I agree with that philosophy but also, I believe in the military saying, "Lessons learned." Meaning the only reason I reflect on the past is to learn how to avoid mistakes and improve upon our actions in the future."

As Edward filed the document in a file marked confidential, he thanked Alexei for agreeing to bury the document and not disclosing its contents. Edward gave Alexei a complete tour of the royal library and a look at some manuscripts from his family dating back to the 1700's. After spending a few hours together, Edward dropped Alexei at Buckingham palace. "Don't you live here with your family Edward?" "No Alexei, my wife Sophie and I live with our two children at Bagshot Park, approximately thirty miles from London. Our home is big but much more cosey and private than Buckingham Palace. King William the IV and other royalties lived there over two hundred years ago. You are welcome to visit any time."

Having a desire to learn more about British royalty, Alexei asks Edward why the title Earl is bestowed upon him and not the title of Duke. "I chose the title of Earl because of its connotations with one of my favorite films, Shakespeare in Love. My mother, however, wanted me to take the title "Duke of Edinburgh" when my father died to continue his work. "Alexei looked in wonderment at Edward. His philosophy was not that much different than his own. "That is very fascinating Edward and a point of view that I share and can respect."

When Alexei entered his quarters, he discovered Lina was fast asleep in his bed. She was quite tired due to all the pomp and ceremony that occurred that day. He quietly got ready and slipped into bed, giving her a kiss on the forehead. She half opened her eyes long enough to give Alexei a smile. She then reached up and pulled him towards her for a hug and passionate kiss. He laid alongside her for a long time holding her in his arms, not waking until the next morning.

Alexei, along with Lina and Gorbousky, prepared for their long journey home. Picking up a newspaper at the airport, they were dismayed to see that Vladimir spoke again about inflicting upon the Ukrainian people whatever it took to bring Ukraine to its knees, including the possible use of Tactical nuclear weapons.

From his military background, Alexei knew the devastation caused by a nuclear weapon. To gain some background on Russia's nuclear capabilities, he asks Gorbousky to brief him on the capability of Russian nuclear weapons. Gorbousky goes over the details with Alexei. "Fifty percent of nuclear weapons were eliminated under my successor but some 7,000 are still stored throughout Russia. Most are short-ranged and designed to be used on the battlefield against troop formations, tanks, or military installations and bunkers. The ultimate risk is that the one-time use of a tactical nuclear might prompt an escalation of an all-out nuclear war. Several nuclear explosions over modern cities would kill tens of millions of people. Casualties from a major nuclear war between the US and Russia would reach hundreds of millions and could destroy life as we know it."

Alexei looks stunned at what Gorbousky just said, making it all that more important to enact his plan as soon as possible to remove Vladimir from office and eliminate the threat of nuclear proliferation. "We need to get back to Russia as soon as we can. Call the crew to get ready to leave as soon as we reach the airport Joey." Alexei phoned Prince Edward and gave him a brief overview of their dilemma. Hearing of Alexei's need for a hasty departure, Prince Edward made available one of his top drivers and waited to bid him farewell. Alexei and Edward gave one another a hardy handshake and Edward bade them God speed and told Alexei to let him know if there was anything he could do on his end, including expediting their take off.

CHAPTER 24

FORMULATING THE PLAN

Upon arriving at the airport, Alexei's crew informed him
that they encountered the same problem on their return to Moscow as
they did on reaching London. With hundreds of Russian diplomats
being asked to leave European nations, the journey back home for
Russian based aircraft is not as simple as flying from point A to point
B. "Russian aircraft now must use an extreme circuitous route. Instead
of simply flying a straight flight path across Poland into the Russian
capital, Russian aircraft now need to skirt the European mainland by
flying over the Baltic Sea before being able to enter Russian airspace."
(93) Prince Edward expedited the clearance of Alexei's aircraft
through British air space but there was not enough time to do the same
with other NATO countries.

With the high-speed capability of the Ilyushin aircraft, the flight
across the European continent into Moscow would normally have been
a short routine flight. Now hours have been added to their flight time
because of the current airspace restrictions. Likewise, Alexei's aircraft
will have to abide by the same restrictions. Alexei and Gorbousky are
concerned that such a delay could dramatically affect their averting a
catastrophic event for the European continent and the Russian people.
The only way they could communicate was by phone and their concern
was that Vladimir's people could listen in on whatever
communications they may send.

As soon as they entered Russian airspace, they were greeted by a
Russian Sukhoi SU-30 fighter. The twin seat, fighter is primarily used

for tactical deployment against ground and naval targets. (94) It is not as effective when used for air-to-air combat. This is one of three types of aircraft that was shot down by the Ukrainian air force. Analysts noted that the reason for their being shot down was due to the absence of backup support to the Russian aircraft and the enduring strength of Ukrainian air-defenses, as well as Russian air-warfare doctrine that assigns warplanes to bomb preplanned targets instead of training its pilots to think and act independently. (93)

Alexei and Joey were not pleased to see the Russian fighter for they could not help wondering if it was sent by Vladimir to intercept their aircraft. Both Alexei and Gorbousky went up to the cockpit of their aircraft to listen in on the conversation between the fighter pilot and their pilots. The fighter pilot informed Alexei's pilots that he had orders to escort them to a military base close to the Baltic Sea, Chernyakhovsk Air Base. When asked who gave the order and why a change in course, the only excuse given by the fighter pilot was to clear their aircraft for entrance into Russian air space. "The military base where they may be forced to land is located southwest of the city of Chernyakhovsk and is a medium sized interceptor airfield." (95) Hearing all this, their worst fears were confirmed that this action was the doing of Vladimir. With Lina aboard, they knew that Vladimir would never shoot down their aircraft but could force it to land. If they landed, they surmised that Vladimir would abscond with Lina and detain or even incarcerate them.

Alexei and Gorbousky looked at one another with a puzzled look. Gorbousky then spoke up. He directed the pilot to hand him the air to surface phone. Making a call to General Leopold Ivoshovsky, Gorbousky explained their predicament. Ivoshovsky took immediate control of the situation. "The regional commander over that area used to serve for me. I will ask him to intercede. As Vladimir's fighter came from another air base, my friend will not be held accountable because the fighter that has intercepted your aircraft has no authority over the air space you have entered. My friend is tasked to protect Russian aircraft in your sector and by his interceding will not put him at risk with Vladimir. Again, the fighter pilot radioed the order to land their aircraft at the military base. To give them more time, Alexei's pilot said that he was waiting for air traffic controllers to change his course.

A half hour passed and from the fighter pilot's communications, they could see that he was getting very impatient. Suddenly two Sukhoi Su-34 fighter jets appeared on the horizon.

Photo 24-Russian Sukhoi Su-34 Fighter Jet

When it comes to a dog fight between fighter jets, the Sukhoi Su-34 is far superior to the Sukhoi Su-30 being flown by Vladimir's pilot. As superior an aircraft fighter it is, it was ironic that "the Ukrainian defense ministry claimed its forces shot down three Russian air force Sukhoi Su-34 fighter-bombers on Thursday, extending an unprecedented streak of aerial kills that allegedly has cost the Russians 13 warplanes in 11 days: 10 Su-34s, a pair of Sukhoi Su-35 fighters and a rare Beriev A-50 radar plane."(96)

It is a multirole fighter for all weather and designed for air-to-air interdiction. The Su-34's climbed on each side of the Su-30 and ordered the pilot to stand down. At first, the Su-30 fighter tried to resist but could not give valid reasons why he was way out of his surveillance air space. As he had an oversight into air space near Moscow, he could

219

not justify the reason for being way outside his area of responsibility. At the same time, he was sworn to secret as to who tasked him to intercept Alexei's aircraft. The only alternative open to him was to pull away and return to patrolling his air space north of Moscow. As a result of the unauthorized encounter by the Su-30, the two Su-34's was given clearance to escort Alexei's aircraft until it landed safely in Moscow.

As soon as his aircraft landed, Alexei and Joey started organizing a meeting with the Russian leaders that agreed to support his plan to remove Vladimir from power. He tasked Joey to locate a place where they could safely meet without any prying eyes or ears. He then made sure that Lina safely reached her home. Prior to her departure, she gave Alexei a big hug and passionate kiss.

Upon arriving at her home, she found Vladimir waiting for her. "Once again, you jilted me for Alexei!" "No, I did not Vladimir. You approved my being a member of the Russian delegation to Great Britain. I like Alexei very much, but we have never been intimate. Unlike you, he takes the time to have fun with me and knows how to treat a lady." Hearing this infuriates Vladimir. He orders his security to forcibly put Lina into his Limo. Lina struggles but Vladimir's bodyguards are too strong to ward them off. Lina sits on the far side of the back seat with her arms folded in disgust. She warns Valdimir and his security about abducting her against her will. "You are doing an act of Kidnapping that the Russian courts impose stringent sentences on Kidnappers." Vladimir ignores Lina but you could sense that his security was concerned about what she just said. Vladimir orders his bodyguards to drive to his costal palace.

In the meantime, Joey was busy working on freeing Michail from prison. He called Koskovich who agreed to broker his escape. "Russia is among the countries with the highest number of prisoners. Hundreds of thousands of inmates are supervised by an elaborate apparatus of the Federal Penitentiary Service (FSIN). This extended system is used as a tool for exercising control over society and solidifying their power.

It impacts the how shared norms and values are being formed in Russian.

At present, over 467,000 individuals are incarcerated in Russia's prisons. In terms of the number of prisoners per 100,000 inhabitants, Russia is ranked first in Europe and 17th globally. The present number of inmates in Russia's prisons is among the lowest in the country's history and has been gradually declining over recent years. A decade ago, the number of prisoners in Russia was almost double the present figure. The decrease in the number of inmates has been linked to the fact that the courts pronounce prison sentences for minor crimes less frequently and tend to apply other penalties." (97)

In the case of Navalka, his imprisonment was strictly political. The prison where he was imprisoned was not that fortified because of its remote location in Siberia. The superintendent warned the new prisoners that they would never survive the harsh terrain of Siberia should they even succeed in escaping.

To arrange Navalka's escape, Kodkavich had some of the guards paid to look the other way while he escaped at the back end of a laundry truck that entered the prison every day. The guards arranged for Navalka to work in the prison's laundry so he could hide in a laundry bag. The prison changing of the guard at the same time made his escape that much easier.

The laundry truck drove through the gates to pick up the laundry right on schedule. The truck was given only a cursory look before it drove out the gates. So as not to give away the location of the meeting place, the driver dropped Navalka off miles from the prison where he was picked up by one of Kodkavich's men who hid him temporarily. Navalka looked forward to enjoying a hot meal and warm bed compared to the awful time he spent in a stark prison that had little heat and only essentials for survival.

As for Joey seeking a safe place for the Russian leaders to meet, he eventually secured a secluded and easy to protect place that was owned by Oleg, a former summer palace on a mountain top. The palace had towers manned by a highly trusted staff devoted to protecting Oleg and any of his guests. It had one road in and out that twisted down a mountain side and had enough rooms capable of housing all who were to attend. The structure was built of concrete anchored into the mountain with panoramic views from all sides, making protection easy to provide. To enhance security and screen intruders, there was an old mansion located at the base of the mountain just on the other side of the gate. The complex is reachable by car or there is a helicopter pad that can accommodate two helicopters.

Alexei had Joey send messages to their coalition of leaders to meet at Oleg's retreat in three days. Word came back that they all agreed to meet and even the crime boss Kodkavich planned to join them.

Finally, the day had come for all to arrive. Alexei was the first to arrive and was greeted by Oleg and Ferdinand. Alexei's and Joey's security force mixed in with the others now in place. What really gave them protection, however, was the armed guards that came with the former crime boss Kodavich and the security teams retained by other Russian leaders. Kodavich brought an elite team of former special ops soldiers trained in covert warfare and equipped with more than the basic weapons. They were military members of the Soviet Union's Spetsnaz GRU, special operations units that were also trained in preserving military intelligence. Induction into Spetsnaz is a brutal, 5-month long process designed to strip away the dignity of a soldier and instill extreme toughness. There is a high level of emphasis on the sheer strength of soldiers during combat missions, a commonly used tactic to keep the enemy guessing. Spetsnaz training includes assault course work under live fire, martial arts instruction with live bladed weapons, how to be stealth like, including the expert use of weaponry such as the ballistic knife and the more mundane entrenching tool, which results in many recruits receiving minor stabs and flesh wounds. The lethal effectiveness of one special ops soldier is equivalent to the combat effectiveness of twenty basic soldiers. (98) They are highly loyal to Kodavich and came armed with stingers and fully automatic weapons.

Some of the special operations men were posted at the entrance at the foot of the mountain and in the old mansion with their high-tech surveillance equipment and weaponry. Nothing could get past them. The palace was fortified as strong as Camp David, the President's personal retreat in the United States.

Both Kodavich and Oleg hand-picked their security people, all of which were members of elite Russian forces and represent the best of those forces. All had to possess the highest security clearances during their military tenure before Kodavich would hire them.

CHAPTER 25

BUILDING THE COALITION

Oleg, Ferdinand, and Alexei greeted everyone upon their arrival. They were particularly surprised by how highly polished and well-spoken Kodavich was. This was attributed to the fact that his parents sent him to an American university and demanded that he earn a college degree before returning to join the family business of crime, After Kodavich became the godfather of the family, he opted to leave the crime syndicate and take his family businesses into a realm of law-biding legitimacy.

Long stretch limos wound up the compound's two-mile-long road to unload their charges, most having SUV chase cars following with security. Each was assigned a room and asked to join everyone in the mansion's conference room for cocktails and refreshments. The first night was dedicated to giving everyone the opportunity to get to know one another and each gave their own introduction and background. Prior to and during dinner, the leaders were treated to Russian Oestra Caviar which is one of the best kinds of caviar that you can buy. They were also served various wines and liquors including Yorsh which is a popular Russian mixed beverage made with a combination of beer and vodka. After savoring the good food and drink and telling stories of the old Russia, everyone turned in for the night. Before retiring to their respective bedrooms, each of the participants were given a packet that outlined the plan proposed by Alexei.

Everyone awoke early to the typical Russian breakfast, big & thin pancakes (Blini), cottage cheese pancakes (Syrniki), and buckwheat porridge (Kasha). Russia was traditionally a tea drinking country, but coffee is fast becoming a preferred drink. During the time of the Soviet Union, most people were choosing black tea as their preferred hot beverage for breakfast, lunch, or dinner.

The meeting started early the next morning. Each had a more detailed packet of Alexei's plan dropped in front of them and Alexei had a slide presentation on a screen ready to roll. Alexei's goal was to have them fill in some of the blanks as to who could execute what part of the plan. All were silent for several minutes while reviewing the plan. Oleg first welcomed everyone to his home and then introduced Alexei even though they all personally met with him before today's meeting.

Alexei had the safety of Lina on his mind. After the ordeals she went through with Vladimir, he was concerned that Vladimir might try to force himself on her again. Alexei repeatedly tried phoning her. After numerous failed attempts to reach her by phone, he starts to think the worst. Before starting his presentation. he takes Joey aside and asks him to track her down.

Alexei opened his presentation, thanking everyone for agreeing to participate in such a risky mission. When making his presentation, he felt it was extremely important not to sugar coat what could befall anyone who participated. "Like you, I am willing to put my life on the line for not only those of the Ukrainian people but also for the soldiers and civilian population of our mother Russia."

Alexei gives an overview of the Ukrainian casualties reported to date. "The total number of Ukrainian and Russian troops killed or wounded since the war in Ukraine began 18 months ago is nearing 500,000, U.S. officials said, a staggering toll as Russia assaults its next-door neighbor and tries to seize more territory. The number of refugees has surpassed 6.6 million." (99)

Russia is reconstituting its force in the short term by refurbishing older equipment at sufficient rates, mobilizing personnel, and recruiting volunteers. Most of Russia's equipment delivered to the front lines is refurbished equipment. It is suitable for soldiers' needs but is qualitatively worse than newer equipment. If early 2024 loss rates continue, Russia risks depleting available Soviet-era stockpiles for certain types of equipment in 2026." (100)

Alexei next reports on the economic impact of the war. "Vladimir has devastated Russia's economy that will take years to recover. He continues to lie to the Russian people that his invasion is about peace keeping when it is about satisfying his ego to resurrect the Soviet Union. He must be stopped at all costs before the damage has gone too far to repair. He has put the entire world at risk with his threats of nuclear retaliation if he deems necessary. If he launches tactical nuclear weapons like he has threatened to do, it could catapult us into an all-out nuclear war.

Just then, Ferdinand and Oleg chimed in to reinforce the plea by Alexei. Ferdinand was the first to speak. "I know we are all in agreement that this unwarranted war must be stopped, and it is time to impeach President Vladimir. We have enough influence in this room to accomplish this and to stop his insanity and each of us can play a key role."

Oleg was the next to speak. "Just lending my mountain retreat to host this meeting shows my resolve to take on the task ahead of us. I am sure you would not have come unless you felt the same way as me."

All nodded their heads yes while also lifting their drinks in agreement.

Ferdinand spoke again. "You all know Alexei as the Czar, but you may not know his background where he served at the Pentagon at the highest level of the command structure for three Chairman of the Joint Chiefs of staff and the Secretary of Defense. While there, he was part of a team that helped formulate a plan to proliferate the wars in Afghanistan and Iraq. He also helped craft homeland defense. He is now willing to apply his military skills to formulate a plan to change the course of this war and force a change in leadership. Please present your plan Alexei.

"Thank you for your introduction, Ferdinand. Timing on this mission is everything. Everyone will have to pull their weight and implement their part of the plan at precisely the same time. Each of your roles is outlined in the packets we left on the table. Feel free to volunteer if you wish to accomplish other components of the plan or change specifics of the plan.

"The first strategy is to refute Vladimir's contention that he is going into Ukraine to keep the peace. "As you know, one of the United Nations missions is peace keeping. They can muster a force of anywhere from 67,000 to over 100,000 among their member nations." (101) We need to get the United States to ask for a vote in the UN to agree to send in a peace keeping force into Ukraine. The UN can then demand that Vladimir pull his forces out of Ukraine in place of the UN peace keeping force. Even if he refuses, it will further expose Vladimir as to his true intention, to rebuild the empire of the Soviet Union. I have taken it upon myself to send an emissary to the U.S. embassy in Poland to make the request which hopefully should occur in three-four days.

"If the United Nations does not act in a timely manner, we need to have a plan B in place and that is to forcibly remove Vladimir from office as allowed by the Russian constitution and under the auspices that he is not fit to lead Russia through this turmoil he has started. So that we do not breach the Russian constitution, we must request the Duma to call for a vote to impeach him before forcibly removing him."

"In accordance with the current "Russian constitution, the removal from office of the President is regulated by article 93 of the Constitution. It provides for impeachment by the State parliament (the Duma) and should be accompanied by the opinion of the Supreme Court of Russia and the Constitutional Court of Russia After indictment, the decision to remove a president from office is voted on by the Federation Council. The decision of the State Duma to indict

227

and the decision of the Federation Council to remove the President from office must be accepted by two thirds of the respective chambers (300 and 114 votes respectively). The initiative to vote on indictment must be supported by no fewer than one third (150) of deputies of the State Duma and the conclusion of a special Commission formed by the State Duma. The decision of the Federation Council on removal from office of the President of the Russian Federation must be accepted by vote no later than three months after the bringing of charges by the State Duma against the President. If within this period the Federation Council does not vote for removal, charges against the President shall be considered rejected. As you can see, time will be of the essence to have the Federation Council vote for his removal." (102)

To get the Duma to act, someone will have to judge Vladimir incompetent, or he does something that places our country at risk. Who among you is best to initiate a vote of incompetency once we gather enough evidence?

Gorbousky raises his hand. "There are many members of parliament that owe allegiance to me. I personally got them elected and they owe allegiance to me more than Vladimir. I will lobby the Duma for his impeachment. Ferdinand, you, and Oleg contribute considerable money to get them elected and spend a lot on entertainment to buy their votes. I think the two of you can be very instrumental to garnering the necessary votes."

Ferdinand and Oleg nodded in agreement to join Gobousky in procuring votes in the Duma for Vladimir's impeachment.

Alexei gives the three of them a thumbs up. "Even if we are successful in getting all the powers to be to vote for his impeachment, we may still have to initiate plan B. Vladimir still has a good deal of allegiance among those military and political leaders that reap his gifts of expensive homes and contribute towards their lavish lifestyles. They may stage a coup to keep him in the office. In that event, the Duma will have to direct us to forcibly remove him from office if he does not go voluntarily.

Plan B needs to have a military force component. We need one of you to neutralize the military from intervening if we must forcibly remove Vladimir from office. Immediately Generals Trachesky and Ivankoff raised their hands.

General Trachesky stands up to speak. "I am not certain that we can enlist the support of the Chief of the General Staff, Valen Serasino. Along with General Ivankoff, however, we can muster enough of those generals under him to ward off a military coup. Many of those generals served under us when they were junior officers. Because of us, they quickly rose through the ranks and owe their allegiance to us and Russia. General Ivankoff agreed with Trachesky by nodding his head in a yes affirmation.

Alexei also explained how they need to find a way to divert any tactical nuclear missiles that Vladimir may launch. "I once also served at the military's Space and Missile Systems center in El Segundo California. They may be able to give us directions on how to interfere with the launch systems should Vladimir decide to launch tactical nuclear warheads. I think it can be done by jamming the satellite's guiding system for those missiles and then inputting our own coordinates. I spoke to the U.S. Presidents chief of staff about our overall plan while attending the services for the Queen. I will reach out to him again to see if he can gain approval for NATO to intercede to safely divert those missiles."

"While serving at Space and Missile Systems, I learned that Northern Defense systems has a system called DIVERSION, where they use it to protect the United States from a wide range of manned and unmanned air and missile threats." "Their web site says they do it by integrating sensors, weapons, and command and control to acquire, track, verify, engage, and defeat current and evolving threats. They refer specifically to the maneuver of short-range air defense missiles and display a counter hypersonic system on their web site." (103)

"We need to enlist the support of NATO to use this system that can not only jam the launch of a missile but can also divert it to another target. I can think of a great target for diverting those missiles. The target that I am thinking about is in East Asia, on the Northern part of a peninsula that is between the East Sea of Japan and the Yellow Sea, North Korea's military bases. With their being a thorn in the side of neighboring countries and North American countries, we would be doing a great service if we can divert any launches to take out their ballistic missile bases. Because their bases are so isolated and protected, there are no civilians living within hundreds of miles of their bases, virtually eliminating the possibility of civilian casualties. I will see if I can contact America's Secretary of Defense to hopefully set up a diversion system using their systems."

All the Russian leaders were especially excited about this possibility and gave it a thumbs up to this idea. Their only reservation was the possibility of North Korea retaliating with one of their nuclear weapons. Alexei assured them that he had a follow-up plan to avert this from happening.

Alexei goes to the next slide in his plan. "The truthful broadcast of what is going on in Ukraine is of great importance. Once the people learn why Vladimir invaded a peace-loving nation and the devastation, he has caused the Ukrainian people as well as the casualties among our soldiers, they will rally to our side and want Vladimir's head. Ferdinand and Oleg have already agreed to bring this about. They own two of the largest TV stations and can give you some oversight as to how they will broadcast it using television and radio stations across Russia.

Ferdinand and Oleg nod their heads in agreement and start their brief. "As you know, television is the most popular medium in Russia, with 74% of the population watching national television channels routinely and 59% routinely watching regional channels. There are 3300 television channels in total. Before going digital television, three channels have a nationwide outreach, reaching over ninety percent of the Russian territory. We have access to those channels." (104)

"The Rights and Freedoms of the Person and Citizen of Russia is provided for in the Russian Constitution. Where Vladimir has sadly been able to keep the truth of the Ukraine war from the people is where he amended the Constitution to permit this right to be limited when in the judgement of the government, it is better to protect the Constitution and morality of the people by limiting their access to the news. His amendment to the Constitution provides him with the power to limit freedom of speech and establish limits for its expression." (105) "We can circumvent his control over nuclear weapons by using the Soviet communication satellite, Molniya.

Photo 25-Russian Communications Satellite Molniya

"Molniya was a first-generation Russian communications satellite (COMSAT) orbited to assess and perfect a system of radio communications and television broadcasting using earth satellites as active transponders and to experiment with the system in practical use.
The basic function of the satellite was to relay television programs and long-distance two-way multichannel telephone, photo telephone, and telegraph links from Moscow to the various standard ground receiving stations in the 'Orbita' system." (106) We feel we can easily jam those stations long enough

for us to broadcast the truth about the Ukraine war." Once again, all the leaders nodded their approval.

Ferdinand and Oleg sit down, and Alexei returns to the podium to bring up his next slide. "We also need the churches to get the word out about the atrocities being inflicted on the Ukrainian people and to rally the people against Vladimir and any elected official that supports it. To accomplish this, we need to remove Vladimir's religious puppet, Patriarch Chrill, as leader of the Russian Orthodox church and replace him with one that is sympathetic to our cause. We think the best replacement for him would be the leader of the Russian Orthodox church in Ukraine." Before Alexei could go on, he was interrupted by the former crime boss, Kodavas.

"You need to say no more Alexei. I will handle Chrill. Along with my former colleagues, we channeled more money than Vladimir into the daily operations of the church. I am not a fan of Chrill and his ridiculous position on supporting the invasion of Ukraine. The anointed successor to Chrill holds a completely opposite view on the war. He is 100% against it. I think we can coerce Chrill to retire and step aside now for his successor."

Kodavich volunteers more to support the overall plan. "We can also provide much input into removing some of those high-ranking generals who supports Vladimir. The location of their homes is known to us, and they are not heavily fortified or guarded. The General Staff of the Armed Forces of the Russian Federation is equivalent to America's Chairman of the Joint Chiefs of Staff. He leads the military staff of the Russian Armed Forces, overseeing operational command of the armed forces under the Russian Ministry of Defense. The General Staff Building is located in Moscow on Znamenka Street in the Arbat District. Together with the Main Building of the Ministry of Defense and several Staff directorate office buildings nearby, it forms the so-called Arbat military district, which is the highest supreme command of the Russian Armed Forces. After dropping off their passengers at the Kremlin, most of their Limo drivers go straight to the hotels to earn money by using their vehicles as cabs. My people can intercept the drivers and then subdue the generals before they realize that the driver is not their own. Leave this part of the plan up to us."

Alexei nods his approval. "The is great to hear Simon and we will also need the input of your people to help shut down communications among the staff of Vladimir so they cannot rally the troops."

Alexei resumes his slide presentation. "Now comes the part that you will play Michail. We need you to go on national television to tell the true story to the Russian people. When we give the word, Ferdinand and Oleg will conceal your broadcast location so the authorities cannot stop you from broadcasting the truth."

Michail chokes up with emotion. "Thank you for arranging for my freedom and your protection. I look forward to supporting your plan by telling the truth about Vladimir to the Russian people."

While making his closing remarks, Alexei could not get Lina's whereabouts off his mind. "We will realize the least resistances by launching our plan when some of Vladimir's security forces will be on leave. As far as communicating with one another, Joey will hand out cell phones that have a top-secret security frequency. Please do not use them for personal use, only use them for communicating amongst ourselves. This concludes the meeting for today."

Everyone stays around for an hour having some refreshments and getting to know one another better. Suddenly, Joey enters the room and takes Alexei aside. "Neighbors told me that Vladimir forced Lina into his car and drove away with her. Before leaving, they overheard him say that he was taking her to his mansion on the Baltic Sea."

CHAPTER 26

PLANNING THE RESCUE

Alexei shows great concern. He turns quickly to look for Kodkavich before he goes out the door. Alexei hastily takes him aside. "I will need some of your best men to rescue a damsel in distress Simon. The mission will be risky and challenging. It will involve rescuing someone I care very about from the clutches of her former boyfriend, Vladimir. The men you provide must be trained in stealth like tactics and extremely trustworthy and faithful to whatever mission they undertake. I will also need them armed with state-of-the art weapons." Seeing the worry on the face of Alexei, Kodavich readily consents to providing the men and assures Alexei that all his security people are among the best of those who have a background in special ops. Alexei thanks him and refers Joey as the point of contact that will coordinate when he needs the men.

On his way back to his quarters, Alexei learns from the radio that Vladimir is using his media network to launch nationwide propaganda against him. He is blaming the casualties and failures of the war on Alexei. Hearing this, Alexei directed his driver to take him straight to the Kremlin with Joey and his security in tow. Upon his arrival, Joey and his team led the way up to Vladimir's office, pushing the Kremlin security guards to the side.

Vladimir prepared himself for Alexei's arrival by beefing up his security in the hallways leading to his office. As a result, Alexei and Joey could not get past the large bronze doors that leads into Vladimir's office.

Realizing it may be a mistake for him to not meet with Alexei, Vladimir waved his security off and beckoned for Alexei to enter his office but without Joey and his security. Vladimir distanced himself from Alexei as he did with all visitors by sitting at one end of a long table and Alexei sitting at the other end. Alexei accepted this as Vladimir's standard operating procedure.

With an angry look on his face, Alexei tears into Vladimir. "What gives you the right to blame me for your failures Vladimir? "

Vladimir leans forward in his chair with his hands resting face down on the table. Both postures of the men are confrontational.

Vladimir glares at Alexei while explaining why he has the right to blame him for the failures in Ukraine. "As Czar of Russia, you are at the top of the food chain. Referring to Russia's Supreme court ruling in 2008, the court ruled for full rehabilitation of Russia's last czar and his responsibility to oversee matters of state. Furthermore, the Russian Orthodox Church sanctified your family in 2000, recognizing the last Czar as a beacon of the Russian Orthodox faith. This sanctification makes you the current Czar responsible for all good or evil. Vladimir invokes a saying by a former U.S. President "The Buck Stops here" and the buck concerning Ukraine now stops with you Alexei."

Alexei places both his hands firmly on the conference table. "Your analogy is preposterous and ill-thought-out Vladimir. First, I was not even crowned Czar until after you encircled the borders of Ukraine with troops. To re-coin an old saying, "You seem to want to point the finger at the wrong person, when you should be pointing the thumb"! According to the amendment you crafted to the constitution, it may have granted me some oversight but never gave me the power to cause or avert any adverse actions in Ukraine."

"In the U.S. military we had a saying "Lessons Learned," meaning you learn not to make the same mistakes as your predecessors. You evidently do not subscribe to such a philosophy.

You should also take a page from Russian history where Nicholas was overthrown and executed. With your lavish lifestyle, place, and autocratic rule, I would venture to say that you have become a Czar like ruler. If you keep going down this path, you will realize the same result. I am pleading, for the sake of our people, stop this war now!"

Each of the men are now standing with their fists leaning on the table. Vladimir looks at a message that he received from the United Nations.

"It is ironic that I received a message from the UN that if I contend that my forces are in Ukraine for peace keeping Alexei, the UN is willing to enact its peace keeping role. They say that they are willing to commit the peace keeping troops, making it unnecessary for Russia to expend our troops or resources and thus allowing us to pull our forces out of Ukraine"

Vladimir sits back in his seat at the other end of the table and laughs. He takes Alexei out on the balcony and points to the West towards some missile silos that house tactical nuclear weapons. "Allow me to show you something Alexei. You see those silos. They are loaded with tactical nuclear weapons. They were put there to protect Moscow from invasion. If the United Nations tries to intercede, I will target those weapons to hit the capital of Ukraine and other cities. That will not only end the war, but it

Photo 26-Loading ICBM into Silo

will topple Ukraine's leadership. If the United Nations enters Ukraine, they will also pay the ultimate price."

"In addition to the possibility of using tactical nuclear missiles, I have appointed "a new commander in charge of my forces in Ukraine. The new general I have put in charge has a reputation for brutality, even more so than the previous generals in charge. My new commander played a major role in my Syria assault. Our combat aircraft, under his watch, caused widespread devastation in the rebel held areas. He is a close confident to me and what I especially like about him is he has never had any political ambitions." (107) He has always executed a plan exactly as I wanted.

Analysts say the new general's appointment is highly unlikely to change how Russian forces are conducting the war but that it speaks to Vladimir's dissatisfaction with previous command operations. It is also, in part, meant to appease the pro-war base within Russia itself, according to the Institute for the Study of War (ISW) think-tank.

"A Chechen leader has called for Russia to "take more drastic measures including the use of "low-yield nuclear weapons" in Ukraine. Putin welcomed the appointment of the new general, who first saw service in Afghanistan in the 1980s before commanding a unit in the 2nd Chechen War. Praise came from Vladimir's inner circle that the General is notorious for crushing all forms of dissent." (108)

Alexei pointed his finger at Vladimir and chastised him for his new direction in the war. "Are you crazy Vladimir! Such an act will start World War III and devastate not only Ukraine with radioactive fall-out, but the radiation will contaminate much of Western Russia and bordering countries north and south. You will go down in history worse than Hitler!"

"As for your new general, some of his junior officers left their careers in the armed forces after serving under him in Syria because his political views and harsh military tactics conflicted with theirs."

Vladimir turns to face Alexei. "Better dead than looser. I am gambling on it as being my ace at the negotiating tables next time our people sit down with Ukraine negotiators. I cannot and will not lose this war. I am prepared to launch those weapons if all else fails. Our people were viewing me poorly, my approval rating was plummeting prior to the war. Now it soared to 80% after the start of the war. The people love me Alexei."

"You are delusional Vladimir. We both know that you fabricated that rating by controlling the media. If the people knew the truth, they would hang you in effigy in the middle of red square. Even the parents of all those innocent young soldiers you killed needlessly have no idea their sons and daughters are dead. Do you realize that your orders have turned some of our young soldiers into killers and rapists? Some of them are killing unarmed Ukrainian civilians and over three hundred young children have been targeted by your missiles for slaughter. Their blood and the blood of our youth are on your hands Vladimir!"

"You need to read the global tea leaves Vladimir. A median of 85% across eighteen countries express an unfavorable opinion of Russia, with the majorities in most nations saying they have a very unfavorable opinion of Russia, with majorities in most nations saying they have a *very* unfavorable opinion of Russia." (109)

"I do not care Alexei. I only care about the admiration of the Russian people. Unlike the Czars that have gone before you, you are nothing but a figure head and cannot stop me."

"Maybe so, but I have the admiration of the people. Whereas you have a false following because of the lies you have perpetrated on the people." The two men are glaring with anger and hate for one another.

Vladimir suddenly brings the issue of Lina into their conversation. "And what about Lina? You have stolen her affection and turned her against me. You did not respect the relationship that I have with her."

"Yes, what about Lina? Where is she now, Vladimir? I was told that she had not been heard from for days. I have respected whatever you consider having a relationship with Lina, but your idea of a relationship is a controlling one Vladimir. The time the two of you have been together was nothing but stress for her. She feels used and abused by you."

"Be careful what you say and do Alexei. Someday, you may eat or drink something that may give you indigestion. I consider you simply as a guest in my country, not a true Russian."

Alexei is now to the point where he may lose his cool. He grits his teeth and raises his finger in a threatening gesture to Vladimir. "Do not even think about it Vladimir. I have had enough of your ranting. I will leave you with the thought that other regimes like yours have gone down in flames. Remember the Libyan Dictator who thought he was invisible, only to be beaten to death and his body dragged through the streets. I cannot understand it Vladimir. I have seen photos of you praying with the head of the Church, yet you seem to have no fear of God."

"Now we better understand one another Alexei. With that, I bid you farewell."   Alexei now turns to leave without both men saying anymore. Alexei exits in a huff to Red Square and a dark and dismal day which strangely depicts the mood between the two men.

CHAPTER 27

UKRAINE ATTACKS RUSSIA

The next day became a nightmare for Putin and the Russian people. Word quickly spread throughout Russia that "Ukraine launched one of its biggest-ever drone attacks on Russia over

the weekend, hitting a refinery and power station deep inside the country, according to videos posted on social media and geolocated by CNN.

Photo 27-Drone carrying four missiles

Despite the effects of the attack, Russia's biggest advantage is manpower and it has shown a willingness to throw soldiers at Ukrainian positions to gain a few meters at a time. About 1,200 Russian soldiers were being killed or wounded every day in May and June, the highest rate since the beginning of the war, according to Western officials.

The Russian Defense Ministry acknowledged the size of the Ukrainian attack, but downplayed its effectiveness, saying Sunday that 158 Ukrainian UAVs (unmanned aerial vehicles) "were destroyed and intercepted by on-duty air defense" overnight in 15 regions, including over the capital." (110)

The Ukrainian drone strikes follow others in the past week, including one last Thursday that set fire to oil reservoirs at a refinery in the Rostov region of Russia, according to the Ukrainian Defense Ministry.

The recent wave of Ukrainian attacks on Russian territory began last month when Kyiv's troops launched a cross-border incursion into the Kursk region on August 6. Just on Monday, Russian President Vladimir Putin acknowledged that "people are going through tough ordeals, especially in the Kursk region," as Ukrainian forces attempt to "destabilize the situation along the border." But the attack has not stifled Russia's offensive in the eastern Donbas region, added Putin. Ukrainian President Volodymyr Zelensky the Kursk offensive is going "according to plan," but admitted "difficulty" in the eastern Ukrainian cities of Pokrovsk and Toretsk.

Zelensky said the most recent drone assaults deep inside Russia Zelensky announced last month that his country has a new jet-powered drone that can strike deep into Russia. He said the Palianytsia "missile-drone" had been used in combat for the first time and was much faster and more powerful than the country's existing fleet of drones, according to Ukrainian state media.

The Ukrainian president said he would not give any more specific details on the Palianytsia. But he hailed the new weapon's "long-range" capabilities, hinting that it may surpass the up to (932 miles) range of Ukraine's current drone fleet.

Just in the past week, Russia has launched over 160 missiles of various types, 780 guided aerial bombs, and 400 strike UAVs of different kinds against our people," Zelensky said in a post on X.

On Monday, at least three people were wounded by strikes in Kyiv, as well as the eastern Kharkiv and Sumy regions, according to Ukrainian authorities. Those came after 41 people were injured following a Russian attack on civilian infrastructure in Kharkiv, Ukraine's second-largest city, local authorities said.

"Russia is once again terrorizing Kharkiv, striking civilian infrastructure and the city itself," Zelensky said on X, calling on allies to "give Ukraine everything it needs to defend itself." It is entirely justified for Ukrainians to respond to Russian terror by any means necessary to stop it," Zelensky said, reiterating his call for Western countries to lift restrictions on the use of long-range weapons, which have that prevented their use to hit targets inside Russia.

"This includes decisions to carry out long-range strikes on Russia's missile launch sites, destroy Russian military logistics, and conduct joint efforts to shoot down missiles and drones – everything that will help us resist Russian evil," Zelensky said. Russia has repeatedly targeted Ukraine's energy infrastructure with missile and drone attacks since its invasion. Ukrainian Defense Minister Rustem Umerov told CNN last week that he has presented the Biden administration with a list of targets inside Russia that Kyiv wants to hit with US-supplied weapons, including the Army Tactical Missile Systems (ATACMS).

Fired from mobile launchers, ATACMS have a range of up to three hundred kilometers (186 miles) and can deploy single high-explosive warheads or up to nine hundred submunitions. Ukraine's Foreign Minister Dmytro Kuleba also urged allies to "abandon baseless fears" and "lift restrictions on the country's legitimate right to self-defense." "Ukraine is forced to fight with hands tied behind its back," Kuleba said on Monday.

Umerov has pushed back on the assessments, saying Ukraine has presented the US a list of targets they would use ATACMS to strike. An analysis last month from a Washington-based think tank, the Institute for the Study of War (ISW), supported Ukrainian claims there are high-value targets inside Russia within range of ATAMCS. ISW said it had identified 233 Russian targets – "large military bases, communications stations, logistics centers, repair facilities, fuel depots, ammunition warehouses, and permanent headquarters" – in range of ATACMS that are immobile assets, meaning Moscow cannot move them out of harm's way. And ISW said Ukraine would only need to use ATACMS to strike some of those targets to have a significant impact on Russia's ability to fight.

While it pushes for the US to lift the ATACMS restrictions, Ukraine has been developing new longer-range indigenous weapons. Zelensky said the Palianytsia "missile-drone" had been used in combat for the first time and was much faster and more powerful than the country's existing fleet of drones.

Ukraine's president said he would not give any more specific details on Palianytsia, hinting that it may surpass the range of Ukraine's current drone fleet." (110)

CHAPTER 28

VLADIMIR BECOMES DESPERATE

Shortly after returning to his quarters, he finds Joey glued to the television set. The news media is carrying a news conference Vladimir is giving on national television. As a result of Ukraine's attacks on Russia, Vladimir is announcing the partial military mobilization of Russia's reservists. He was contemplating on doing this even before he met with Alexei but said nothing. Alexei shakes his head in disbelief. "I wonder if he confided with the Parliament. Another example of his untrusting demeaner and clandestine approach."

"I would speculate that his forces have experienced serious setbacks in Ukraine, and he needs reinforcements Joey. We need to learn more about the makeup of Russia's reserve forces." Alexei then goes online to learn more about the size of Russia's military. He reads to Joey that "Russia has the world's fifth-largest military in terms of active-duty personnel, with at least two million reserve personnel. The reservists are assigned to active units and can quickly integrate with them if mobilized. The Russian military, like the U.S. forces, is divided into the following services: the Russian Ground Forces, the Russian Navy, and the Russian Air Force. There are also three independent arms of service: Strategic Missile Troops, Russian Aerospace Defense Forces, and the Russian Airborne Troops."

Knowing that Vladimir would not permit stories that would hurt his invasion of Ukraine, Alexei also surfs the internet for information from European or U.S. news media. He finds a follow-up story that is aired on the internet. "In an effort to avoid being deployed into a war that has left thousands of soldiers dead or wounded, "Russian men are starting to flee Russia. Thousands of Russians flee to neighboring countries to avoid Vladimir's military draft. Georgia, Kazakhstan, and Mongolia are witnessing a massive influx of Russians fleeing their country to avoid being drafted into Moscow's invasion of Ukraine following Vladimir's mobilization order, which has prompted unprecedented anger and opposition in parts of the country. "(111)

"A search on Yandex Maps shows a build-up of vehicles near the southern border, suggesting Russians are fleeing in response to the decree that reservists will be called up to fight in Ukraine" (112)

"In addition to all this, the news is reporting that Vladimir has threatened to use nuclear weapons if Ukraine continues its aggression. "An ex-CIA office said that Vladimir is backed into a corner. Given all his setbacks, he is very unlikely to deescalate. The chances of his resorting to the use of tactical nuclear weapons are increasing." (113)

Alexei sits in front of Joey talking about what they need to do to stop Vladimir. "Vladimir is a mad man, Joey. He is desperate and will do anything to get his way. In his twisted mind, he feels justified to use tactical nuclear weapons to win in Ukraine. We need to act quickly. One way to separate him from his large security force is to get him away from the Kremlin. If we can free Lina, it will lure him to her where we can capture him. Get a hold of Kodkavich. Tell him we will need his best special ops people."

As Joey gets up to leave, Alexei continues to strategize. "We need to get word to NORAD and brief them on our plan. They in turn need to task Northern Defenses to modify their hyper sonics system so that it can attempt to divert any tactical missile that Vladimir may launch. I will use my contacts at the Pentagon to start the ball rolling."

"North American Aerospace Defense Command (NORAD) is a combined organization of the United States and Canada that provides aerospace warning, air sovereignty, and protection for Canada and the continental United States." (114) Just then, one of the security men entered the room. He told Alexei that there was a doctor in the waiting room to see him and it is especially important. Alexei asks Joey to show him in after clearing him through security. The doctor enters. "How can I help you, Doctor?"

"No, it is how I can help you your Highness. I am Doctor Jervalny, one of the former doctors who took care of President Vladimir. Along with other doctors, I treated him for throat cancer. Besides being a general practitioner, one of my specialties is psychiatry. While the other doctors treated his cancer, I observed his behavior. I discovered that the President is suffering from schizophrenia, gross disorganization, diminished emotional expression, and most importantly he has a paranoid personality disorder. When you have paranoid personality disorders, you may feel as if you do not know who you can trust. It can be hard to identify whom you should and should not believe when it comes to your own truths and even information about your diagnosis. As a result of Covid 19, he has also become a germophobe. All these disorders account for his distancing himself from visitors and his erratic behavior. "

Alexei listens intently to the doctor's prognosis intently. "Can his mental condition impair his judgement, Doctor? The reason I ask is that the Russian President can give the order to launch a nuclear weapon and unlike the United States, there is little checks and balance system to validate a launch."

"Yes, your highness, his condition can impair his judgement. Because I told him about his condition, he tried to poison me with a military-grade nerve agent, Novichok. After becoming deathly sick from it, I took refuge at my friend's cabin in the forest."

"Soon, we are going to need you to tell your story to the Russian Parliament and on national television doctor. Until then, my security people will take you to another mountain top home where we will call upon you to give testimony." The doctor thanks Alexei and goes off with two of Alexei's security men. Alexei then turns to Joey.

"We need to get word to the NATO countries alerting them to what may happen Joey. It would be like Armageddon if Vladimir launched a nuclear weapon. The United States may be able to interfere with the guidance systems if he was to launch. With Vladimir having cancer, he may have a death wish and does not care if he takes the people of Russia with him."

"I will get right on it Alexei." "And Joey, we need to devise an escape plan to free Lina. See if we can find any of the builders or workers that built Vladimir's Ocean Mansion and if they have any building plans." Joey departs the room to see what he can find.

Alexei has two phones, one that is connected to the Russian grid and the other that he used when living in the United States that is still connected to the U.S. grid system. The one connected to the American system has all the contacts when he served at the Pentagon on the Joint Chiefs of Staff, including the National Military Command Center (NMCC) and the Secretary of Defense's (SECDEF) Executive Support Center (ESC). He immediately phones the ESC and identifies himself with the same codes he used while serving at the Pentagon. He asks to speak to the Executive Officer for the SECDEF and/or the Exec Officer for the Chairman of the Joint Chiefs of Staff. Both are high ranking officers, bearing at least an Admiral's or General's rank. After he is cleared by the ESC, the SECDEF'S Exec Officer picks up the phone. Alexei briefs him on all that has transpired and what he needs from NORAD. He further urges him to verify what he is saying is true with the Presidents Chief of Staff, who he briefed when at the services for the queen. The SECDEF's chief of staff said that he would get back to him after he confirms his conversation with the President's Chief of Staff and receives the go ahead from the White House, Department of State, and the Department of Defense. With the action having such high security ramifications affecting other nations, all must concur on the action before it is referred to the President for final approval.

When something of national security arises, the issue is chopped off (signed off) by all at the Department of Defense, State Department, the White House, and whatever agencies that may be involved before any actions can be initiated. Sometimes the action may be passed by another country via its President or Prime Minister. When this is the case, the President is the only one that will make that call. Alexei's knows that it normally takes considerable time before an action is approved. He also knows that in cases that involves significant national security, it can be expedited. Alexei nervously waits for the Exec Officer to get back to him. In a matter of hours, he receives the phone call he has been waiting for and hopefully all systems are a go.

The voice on the other end of the phone this time is the Secretary of Defense. "We have received approval to go ahead with what you ask your eminence and are patching a conference call through to NORAD's hardened command center at Cheyenne Mountain.

Photo 28-Cheyenne Mountain

The Cheyenne Mountain Complex is located at Cheyenne Mountain Air Force Station (CMAFS), a short distance from NORAD and USNORTHCOM headquarters at Peterson Air Force Base in Colorado Springs. It is owned and operated by Air Force Space Command. Cheyenne Mountain (Photo 25) is in Colorado, southwest of downtown Colorado Springs. At the height of the Cold War in the late 1950s, the idea of a hardened command and control

248

center was conceptualized as a defense against long-range Soviet bombers. The Army Corps of Engineers supervised the construction of an operational center within the granite mountain. The Cheyenne Mountain facility became fully operational as the NORAD Combat Operations Center. (115)

The NORAD commander is surprised to receive a phone call from the SECDEF and the Czar of Russia. The SECDEF directs the commander to speak openly with Alexei. Alexei explains what he needs from NORAD if Vladimir decides to launch a nuclear weapon. Alexei says that he will give the commander coordinates where to divert the weapon. The SECDEF and NORAD commander assured their support. Alexei notes that the targeted area will not be aware of NORAD's involvement because the launch will originate from Russia.

Having hardly slept the night before, Alexei is awoken by Joey early the next morning. "We are in luck Alexei; I found the builder and he has the original plans. "Show him in Joey." The builder enters the room and is awestruck that he is in the presence of the new Czar. He gives a light bow, but Alexei makes motions for him to stand up.

"We need you to swear to secrecy about what we do here today." The builder Promises to do so and unfolds his plans and Alexei as several questions. "Where do these underground tunnels lead? "They lead to the beach beneath the building 'Czar Alexei. They connect utilities and the other for an escape tunnel. Vladimir wanted them positioned so they would lead to different house locations."

Alexei thanked the builder for his input and offered to pay him for his efforts. "No, your excellency. I do not want any payment. "If I would have known he was going to invade Ukraine, I would have given him a piece of my mind. My only son was drafted and is fighting in Ukraine, and we fear for his life."

CHAPTER 29

THE RESCUE

After the builder left, Vladimir made the trip to Oleg's Mountain top resort where the special ops team was waiting for him. All were muscular and heavily armed with the best in high-tech weaponry, including night glasses and laser guided weapons. Depending on the mission, commandos sometimes carry an assortment of other equipment, such as breaching materials, night-vision goggles, anti-tank missiles, grenade launchers, vests, first aid kits, knives, watches, GPS devices, helmets, belts, rope slings for scaling walls.

The commandos were dressed in Type II uniforms, a desert digital camouflage uniform of four colors worn by Special Warfare Operators. Additionally, they kept in their pockets – a pen and notepad, maps, GPS device, knives, grenades, and a flashlight – so that they are ready for whatever situation they may confront. The special ops team could not understand, however, why Alexei asked them to bring stun guns used to put large animals to sleep and grappling hooks. Alexei lays the plans out and the team leader gives them a quick look over before making any comments.

The team leader then scrutinizes the plan with his men and takes comments from them. "I know this beach head in front of the building. It has numerous boulders jutting out of the water, making it extremely difficult to navigate through treacherous waters. The coastline is not as accessible as it might first appear. Moreso it is extremely dangerous and surrounded by steep cliffs. Known as one of Russia's deadliest locations for shark attacks, there have been several fatal attacks here, including one not long ago when the victim was seized in waist-deep water and dragged out to sea. No wonder Vladimir selected this location to build. It would be difficult to scale the cliffs but not impossible for scaled special ops people like us."

Alexei sympathizes with the team and tries to console them. "I cannot do anything about the sharks but take a closer look at those openings at the base of the cliffs. They were designed to look like caves, but they are really escape tunnels that lead into different parts of the palace. Only three of your team that comes in from the sea must scale the cliffs to take out the perimeter guards. After the mission is completed, your sea team will stay in place beneath the tunnels to wait for further orders. Make sure you bring enough MRE provisions and overnight gear to sustain yourselves for a long wait because the last part of our plan is to wait for Vladimir to hastily come to his palace to learn the whereabouts of Lina. Hopefully, it will happen sooner rather than later."

Alexei goes on to compare his plan to another plan that involved the killing of the world's most wanted terrorist, Bin Laden. "We tried to learn from other assault plans like the one that captured and killed Bin Laden. From what I have studied, "U.S. Special Forces raided an al-Qaeda compound in Abbottabad, Pakistan, and killed the world's most wanted terrorist: Osama bin Laden. The entire operation, which lasted only 40 minutes from start to finish, was the culmination of years of calculated planning and training. Ultimately, bin Laden was found and killed within nine minutes, and SEAL Team Six was credited with carrying out a nearly flawless mission." (115)

"I believe the orders were to not take bin laden alive, they were to execute him and spread his ashes in the sea. Reason being is that they did not want him around to give his followers the excuse to take hostages throughout the world in exchange for his release."

"Because many of those soldiers guarding Vladimir's compound are innocent young Russian soldiers, we want to avoid any casualties at all costs. Now you can understand the reason that we requested that you are armed with stun guns. Unlike the plan to capture bin laden, we only have one day to train for the assault on Vladimir's compound. Otherwise, we could take some of the lessons learned by the assault plan on Bin Laden's compound. For one thing, they came in by helicopter which alerted Bin Laden and his men to defend the compound. We will not assault the compound by helicopter. Instead, we will leave our vehicles ten miles out and come in by land and sea. Another good thing is that the moon will be shining at your backs, giving your men better vision to safely land on the beach and scale the cliffs. At the same time, the bright light of the moon will blur the visions of the guards, making it easier and safer for us to overtake them. Hopefully, the night conditions will allow the moon to shine through some cloud coverage, making our assault stealth-like by sea and by land."

Alexei continues his analogy of the assault to kill Bin Laden. "The navy seals went from the ground floor up to the third floor, giving Bin Laden and his guards time to prepare. To avoid alerting the guards, we will use the downspouts and grappling hooks to scale the building to the roof and then enter through the large skylights on the roof. This will give us the advantage to access the palace from the ground floor up and the roof down, giving us the element of surprise."

"Lastly, the Seals had a force of twenty-four men where we will only be using twelve men, more skilled in guerilla warfare. Six will come in by sea and twelve by land. Although it is a smaller force, it will make our movements stealthier and more undetected." Alexei points to the team leader. "You will need to pick the most experienced special ops men amongst you for the six that will come in by sea. Especially as they will need to know how to maneuver through waters that are treacherous, choppy, and loaded with sharks."

The Team leader assures that all his men are experienced for any mission. He counts only twelve of the special ops people that will accompany him. "Six by sea and twelve by land. I only count twelve of us?"

Alexei pats the team leader on the back. "Your count is correct, but I would not ask you to do such a risky mission unless I came along as part of the team. Joey and I, along with four of my best security people, will be joining the land assault but in a different way. We need to be there so Lina has no fear for her life. My team and I will be coming through the front door. Again, the reason for the stun guns is that we must be careful not to kill any of Vladimir's guards. Whatever their assignment, they are still our people."

The team leader asks another pertinent question while reviewing the plans. "How are you going to get through the front with those heavy bronze doors? The front of the palace is built like a fortress and non-penetrable and the walls would be difficult to scale. Why would the guards allow you entry without being challenged?"

Alexei acknowledges his question as good and valid. "We have done extensive research and have inside information on the operation of Vladimir's palace. He has six cleaning people who come every night to assist the permanent staff to clean the palace. They are not necessarily the same people every night so the guards will not know the difference. We plan to intercept them and buy them off with more money they can earn in several months. That way, I and five others can walk through the front door with no resistance. Security is only beefed up when Vladimir is on site. Otherwise, there is only a small garrison of guards when he is not in residence."

The team leader interjects. "As they say, sounds like a plan." "Do you realize your eminence that you will follow the leads of some Czars that have gone before you, like Peter the Great, who also led his men into battle?" Alexei wrinkles his lip to the side. "I just hope that we are as successful as them. Then we agree. It is a go for tomorrow night. You and your team get a good dinner and a good night's sleep. May we all make it out alive."

Morning came faster than normal. This time Alexei got a good night's sleep. The team was already up and having breakfast and talking about the mission.   All stood as Alexei entered the room, giving him a welcome befitting a Czar. Alexei being his humble self, bade them all to be seated. After having a friendly breakfast, they went over the plan once again. Each acknowledged that they understood the plan and particularly each of their parts. The sea assault team dawned wet suits and the land team dressed in BDU combat dress. Alexei and his team prepared to leave to intercept the cleaning people. All synchronized their watches, checked their weapons and equipment before departing. Alexei again reminds them that they need to accomplish this mission without any bloodshed. All agree.

The sea team boarded a fast speed boat equipped with a raft and scuba tanks. The rocks prevent boats from getting too close to the beach. To readily access the beach and go undetected, they went stealth by boarding rafts about a couple miles out from the beach. Although the moon and stars gave them a bright path, the waters themselves were mirky and turbulent that night. Because of the jutting rocks, the sea team had to disembark from their rafts ten yards from the beach and wade through the murky waters up to their waists with their weapons and equipment held high above their heads.

As they started towards the shore, a fin appeared behind them. From what they could see in the moonlight, it was a great white shark. The great white shark is responsible for the most unprovoked attacks of any other shark in the world, according to the Florida Museum. There have been 333 recorded great white shark attacks in history; fifty-two of them were fatal. The biggest great white ever recorded was twenty feet long and weighed approximately 4,500 pounds. This one was only ten feet long but hungry enough to attack them and big enough to drag any one of them out to sea. It was not stopping until it wetted its appetite. The one special ops guy among them was a former navy seal, John, who hired on as a mercenary. He dealt with sharks in the past and volunteered to take this one on. He tossed his pack and weapon to one of his other comrades and turned to take on the shark. John was able to step aside to have the shark miss him. He then grabbed hold of the Shark's fin and stabbed the mammal in both eyes and slashed one of its gills with his knife, making the shark helpless, thrashing wildly in the surf. Other sharks fed on the wounded shark and dragged it under the dark waters, diverting further attacks by other sharks. The sea team finished navigating the rocky beach and made it safely to the tunnels.

The land team drove to within ten miles of the rear of the palace as planned. So as not to be identified, Alexei did not join in intercepting the cleaners and buying them off. Two security people were left with the cleaning people to hold them until after completing the mission.

Alexei's team reached the palace front doors of his palace *(Photo 25)* while the other two assumed their position as directed.

Photo 29-Vladimir Oceanside Palace

Joey taps Alexei on the shoulder and whispers into his ear. "Look into the main dining room Alexei. There is Lina having dinner. She really has a forlorn look on her face."

Alexei used a hooded sweatshirt to disguise himself and spoke fluent Russian on behalf of the cleaning team. Upon being checked by the Palace guards, they were granted entry. Opening the doors, the guards could not discern them from the cleaning people. The team hid their stunned guns in the cleaning equipment.

The sea and land team waited for a signal from Alexei that his team had entered the palace. The sea team split up. Three had to cut through the gates to the tunnel on the beach and the remainder had to scale the cliffs to help take out the perimeter guards surrounding the palace. The land team scaled the palace walls from the rear after they helped the sea team subdue the perimeter guards. Joey sends a signal to the other two teams to start their assaults and whispers to Alexei.

They start sizing up the security guards, counting four on the first floor. The rooms were luxurious and elegantly furnished with expensive tapestries and paintings. It also had a full staff of servants.

Alexei nods towards the guards and quietly says to Joey. "As I said before, these guards are young, and I want to avoid killing any of them. Disperse our people to work like their cleaning near each guard. They can get the drop on them at my command without shedding any blood."

Once the sea team makes it to the roof, they easily subdue the roof guards and work their way down to the ground floor, overtaking and subduing guards as they go. Once Alexei knows that most of the palace is under their control, he gives the signal to subdue the remaining guards on the ground floor. As all guards are overtaken, Lina stands up and is frightened until Alexei removes his hood and she recognizes him. She runs into his arms and sobs with joy to see him.

"Oh Alexei, you did not forget me. It has been terrible locked up in this mausoleum and having to put up with the rantings of Vladimir. I hate Vladimir for thinking he can imprison me as if I was his possession."

"We must quickly leave Lina. One of the guards could have sounded the alarm for backup forces. We cannot afford to hesitate for a moment."

As they start walking towards the front door, two young guards they missed challenges them with fully automatic weapons. Guns drawn, the guards and Alexei stare down one another. Suddenly the guards recognize Alexei as the Czar. Now, Alexei may be forced to give Joey the signal to kill these two young soldiers to keep them from telling Vladimir. The young guards lower their weapons without confrontation and address Alexei.

"We have seen you on television. You are the new Czar of Russia, our hope for a brighter and freer future." Hearing this, Alexei had all the guards gathered in the main hall of the palace, asking them to swear loyalty to the cause. Two of them spoke up. "Many of us young people no longer revere Vladimir. He is autocratic and killed many of our young friends by sending them into a war we did not have to fight. He has not been kind or generous to those of us who have protected his palace. We have stood at attention while he lavishly entertains his guest. Do you see those tents outside the walls? That is where we sleep. On some freezing nights. we do not even get a hot meal. Most of us have not seen our families for months because he does not want to change the guards in the hope of keeping assassins from penetrating our ranks. He treats us with no respect. We want to serve a nobler cause. Tie us up and we will report that it was Ukrainians that stormed the palace. If ever you return, we will be your inside connection."

Alexei thanked them and had them fire their weapons as if they warded off the intruders. He also asked that they do not report anything to Vladimir until he gives the word. He lets them in on his plan to return when Vladimir is told about what has happened to Lina and his palace. "Afterwards, I assure you that you will not be serving long hours and eating cold meals, and you will be given ample time to be with your families and friends. Also, I will have you promoted to the next rank with the accorded increase in salary to go with it once we oust Vladimir from power. Lastly, you will no longer sleep in tents. Like American soldiers who invaded Iraq, you are welcome to sleep in the comfortable bedrooms of Vladimir's palace. One other point, each of you can help yourself to an artifact to compensate you for all those cold meals. The guards' eyes lit up at this and thanked Alexei. "We thank you for your thoughtfulness. You have our dedication and loyalty."

Vladimir was counting on the Ukrainians to rally around him when he invaded their country. Instead, he discovered the Ukrainians would rather fight to the death to save their homeland.

All this was a surprise to Alexei and Joey, and they could not have hoped for a better result, especially as there was not one casualty that resulted from their assault on the palace. The last part of the plan is to draw Vladimir out from the heavily guarded Kremlin walls once he learned of the assault on his mansion. Alexei directed the sea and land teams to hold up in the tunnel leading from the beach to await the signal to again move on the mansion once Vladimir arrives. While waiting for that time to come, Alexei asked Joey to make certain that plenty of good food was stocked at the palace for the guards and his men in the tunnel had the same plus comfortable sleeping accommodations. Alexei departed, taking Lina to Oleg's Mountain retreat, and asked Joey to have the Russian leaders to meet him at the mansion. Upon arriving at the Mountain fortress, he assures Lina that she will be safe.

Lina is still shaking and holds on tight to Alexei. "What happens now Alexei. I have seen the dark side of Vladimir and am afraid for you and Russia. He will stop at nothing to get what he wants." "We plan to stop him, Lina. It is only a matter of time."

CHAPTER 30,

ENACTING THE PLAN

Alexei leaves Lina in one part of the mansion and goes to the great room to wait for the Russian leaders to return to the mountain top. Before he leaves her, she hugs him and gives him a long embrace and passionate kiss. He returns the same.

The Russian leaders reach the mountain top to be briefed by Alexei. They gathered in the great room and waited for Alexei to address them. Alexei starts with an emphatic statement. "It is now time to place in action the overthrow of Vladimir. We have learned a lot about the condition of Vladimir, including that he has become mentally deranged. He told me that, if necessary to win the war, he will take out key Ukrainian cities by using tactical nuclear weapons. Unlike the United States, he alone can give the order to launch nuclear weapons. My sons sent me news feeds from the United States. Look at the screen on the wall and I will show you the atrocities being perpetrated on the Ukrainian people."

You could hear disheartening remarks and expressions of serious concern among the leaders as to what they saw. Even their far-reaching influence could not stop Vladimir from pulling the trigger that would launch nuclear weapons. All looked to Alexei for answers. Alexei ponders while holding his chin and waving one finger in the air. "As you can see, Vladimir and his generals have been committing war crimes. Removing him from power will not be enough. We must prove to the people that he has been lying by bringing him and his generals to trial for war crimes."

"We need to follow the same plan we used to get to the inside of Vladimir's palace to save Lina. Also, we must get our people in those nuclear launch silos. Who among you can get information on how and when they change their watch."

Generals Ivankoff speaks up followed by General Trachesky. "When I was a young officer, the silos came under my command. I knew the system then, but I do not know if it is still in place. As an alumnus of that command, however, I may be able to glean the information from one of the officers." General Trachesky interjects. "I can also check with my contacts."

Alexei remarks about how time is of the essence. "We do not have much time. We cannot depend on how long there will be a lull in the fighting. For now, we do not know the mindset of Vladimir. He may be reluctant to wreak havoc on Ukraine because he believes that Lina is held captive by them, or he may take steps because he feels that me and Lina deceived him. If he launches even one of those nuclear missiles, the retaliation on Russia will destroy Russia as we know it

While waiting to learn if the silos have been secured, we now need to get everything in place soon. One other important thing we need to put in place is to neutralize Vladimir's General Chief of Staff and other key Generals. That is the part that you will play Simon. "Leave that to me Alexei. As we discussed, my men will capture them by replacing their chauffeurs."

Alexis turns to Gorbousky. "Have you been lobbying the Duma to gain enough votes for impeaching Vladimir?" "My people said if we can prove anything that he has done to put Russian in peril, they can garner enough votes to impeach him. This would include him committing war crimes, lying to our people, or using unnecessary force in Ukraine such as the launch of a nuclear missile. They are willing to accept the decision of our high court or a ruling from the International Criminal Court. "

The International Criminal Court is an international tribunal seated in the Hague, Netherlands. It is the first international court with authority to prosecute individuals for the international crimes of genocide crimes against humanity, war crimes and the crime of aggression.

"Ferdinand and Oleg, do you have the people in place that we discussed to air the truth using the news media?" "We are ready Alexei. We are going to use everyone here to speak to the nation and we also want to use Lina. Her youth and stellar reputation as an Olympic gold medalist will hopefully get the youth on board."

Alexei feels comfortable that everyone is doing what they promised. "Okay, we implement the rest of our plan soon. Everyone be well rested and ready. The timing of implementing each segment of the plan is critical." Each of the participants is given another set of top-secret phones and communication codes. Alexei ends the meeting.

Returning to his room, he finds Lina waiting for him. She gives him a hug and a kiss. "I want to stay with you tonight, Alexei." I want you more than you want me Lina, but do you realize that like Vladimir, I am much older than you Lina. I would, however, like to feel your warmth next to me if you would like to sleep with me tonight."

The night sleeping together was very romantic. Like two children having a sleep over, Alexei and Lina slept passionately holding one another. Occasionally each would wake and give the other a kiss on the back or the cheek. Alexei would sometimes wrap his arms around Lina and Lina would snuggle up with her back to his front.

The morning sun shines on Alexei and Lina and finds them tenderly wrapped in one another's arms, flesh against flesh. Alexei awoke earlier and just laid there gazing lovingly into her face. He has never felt such love since the loss of his beloved wife. Lina opens her eyes peering into Alexei's, smiles, and whispers into his ear that she loves him. He in turn says the same. "This is the nicest evening I have ever spent with anyone in bed. I never felt such love for someone without making love to them. I love you Alexei." Alexei paraphrases an old line from the movie Ghost and simply replies "DITTO"

Lina giggles like a little girl at Alexei's response and comments. "Like in the movie Ghost, however, I hope you do not have to die to get you to say I love you too Lina." Alexei showers within the eye shot of Lina. She sits at the end of the bed with her long hair glimmering in the sunshine. Alexei walks out of the bathroom and stops in his tracks, marveling at her innocence and beauty.

Lina giggles again. "I cannot believe that I slept in the arms of the Russian Czar, and nothing sexual happened. What a terrible movie this would make. On the contrary Lina, we made love in a different way last night just by lovingly holding one another."

After Alexei gets dressed, he kisses and hugs Lina. She kisses him back and holds onto him. "I want us to spend a couple of days together before you go after Vladimir Alexei. If he finds out that we are together, he will do everything he can to kill the both of us. I have a special place where we can go to get away from all this mayhem for a couple of days. Its only 124 miles from Moscow. A safe and picturesque place that only the locals frequent. Will you go with me Alexei?" Alexei looks into her earnest eyes and recalls her telling him how Vladimir always put all else before her. "Yes Lina, I am in!" Lina breaks her stare, and a smile comes over her face. "I will make the plans Alexei, including matching Joey with my trustworthy cousin."

Alexei goes to the dining room to have breakfast with the leaders that stayed overnight. They exchange more information and get on their way to putting their parts of the plan into action.

Alexei and Lina spend another night snuggling with one another. When Lina opened her eyes, Alexei was gone.

CHAPTER 31

ALEXEI MEETS THE FAMILY

As Lina was up and about, the door opened, and Alexei stood in front of Lina dressed in Denim pants, a leather jacket, helmet, gloves, holding another leather coat and helmet in his hands. He also had some saddle bags that would normally attach to a bike or motorcycle. Lina looked at him with a puzzled look but finally figured it out. Alexei hands Lina all that he had in in hands. "Please put these on Lina." Knowing Lina's size, Alexei had Joey go out and purchase her the essentials she needed for the weekend. Before leaving the mountain retreat with Lina, Joey stops them and holds his hands on both shoulders of Alexei. "I hope you know what you are doing Alexei. With me as your only security, we will be vulnerable." Lina exclaimed that where they are going, there is little news that will reveal the identity of Alexei. "We can ride avoiding the main roads, Joey.

Lina was becoming very anticipative as to how they would be traveling. As soon as they walked out the door, her eyes widened when she saw their mode of travel was a Harley motorcycle (Photo 27).

Photo 30-Two couples on motorcycle

Joey discovered that two of the special Ops men had motorcycles and were more than willing to loan them to Joey and for one his friends. With the four of them wearing helmets, they were unrecognizable. Alexei asked Lina the name of the place they were headed for, but she said it was a surprise, and she would give him directions as they traveled. Lina tucks her long flowing hair under the helmet.

To avoid being spotted, they used the alley ways to travel out of Moscow. About fifty miles out of the city, they stopped at a small village to pick up Lina's cousin. Joey could not believe his eyes. Like Lina, her cousin was a cute brunette with a fun-like personality. She climbed behind Joey and the four of them were off traveling at high speeds. Alexei had no idea of their destination but could sense that Lina was taking them toward the coast. After about a three-hour ride, they finally reached their destination, a small village by the name of Myshkin.

"Myshkin is located on the left bank of the Volga River 39 km far from Uglich. Being quiet and cozy, Myshkin will give you an idea of what a typical Russian provincial town is. Being remote from the major tourist centers, the town is closely surrounded by protected pine forests. *There are no plants or factories in this green town.* With population of 6,000, Myshkin is believed one of the smallest Russian towns. (116)

Lina directed Alexei to pull up to a large country inn on the outside of the village. The four of them dismounted. Alexei and Joey stayed with the motorcycles while Lina and her cousin simply walked through the front door without even knocking. After a few minutes inside, Lina opened the door and waved for Alexei and Joey to enter the Inn. Once inside, Lina introduced Alexei and Joey to her parents and two brothers, using the assumed name John for Alexei so as not to reveal his identity. As her parents had no television, they never recognized Alexei as their new Czar. After a warm welcome, the four of them sat down for a delicious brunch. It was enchanting for Alexei to see Lina in her childhood home, helping her mother with the meal and setting the table. At first, her parents and brothers were stand offish from Alexei and Joey. With his extroverted personality, Alexei quickly won them over. He even washed all the dishes following the meal. Within a short while, Lina's family warmed up to Alexei as if they had known him for many years. Visualizing that Lina may be thinking of Alexei as more than just a date, Lina's mother started asking Alexei many questions and Alexei asked Lina's parents some questions about Lina when she was a little girl growing up

Alexei could sense that the questions from Lina's mother were more fact finding to protect her daughter. "So, John, you were born and raised in the United States? What part of the United States?" "I was born and raised in the Steel Valley." What is your heritage background, your roots John?" "My great grandparents migrated to the United States from Russia in the early 1900's". "What brings you to Russia now John and do you intend to stay." "A job brought me to Russia."

Before Lina's mother could probe further, Alexei asks her about their life in the village. Lina's father chimes in. "We were born and raised here. Besides farming, I am one of the many fishermen who depend on the sea and farming for our livelihood. My two sons are also fishermen and help us run the farm. They went to the university to learn agriculture and decided to stay here. Our farm has grown into one of the largest on the coast. Early on, we sacrificed much when we discovered that Lina was athletic enough to be selected for the Russian Olympic team." "What about your family John. When you say a job brought you to Russia, what type of job?" Alexei was about to answer when Lina chimed in. "John's works in his family business father." Lina's father came right back to ask, "what's your family business?" "My family is in the service industry."

Lina's father seems to want to put Alexei to a test. "My sons will be going out in the morning to fish. Perhaps you would like to join them?" Lina comes over and places her hand on Alexei's shoulder. "This is our time together father. We intend to spend the time here together and tour the countryside. I want to give him the opportunity to get acquainted with my family and show him places where I played as a young girl."

That evening, Alexei plays one of the most favorite Russian card games with the family, "Durak or Fool" while Joey keeps watch on the outside of the Farmhouse. The family keeps asking why Joey does not come in and play with them. Lina explained that he is not feeling well and needs some fresh air. At the end of the evening, Lina's parents were that much more drawn to Alexei. Lina's mother looked at her daughter and then nodded towards Alexei with a smile of approval. Lina smiled back.

The family turned in early because they must start the day before dawn to care for farm animals, followed by a day of fishing. As Lina's family is deeply religious, her mother pairs Alexei and Joey in one bedroom and her daughter and niece in another. This is another attribute of Lina's family that is appreciated by Alexei.

Alexei and Joey are awoken early in the morning by a Rooster. They find a voluptuous breakfast waiting for them when they go into the Kitchen, cooked by Lina and her mother. Again, Alexei washes all the dishes.

After breakfast, Lina sneaks Alexei out the back door so they can be alone for the day. Their first stop was Mishkin's Upper Boulevard which offers rare panoramas of quaint villages, pine forest reserves and the Volga and Yukhoti Rivers. Upper Boulevard is regarded as the most beautiful street in Myshkin, ornately decorated stone mansions coexist with wooden huts to recreate the atmosphere of a small merchant town. Lina holds Alexei's hand as she gives him a tour of what she considered one of her favorite streets to walk as a young girl. "It is where my mother met my father and later it was where he asked her to marry him."

Next, Lina took Alexei to Assumption cathedral. Her reason for taking him to Assumption cathedral was because it was visited by one of Alexei's ancestors, Tsarevich Alexander who became the future Emperor Alexander III.

Lastly, she wanted Alexei to see Nikolsky Cathedral (Photo 27) because it had a special place in her heart. It is the oldest stone building in the city, built in 1766. It is where her father and mother were married. "You can make a wish by lighting a candle Alexei." Alexei and Lina each picked up a candle and lit it. "What did you wish for Lina?" "Did you not know as a little boy that I can't tell you because my wish may not come true."

After they toured more of the town, they knew it was time to head back to Moscow. Upon returning to the family home of Lina's, Joey was nervously waiting for their return. Line's father asked Joey why he seems so jittery when John is away. "I guess it's just a habit of ours when we looked out for one another as kids growing up in a tough neighborhood." Of course, it was really Joey who felt responsible for protecting Alexei even more so during these trying and difficult times.

After Alexei and Lina were packed and ready to leave, Lina's mother took Lina aside. "I think John would be a good guy for you Lina. He would be better than Vladimir, who your father and I do not like. Do you think John's family business is good enough to support you if you marry him?" Lina breaks out with a smile. "Yes mom, his family business is a good business. It has been around before the turn of the century." Lina's mom turns to Alexei and gives him a big hug. "Please bring your two sons with you the next time you visit." Joey and his date are already on their motorcycles when Alexei and Lina walk out to get on theirs. It is another beautiful sunshine day for the ride back to Moscow. They ride over beautiful tree lined roads and villages on their ride back to Moscow.

Upon dropping off Lina's cousin, Joe is elated that she is willing to see him again. After arriving back at the Mountain top compound, Alexei phones all the leaders to confirm that they are prepared to exercise their part of the plan. He then contacts the lead security at Vladimir's palace and instructs him to report to Vladimir that Lina has been taken hostage by Ukrainian commandos and his palace has been ransacked. Everything is now in motion to subdue Vladimir.

CHAPTER 32

THE NUCLEAR MISSILE LAUNCH

With the hordes of people leaving Russia to escape military service and public sentiment going against him, Vladimir feels more than ever before that his back is against the wall. He starts to hallucinate that he needs to make a major statement to turn the tide in Ukraine and calls to his office the lead generals overseeing the war.

Following standard procedure for meetings with Vladimir, the generals sit at the far end of the table where Vladimir sits at the other end. This time Vladimir stands to emphasize what he is about to say. "It is time to take the next step to bring Ukraine to its knees. We will target one of their military bases with a tactical nuclear weapon to show we mean business and do whatever it takes to win this war. I want you to prepare a tactical nuclear warhead for launch upon my orders. After launching the one warhead, prepare to launch others if it does not get their attention. What base do you suggest that we target?"

The generals take some time to study the war map of Ukraine. The consensus was to hit the "Kulbakino is an air base of the Ukrainian Air Force located near Mykolaiv, Mykolaiv Oblast, Ukraine. The base is home to the 299th Tactical Aviation Brigade, which flies Sukhoi Su-24M, Sukhoi Su-25, Aero L-39C Albatros and Aero L-39M aircraft." (117) Because of its location in south central Ukraine, they felt it will do the least collateral damage and any nuclear cloud that results will not affect the borders of Russia. Looking at one another, however, the generals try hopelessly to try reasoning with Vladimir. They could see that nothing they could say would change Vladimir's mind. Vladimir approved the target and went into his office to address the nation before all the television cameras.

Joey brings Alexei's attention to Vladimir's broadcast. "My fellow countrymen, I first want to remind you why we took military action against Ukraine. First, we were concerned about the expansion of the North Atlantic Treaty Organization into Eastern Europe and former Soviet Republics, especially when Ukraine is so close to our boarders. Secondly, there is evidence that Ukraine committed genocide. Third, Ukraine has never had its own authentic statehood and is therefore still part of Russia. Fourth, Ukraine has the desire to obtain nuclear weapons, thus posing a threat to Russia. After many months of trying to address these threats, we have concluded that we need to take more drastic measures. We have given the order to use a limited nuclear warhead against the Ukrainian military."

The television fades out to a video of Russian military parades, fighter flights flying in formation, and the Russian national anthem. Vladimir kept using the word "we" in his broadcast to the nation because he wanted to give the impression that he alone did not make the decision. He wanted the Russian people think it was a consensus of his generals and other elected officials.

People throughout Russia came out of their homes and shops to talk amongst themselves about what Vladimir just said. Even the Russian Parliament was caught off guard. They were extremely upset that Vladimir did not consult with them first before taking such a drastic step and were starting to wonder if it was true that Vladimir may be deranged. The whole of Russia was dead set against using a nuclear weapon of any kind and feared that the launch of one would lead to a world-wide nuclear war.

A senior researcher at the United Nations Institute for Disarmament Research in Geneva, said on Twitter that the order might have activated Russia's nuclear command and control system, opening communication channels for any eventual launch order. Alternatively, he added that Russians might ramp up their nuclear facilities.

As soon as Vladimir mentioned using limited nuclear warheads, Alexei was on the phone to alert NORAD, who was in the final stages of developing a diversion system. He gives the coordinates to divert the missile. The target is a military base of the country posing the greatest to South Korea and other NATO countries. It is South Korea's newest missile base, having the capability of deploying intercontinental ballistic missiles. NORAD and the U.S. Command are pleased with the target because they have wanted to take it out long ago. With a missile coming from Russia, no blame can be placed on the United States. As far as Vladimir launching from other Russian Missile silos were concerned,

General Ivankoff briefs Alexei on the process for Russia to launch a nuclear missile. "A 2020 document called "Basic Principles of State Policy of the Russian Federation on Nuclear Deterrence" (118) says the Russian president makes the decision to use nuclear weapons. The 2020 doctrine presents four scenarios which might justify the use of Russian nuclear weapons, the use of nuclear weapons against Russia, launch of ballistic missiles aimed at Russia, an attack that would undermine Russia's nuclear forces, and the use of conventional weapons against Russia. As far as he could see, none of these scenarios were violated to justify Vladimir using a nuclear warhead. Alexei calls Gorbousky and asks that he contact the leadership in Parliament to disseminate it among their members. "I will do so immediately Alexei."

General Ivakoff explains the use of a small briefcase, known as the Cheget. "The briefcase is always kept close to the president of Russia, linking him to the command-and-control network of Russia's strategic nuclear forces. The Cheget does not contain a nuclear launch button but rather transmits launch orders to the central military command, the General Staff. The Russian General Staff has access to the launch codes and has two methods of launching nuclear warheads. It can send authorization codes to individual weapons commanders, who would then execute the launch procedures. There is also a backup system, known as Perimeter, which allows the General Staff to directly initiate the launch of land-based missiles, bypassing all the immediate command posts.

Ivakoff explains Russia's arsenal. "It is estimated that Russia has 5,977 nuclear warheads, more than any other country. Of these, 1,588 are deployed and ready for use. Its missiles can be fired from the land, by submarines and by airplanes. Vladimir oversaw a coordinated test of Russia's nuclear forces on Feb. 19 shortly before ordering troops into Ukraine. To date, the only use of nuclear weapons was when the atomic bombs were dropped on the Japan by the United States in 1945, at the end of World War Two." (119)

Today, a deployed intercontinental-range nuclear weapon that is loaded onto an intercontinental-range ballistic missile can reach the United States from Russia in approximately 30 minutes. Any country, including the US, only has a limited ability to destroy an incoming nuclear intercontinental ballistic missile as reported in a study released last month by the American Physical Society. The US, however, has the best interception systems for destroying a nuclear warhead." (120)

A Minuteman III intercontinental ballistic missile. Sitting atop the towering missile is its polished silver nuclear warhead, capable of hitting any spot in the world, with booster rockets that can propel the missile to 15,000 miles per hour. (121)

Alexei shakes his head in amazement after hearing what General Ivankoff has just said. "It makes it all that more important to divert any missile Vladirmir may launch and to shut down those other missile silos as soon as possible."

In the meantime, Kodakavich has kidnapped Vladimir's top generals. Ivankoff and Trachesky have arranged to switch the Missileers who control the nuclear silos with their own people. General Ivankoff takes steps to eliminate the possibility of Vladimir launching from other missile silos by using his military connections to have them locked down.

Having his back to the wall with his failures to take Ukraine, Vladimir reaches for the Cheget brief case to insert the codes to authorize the launch of one missile by the command-and-control network of Russia's strategic nuclear forces. Once the code and the target were verified, the countdown to launch was set in place. Unknowingly to Vladimir, one of his officers responsible for carrying the Cheget briefcase was loyal to Trachesky and dead set against launching a nuclear warhead. Once the officer alerted Trachesky that Vladimir accessed his briefcase to launch one nuclear warhead, Trachesky asked the officer to scramble the remaining codes in the Cheget briefcase so Vladimir could no longer access the codes to launch other missiles.

Vladimir goes to his command post to view the launch and the destruction when it reaches its target. Except for Vladimir, you could feel the tension among his staff who are not supportive of his decision to launch a nuclear weapon. The Russian command post controllers set the coordinate for the air base in Ukraine, 48.3794° N, 31.1656° E. The geographic coordinate system enables missileers to target any place in the world using their latitude and longitude. The countdown starts at ten and the missile is on its way at one. In the meantime, NORAD reset the coordinates for the target in North Korea.

After ten minutes into the launch, the controllers in the command post have expressions of confusion on their face. They recheck their coordinates and they discover that the missile is on its way to a target other than the coordinates they set for Ukraine. The lead controller turns to brief Vladimir. "Something has gone amiss Mr. President. The

Photo 31-Russian Soyuz Booster Rocket

path of the missile is showing a target that has a coordinate of 40.3399° N, 127.5101° E instead of a Ukrainian coordinate of 48.3794° N, 31.1656° E.

Vladimir's eyes widen. What do you mean, it is heading for a different coordinate. "Where is the location of coordinate 40.3399° N, 127.5101° E?" The lead controller rechecks his target and slowly turns around again with a worried look on his face. "That coordinate Mr. President is the one for the northern Peninsula of Korea. To be more exact Mr. President, it is a military base in North Korea."

Vladimir jumps out of his chair and yells at the controllers to make the correction. "We cannot nuke North Korea. Change the direction of the missile now!" The controllers try everything to change it but to no avail. "There is nothing we can do to change it Mr. President. For some reason, we have no control over the path of the missile."

Vladimir eyes widen again, and his mouth drops open. He lunges to look over the controller's shoulder to get a better look at the coordinates and a view from the camera mounted on the nose cone of the missile. "How long will it take for the missile to reach its target?." The controllers take another look at their calculations. "In less than one hour Mr. President."

Vladimir wraps his cheeks with both hands in utter confusion and then orders Sanyo to get the leaders of North Korea on the hot line. Sanyo does so within minutes and hands the phone to Vladimir who in turn speaks to the President of North Korea. "There has been a huge

274

mistake. A missile armed with a nuclear warhead that we just launched is headed for your largest missile base and there is nothing we can do to change its course." There was silence on the other end of the phone because Vladimir forgot that he was speaking in Russian, and the North Korean leaders did not understand him. Vladimir suddenly realizes that they cannot interpret his language but has limited time to find an interpreter that speaks the North Korean language. The missile also breaches air space over China while headed for North Korea. Both North Korea and China picks up the missile on its radar systems.

The hot lines to China and North Korea are continuously ringing off the hook. Vladimir first picks up the phone from North Korea to hear a Russian speaking interpreter on the line. "Why have you launched a missile against us!?" Vladimir blurts back that it was a mistake. North Korea shouts back to change its course! With a noticeable quiver in his voice, Vladimir tells them that his controllers cannot change its course. The North Koreans warn Vladimir that they will have no choice but to retaliate if the missile hits anywhere in their country and hangs up the phone.

Vladimir next takes a call from China. This time it is the President of China asking Vladimir why he breached their air space with a missile. "What type of warhead is on that missile and is that missile meant for us or for another country!?" By the time Vladimir explains the mishap, he and the controllers see images sent from the camera on the nose cone of their missile headed dead on target to the North Korean air base. Within minutes there is a flash explosion, and the screen goes black. Vladimir slumps back into his chair and drops the phone. After sitting there for a few minutes in a daze, he quickly picks up the phone to assure the Chinese president that it was all a mistake, and the missile was not meant to strike China or North Korea for that matter. China has already confirmed the hit and that it was carrying a limited nuclear warhead. The President of China loses control and yells uncontrollably at Vladimir, calling him an imbecile. He warns

Vladimir not to make another mistake or he will give China no alternative but to retaliate using the same type of weapon.

The controllers and Vladimir desperately try to get an image of North Korea from one of their satellites. When they succeed, they see an image of a cloud lingering over the largest missile base of North Korea. It is larger than normal because North Korea had some nukes there to test. Vladimir and the controllers cannot believe their eyes. Their hot line rings again and this time it is an interpreter for the President of North Korea. The interpreter prepares to repeat the words of the North Korean President. Before he can speak, Vladimir desperately tries to explain that it was a mistake. When the President of North Korea speaks through the interpreter, he informs Vladimir regardless of whether it was a mistake, he leaves them no choice but to save face by retaliating and hangs up the phone. Vladimir sits there dazed without saying a word. He tries to get the leaders of North Korea back on the phone, but his people cannot make contact. Vladimir then summons his logistics people to learn more about the launch capabilities of the North Koreans and how Russia can avert a strike.

The logistics people brief Vladimir that their defense systems have limited guidance systems to ward off a missile attack. As far as the capability of North Korea's missiles, the last time North Korea tested a nuclear bomb was in 2017. "The explosion at its Punggye-ri test site had a force, or "yield", of between 100-370 kilotons. A 100-kiloton bomb is six times more powerful than the one the US dropped on Hiroshima in 1945. "(122) The only good news the Russian control centers had was that their satellites revealed that North Korea had only one missile ready to launch which had the capability to reach Russia. The others would take a day or two to get them ready for launch.

Sanyo gives his opinion on what needs to be done. "It is your sworn duty to alert the Russian people to prepare themselves for a possible nuclear attack." Vladimir looks out the window and then speaks. "There is no reason to concern the people right now. We will wait to see if North Korea retaliates" "But Vladimir, we will only have an hour or less to prepare if North Korea launches." "That's my decision, we will wait and see." Everyone in the control room looked away from Vladimir in disapproval.

In the meantime, NORAD is using their satellites to monitor the results of the missile strike and keep Alexei informed. They know from classified documents that a 10-megaton bomb detonated at an optimal altitude might do medium damage to 9.4 miles from ground zero, but a 100-megaton bomb will do the same amount of damage to 20.3 surrounding miles. The reason for NORAD picking the one missile site of North Korea is that they wanted no collateral damage of civilian populations. They knew that North Korea picked the location for their number one missile base because there are no people living or allowed to live for that matter, within one hundred miles of the base and that would mean no collateral damage to civilian populations. NORAD monitors the other missile base that has the capability to launch their only nuclear weapon. Surveillance from their satellite reveals that they are preparing a launch. Again, no collateral damage will result because no civilian populations are within one hundred miles of the base.

NORAD alerts Alexei who in turn calls Sanyo to ask him to prepare the Russian people to cover up. Sanyo questions Alexei. "How do you know that we launched, and that North Korea is going to definitely retaliate." "Remember that I served at the highest level of the command structure at the Pentagon. I have contacts there that keep me abreast of what is going on around the globe Sanyo. Is President Vladimir going to alert the Russian people or not about a possible nuclear missile attack?" Sanyo hesitates but knows that it is the duty of Russia's President to protect the people and if he does not, it is an impeachable offense. "No Alexei, he is not. His thoughts are to wait for them to launch." "I am telling you right now Sanyo that they are preparing to launch an attack on Russia with a nuclear warhead!"

"What do you want of me Alexei. I urged Vladimir to go on the air to warn the people and he refused. "What about you going on the air to warn the people Alexei?" "You know that the television studios will not allow anyone broadcast unless the administration approves it Sanyo." "Who do you think I am Alexei? I am the administration and can approve your broadcast." Alexei puts forth a major question to Sanyo. "You are willing to put yourself at risk if you cross Vladimir?" "The way I see it now Alexei is that Vladimir's time as President is very limited. I first owe allegiance to the people. I will send a message to the stations to let you broadcast a message to the country."

Knowing that there is no other option, Alexei agrees to go on air. He calls Oleg and Ferdinand to ask to use one of their studios and they agree. Knowing that Sanyo is signing his death warrant, Alexei clears it with Oleg and Ferdinand to allow Sanyo to take refuge at the Mountain-top compound. They agree.

While Alexei readies himself to address the nation, Sanyo orders the military to stand up its missile defense systems. The military sends an encrypted message to all military bases to prepare their anti-ballistic missile systems, the A-235 system, which is designed to intercept incoming warheads targeted at striking its capital or other major cities. System A-235 PL-19 *Nudol* (Russian: Система А-235 / ПЛ-19-181М / Нудоль) is a Russian hypersonic anti-ballistic missile and anti-satellite weapon system in development. It is designed to deflect a nuclear attack on Moscow and other regions within European Russia. Russia has three anti-ballistic missiles. (123)

Alexei arrives at the studio and prepares to address the nation. "My fellow Russians, our President has placed our nation in jeopardy by launching a nuclear missile at a target in Ukraine that went astray, causing massive damages to one of North Korea's military bases. You must prepare for the possible retaliation from North Korea. I am doing everything that I can to avoid this catastrophe. In case all fails, our experts on training the military how to protect themselves will now provide you with some valuable information on self-protection.

A weapons defense trainer enters the broadcast booth and starts his presentation to protect the people of Russia. "You'll need to shield yourself from the thermal and nuclear radiation, as you could die if exposed. However, you must find somewhere safe – you do not want to be crushed in a building destroyed by the blast wave. Get indoors, and preferably into a reinforced bunker or basement. Stock up on non-perishable food, water, and first aid supplies, if possible. Seek shelter indoors immediately. If you cannot get to a basement, find a central part of a concrete building. Remove contaminated clothing and wipe off or wash unprotected skin if you were outside after the fallout arrived. If you are outdoors and there are no nearby buildings when the explosion occurs "take cover from the blast behind anything that might offer protection." "Lie face down to protect exposed skin from the heat and flying debris," or if you are in a vehicle, "stop safely, and duck down within the vehicle. If in a building, seek central corridors on lower floors of the building which will also provide good protection." (124)

After the trainers were finished with their instructions, Alexei came back on the air. "Hopefully, we have learned that war is not an answer to solving disagreements between two nations. To quote a past President of the United States, "If we do not eradicate war from the face of our earth, war will eradicate us from the face of our earth (*President Harry Truman*)." Upon completing his broadcast, Alexei returned to the Mountain top retreat to interact with NORAD.

NORAD was waiting for Alexei to tune in on their communication channel. As soon as Alexei made contact, NORAD briefed him on what they are picking up from their satellite surveillance of the North Korean continent. The satellite has pinpointed considerable activity from one of their other bases where they launch missiles, P'unggye-ri in northwest North Korea. This base was a former Japanese Army Air Service base taken over by the North Koreans. "The Punggye-ri Nuclear Test Facility is North Korea's only nuclear test site and was the location of the 2006, 2009, 2013, January 2016, September 2016, and September 2017 nuclear tests. [1] The facility is in mountainous terrain with three visible tunnel entrances known as the South Portal." (125) NORAD reported to Alexei that they are readying a missile launch.

Alexei asks if they can do the same maneuver with the missile that they used for the one launched by Vladimir? "Perhaps you could make the missile do a boomerang maneuver where it would return to the North Korean base that launched it?" NORAD responds that they can try but they first need approval from Washington to divert the missile. Alexei urges them to expedite the approval because time is working against them. The process of gaining approval for such an action would normally take more than a day. Because of the underlying concerns to get it through as soon as possible, however, NORAD knew they must push the right buttons as soon as possible. After all agencies have chopped off (military jargon for signed off), NORAD said Washington gave them the okay and everything is a go for trying to divert the launch.

The White House gave their approval and requested that allied intelligence agencies step up efforts to detect any North Korea and Russian military moves or communications that might signal the launch of nuclear weapons. NORAD and the Allies task additional U.S. and allied intelligence assets. This would include aircraft, space assets, and satellites connected to cyberspace. Outside military installations, they also tasked commercial Earth-imaging satellites. Based on satellite imagery, they zeroed in on the launch site of North Korea's missile base. They were pleased to see that the base is far from civilian populations, thus confirming that they will avoid any collateral damage to civilian populations.

Meanwhile, North Korea was preparing to launch. It intended to use one of their most powerful Intercontinental Ballistic Missile (ICBM). In a test launch of two of its long-range cruise missiles to a dummy target, 1118 miles away at an average speed of 447 mph. (126)

It can reach great distances such as New York City and Moscow. The countdown begins. NORAD picks up North Korea's launch while

Russia positioned its systems to intercept it. The countdown hits one and the missile lifts off its launch pad.

Because their missile had limited distance, North Korea had to set its course over the northeastern region of China and part of Mongolia. Normal protocol is for one country to request and receive approval for passage through another country's airspace, especially one that is supposed to be their ally. North Korea sent a message to Beijing that the path of their missile would penetrate its air space but did not wait to receive their approval. China put its air defenses on high alert when it picked up North Korea's missile on its satellites. After they concluded that it was lunched from North Korea, they immediately phoned the General Secretary of North Korea to warn him that they breached China's air space without permission and requested specifics on what the missile was carrying. The General Secretary had his people send specifics on the missile content. As soon as China, learned that it was carrying a nuclear missile, it sent anti-ballistic missiles to take it down. As it would soon be over more populated areas of China, they had a very narrow window. China's missiles were unable to gain enough air speed to catch and destroy North Korea's missile.

Shortly thereafter, the leader of China contacted the General Secretary of North Korea and read him the riot act. An intense argument ensued, and North Korea's General Secretary hung the phone up on China's premier. At the delight of NATO and its allies, this would tarnish future relations between China and North Korea.

As his last act as Chief of staff and before Vladimir can locate his whereabouts, Sanyo sends a message to launch anti-ballistic missiles to take down the North Korean missile. Russia launches but again their missiles fail to take down the nuclear warhead enroute to Moscow.

The last hope to stop the missile is NORAD. NORAD jams the guidance systems of North Korea and takes over the guidance system of its missile. They input the coordinates of the base where the missile was launched, 41°16'47.87"N 129°5'10.51"E. Cheers come from the controllers in the NORAD command post when they see the missile reversing its course. The guidance for the missile was being overseen by top generals in the North Korean command post where the missile was launched. One of the North Korean controllers in the command post turns to the generals and reports that there seems to be something wrong with the target coordinates for their missile. The missile seems to be turning in a boomerang effect and changing its coordinates. We put in the coordinates for Moscow, 55.7558° N, 37.6173° E but the target coordinates appear to now be 41°16'47.87"N 129°5'10.51"E, which is the location of our launch site and our command post. The general's eyes widened, and fear came across their faces. It was too late to ring the alarm to evacuate. They froze in place until the missile hit. All went black across their grid. Upon the North Korean General Secretary receiving notice of its failure, he gave the order to stand down any further attempts to launch another missile. Throughout Russia, the people are exuberant that there no longer is a threat of a nuclear strike. They chant Alexei name and start demonstrating against Vladimir and call for his resignation.

Vladimir is watching all this from his office and has called Sanyo numerous times to come to his office. Knowing that Sanyo acted without his approval, he is livid and wants to deal with him accordingly. He then receives a call from the guards at his dacha on the sea. They report that his palace has been overtaken by Ukrainian commandos. They kidnapped Lina and ransacked his palace. Out of frustration, Vladimir throws the phone on the ground and stands up from his desk. He orders his security to ready his helicopter and his escort. "We leave at once for my home on the sea." His head of security holds his hands up in a stopping motion. "This is the weekend Mr. President, and we only have a handful of security guards that can accompany you and there is not enough time to assemble a viable escort of security guards for your protection." Allowing his emotions to take over his common sense, Vladimir screams at his head of security. "I don't care, I want to leave within the hour."

In the meantime, his twisted mental state starts to take over his thought processes. With what he perceives as past interludes between Alexei and Lina, he starts wondering if Lina was taken to Ukraine against her Will or did, she go willingly.

Normally, Vladimir travels with a large security contingency but in his haste, he does not allow his head of security enough time to assemble a larger security force. Only one helicopter with six security people accompanied Vladimir. The President of Russia travels in a helicopter equivalent to Marine One In addition to its most common role as a transport helicopter, the Mi-8 is also used as an airborne command post, armed gunship, and reconnaissance platform. (127) Vladimir's head of security is counting on the guards at the palace to add to his protection.

CHAPTER 33

THE IMPEACHMENT

Alexei and his special ops people received words that Vladimir is on his way to the coast. Alexei alerts his commandos in the tunnel to ready themselves for another assault. Alexei and Joey's team leaves at once to intercept Vladimir moments after his arrival. Upon Vladimir's arrival, he hastily enters the mansion. He yells and berates the guards, calling them incompetent and all kinds of names. The guards stand with their eyes downcast, hating the way Vladimir has treated them in the past and how he is berating them now.

Vladimir paces up and down reading them the riot act as the guards stand at attention while three of the six security people he brought keeps them at attention. "How did you let this happen! How did you survive without a fight? You should have given your lives to protect my property and Lina! My property is far more important than your lives! You are all useless! I will have you all horse whipped and imprisoned for dereliction of duty!"

Just then, one of Alexei's two teams scale the cliffs (Photo 29) to overtake and disarm three of Vladimir's security people waiting outside next to his helicopter. The other team ascends into the mansion from the tunnels and at the surprise of Vladimir and his three remaining

Photo 32-Soldiers climbing a Cliff

security people, the team overtakes them while keeping a watch on Vladimir. Alexei and Joey's helicopters land at the same time. Vladimir yells at his security guarding his helicopter and barks orders for his palace guards to defend him. "Do not just stand there! Defend your President! Shield me and shoot them!"

The Guard leader shakes his head no. "We no longer follow your orders Mr. President. We are tired of your ranting and the way you have treated us these past years while we have protected you and this so-called palace! To boot, we have lost good friends and children, killed in your senseless war on Ukraine. We now owe our allegiance to our new Czar, Alexei!"

At that moment, Alexei and Joey enter the mansion. Vladimir turns to confront them, shouting obscenities and calling them traders to him and Russia. "So, you are behind all this Alexei! Remember what I showed you on your last visit to my office, those silos loaded with Tactical missiles!"

Vladimir reaches in his pocket for his phone and yells in the command code to launch the missiles but there is no confirmation of a launch from the silos. He repeats himself several times but again receives no confirmation of a launch. Frustrated he looks at his phone to see if there is a signal. Alexei shows Vladimir his phone. "There will be no launch because we now control those nuclear silos Vladimir. Our people have taken them over."

Vladimir desperately tries to draw a pistol from one of the guards, but the guard overpowers him and pushes him to the floor. Vladimir sits there in bewilderment, repeatedly saying "I am the President of Russia, and you must obey my orders." The instability of his mental state is now showing and all present now realize that they have been taking orders from a deranged man. Alexei helps Vladimir to his feet and tries to be as kind as possible. "Come with us Vladimir. We need to get you some help." Vladimir tries to resist but the guards have a tight grip on his arms. "I do not need help," repeating that he is the President of Russia and will have their heads if they do not release him. He looks around hoping to see Lina. "And where is my Lina? I want to talk with Lina. Surely, she has not abandoned me."

Finally, after Vladimir realizes that he has been put under custody, he droops his head in despair. Some of Alexei's security takes him back to the Kremlin in the same helicopter that brought him. Once back at the Kremlin, he is placed under house arrest while the Russian parliament debates on whether to impeach him and have him stand trial. The crimes that an international tribunal might consider are obvious enough. Vladimir's unprovoked violation of Ukrainian sovereignty is a clear-cut case of the crime of aggression, defined in international law as the use of armed force by a state against another state's sovereignty, territorial integrity, or political independence of another state.

The record thus far indicates that Vladimir has intentionally ordered the terrorizing of civilian populations and by any measure, that is a war crime. The frequency and intensity of his attacks on civilians may rise to the level of a crime against humanity, legally defined as certain acts committed as part of a widespread or systematic attack on a civilian population. The actions of his military—murder of civilians, sexual crimes, forced deportation—may even meet the standards of the crime of genocide: actions committed with intent to destroy, in whole or in part, a national group as such. (128)

Moreover, Vladimir could be impeached for not alerting the Russian people of imminent attack of a nuclear missile and ordering his security to apprehend Lina without just cause. This could constitute kidnapping and carry severe punishment. Following many hours of debate, the Russian Parliament decides to delay impeachment proceedings dependent on the outcome of Vladimir being tried by their Supreme Court.

Alexei researches the impeachment process and what will happen if Vladimir is impeached and removed from office.

"Article 93 of the Russian Constitution states that "The President of the Russian Federation may be impeached by the Council of Federation only on the basis of charges of high treason or of another grave crime brought by the State Duma and confirmed by a resolution of the Supreme Court of the Russian Federation on the existence of indications of a crime in the actions of the President of the Russian Federation and by a resolution of the Constitutional Court of the Russian Federation confirming that the established procedure for bringing charges has been observed. The decision of the State Duma to bring charges and the decision of the Council of Federation to impeach the President must be adopted by two-thirds of votes of the total number of members of each chamber on the initiative of not less than one third of deputies of the State Duma and on the basis of a resolution of a special commission set up by the State Duma."

Article 92 states that where the President of the Russian Federation is unable to fulfil his (her) duties, they shall be temporarily delegated to the Chairman of the Government of the Russian Federation. The Acting President of the Russian Federation shall not have the right to dissolve the State Duma, call a referendum or to submit proposals for amendments to and the revision of the provisions of the Constitution of the Russian Federation." (129)

While this was all going on, Ferdinand and Oleg started broadcasting the truth, using the leaders and role models suggested by Alexei to deliver the message. Along with the message, a series of photos and movie clips are shown of the atrocities committed at the direction of Vladimir. Bodies of young Russian soldiers are also depicted in the photos and movie clips. All throughout Russia, the people are shocked at what they see and cannot believe that they have been lied to all this time.

It all was falling into place, including the recent ruling by the ICC finding Vladimir and his generals guilty of war crimes. This ruling is also broadcasted across Russia by the news media. Such an indictment further legitimized the decree by the Duma and the Russian courts to try Vladimir for impeachment and his removal from office.

Alexei addresses the leaders at the mansion. "We now need to request that the Prime Minister issue a cease fire in Ukraine while the Russian courts try Vladimir and his generals. If we get a favorable ruling, the only thing that can save Vladimir from a life sentence is their finding him insane.

Gorbousky chimes in. "I was able to arrange with the Russian Supreme court the expediting of Vladimir's trial and that of the Generals. They have agreed to hold it starting tomorrow." The leaders find this exhilarating and retire for the night to their quarters.

"Russia's highest judicial body is the Supreme Court, which supervises the activities of all other judicial bodies and serves as the final court of appeal. The Supreme Court has been supplemented since 1991 by a Constitutional Court, established to review Russian laws and treaties. The Constitutional Court is presided over by 19 judges, who are nominated by the president and approved by the Federation Council and appointed to life terms. The Russian legal system has attempted to overcome the repression practiced during the Soviet era by requiring public trials and guaranteeing a defense for the accused."

The Constitutional court deals with disputes concerning the constitutionality of certain legal acts and is a separate judicial body in the Russian court system. Commercial courts deal with just what they sound like, matters of economic concern. Regional courts include magistrate and resolve minor matters. The Supreme court is the court of cessation and the supervisory court which could make a final decision or overturn a lower court's decision." (130) Normally, Vladimir would be tried in the Constitutional court but to avoid any appeals by Vladimir, the Constitutional court deferred his case to the Supreme court of Russia.

Alexei goes back to his room to find Lina waiting for him. She is sitting at the end of the bed just like he left her the last time. She kiddingly tells him that they have some unfinished business from the last time they spent the night together. She is dressed in a silk top that has one side dropped below her shoulder. Her hair is down over her shoulders, leaning back on the bed. She takes Alexei hand in hers and gently pulls him over to the bed. Alexei tries hard to resist but Lina is very persistent and not ready to give up. You could sense a tremor in both their voices. Finally, Lina agrees to give Alexei space and starts out the door. What is not obvious is the innocence of the two who only had one serious relationship in each of their lives. Alexei was always on military duty and Lina trained most of her life for Olympic competitions and never really had true love. Vladimir was more in love with her beauty than with her spiritually and Lina was more infatuated with his position.

Alexei suddenly realizes that he loves Lina and can no longer resist her. Before she can go out the door, he takes her by her hand and lovingly pulls her back into the room. He pulls back her hair and gently brings her body against his. He starts showering her with passionate kisses and she returns the same. "I have been wanting to do this since the first time I saw you Lina and each time we were together, it became more difficult for me to resist." "I feel the same Alexei."

The two continue to shower one another with kisses and start to slowly undress one another. They continue their hugs and kisses while Alexei picks her up and gently lays her in the center of the bed, holding her against himself until they melt into one another's bodies.

After a long night of love making, they fall asleep in each other's arms. Alexei wakes first to ready himself for the trial of Vladimir. He receives word from the Kremlin that Vladimir is already on his way to the Supreme Court of Russia. Alexei leans over to passionately kiss Lina before going for breakfast. Before taking a second step, she pulls him back towards her to tenderly return the kiss and whispers in his ear how much she loves him.

Gorbousky walks out into the hallway from his room at the same time as Alexei leaves his room. Besides wishing Alexei good morning, he smiles and makes a comment about when he and his wife were deeply in love with each other. "I remember when I spent the first night with my wife when we were passionately in love."

CHAPTER 34

THE TRIAL

Upon Alexei joins everyone for breakfast, Joey hurriedly enters the dining room to announce that "CNN is reporting that announces that the News is reporting that missiles rained down on Israel as Iran launched an attack on Tuesday and that Israel vows "very strong response to Iran missile Attack." Everyone looks at one another in astonishment, wondering how this will affect their rebuilding of Russia's government." (131) Alexei stands up and calms the mood by saying we cannot allow world events interfere with our establishing a bright and new future for Russia. My heart goes out, however, to all the soldiers and innocent people that will suffer because of the ignorance and egos of their leaders. Everyone raises their water glass in a sign of agreement.

After Alexei and the leaders finish a full breakfast, they all leave for the Supreme court of Russia. All the leadership team had to do to incriminate Vladimir was to validate the case files accumulated by the ICC and present them to Russia's Supreme Court. As the evidence was undeniably stacked against Vladimir, the trial should move very quickly. Besides lying to the Russian people, Vladimir will be charged with war crimes.

The International Criminal Court has specific definitions for genocide, war crimes, crimes against humanity and the crime of aggression. Read about them in this guide published by the ICC.

Specifically, targeting civilian populations, violating the Geneva Conventions, targeting specific groups of people and more could be potential Russian war crimes. Khan said there can be justified attacks in civilian areas if they are being used to launch attacks. But even then, he said, attacks in civilian areas cannot be disproportionate. There is a method of gathering evidence from testimony, satellite images and elsewhere to meet a burden of proof. (132)

All that Alexei could think about while the trial commenced was pulling back all the troops in Ukraine so no more atrocities could occur, and blood would not be spilled by the military on both sides. At the same time, he wanted to curve the economic costs of the war. The cost was starting to seriously concern not only Russia, but America and other Western countries that were embroiled with economic problems. The global economy was heading fast into a recession.

The courtroom was packed, and thousands of Russians gathered outside to watch on a large screen what was transpiring inside. Ferdinand and Oleg arranged for the trial to be broadcast on all major television networks and the judge's permitted coverage by U.S. and other foreign television networks.

The judges enter the court room. The clerk of Courts calls for everyone to rise and pronounces that the court is in session. The judge calls Vladimir Dimitri to come before the court and the clerk reads the charges against him, war crimes. He asks Vladimir how he pleads, guilty or not guilty as charged. Vladimir gives a stance of defiance and firmly pleads "Not Guilty!" The trial starts.

The Prosecutors calls Vladimir to the stands and shows film clips from Ukraine of killing civilians and bombing of Ukraine schools and hospitals. Included are photos of the bodies of children and old people lying dead on the streets. It shows some Russian soldiers killing adults and children in cold blood, and their raping of young women.

This was the first time that the Russian people saw these photos. Now seeing them for the first time, the people in the courtroom and those outside it gasped at the horrors they saw.

The prosecution calls Vladimir to the stand for questioning. "Vladimir, did you give orders or allow such atrocities as depicted in these film clips? Were you aware that this was being inflicted by your troops? Vladimir stands and points his finger in defiance. "I did not order or permit such attacks and was not aware of them. I have been falsely accused of ordering such atrocities." "You may step down Mr. President"

The prosecuting attorney next calls the President of Russia's Parliament and puts forth a question to him. "Who is the supreme commander of the Russian military? The Parliament President points to Vladimir. "According to Article 87 of our constitution, the president of Russia, is Supreme Commander-in-Chief of the Armed Forces of the Russian Federation." Pointing to Vladimir again. "He holds ultimate commanding authority and responsibility over the Russian Armed Forces"

The Prosecuting attorney thanks him for clarifying who is responsible for the actions of the military. "You may step down"

The prosecution calls to stand the President's Chief of the General Staff, General Gerasin. General Gerasin takes the witness stand.

"General Gerasin, who was directing the overall proliferation of the war on Ukraine and were orders ever given to target civilians, hospitals, homes, and schools?"

General Gerasin points to Vladimir. "Why that would have been the President. He gave the orders to kill civilians if necessary and to target schools and hospitals. He told us that because the President of Ukraine urged Ukraine civilians to fight, we were justified in treating civilians as combatants and they should be shot on sight. When we were not making much headway, he even urged us to target civilians even if they were not combatants." Vladimir jumps to his feet yelling that the General is lying! The general yells back. "You are the liar,

President Vladimir. Many a time, you directed us to target civilian targets and even schools and hospitals!" The judge scolds Vladimir. "Sit down and restrain yourself."

"You may step down General Gerasin. The prosecution now calls the first Deputy Chief of the General Staff, Colonel General Bogman. General Bogman, were you present in all meetings with the President and General Gerasin. In fact, here are photos that show the three of you conferring on the war in the President's office."

"Yes, I was present but as a lower ranking officer, I had no input or say. In fact, I was shocked at what transpired in those meetings. I was denied any input to condone or refute any orders or decisions. All major decisions were made by President Vladimir. Other military officers that was present only gave suggestions and advice. What marching orders were you and General Gerasin given and who initiated those orders?"

"The orders were to do whatever necessary to bring the Ukrainian people to their knees even if it meant bombing civilian targets. The higher-ranking generals in the meeting questioned President Vladimir on his choice of targets and reminded him that it was against the Geneva Convention. He retorted that he would bare sole responsibility for issuing such orders. He said to show no mercy, annihilate the cities and its people if necessary."

Again, Vladimir yelled out calling Bogman and Gerasin traitors. Again, the judge told Vladimir to refrain himself. You may step down General Bogman. The prosecution now calls the President's chief of staff, Jon Sanyo."

A long time has passed since Vladimir laid eyes on Sanyo. Vladimir was surprised that Sanyo was going to testify against him. Vladimir started squirming in his seat. Sanyo glanced at both Vladimir and Alexei. He nodded at Alexei and looked away from Vladimir, giving an advanced sign that his testimony would not bode well for Vladimir.

"Mr. Sanyo, you were privy to all that went on in the strategy meetings of the Ukraine war, were you not." "Yes, I attended them as ordered by the President."

"Who grafted the orders to bomb civilian targets and kill noncombatants? Please point to that person if he is present in the court room." Immediately, Sanyo points to Vladimir. "He is sitting there. Not only did he issue the orders, but he wanted to blame it on Czar Alexei. I am here to testify that the Czar had nothing to do with it. The Czar tried to stop Vladimir. I had to do Vladimir's bidding because he threatened to kill me and my family."

Again, Vladimir bursts out in uncontrollable and insane rage. The head judge warns Vladimir that he is not to interrupt the proceedings again or he will be gagged.

The prosecuting attorney again pressed Sanyo for his input as to whether it was warranted to launch weapons of mass destruction. "In my opinion, it was not necessary." The judge ordered that his one comment be stricken from the record because it was an opinion.

The prosecuting attorney rephrased his question. "Did you urge the President to warn the Russian people when it appeared that a nuclear attack from North Korea was imminent?" "Yes, I urged him to make a national announcement using our television networks, but he refused. Knowing the devastation it could cause; I took matters into my own hands by asking Czar Alexei to make that broadcast." If the Czar had not done so and that missile would have reached Moscow, millions would have perished needlessly!"

"You may step down Mr. Sanyo." To the surprise of Vladimir, the prosecution called Lina.

Russia's criminal code has an abduction/kidnapping law which carries a prison sentence of up to fifteen years, thus the reason for calling Lina who was technically abducted by Vladimir. The prosecutor interrogates Lina if she was abducted by President Vladimir or voluntarily went to President Vladimir's villa on the coast. "I was abducted by President Vladimir who sits there." Lina pointed to

Vladimir. "It was President Vladimir who abducted me! I was freed by our Czar."

The reason for the prosecuting attorney introducing Lina was to add another count to Vladimir's crimes so if others did not stick the one for abduction would. Vladimir's defense attorney cross examined Lina, trying to discredit her allegation but did little to do so.

Lastly, the prosecuting attorney called the commander of the guards at Vladimir's dacha. "Did President Vladimir ever hold anyone captive in his summer dacha? If so, could you please point that person out if they are present in this courtroom." The commander of the guard lifts his hand and points his finger at Lina. "He held that lady against her will at his summer palace. We were ordered by President Vladimir to keep her captive until he said otherwise."

Next, the prosecuting attorneys called Dr. Jervalny. As Dr. Jervalny comes to the stand, Vladimir starts to squirm again. The prosecution starts with asking Dr. Jervalny his name and how he came to know Vladimir and what his areas of specialty were. "Along with other doctors, I was a long-time physician treating him for a specific medical condition. Looking at the Presiding Judge, Dr. Jervalny asks if he can break doctor to patient confidentiality. The Judge gives his consent. "If your testimony is pertinent to this case and whatever you reveal is not directly relevant to your specific treatment, you can talk openly." Dr. Jervalny outlined his areas of expertise, including his background in psychiatry. The prosecutor asks Dr. Jervalny if he treated President Vladimir for any mental disorders. "No, I did not." "Then you can talk freely of what you observed when it comes to his behavior Dr. Jervalny." Dr. Jervalny felt relieved that he will not violate his hypocritic oath if he discusses what he observed about Vladimir's behavior. "I observed some erratic behavior from President Vladimir. In my professional opinion, the President is suffering from schizophrenia, gross disorganization, diminished emotional expression, overshadowing all the rest, he must have paranoid personality disorder. Paranoid personality disorder is a condition that you feel you do not know who you can trust. He may also be a germophobic. All this may account for Vladimir distancing himself from others.

Vladimir again yells out that what he is hearing is preposterous. The presiding judge gives him another warning.

The prosecuting attorney asks the president judge if he can approach the bench. "Your honor, I would like to show a brief film that will wrap up my case against the President." The president judge gives his approval to show the film.

The courtroom goes dark as a screen lights up with a video. "First it shows a segment of a ship loading stolen grain in a Ukrainian port sanctioned by Vladimir." Second are photographs of ten sites in a town called Izium where civilians and soldiers have been tortured." (132) "Third were photos of an attack on the village of Chaplyne which was one of the deadliest and came when the villagers were peacefully celebrating Independence Day. Fourth were slides showing a deadly attack on a nursing home. Fifth was the destruction of schools. Sixth showed a fifteen-year-old boy telling the story of Russian soldiers trying to execute him. Seventh were photos of more than four hundred civilian corpses discovered in mass graves." (133)

The president judge called for an end to the video. "We have seen enough Mr. Prosecutor. Do you have anything else to present?" "No, your honor."

The defense attorneys for Vladimir were perplexed, trying to find anything else that will vindicate Vladimir or at least reduce whatever sentence that may be handed down. After exhausting all its excuses and knowing it had little rebuttal except to ask for leniency due to insanity, the defense attorneys had no alternative but to rest its case, after giving its closing arguments.

The judges stood to leave the courtroom to determine if Vladimir's fate. In his twisted mind, Vladimir thought the trial was over and started to leave the courtroom. The presiding judge ordered Vladimir to stay in place. Vladimir turned and simply asked why he should stay. "The hearing is over, is it not? I have a lot of work to do back at the Kremlin and need to get on with it." The presiding judge directed the security guards to hold Vladimir in place.

Vladimir started to get out of control. "Why are you holding me? I did nothing wrong. Yes, I did all what they said. I did it for Russia. I had civilians targeted and approved hitting schools and nursing homes with missiles. This is what I was trained to do as a KGB agent. I took an oath to do whatever it takes to protect our mother land! I am the President of Russia and need to go back to my office! "Two security guards subdue Vladimir and pull him back to his seat. You could not hear a pin drop in the courtroom. All in the courtroom or watched the trial on television now realize more than ever why Vladimir is psychotic. You could hear whispers throughout the courtroom where people were pitying him.

The judges left the courtroom to deliberate their verdict only to return within an hour. The court tip staff asked Vladimir to rise and face the judges. When the presiding judge addressed Vladimir as Mister and not President, everyone knew what the ruling would be, including Vladimir. Vladimir's head dropped.

The tipstaff asks all to rise and for Vladimir to face the judges but he refused. Two security guards grabbed Vladimir by his arms and lifted him to his feet. The Presiding judge gazes upon Vladimir. "Vladimir Dimitri, we find you guilty of war crimes and violating your oath of office and the constitution of Russia. Your actions have placed our people in harm's way and unnecessarily caused the lives of our soldiers and the lives of innocent people of other countries. What sentence we are about to hand down does not nearly compensate the people of Ukraine or Russia for their losses. "

Turning again to Vladimir, the presiding judge decrees his sentence. "Because we cannot even begin to believe that any sane person would have caused such atrocities and destruction as you, we cannot sentence you to be executed. We can, however, sentence you to imprisonment at one of the most hard-core prisons in Russia, the

Butyrka Prison. There you will undergo psychiatric treatment." At the same time, the International criminal court finds Vladimir guilty of war crimes after reviewing all the evidence presented to them

Having received his sentence, Vladimir is reluctantly led out of the courtroom with his arms and legs chackled in chains through a back door to a waiting van. The scene outside is likened to the demonstrations outside Czar Nicholas's palace in the early 1900's when he was forced to abdicate his throne. People surround the courthouse chanting shame on Vladimir.

The lead prosecutor spoke briefly with Alexei and others before departing the courtroom. "Vladimir may have been better off if they had executed him. In the center of Moscow lies a prison infamous for the inhumane treatment of inmates. Since its first incarnation 250 years ago, Butyrka Prison has been home to a long history of harsh living conditions, human rights violations, and spectacular escape attempts. (132) Its famous inmates once included the revolutionary poet Vladimir Mayakovsky, the founder of the KGB Felix Dzerzhinsky, and the poet Aleksandr Solzhenitsyn. Any prisoners Vladimir committed to the prison may kill him. He may wish he were dead.

Photo 33-Russian Prison-Butyrka Prison

Russia's Duma (the parliament) invoked Article 93 of their constitution, unanimously voting to impeach Vladimir. They followed on to vote to invoke Article 92 of their constitution to appoint a temporary replacement for Vladimir. They adhere to Article 92 by appointing the Chairman of the Government of the Russian Federation temporary president until a new one can be elected. Parliament also degreed that Sanyo will continue as chief of staff while the prime minister puts his ministers in place. Alexei felt that it was a good move by the parliament because the Chairman may not have spoken against the invasion of Russa, but everyone knew that he was not supportive of it. The Chairman of the Russian Federation ordered a cease fire in Ukraine and to start withdrawing Russian troops from Ukraine The countries of the world stopped sanctions against Russia.

Alexei and the leaders on his team returned to Oleg's Mountain hideaway for a celebration and reflection on the new direction of Russia. All those involved in the overthrow of Vladimir joined them.

Gorbousky lifted his glass in toast fashion and specifically toasted Alexei, suggesting that Alexei would make a great President as well as a fantastic Czar. Alexei quickly retorts. "One title is enough Mikal. "

"Join me in a toast to the best thing that has happened to Russia in years, except for me (laughing kiddingly when referring to himself). And of course, that person is Czar Alexei. If Alexei would have been Czar during the time of his great grandfather Nicholas, the likes of communism and Vladimir would not have befallen Russia." Winking at Alexei, Gorbousky holds his glass in the air. "Perhaps the Czar and President of Russia can be one in the same."

CHAPTER 35

THE PROPOSAL

Now that Vladimir has been incarcerated, Lina leaves the mountain top to check on her apartment. Alexei returns to his apartment at the Kremlin to catch up on his correspondence and checks his calendar.

Alexei had formal audiences with dignitaries that day and therefore needed to dress in his formal dress as the Czar would wear. As he was donning his formal uniform including jacket with epaulettes and medals, Nikolai informs Alexei that his niece Katey and her husband Steve was in his waiting room. Alexei suddenly realizes that he invited them to visit him in Russia. Alexei goes to greet them. His niece is stunning, and her husband is handsome, having the appearance of two movie stars. Being a history buff of the military, Steve asks Alexei if he could see the armament room. "Of course, Steve, I will give you a personal tour." Before leaving his apartment, Alexei asks Nikolai to bring some refreshments for his niece.

Upon Alexei and Steven leaving, Katey answers a knock at the apartment door while Alexei is gone. Katey opens the door, and both ladies have a surprise look on their face, with Lina thinking that Alexei is cheating on her with another lady. Not wanting to be confrontational, she hurriedly excuses herself without giving Katey a chance to introduce herself.

Upon Alexei returning to his apartment, Katey informs her uncle of his visitor, and the surprise look on her face when she saw her in his apartment. Alexei's eyes widen and thinks the worst. "She must think that I am cheating on her with you Katey. I must explain." He calls her cell phone several times but no answer. "The two of you must come with me to Lina's apartment so I can introduce you as my niece." Before going, he tries several times to reach her by phone but again no answer. Alexei asks Nikolai to bring up his limo. This time, Alexei is escorted with two SUV's full of security, one in back and one in front of his limo.

Upon arriving at Lina's apartment, she is nowhere to be found. Joey suggests calling her cousin. "Her cousin told him that she left for her parent's Inn because she was upset about you cheating on her with a young woman she met in your apartment. Her cousin said that Lina has been hurt too many times in the past and it is difficult for her to deal with another."

Alexei climbs back into his limo and directs his driver to take him to the home of Lina's parents. This time, the driver took the main highways and made good time. It was very strange to see these three large black vehicles drive through the village and up to the Inn of Lina's parents. People in the village noticed the seal of the Czar on the side of the vehicles. Some decided to follow the caravan.

Photo 34-Russian Hall and Inn

When the vehicles wound up the graveled long road to the country Inn of Lina's family (Photo 31), her family came out to see what the commotion was all about. Alexei stood in front of them dressed in his formal Czar dress. The family was stunned to see the caravan, security, and John standing before them dressed like royalty. "What is this all about John." "Forgive me for not telling you when I last visited your home. My name is Alexei, and my family business is being Czar."

The family was shocked and did not know what to say except they did not appreciate the way Alexei treated their daughter. "Czar or no Czar, we do not want our daughter involved with the likes of you John or whatever your name is. Alexei tried to explain what happened but could not get a word in whatsoever. "She does not want to see you ever again." As the parents and brothers continued to berate Alexei, Katey and Steve quietly walked around everyone through the front door, appearing moments later. Alexei was relieved to see them together and simply said to Lina. "I see that you have met my niece, Katey." "Yes, I have Alexei, and I apologize for ever doubting you."

Lina steps in front of Alexei and softly caresses his hand, giving him a loving kiss. He in turn returns a kiss and gives a sigh of relief.

One of the attributes that Alexei loved about Lina was her intelligence and cleverness. Lina exhibited her cleverness again by placing her arms around Alexei and whispering in his ear. "Now about that conversation that you agreed to have when Vladimir is ousted from power. I do not notice any ring on my finger. I recall the saying used for your hometown football team, the Pittsburgh Steelers. After earning four rings, Pittsburghers kept saying they wanted one more for the Thumb. Well, I was hoping to have one for my finger.

All the neighbors and Lina's parents suddenly realize that the Czar of Russia and their daughter were standing before them. At first Alexei was ambivalent to what was going on around him. He only had eyes for Lina. Suddenly, Alexei came out of his daze, and he reached into his pocket. "Well, I guess if this is where it has to be, then so be it." Alexei gets down on one knee and opens the small box he pulled out of his pocket. "What do you say Lina? Will this fit that ring finger of yours?" "It's the perfect size Alexei."

Lina laughed and gave Alexei a big kiss and a hug. She professed her love for him and this time he did not say ditto. Alexei wrapped his arms around her and gave her a passionate kiss. You could hear Lina's mother comment. "I hope nothing happens to his family business like what happened to the last Czar of Russia and that he will continue to wash the dishes." Overhearing what she just said, Joey came over laughing and whispered in the mother's ear. "I have known Alexei for years and you can bet on the fact that his family business will survive for as long as Russia survives, and he will wash the dishes for Lina!"

REFERENCES

1. History.com, Romanov family, Original Sept 21, 2017, updated August 15, 2024, by History editors
2. Alexander Palace, Nicholas Diaries and Letters, 1917 Diary of Nicholas II, The Abdication and beyond
3. Tumblr, Romanov Facts
4. The Alexander Palace by I.Bott & V.Faybisovich 1977
5. Britannica, Bloody Sunday, Tsar Nicholas II, Protestors, Massacre
6. Britannica, Alexandra, Empress consort of Russia, Written and fact-checked by Editors
7. Library of Congress, the murder of Rasputin, headlines & heroes
8. Smithsonian Magazine, What really happened during the murder of Rasputin
9. Britannica, How did Catherine the Great come to power
10. History.com, Why the British Royal Crown failed to save the Romanovs
11. Britannica, Russian Provisional government-facts, history, & Summary
12. History.com, Russian Revolution, causes, timeline & Bolsheviks
13. History.com, Why Czar Nicholas II and the Romanovs were murdered
14. Alexander palace.org, Russian history websites, The executioner, Yurovsky's account
15. History.com, Russian revolution, by History.com editors updated March 27, 2024
16. Britannica, Did Duchess Anastasia survive her family's execution?
17. Emigration, Russian Empire, International Encyclopedia of the First World War, by Siobhan Peeling

18. "Overview + History | Ellis Island". Statue of Liberty & Ellis Island. March 4, 2020. Archived from the original on September 18, 2021. Retrieved September 10,2021.

19. CNBC, Putin's popularity rating falls to lowest level in over two decades amid coronavirus outbreak, published May 2, 2020

20. Britannica, Vladimir Putin, President of Russia, written by Michael Ray

21. Britannica, Vladimir Putin, Biography KGB, Political Career and Facts by Michael Ray

22. [Kremlin]. Vaster Etymological dictionary. Archived from the original on 4 December 2022. Retrieved 2 June 2014.

23. Wilson Center, Nikolay Egorychev's notes and the end of the Soviet-Afghan War

24. CNN, Worlds largest plane destroyed in Ukraine, by Jack Guy Feb 2022

25. Passenger search, Statue of Liberty, and Ellis Island

26. Secret Pittsburgh, About the Homestead Pump House

27. Britannica, Kremlin, Moscow, Architecture, History, fat checked by Britannica editors

28. Wikipedia, Presidential administration of Russia

29. "On First Person this week, New Yorker staff writer Masha Gessen on how Vladimir Putin plans to rule Russia forever". "'It's a remarkable feat.' in power since 1999, how Vladimir Putin became a Russian leader rivaled only by Josef Stalin"

30. Reuters, Troop deaths, injuries in Ukraine war nearing 500,000, New York Time citing Ukraine officials

31. Time, A former supreme commander of NATO on what Putin's up to in the Ukraine

32. JSTOR, The new NATO prepared for Russian Hybrid War

33. Wikipedia, Federal State Statistics Service. Archived from the original on 1 September 2022. Retrieved 1

September 2022. "Major Agglomerations of the World - Population Statistics and Maps". Archived from the original on 7 July 2023. Retrieved 2 May 2023. Akishin, Alexander (17 August 2017)."A 3-Hour Commute: A Close Look At Moscow The Megapolis".*Strelka Mag.* Archived from the original on 17 April 2021. Retrieved 23 May 2020

34. Britannica, The inner city, Moscow, Capital, Kremlin, Red Square, written by Richard Anthony French and Kathleen Berton Murrell

35. Russia Beyond, Can you afford to live in Moscow, Ksenia Zubacheva

36. Johnson's Russia list, Percentage of Russians who speak English doubles to 30%

37. The Atlantic, The Soviet War in Afghanistan, 1979-1989, Alan Taylor

38. PBS, Ruble plummets amid global sanctions, sending Russians to Banks and ATMs

39. The Moscow Times, Birds of prey fly high over Moscow on World Falconry Day

40. History, Kaiser Wilhelm, and Czar Nicholas exchange frantic telegrams

41. Britannica, St. Petersburg map, points of interest & History, Daily Maverick

42. "Article 22. Permanent seat of the Supreme Court of the Russian Federation (Edition as of 2 August 2019)". *Collection of federal laws of the Russian Federation* (in Russian). Retrieved 21 January 2022. *Gauslaa, Jon (11 September 2002). "Supreme Court 2000: The reputation of the Presidium". Bellona Foundation. Archived from the original on 25 December 2004. Foglesong, Todd, The Dynamics of Judicial Independence in Russia*

43. Britannica, Winter Palace, Baroque Architecture, Hermitage Museum

44. Ukrainer, Centuries of tyranny in Russia: history of Ivan the Terrible, the first Moscow Tsar,

45. Francois Veldi, The Title of Emperor, section "Russia". See also Chancery of the Committee of Ministers, St. Petersburg: *Statesman's Handbook for Russia: 1896*, Section "On the Prerogatives of the Sovereign Power". Wikipedia-Red Porch, "Red Porch" – news·newspapers·books·scholar·JSTOR*(Dec. 2009)*

46. The Czar crown, A symbol of Imperial Spender. Adastra Jewelry https://adastrajewelry.com/blog/the-imperial-Crown-of-Russia

47. Wilson Center Has Vladimir Putin Always Been Corrupt? And Does it Matter?

48. Carnegie Europe, Fighting a Culture of Corruption in Ukraine, By Thomas de Waal Senior Fellow, Published on April 18, 2016

49. Hillsdale College Imprimis, Complications of the Ukraine War, by Christopher Caldwell, Crimea referendum: Voters back Russia union, 16 March 2014

50. Trove newspapers, May 8 1986, The Coronation of the Czar

51. Wikipedia, Order of St. Andrew, Jean-Henri Schnitzler. Secret History of the Court and Government of Russia Under the emperors Alexander and Nicholas

52. Gilbert's Royal Books, Last Coronation of a Russian Tsar.

53. Wikipedia, Coronation of the Russian Monarch

54. History.com, Romanov family

55. NPR, The mysterious disappearance of the Russian Crown Jewels, Dec 2012, by Corey Flintoff

56. Alexander Palace, The home of the last Tsar-Romanov and Russian History.

57. Russia Beyond and the New York Times

58. Drayton, James (20 June 2012). "Sviyazhsk". *home to roam*. Retrieved 11 July 2012.

59. Exoticca, Russia villages beyond Moscow and St. Petersburg

60. Oxford Reference, Dwight D. Eisenhower 1890–1969 American Republican statesman, 34th President 1953–61

61. Russia beyond, Why was the Russian Tsar considered an emissary of God, Georgy Manaev

62. HorusExploreDeitiesofAncientEgyptegyptianmuseum.org/deities-horus

63. Tsarist Government, alphahistory.com

64. UK Parliament, Parliament, and crown

65. Why the Royals must adhere to strict dining rules, according to an etiquette expert, Marie Claire

66. Wikipedia, Coronation of the Russian monarch

67. European Royal History, My favorite crowns, #6, The imperial crown of Russia, Part II

68. Liebmann, pg. 200. At The Royal Passion-Bearer: Tsar-Martyr Nicholas Alexandrovich Romanov II, pg. 4

69. Wikipedia, Coronations in Europe

70. Tsar Nicholas.org, Bokhanov, A.N. Diaries & Letters, Nicholas II, Novo-Romanov Archives, Nicholas II's Diaries 1984-1918

71. Britannica and Travel all Russia, St. Basil the blessed church, Moscow

72. , Gwendolyn Leick (2013). *Tombs of the Great Leaders: A Contemporary Guide*. Reaktion Books. p. 39. ISBN 978-1780232263. Tumarkin, Nina (1997). *Lenin Lives! The Lenin Cult in Soviet Russia* (enlarged ed.). Cambridge, Massachusetts: Harvard University Press. pp. 180, 191–194. ISBN 978-0674524316.

73. Maslenitsa festival in Russia - when the pancakes never end Maslenitsa Festival - What To Expect During Russia's Pancake Festival (56thparallel.com)

74. *Galayda, A. (11 February 2020). "Why the only Bolshoi Theater school outside Russia is in Brazil". Russia Beyond the Headlines. Retrieved 19 February2020.*

75. Circopedia: The Free Encyclopedia of the International Circus, s.v. "Moscow Circus." [1] (Accessed May 3, 2011) Dabars, Z. (2002). The Russian Way: Aspects of Behavior, Attitudes, and Customs of the Russians. United States: McGraw-Hill

76. *Kasler, Peter Alan (1992). Glock: The New Wave in Combat Handguns. Boulder, Colorado: Paladin Press. ISBN 978-0-873646499.*

77. The first oligarch dies, his kleptocracy thrives". *Reuters.* Retrieved 15 May 2024.

78. MoscowCanal, culture.google.com/entity/Moscow-canal

79. Federal Reserve bank of Dallas, Russian ruble buckles under trade sanctions, declining export earnings, J. Scott Davis, and Kunal Patel

80. R. Street, Why Swift sanctions on Russia might not be enough, by Philip Rossetti

81. Mallory, Stephen L. *Understanding Organized Crime.* Jones and Bartlett Publishers, 2007, p. 73-87.

82. St. Petersburg.com, Tombs of the Peter and Paul Fortress by Philip Rossetti, www.unofficialroyalty.com/royal-burial-sites

83. Unofficial Royalty, Romanov burial sites, by Susan Flantzer

84. Revision of article that appeared in The New York Times

85. U.S. State Department, 2022 report on International religious freedom, Ukraine

86. Mallory, Stephen L. *Understanding Organized Crime.* Jones and Bartlett Publishers, 2007, p. 73-87. Russian mafia abroad is a myth – head of Russian Interpol bureau". Interfax.com.ua. 23 December 2009. Archived from the original on 5 July 2012. Retrieved 16 July 2012.

87. Moscow Sotheby's International Realty

88. Ilyushin IL-96-300, Aeroflot JP5926424.,
    https://cdn.jetphotos.com/full/1/73785_1172235533.jpg

89. Royal Residences: Buckingham Palace, The Royal
    family, Royal Residences: Buckingham Palace | The
    Royal Family

90. Reuters, Queen Elizabeth's funeral watched by 11.4
    million people in U.S. -Nielsen, by Lisa Richwine

91. Royal Collection Trust, A History. A history of the Royal
    Library

92. History, Why the British Royal Crown failed to save the
    Romanovs Russian aircraft now

93. Forbes, Russian aircraft now must use an extreme
    circuitous route

94. Outlook 2010: Reorganization Nears Completion, But
    Russian Industry Still Has Far To Go". *Aviation Week &
    Space Technology*. Vol. 172, no. 4. 25 January 2010.
    Archived from the original on 14 October 2017.
    Retrieved 24 November 2015.

95. "6th Air and Air Defence Army - Russian Naval Aviation -
    Baltic Sea Fleet". Eastern Orbat. Retrieved 1 January 2023.

96. Forbes, Which Is Why Ukraine Is Shooting Them Down—
    As Fast As It Can, by David Axe

97. OSW, Center for Eastern Studies, Russia behind bars: the
    peculiarities of the Russian prison, by Jan Strzelecki

98. systemaspetsnaz.com, Russian martial arts, hand to hand
    combat of Russian Special forces

99. The New York Times, Troop Deaths and Injuries in
    Ukraine War Near 500,000, U.S. Officials Say, By Helene
    CooperThomas Gibbons-NeffEric Schmitt and Julian E.
    Barnes

100. Carnegie Russia Eurasia Center, Russian military
    reconstitution 2030 Pathways and Prospects, by Dara
    Massicot, Published on Sept 12, 2024

101. United Nations Peacekeeping

102. The constitution of the Russia Federation, President of the Russia Federation Chapter 4,

103. Northrup Grumman, SHORAD, Northrop Grumman's short range defense capabilities protect U.S. and allied forces from a wide range of manned and unmanned air and missile threats

104. DBedia, About television in Russia,

105. The constitution of the Russia Federation, President of the Russia Federation

106. National Aeronautics and Space Administration

107. CNN, Sergey Surovikin, Russia's new top commander in Ukraine, By Sarah Dean

108. World Stock Market, CNN, They hated him, ex-serviceman recalls when he served new Russian commander in Ukraine

109. Pew Research Foundation, Ratings for Russia drop to record lows, by Richard Wike, Janell Fetterolf, Moira Fagan, and Sneha Gubbala

110. CNN, Ukraine carries out one of its biggest ever drone attacks on Russia. By Brad Lendon Alex Marquardt, Isaac Yee, Darya Tarasova, Maria Kostenko, Chris Liakos and Brad Anna Bernova contributed to this report

111. Russian Draft Dodgers Fleeing to West in Record Numbers by Ellie Cook

112. Newsweek, six miles of traffic at Russia's Georgia Border amid Mobilization , by Isabel van Brugen

113. Putin warns again that Russia is ready to use nuclear weapons if its sovereignty is threatened, by Associated Press

114. About Norad, North American Aerospace Defense Command

115. History, How Seal Team Six took out Osama bin Laden, by Julie Marks

116. Russia Guide, Myshkin - Travel Russia Guide (russiaeguide.com)

117. Ukraine Air Force". Scramble.nl. Retrieved 26 February 2022.

118. Ministry of Foreign affairs of Russia, Basic Principles of State Policy of the Russian

119. Reuters, Federation on Nuclear Deterrence, The chain of command for potential Russian nuclear strikes

120. Boston Globe, After four decades and $200 billion, the US missile defense system is no match for a Russian Nuclear attack, by Puzzanghera

121. CNN, Exclusive, an inside look at America's aging ballistic missile arsenal by Oren Liebermann

122. BBC, North Korea, What missiles does it have?

123. "S-500 or A-235? Russia Tests Advanced New Missile Defence System With Extreme Range". Military Watch. 5 June 2019. Diplomat, Ankit Panda, The. "Russia Conducts New Test of 'Nudol' Anti-Satellite System". The Diplomat. Retrieved 21 January 2019.

124. The Week

125. CNN, North Korea test fires ballistic missile with potential to reach entire US, Japan says, by Brad Lendon and Gawon Bae,

126. Jalopnik, The President of Russia travels in a helicopter equivalent to Marine one. It is an updated version of the tried and true Russian rotary wing workhorse, the Mil Helicopter Plan

127. Jalopnik, The President of Russia travels in a helicopter equivalent to Marine one. It is an updated version of the tried-and-true Russian rotary wing workhorse, the Mil Helicopter Plan

128. Boston Review, How the International Court could prosecute Putin

129. Constitution of the Russian Federation, Official Website of the Government of the Russian Federation / The Russian Government

130. Britannica, Justice of Russia in Russia, government, and society, written by Marc Raeff and Yuri V. Medvedkov

131. CNN, missiles rained down on Israel as Iran launched an attack on Tuesday

132. CNN, How war crimes prosecutions work, by Zachary B. Wolf, CNN, War Crimes Watch: Targeting schools, Russia bombs the future, by JASON DEAREN, JULIET LINDERMAN and OLEKSANDR STASHEVSKYI , CNN

133. CNN, Satellite images appear to show Russian ships loading up, PBS Frontline, Russia Smuggling Ukrainian Grain to Help Pay for Putin's War By Michael Biesecker, Sarah El Deeb, Beatrice Dupuy

134. The Seattle Times, ten torture sites in one town, Russia sowed pain, fear in Izium Associated Press

135. Center for European policy analysis, Russian Limbo, Butyrba Prison

PHOTOS

1. Alexander Palace. Pushkin. Александровский дворец. Пушкин (9061172848)Wikimedia, Andrey Korchagin, https://en.wikipedia.org/.

2. Czar Nicholas ii and family, Library of Congress's Prints and Photographs division, under the digital ID ggbain.14545

3. King George V and Czar Nicholas ii, Wikimedia Commons, public domain in the United States

4. Ipatiev house Public Domain, Wikimedia Commons http://www.searchfoundationinc.org/1977, Unknown author, original uploader was Crimea at Hungarian Wikipedia

5. Ellis Island, Wikimedia Commons, by Ken Thomas

6. Air Force Basic Training Photo, U.S. Public Affairs, Wikimedia Commons

7. Red Square covered with snow, Wikimedia Commons, Thomas Taylor Hammond (1920-1993)

8. Antonov An-225 Mriya Russian aircraft, Wikimedia Commons, https://armyinform.com.ua/2019/12/21-grudnya-1988-roku-an-225-mriya-vpershe-pidnyavsya-v-nebo, creativecommons.org/licenses

9. Mifflin Street Block Party, Creative Commons Attribution-Share Alike 2.0 Generic license, Mark Sadowski from Madison, Wisconsin

10. From Ukraine to DR Congo cargo plane An-124 "Ruslan" for Ukrainian peacekeepers delivered helicopters and aviation assets, Kārlis Dambrāns from Latvia

11. Grand Kremlin Palace Aleksandr hall, licensed under the Creative Commons Attribution 3.0 Unported license, Wikimedia Commons

12. Lenin's Tomb, Gan-Shmuel archive via the PikiWiki - Israel free image collection project, United States public domain tag

13. Buildings of Supreme Court of Russian Federation in St Petersburg, licensed under the Creative Commons Attribution-Share Alike 4.0 International license, by Maxim atayants

14. Aerial-SPB-Winter Palace, licensed under the Creative Commons Attribution-Share Alike 4.0 International license, Andrew Shiva / Wikipedia / CC BY-SA 4.0

15. Russian Crown Jewels, Wikimedia, http://fotki.yandex.ru/users/wise-cat/view/770000/

16. 2019-07-26-Moscow-3182-Tomb of the Unknown Soldier, Don-vin, Wikipedia Cathedral of Dormition, Wikimedia Commons, Creative Commons - Wikipedia

17. Cathedral of Dormition, Wikimedia Commons, Pedro Szekely https://www.flickr.com/photos/pedrosz/.org/licenses

18. Photograph of Princess Diana dancing with John Travolta at a White House dinner for the Prince and Princess of Wales, National Archives and Records Administration, cataloged under the National Archives Identifier (NAID) 198569

19. Moscow at night Red Square St. Basil Cathedral in 1985 wit, Gottfried Hoffmann

20. Moscow State Circus, Wikimedia Commons, https://creativecommons.org/licenses, Kim Fyson

21. Luxury yacht Tango in Barcelona, Wikimedia Commons, Creative Commons - Wikipedia

22. Peter and Paul Cathedral, Peter and Paul Fortres, 1733, Creative Commons Attribution 2.0 Generic license, Wikimedia Commons Andrew Shiva / Wikipedia /

23. Buckingham Palace aerial view 2016, , SAC Matthew 'Gerry' Gerrard RAF/© MoD Crown Copyright 2016, Open Government Licence version 1.0

24. Russian Air Force Sukhoi Su-34 Beltyukov, http://www.airliners.net/photo/Russia---Air/Sukhoi-Su-34/2094240, Alex Beltyukov websites (mil.ru, минобороны.рф) of the Ministry of Defence of the Russian Federation, Atribute Mil.Ru

25. Molniya 1 in Kaluga, Wikimedia commons, Attribution 4.0 International license, Stolbovsky

26. Loading an ICBM container into a missile silo, Ministry of Defense of the Russian Federation, https://structure.mil.ru/structure/forces/strategic_rocket /weapons/more, mil.ru

27. GIDS Shahpar 2 Drone, Creative Commons Attribution-Share Alike 4.0 International license, Hezmok Media

28. CMSAF visits Cheyenne Mountain SFS, the image or file is in the public domain in the United States, Wikimedia Commons, the image or file is in the public domain in the United States

29. Putin's palace residence, Wikimedia Commons http//ruleaks.net/1901

30. Motorcycle Riders Wikimedia Commons, https://www.dvidshub.net/image/27340ID 100424-A-2848B- Taken by Sgt David Bruce

31. Soyuz 18 booster, Wikimedia Commons, Great Images in NASA, User Audin on en.wikipedia

32. Soldiers from the 86th Infantry Brigade Combat Team (Mountain) practice their mountain skills with Kosovo Security Forces, U.S. Army photo by Sgt. 1st Class Jason Alvarez

33. Butyrka prison, Wikimedia Commons, Butyrka_prison.jpg: Stanislav Kozlovskiy

34. Approach to Russia Hall, Wikimedia Commons, Whysports, https://en.wikipedia.org/wiki

Czar Nicholas photo, Wikimedia Commons, W. & D. Downey, London, Cover Image by Nikita Karimov

THE AUTHOR MATT DROZD

The Author, Matt Drozd, served at the Pentagon and the Department of State during 9-11. He served at the highest level of the military command for three Chairman of the Joint Chiefs of Staff, the Secretary of Defense Donald Rumsfeld, and when Colin Powell was Secretary of State. He has an impeccable reputation as a highly decorated veteran who protected our embassies and troops. He received several defense meritorious service awards including one for saving the lives of sailors injured when the USS Cole was attacked by terrorists. Lt Colonel Drozd was a key member of the team that crafted Homeland Security and was referred to be Secretary of the Army. In addition to his military prowess, he was the program controller for ABC world network news and worked with such notable Anchors as Peter Jennings.

www.mattdrozdbooks.com

OTHER NOVELS BY MATT DROZD
www.mattdrozdbooks.com

Save our Country A fictional novel blended with intrigue, romance, and historical facts. A powerful and captivating drama based on extensive research on the process of electing the President of the United States. Readers will begin their journey starting with the author of our Declaration of Independence and ending with the election of an unorthodox candidate as our next President. Along the way, the reader will learn about the different leadership styles of past presidents and the candidates that are now vying for the highest office in the land. The Author has unraveled the mystery of what to look for when selecting the best candidate that will become the most powerful leader of the free world. *Save our Country* is more than an entertaining and intriguing story. It is a call to action, urging the silent majority to make their voices be heard and lays out a road map for political campaigns of independent candidates. It surprise ending only occurred once in our nation's history.

BEHIND THE SCENES OF 911

(Photos provided by Wikimedia Commons)

The Author, Matt Drozd, served at the Pentagon for three Chairman of the Joint Chiefs of Staff, the Secretary of the Air Force, and the Secretary of Defense. While serving at the Pentagon, he also served in the State Department when Colin Powell was Secretary of State. His serving at the highest level of the military and State Department will reveal to the reader what transpired behind the scenes of 9-11. In addition to his military and foreign affairs prowess, the author was the Program Controller for ABC World News. Behind the Scenes is an intriguing look into how our military responded to what became one of the most catastrophic events in our nation's history.